Praise for *Buffalo Boy and Geronimo*

"Nothing in the publisher's biography of Janko suggests he is a poet,
but his book is what used to be called, admiringly, 'a poet's novel.'
Readers who seek a complex plot won't find it here, but the lives of the two
antiheroes . . . are rendered in such rich textures that one sometimes feels
Virginia Woolf is writing them."—*Los Angeles Times Book Review*

"An anti-war novel certainly, but very much its own kind. . . . Folkloric in
approach, it's sustained by prose that is often lyrical, though never
self-conscious."—*Kirkus Reviews* (starred review)

"In a sense, nature can be considered the protagonist of Janko's novel,
as well as its theme. . . . *Buffalo Boy and Geronimo* suggests that spiritual
communion with the universe will enable us to transcend our differences, be
they political, racial, or societal. Janko's novel also implies that all life should
be treated with dignity and respect, and it challenges us to worship the very
ground upon which we tread."—*San Francisco Chronicle*

"Set in Vietnam during the war, this simple tale achieves depth through its
language and naturalistic detail. . . . This book deserves to enter the canon
of masterly, penetrating works about this still controversial era.
Recommended for most collections."—*Library Journal*

"Humans and animals, even plant life of this war-ravaged land, are shown
reverence in Janko's ambitious work. . . . What puts him a cut above most fiction
about the Vietnam War is his ability to engage the readers in the atmosphere
of its people and environment."—*Hartford Courant*

"James Janko was an infantry platoon medic during the Vietnam War,
one of the most perilous combat occupations of that search-and-destroy
conflict. . . . His *Buffalo Boy and Geronimo* provides a startlingly fresh look at that
often-examined conflict with his focus on its great environmental costs through
the eyes of two characters on opposing sides."—*Seattle Post-Intelligencer*

Praise for *The Clubhouse Thief*

"Reading *The Clubhouse Thief* is akin to listening to a Gustav Mahler symphony. Mahler's symphonies have broad parallels to real life in the world; they meditate on nature, politics, religion, joy, death, suffering, identity, poetry, and literature. Mr. Janko's novel has the same type of broad parallels, using baseball as his modus operandi."—*Windy City Reviews*

"Janko delivers a meditative and lyrical baseball novel. . . . His prose is by turns thoughtful and poetic, and over the course of the story, he weaves together a multitude of voices. Each character has his or her own finely wrought cadence, and their actions throughout the plot are believable and well-earned. . . . A spirited vision of America and its national game."—*Kirkus Reviews*

WHAT WE
DON'T TALK ABOUT

JAMES JANKO

THE UNIVERSITY OF WISCONSIN PRESS

The University of Wisconsin Press
728 State Street, Suite 443
Madison, Wisconsin 53706
uwpress.wisc.edu

Gray's Inn House, 127 Clerkenwell Road
London ECIR 5DB, United Kingdom
eurospanbookstore.com

Printed in the United States of America
This book may be available in a digital edition.

Library of Congress Cataloging-in-Publication Data

Names: Janko, James, 1949- author.
Title: What we don't talk about / James Janko.
Description: Madison, Wisconsin : The University of Wisconsin Press, [2022]
Identifiers: LCCN 2022007576 | ISBN 9780299340049 (paperback)
Subjects: LCGFT: Fiction. | Novels.
Classification: LCC PS3610.A5697 W47 2022 | DDC 813/.6—dc23/eng/20220414
LC record available at https://lccn.loc.gov/2022007576

This is a work of fiction. Names, characters, places, and incidents either
are the product of the author's imagination or are used fictitiously, and any
resemblance to actual persons living or dead, businesses, companies,
events, or locales is entirely coincidental.
During the 1960s, the terms "colored" and "Negro" were commonly used
and were not considered offensive. The racial slurs that do occur in *What We
Don't Talk About* are integral to the story. The intention is to portray the
language of racism accurately rather than mask it with euphemisms.

For Uong Chanpidor,
for family and friends in Illinois,
and in memory of Robert Ray Boeskool

Tens of thousands of northern towns prohibited the presence of
Black people after sundown from the 1890s until the 1980s. In Illinois alone,
there were more than 430 confirmed "sundown towns" during the
civil rights movement of the 1960s.

Whites from the traditional South expressed astonishment at the practice.
Why expel your maid? . . . The traditional South has almost no independent
sundown towns, and never did.

—JAMES W. LOEWEN, *Sundown Towns:*
A Hidden Dimension of American Racism

Contents

PART I

Orville, Illinois

(1962–1963)

You could listen patiently for a hundred years and never hardly catch
more than shards and shreds of the incalculable ocean of stories just in this
one town. . . . But you sure can try to catch a few, yes?

—BRIAN DOYLE, *Mink River*

Summer Eve

"Lord, give me cards warm as whiskey,
greenbacks and silver, a horse and three acres,
and a girl ripe as June."

Fenza sang this song to the setting sun and the Illinois River. There was no girl in sight, only his sidekick, Gus Zeul, and there was no horse or three acres. He sipped spirits from a Mason jar, a blend of Wild Turkey and grape Kool-Aid. The boy had copped the booze from his father's liquor cabinet. He stole the song, too, from Sy Clausen, a gambler who once drew a knife on a man after losing $650 in a euchre game.

At twilight, the boys gravitated to their usual haunt, the trunk of a fallen cottonwood near the cove where town girls swam and sunbathed on hot afternoons. At age thirteen, they resembled the clientele at Orville watering holes, the regulars who found their way to the same bar stools for cool drinks and conversation on summer eves. Tonight they had enough booze to get tipsy, and they also had the river, the sky, and the good fortune of having no one to impress. The river cut a dark path through a green world. The town rose on the hill behind them, a few lights in the quiet dusk.

∼

A pickup crept along the riverfront road. Fenza saw it first, a Chevrolet missing its front bumper, a heap maybe on its way to the junkyard east of town. Puffs of smoke oozed up from the hood. The muffler scraped and sparked over the crooked bricks of Canal Street. Whose truck, and who was driving? The half-light of dusk left room for wonder. Fenza stood, took one step forward, and then he saw him: a Black man bent down behind the wheel.

He caught a breath. The few coloreds who visited these parts on summer days fished the far side of the river and stayed clear of town. At dusk, they'd always had the good sense to disappear, drift down the river roads to Peoria, or head up Route 6 toward Chicago. The driver of this heap must have thought he could ease through Orville without being noticed. No, pay the toll, thought Fenza, empty your pockets. The Chevy sputtered to a halt some fifty feet from where the boys kept watch.

The Negro stepped out and left the door half open. He was a gray-haired fellow, almost bald, trousers hanging low on narrow hips, a white shirt drawing a wedge of light like the wing of a moth. The sky had gone dark gray, the steeple up the hill pitch black. The man raised the hood of his heap and leaned over, burying his face in a cloud of steam.

Shit for luck. Radiator overheated. Leaky sonofabitch, thirsty as July. The man mumbled, shook his head, and glanced toward the river. He stepped aside and pressed his hands to his hips.

Gus nudged Fenza. "You leave him be."

"You see me botherin' anyone?"

"Don't start."

"It's damn near dark."

"You afraid of him?"

Fenza edged forward. "Hey," he called. "Hey, old man."

The Negro stood motionless.

"You know where you are?" said Fenza.

No response.

"You got maybe three minutes to disappear."

The old man gave the town on the hill a single glance. The headlamps of a car slanted up a steep road toward a church. Every town in these parts boasted a hilltop church, a hint of Calvary, Jerusalem by the river. Just now, though, he had a mournful feeling about religion in general, crucifixion in particular. These snot-faced boys knew he had no intention to stop in their sundown town. Day or night, they could have their Jerusalem, die in it for all he cared. He was passing through, heading for home before night set in. Like any Negro in these parts, he knew the rules of this ville, plus others like it: a white man's river town was a fortress of invisible gates.

He shut one eye, kept the other fixed on these boys. He knew he could make it home in his truck, just needed some time to let the radiator cool, add some water, and maybe tinker with the battery, tighten loose connections. He'd had a good day fishing the backwaters south of Sells Landing. In the bed of his truck, in a washtub topped with chicken wire, he had three catfish fat as Sunday hams, plus four carp almost as stout. Upriver, at home, he had a small pond out back, and he'd started stocking it with catfish and carp, a few bluegills too, though they were harder to come by. He forced himself to nod and smile for these boys, and the wee one smiled back. "Just need to fetch me some water," said the man, "and be on my way."

The wee boy, the blondie, said, "Mister, you can take your time."

"Huh?"

"You can stay on here long as you like."

Well, that's nice, but what could he like enough to stay for? He cursed himself for not having his bucket, or even a tin cup to fetch water from the river. The water in the washtub was for his fish. Some had sloshed out when he rolled over bumps, so he needed a few gallons to replenish the tub too. He must've left his bucket on the shore where he'd been fishing. He cursed old age, forgetfulness, and everything else that put him in this bind. In a few minutes, after his truck cooled down, he'd open the radiator and fill her up, handful by handful from the river. Yes, he'd sidle shoreward, grab some river, ferry it in cupped hands, drops of it sliding through bent fingers. The boys would see a humble jig crazy for water, and the mere thought of humiliation stoked his fury. He measured his breathing, deep and slow, but he hated these boys. Especially the "nice one" who'd let him stay in this town long as he liked.

He bent over the back of his pickup and opened his tackle box. Humming, his voice almost sweet, he took his knife, the one for gutting fish, and slid it down, blade closed, in his right front pocket. The boys were down the shore a-ways, far enough off that they couldn't see what he'd done. He kept humming a song his grandma used to sing: "Lay me by the waters, sweet Jesus, wrap me in mercy." The river was black, the sun gone, the sky leaning toward night. Wrap me in mercy, Jesus, or open my knife.

The bigger boy, shoulders square, his belly slopping over his belt, started in with a steady stream of complaints. "So, what's the problem here? If you can't move your jalopy, move yourself. Walk. Run. Limp. Get out of this town."

Now the fat boy wobbled his way up the cove, crossed the footbridge over the canal, while the wee one yapped at his heels.

"You let that man be. I *mean* it."

"Roger and out. I'll let him be when he's gone."

They stopped some ten paces from the man and his truck.

"You're still *here?*" said the bully, his eyes mean and small, his pug nose scrunched as though he smelled something sour. The light of the sky was all but drained now. They say the sun, day or night, is ninety-three million miles away.

The old man leaned on his truck. Up the street the blue neon of a bar—MUTTS MARELLI'S TAVERN CASH ONLY—lighted a long window. The door opened, someone entered, and the twang of jukebox gospel drifted over the road: "Save me, O God, for the waters have come in unto my soul."

Mercy. Up ahead by the train station another joint beckoned the townsmen. A gold light flashed on and off over the entry, a lightning bug going nowhere. He sipped a breath and glanced at the blond boy. "I wonder," he said, "where I might borrow a pail for some water." He shrugged. "This old truck," he said, "is thirsty. With a pail or two of water, though, she'll take me home."

Fenza said, "You come here to borrow a pail?"

"I—"

"What you got in that pickup? You been fishin' our river?"

The man nodded.

"I'm a game warden. Any fish you got best be legal."

There was nothing to say to this nor to what followed.

"No way you've got enough money to pay the fine."

The wee boy stepped past his friend or acquaintance. "Ignore him," he said, "even though he's famous." He hitched a thumb toward the big lug. "He's the most messed-up moron from here to hell."

Fenza smiled as though he'd received a compliment. "Might lose my temper, too, if I see someone breakin' the law."

"I ain't—"

"You'll call me sir. Can we get that much straight?"

"I—"

"His name's Fenza," said Gus, "and he's a weakling."

Fenza shoved him.

"You got nothin' to worry about," said Gus. "I'll go get you a pail."

Fence? Was that his name? A high cloud over the river held a rib of light, a streak of ash. The man glanced from the sky to the wee boy hurrying up the road toward Mutts Marelli's, and then he set an eye on Fence. This fat boy wanted to be called sir, but the man had a weapon, a fish-gut knife, and he'd rather cut this cracker than call him sir. When Fence, smiling his dirty smile, took three steps forward, the man thought, Come on then, come on. In one lean second, he could pull his knife, snap the blade, but then what? If he defended himself, cut Fence just enough to stop him, he might die in this godforsaken town.

"Why you passin' through these parts?" said Fence. "You got no kin here."

The man lifted his chin. His spine straightened.

"We got a law," said Fence, "and don't pretend you don't know it."

I know it better than you would.

"You can't be in this town at night."

The man had a notion to kick his truck, put some new dents in it, for he was afraid to direct his anger at Fence and see it spin beyond control. He'd known too many boys like this, backwoods crackers who started their life-long careers in hate the second they slid from their mothers' wombs. The law Fence referred to was unwritten, but it was upheld in Orville and other river towns as though it were the first commandment. The fishing was good in these parts, sometimes better than good. But a Negro had to slide in and out as quiet as a snake.

Fence was edging closer, a hand in his front pocket. He might have a knife, too, a boy like him, and where was that wee one who'd scooted inside the tavern? Maybe he went into that joint not to ask for a pail but to alert the men there was a Negro right out front by the river. A fish-gut knife couldn't fend off a posse of drunks. A fish-gut knife couldn't take on a town.

Fence asked how old he was.

Stay quiet. Stay quiet.

"You deaf, old man?"

No, just smart.

"I say, How old? I say *speak*."

Words are trouble, Fence. You can have them.

"Well, you *smell* old. You *look* old. You're old as a pile of dirt."

You might be right on that, Fence, right for the first time in your mis-spent life. Old as dirt. Old as the sun and the law of the sun, though this wouldn't be the law of Orville. The sun made me black, left you pale. You don't know enough sun to be my brother. The old man played his best card. He'd learned as a child to spook rude white folks with long spells of silence. So he nursed his quiet till his breath made no sound, nor his heart where it lodged too far inside to be heard past his ribs. He wouldn't call this boy sir to save his life. No, he'd flash a knife at Fence, cut him, too, give him a scar to remember him by, if he had no other choice.

Fence was coming forward, smiling, when the other boy banged out of the tavern, a pail in one hand, and slammed the door behind him. The loudness made the man jump. He lost his quiet, his heart pushed clear to his breastbone, but maybe a little noise was safe now, or not even heard.

The boy with the pail headed straight for Fence. "You touch that man, you're done for. You hear me?"

Fence winked. "I may do more than touch him."

"You best get out of my way."

A round face appeared in the window of the tavern. The boy with the pail turned and called over his shoulder, "Be right back, Mr. Marelli. Be right back with your pail."

A short, stocky fellow, maybe Mr. Marelli, stepped outside wiping his hands on a barkeep's apron. His neck craned forward like that of a bird waiting for a worm to rise to the surface of the earth.

The wee boy said, "Fence, out of my way. Out of my way."

Fence held his arms wide.

"You been warned," said the wee boy. "Here's what you get."

He came forward and swung that pail like a sickle, clipped Fence's shins, metal to bone, and scooted by him at a jog.

Fence, wide-eyed, moaned and staggered. He looked toward Marelli's Tavern, beckoned with a raised hand. In the next while he fell to the ground as slow as a sick tree blown one way, then another, by a confused wind.

After the old man eased the cap off the radiator, the blond boy went to work. Darting back and forth from the shoreline to the truck, he poured quart after quart in the thirsty machine. The canal was choked by moss, so he drew water from the river. At one point the man said, "You must be tirin', let me help," but the boy said, "Keep an eye on Fence." The big boy had risen to one knee. "I'll whack him again if he's fool enough to stand."

Fence sat back down. He kept quiet awhile, but he was edgy as a well-banked fire, hot coals beneath ash. The man could feel him gathering strength, gathering the lash of his tongue, too. He started a round of nigger this and nigger that, niggers ruining everything. He bent low, rubbing the raw hurt of his shinbones. And every few seconds, like a clock from hell, he dredged up hatred from whence it came.

The man sucked a long breath through his nostrils. Sweet smells and sour smells, and a smell like a patchwork of cloth left too long in a box. The few times he'd come near these towns, he noticed how this musty smell mixed with the smells of the land, this smell that must come from white folks or what they wear, or from their churches and bars and Main Streets with little stores and eateries, or from all of these things that added up to a sadness impossible to fathom. You slipped away from these towns and the smells changed, lost the sadness or whatever it was, and the river smelled good and the land too, except where some fish or animal lay dead and rotting. Nothing smelled bad for long in the heat of summer. A hunk of rot one week, a dandelion the next. He wondered if white folks had noses to smell their own towns. Sad, sad. Like an old patched-together hanky left too long in a box.

∽

All in all, the wee boy ferried three buckets from the river to the radiator, and four more to the washtub in the bed of the pickup. At one point the old man said, "I thank you, son. I duly thank you."

Fence said, "Who you calling son? You dumb as you look?"

The wee boy, smiling, said, "Son's fine by me." He tipped his face skyward. "Or sun," he said. "That's just as nice."

So he had permission to call this boy son or sun, but he wondered about a birth name. Before he got in his truck and made ready to leave, he asked and was told—Gus Zeul. The boy asked his name in turn. Clarence, Clarence Washington. Gus shook his hand and said, "Well, Mr. Washington, I wish you could stay a while."

The barkeep and a few others had seeped out of the tavern like bad light.

Gus waved them off. "We're fine," he said. "I think we got everything straightened out."

The man took the wheel and the engine turned over on the third try. Riding past the tavern, he sat erect, his eyes on the road. The croupy bark of the muffler, the vibration of the engine, announced his leaving. He rode high in his seat till he was on Route 6, a quarter mile east of Orville. As he slouched for comfort, the town made its last appearance in his rearview mirror, a few lights the color of butter along the river and the outlying fields of soybeans and corn.

The Next Night

Fenza gave Gus Zeul a bloody nose, but then they made up. These boys had been best pals since they were six years old and Fenza saved Gus from drowning. They'd been wading with other kids in Dell's Cove. Gus edged farther out than anyone else, stepped off a ledge, and down he went. Fenza was the only one who saw him go under. He bucked his way to shore, grabbed a piece of driftwood, and hurried back out. He pulled Gus from the Illinois with a long white stick.

Fenza often spoke of this day with regret. Now, half-smiling, he said, "If I could do it over, you know what?"

"I've heard this."

"I'd let your ass drown."

They'd come down to the river again. A yellow moon, almost full, lit the crowns of cottonwoods and willows, and even the boys shone some as they hunched over cane poles propped on logs, lines angled toward deep water. A hundred bats skimmed the river, vanished, and others appeared. Fenza swung his arms like windmills to scatter a swarm of mosquitoes. Bullfrogs hummed in the willow grove.

Two fish in a silver pail. Fenza, given to exaggeration, called them game fish, but they were carp, better known in this town as mud bass. He tilted the pail to let the moon in. One fish rolled on its side, dying, while the other thrashed and churned.

Gus said, "I ever tell you I've seen the bottom of this river?"

"You should've stayed there."

"No, really," said Gus. "The day I almost drowned I saw the Illinois."

"Tell it to Jesus."

"Maybe I have."

"Bullshit."

"Saw it from the bottom up," said Gus. "The most beautiful river in the world."

Fenza spat in the shallows. "Biggest fuck-up of my life," he said. "I should've let you drown."

~

They would've kept fishing till nine thirty, their curfew, had Mrs. Ruth Dempsey stayed home tonight. She wandered down the town's main street, passed J. C. Penney's and Marelli's Tavern, and crossed the footbridge over the Illinois-Michigan Canal. As always, she headed for the river, the strip of beach on the north shore. A spoon in one hand, a pie-pan in the other, she made enough racket to scare off every fish from here to Sells Landing. "Go home," said Fenza, but old Ruth kept coming, banging some hell out of that pan.

Gus had been taught to respect her. He knew from his mom that Mrs. Dempsey had been the secretary of the Women's Auxiliary of the Altar and Rosary Society till she took sick in her mid-twenties. She was his mom's age, thirty-something, but could have passed for sixty. A mop of gray hair hung past her shoulders. She creaked, hobbled, gave off smells, and wore a colorless bathrobe and slippers. Tonight her husband had probably locked her in the house before he left for the taverns. Once or twice a month, always in summer, Mrs. Dempsey escaped her confinement. Quiet as lint, she would creep down Krapalna Street past St. Roch's Church and Sonny's tavern, but as soon as she saw the river she'd let loose a cry, or several cries, and then she'd rattle her pan and sing a refrain that startled Gus no matter how many times he'd heard it wake this town from its slumber on summer evenings:

"I like Indians! I like Blacks! I like tits!"

Orville had been a sundown town for a hundred years. No Blacks after the sun was spent, no Blacks beneath stars. Indians were allowed, though there weren't any, other than those buried in the ground, their bones as anonymous as those of dogs, raccoons, deer. Mrs. Dempsey might be a whole lot happier on an Indian reservation, or in South Chicago. She had no one to play with in this town.

It was always the same. She started off jubilant, raucous, then toned down like she was praying to frogs and fish who might dive for deep water, close their ears, diminish her audience. At present, she tapped her pan with three fingers. She beckoned to the boys with a nod of her head.

Fenza, hunched over, whispered, "You know she's a lesbo? My dad says—"

"Shut up," said Gus.

"Loves girls," said Fenza. "Darkies."

"They're aren't any darkies."

"Her husband wants her dead."

Ruth Dempsey heard the muttering, but not the words. She had a lot on her mind. Whenever she left the shell of husband and home, she had the opportunity to divine Orville's future, ideally for an audience. Just now, one eye on the moon, she ambled down a weedy path to the shore and sat in the ash of an old fire pit, a circle of stones around her. She said, "Well, yes, now we're ready," and threw the boys a glance. They were some thirty feet away, but their ears were so green they might hear anything. She raised the pan and brushed a finger along its rim. The sound was as delicate as the breeze sifting like milkweed over the water and through the trees.

"They're coming," she said, "the Indians and the coloreds." She eased the boys a smile. "You don't need to know what I know—it'll happen anyway." She looked sidewise at Fenza. "Nobody in these parts can hold them back much longer, the Indians and the coloreds. The river, the stars—they've known this for eons. Jesus? He learned a few things the night He was born. He learned all the rest the day He opened His arms and died."

Small sounds sometimes carry a surprising distance. She felt her words pass through Gus as if he were fleshless, without even a skeleton. No bones, she thought. Nothing to get in the way. Only Fenza held firm. This boy had boulders inside him. He was like the town. He was like her husband. It was hard to open Fenza even a crack.

"You hear what I just said?"

She knew he did, though the words got batted down before he could feel them.

"You should let Jesus break into you some night."

He looked out on the water.

"Or the river," she said. "But the river needs more time."

Swaying and pining, she had her Jesus and she had her river. For now she had these boys, too, because their only way back to town was to pass by her and take the footbridge over the canal. They didn't seem keen on edging any closer, especially Fenza. She let this boy know once more that Negroes belonged in this river valley, Indians too, thousands of braves and women and children. "There's big truth and small," she said, "and this one sizes us down to flea-bug midgets."

"Screw yourself."

"You saying something?"

He waved a hand.

"Big truth means can't stop it, never will. See if you can stop the river. Reach with your arms."

Fenza spat.

"See if you can stop the stars."

She gave Fenza the willies, but she also fired his anger. He said to Gus, "Somebody should do her a favor."

"I don't need to hear this."

"She'd be better off in a grave."

Fenza pulled in his line, cleaned the worm off his hook, and tossed the scraps in the shallows. There was only one way to get Crazy Ruth off the river any time soon: find her husband. As always, Mr. Dempsey would lead her to his car and ferry her home.

"You can stay here and babysit if you want," said Fenza. "I'll see if I can find Mr. Dempsey in the taverns."

"Suit yourself."

"I'm taking these fish. It's my bucket."

"All yours."

"You going or staying?"

The old lady inspired in Gus more curiosity than fear. "I'll stay a while."

"You're a lesbo."

"Shut up."

"Don't get too close to her or she'll mess with your dreams."

A pail of mud bass in one hand, a cane pole in the other, Fenza waited till Mrs. Dempsey was staring off across the river before he sidled behind her and made his way over the footbridge and into town.

~

So Gus was alone with her for the first time. The inch of fear inside him soon gave way to wonder. Mrs. Dempsey was stranger than any midget or fat lady in a circus, but so what? She never harmed a soul on the summer nights when she woke the town with her singing and ranting about Indians and Blacks and tits. Embarrassing, sure, but why couldn't people get used to her? Gus's mom, more than once, said, "Will Dempsey's got no right whatsoever to lock *any*one in his home." The town disagreed. Even the chief of police disagreed.

Now Mrs. Dempsey picked up a stone, leaned forward, and tossed it toward the river. The stone made its sound—*plop*—and disappeared.

Gus thought he would teach her to throw. He found a stone, a nice one for skipping, and came forward. He held out his hand to let her see its basic shape, its flatness. "A skipper," he said, and then he threw side-armed and frogged the stone—jump, jump, jump—to deep waters. She marveled, it seemed, and looked from Gus to the river. "Well," she said finally, "you're an Illinois boy, a flat-head. Might take all your life to make yourself round."

〜

Gus backed off until Mr. Dempsey came for her in his brand-new Chevy Impala. On Canal Street, the old fellow left the car idling and tottered across the footbridge and down the path to the beach, a white blanket in his arms. Maybe he feared his wife would take off her clothes, but for now she was decent. Her robe covered her from her throat to mid-calf. Besides, she was too decrepit to draw a lustful eye even if she danced naked for a boy.

Mr. Dempsey greeted Gus with a stiff smile. "Well, here's to another night in Orville, or what's left of it."

"Your wife's fine, sir. No trouble at all."

"Flat-head," she whispered. "This boy's a flat-head."

"Now, Ruth, I think you know his name—Gus Zeul. Let's call him by his name."

"Flat-head."

"Well, you're in one of your moods, I see. All worked up again."

"I don't mind," said Gus.

"Yeah, I wish I could say the same. I don't care to be chasing her around town anymore."

"I understand."

"I'm on call twenty-four hours a day."

Mr. Dempsey presented himself as a gentleman. A deacon at St. Roch's, a foreman at the clock factory, he always wore a starched shirt, fine slacks, and wingtip shoes with pointed toes. He stood by his wife now, but not so near that she might grab him. Gus once saw her do that, shake him by the

14

arm, stare up into dull eyes that revealed nothing. Mr. Dempsey always spooked Gus. The missus? She talked crazy, but seemed harmless as a child.

"Well, what next?" said Mr. Dempsey. "I don't know how to keep her inside where she's safe."

"The Indians are coming."

"Yeah, I bet our friend heard all that," said Mr. Dempsey, and turned to Gus. "This time—and never before as far as I know—she must've crawled through a window." He shook his head. "Had every door in the house latched from outside, so she licked me this other way. Guess I'll have to latch the windows, too, but then what? She might get ornery enough to bust through the glass."

He glanced at his wife. "I need one more favor. Will you ride with me?"

Gus was confused. "Ride where?"

"Along Canal Street," he said, "and up Krapalna to La Harpe." He fidgeted with a button on his shirt. "My wife here, she might jump from the car—she tried that once. If you set yourself in the front seat, though, the passenger side, we'll wedge her between us and she'll be fine."

Gus shut his eyes for a moment. "I can do that, sir."

"Sorry for the bother."

"No bother."

"It will only take a few minutes to get her home."

Gus stood back as Mr. Dempsey crouched behind his wife and gripped her beneath her arms. "Upsy-daisy," he said. "Nice and easy."

"The Indians—"

"Yeah, here they come, Ruthie. And how 'bout if we wait for them at home?"

She joined them with little fuss, with few pronouncements, and they wedged her in the front seat of a car that still smelled of its newness. She leaned toward Gus, nudged his left shoulder, so he crowded the door and gripped the handle. He was more bewildered than afraid. In the light of an oncoming car, he saw bruises on her right forearm, a black-and-blue mark on her neck. She began to tremble when they turned onto La Harpe Street and approached her husband's home.

Mr. Dempsey didn't say a word.

Secret

Jenny Biel was looking through her mother's purse for fifty cents. She found some bills, a one and a five, but she knew better than to take them. She counted the change—twenty-one cents. The only coin worth more than a glance was an Indian head penny. Jenny flipped it high and snatched it from the air—heads. She bet this coin was older than any man in town.

She held it to the light slanting through her parents' bedroom window. The Chief, except for a nose reduced to a small bump, had lost his face, and his headdress and spray of feathers were mostly a blur. Years of use had shaved the date to a single digit—1. THE UNITED STATES OF AMERICA, the imprint around the rim of the coin, was a scrambled alphabet of nine letters. An Indian head in mint condition was worth fifty cents, maybe a dollar. This one was good for penny-candy down at Tony Renh's, or for tossing in a fountain after making a wish.

She needed fifty cents to add to her three dollars in savings. J. C. Penney's had a sale on earrings, and her mother's birthday was tomorrow. Jenny had already looked over the display, and Mrs. Banik, a gray-haired clerk, invited her to put a pair of earrings on layaway. Three dollars down, fifty cents more and they're yours. Jenny was almost fooled. The earrings, crescent-shaped moons, flashed like silver in the electric light of the jewelry case. Mrs. Banik brought them out and let Jenny hold them to her ears and look in a mirror. The girl took her time. What looks good on me, she thought, will look good on my mother. The moons were polished smooth, but they were baubles, as flimsy as the fake gems in a crackerjack box. Mrs. Banik, in a back room, might have carved them from a soup can. Scraps of tin on sale, $3.50. But they were nicely shaped and all Jenny could afford.

She searched the compartments of her mother's purse. A bronze zipper opened a security pocket. No money here, just a photograph of a woman Jenny had never seen. A Negro woman, thin and pretty, her hair shiny and pressed flat to her scalp, no curls but those that frizzed above her ears. She stood in front of a lilac bush and waved to the picture-taker. Head cocked, lips curled in a half smile, she looked more defiant than happy. The sun made her squint, but she kept her chin up, glared, her eyes dark as currants. She wore a loose-fitting dress, bright green, with sequins at her bosom. Jenny would've bet fifty cents the dress was a hand-me-down from an older sister. This girl better eat more if she wanted to fill the crosshatches and pleats and make it her own.

The back of the picture said, *Dear Annie, Your mama love you and understand you.* The ink was faded, almost illegible. The signature was pared down to two letters—GL. Maybe Gladys was her name, or Gloria. Jenny tried to think of other names that begin with GL.

In the next while she sat on her parents' bed and looked at the face of her grandma. A light-skinned Negro with black hair as smoothed and ironed as a Sunday shirt. Grandma GL gave Annie Biel her high cheekbones, her prominent chin, a certain hardness in her eyes. Cheekbones and chin, these were Jenny's too. She had her father's eyes: pale blue, almost gray. She and her mother had delicate skin.

Every morning Annie Biel went to eight o'clock Mass at St. Roch's Church. The clock on the nightstand said 8:51; she was due home in a few minutes. The one time Jenny asked why she was always going to church, Annie said, "To pray for us." Those words meant nothing till now. Maybe her mother was praying that a secret stay a secret the rest of their lives.

～

Jenny went to her room and opened the drapes. She lay on her bed, face up, her head tilted toward the light of a silver maple. The leaves near the crown, as green as the Go of a traffic light, caught the full force of the sun. The trunk was maybe seven shades of gray, not silver, but people called this tree—bark, branches, leaves, roots—a silver maple. Things and words, was there ever a match? GL. That's all Jen knew of grandma's name.

～

She went to the bathroom and leaned over the sink to look in the mirror. A face like her mother's, light-skinned, but fuller in the cheeks, hair longer and straighter, easier to comb. Her mother clipped her own hair shorter than GL's, sheared off every unwanted curl. She and Jen couldn't do anything about those lips, GL's lips. Anyone else in town could get punched in the mouth and still have thinner lips.

Was grandma still alive? Where was she? Chicago? Rockford? Timbuktu? Even with those hard eyes she could've passed for pretty, and today her child and grandchild could do the same. Pretty like silver maples in summer. Pretty like Negroes in Orville. Pretty like a picture that makes you blink, or makes your hand shake as you hold it. Jenny felt her mind turn lean, sharp. A knife to divide one thing from another. Some Negroes were halfway white and halfway pretty. A girl who knew nothing would be a secret to herself.

≈

Jenny stole the Indian head penny and left the earrings to gather dust at J. C. Penney's. She didn't know if her mother's party was the quietest on record, or if the revelry belonged to others. Seven people sat in lawn chairs beneath silver maples that—in any light—weren't silver. People use words any which way.

At dusk, the mosquitoes chased them inside where they crowded around the kitchen table. Grandpa Luke and Grandma Sophie had come all the way from Rockford with a yellow cake they'd bought at some bakery. The cake was almost pretty after Grandma lit the candles and turned off the lights. Sing the birthday song, make a wish. Blow out the candles and share the dark.

After her mother opened her gifts, Jenny asked Grandpa Luke if he knew any Negroes in Rockford.

He leaned back in his chair as if he were farsighted and needed to see her better.

"No, never have," he said. "They live on the west side of town, and that's mostly where they stay."

≈

The next morning, after her mother returned from Mass at St. Roch's Church, Jenny asked, "What did you pray for?"

They sat across from each other at the breakfast table. Her mother, stirring coffee, said, "Half a dozen things. You and me for starters."

"Who else?"

"Your dad always gets his due. Plus two grandmas, two grandpas. Does that make half a dozen?"

"It adds up to seven."

"Well, you're the mathematician. Quick with numbers."

"Grandpa Luke says he doesn't know any Negroes in Rockford."

Annie concealed her discomfort with a smile. "Well, why would he? They live on the west side of the Rock River. Should I pray for them, too?"

Jenny pushed her cereal bowl away from her. "Just the one I call GL."

"*Who?*"

"She's your mom. I saw her picture."

"Jen, you're not making sense. My mom's Sophie, your Grandma Sophie."

"No, she's Negro. I call her GL because those are the first letters of her name."

"That doesn't—"

"*Dear Annie, your mama love you and understand you.* She wrote this on the back of her picture."

"Jen, the world's full of Annies. There are even three in Orville."

"But this one's Negro. Not real dark, but Negro. Don't tell me I don't know what I know."

Annie slapped the table with an open hand.

"You will not speak to your mother this way."

"I'm not sorry yet."

"Then I'll *make* you sorry. What were you doing in my purse?"

Jenny softened. "Fifty cents."

"Huh?"

"I almost had enough money for your birthday gift."

~

Jenny left her Rice Krispies unfinished and went back to bed. After a long silence, she heard her mom doing dishes, the hum of a radio in the background. On most mornings, Annie listened to the country western station or the local Christian station—every song with a message. Jenny lay still, her eyes closed, her hands at her waist. She remembered GL's picture, her hair shiny and dark, her skin gold. Her real grandma was prettier than Sophie, and surely nicer. The only thing Jen liked about Sophie was the clear blue of her eyes.

Blue.

Gold.

High yellow.

Everything looks nice if you dress it in light.

~

Her mother appeared with a tray at noon. She looked older, less pretty, but she had the air of a boss, not a servant. "You barely touched your breakfast," she said. "Don't even think about missing lunch."

Jenny shrugged. "I'm not hungry."

"Then *get* hungry. I'll spoon-feed you if you start whining."

"Mom—"

"Don't try me. Everyone's got to eat."

Jenny, still in her daisy-bloom pajamas, yellow and white, sat up in bed, arranged a pillow between her back and the headboard, and accepted the tray from her mother. She would have to be nice, or at least civil, to find out anything about her grandma. Her mom pulled up a chair beside the bed.

Jenny slurped chicken noodle soup, piping hot. She sipped from a glass of milk.

"Can you promise to keep a secret?"

Jenny drew back for an instant. "Yes."

"Are you sure?"

The girl nodded.

"Can you keep a secret all your life? Will you promise?"

"I don't know what you're about to tell me."

"Something you must never tell anyone, not even your father."

"Okay."

"Okay isn't good enough."

"I won't tell anyone, not even my father."

"Are you sure?"

"Yes."

"Nothing I say will leave this room."

Annie fidgeted with her hands. She kept her eyes down as she spoke of her father, "his delinquency," and the long-ago summer that brought her into this world, ready or not. "From what I can tell," she said, "your grandfather was an ordinary boy, nothing special." She swayed slightly. "I'm not saying you should hold back your respect or your gratitude or anything like that. No, I'm not. I'm just saying Luke was like most boys, goofing off, thinking he was bigger than he was, thinking he could have whatever he liked—just name it. I suppose he was no better or worse than his friends. A man can control himself whereas a boy takes what he wants."

Like what? thought Jenny, but she sort of knew what a boy had in mind. Her mom busied her fingers straightening the hem of her dress.

"Your grandpa's been good to us," said Annie, "and always will be. Only God can judge him for some mistake he made a long time ago."

She waited for her daughter to nod.

"As a boy, Luke didn't cause any harm till—I don't know—he was eighteen or nineteen and coming in late every night." She wiped her hands on her housedress. "You remember the family home along the east shore of the Rock River? Well, Luke must've thought he'd outgrown the whole neighborhood because some nights he crossed the river to the other side." Her eyes flickered, then closed. "A boy looking for trouble generally finds some. Maybe Luke's parents gave the girl some money to keep her child and hush up about the father. That's how things like this get settled. In most cases it's simple, though not mine."

Jenny waited. Her mom's eyes peeped open just enough to let in some light.

"I suppose it's rare for someone like me to be where I am."

Jenny looked straight ahead.

"Had I been darker," said Annie, "I'd be nowhere near this town and neither would you."

Jenny felt a pressure in her stomach.

"Your grandpa married Sophie Mallery three weeks before I was born. I don't know what she knew at the time."

Annie's eyelids twitched.

"You've seen the wedding pictures, the two of them in church. Sophie's a big lady, outweighed your grandpa by thirty pounds. Once I got handed over, all the neighbors must've thought he got her in trouble, or else she went and got *him* in trouble. Well, gossip's just words, Jen. All the hot air in Illinois can't melt itself down to something that's true. You don't have to listen to busybodies to know what's what. No, all you have to do is bide your time, wait and see. I was in high school, a senior, before I realized Sophie loved your Grandpa Luke a whole lot to accept me as her daughter." She flicked a hand: palm up, palm down, as if closing a spigot. "Well, that's what I know, and not much else. Your grandma loved him and forgave him and here we are."

Jenny bit down on her lower lip. She was never fond of "Grandma" Sophie. Alice, her other grandma, hugged her more often. Sophie was stiff, even walked stiff. Like she had a poker up her ass and a determination to hold tight.

Jenny sipped her soup, her hand almost steady. Did GL, her real grandma, give her child away only because Luke's parents filled her purse with money? No, Jen didn't feel this was true, but how could she prove a feeling? Her mom had said, "Maybe they gave the girl some money . . ." *Maybe* is a dizzy word: half shadow, half light. *Maybe* doesn't know whether to bury something or let it rise.

"When did your mom give you her picture?"

"She sent it through the mail," said Annie. "I was around your age when it came to your grandpa's door with my name on it, no one else's."

"That's all? Just a picture?"

"No, she wrote me a letter, too, and told me some of the things I'm telling you. She said she'd sent cards over the years, never forgot my birthday, but I guess Luke or Sophie intercepted my mail, let their guard down just once. Your grandma wrote her address on the letter, didn't write it outside on the envelope where anyone could see it." She smoothed a wrinkle on her dress. "Jen, I slept with that letter one night, slid it under my pillow, but in the morning I got scared and destroyed it, just kept the picture." She almost smiled. "Sure, Sophie and your grandpa know I'm colored, but they don't know *I* know. Sometimes—this might surprise you—I forget all about it. The years come and go and here we are. No different than anyone else in this town."

Now she looked at her daughter straight on for the first time today. "You're a pretty girl, way prettier than I ever was."

Jen had heard this before.

"The boys are already eyeing you. I'm sure you've noticed."

"They're all stupid."

"Yes, Fenza especially. Stay clear of him."

"Ugly as a mud fence."

"It's not his looks that worry me. He's the sort of boy who'll cause trouble all his life."

Jenny half-listened to her mother's warnings, but she refused to be distracted for long. When Annie named other bad boys, or potential bad boys—Butch Yansik, Frankie Reardon—Jenny said, "I don't care about them. How did you meet Dad?"

Annie hesitated. "That's a long time ago."

Jenny, after sipping her milk, said, "Can you say when?"

"Nineteen forty-six."

"In Orville?"

"No, a football game in East Rockford. Dad was Orville's quarterback. After the game, I went with some friends to a hamburger shack and he was there with his teammates."

"Was he cute?"

"Well, yes, and very nice. A gentleman."

"What did he say?"

"Not much. He just smiled a lot."

"Did you go out to his car?"

"Jen, stop it. We'd just met."

"But what happened?"

"Nothing, or next to nothing. He asked for my phone number, but neither of us had a piece of paper. He said, 'No problem, write it on my wrist.'"

Jenny giggled. "I imagine he—"

"Don't imagine too much. Your dad called me the next night, but we didn't see each other for months. We exchanged addresses and became pen pals. He sent me his senior picture and I sent him mine. He wasn't just cute—he was thoughtful and sweet, the opposite of most boys." She sat straighter. "Jen, I loved getting his letters, and I had a big stack of them—at least a dozen—before we began to visit. Your dad would borrow his father's Ford and drive sixty miles to East Rockford, so our first dates were in your grandparents' parlor." She covered her mouth, coughed. "You know what we did? Just listened to country western on the radio, an old Philco your dad called 'our five-star baby grand.' We'd sip colas through straws, or sing along with the songs, and those were *dates*." She touched her daughter's hand, then withdrew. "You won't believe me, but I was happy then. No other boy made me feel safe, respected. Somehow I could see right through him, still can, and he's loved me all these years."

23

Annie, her fingers as busy as the legs of a fly, kept wiping her hands on her housedress. Jenny noticed the wet spots on the beige lap of the dress.

Of course her dad didn't know his wife and child were Negroes, but she asked anyway. Her mother looked out the window a long time before she spoke.

"You must never say a word, or even hint."

"I don't think—"

"You don't *know* what he'd think, but you're smart enough to know what the town would think."

"Mrs. Dempsey would like us."

"No, thanks. That woman belongs in an asylum."

"She likes Negroes."

"Stop it, Jen."

"I think Cassie Zeul's her only friend."

Annie rocked forward in her chair. "Let's forget about Mrs. Dempsey and Cassie Zeul. This is about you and me, no one else."

"And what about Dad?"

"This isn't about him either, though I love him dearly."

Jenny paused. "Me too."

"You'll need to learn the ropes real fast, won't you?"

"I don't know."

Annie breathed in. "Things could get hard for us, harder than you imagine."

"Were you ever going to tell me about my grandma?"

"No, why would I? I all but forgot I had her picture."

"Really?"

"It hasn't meant anything to me in years."

Annie rose from her chair and paced back and forth near the window. "Orville's a decent town."

"It could be worse."

"It could be a lot worse. You'll disappoint me if you take this town for granted."

Jen shrugged. "I'd like to meet my grandma."

"Well, you won't. I don't know where she is, or if she's alive."

"She *looks* alive."

"That's a long time ago. If your grandma's still somewhere on this earth, rest assured her days are more difficult than ours."

Jen set the tray on her nightstand and swung her legs over the side of the bed. Her mom, still pacing, gestured toward the window and the alleyway out back.

"You ever seen a Negro in Orville?"

"Just you and me."

"Jen, it's not nice to take a serious question and make it smile."

"I'm not smiling."

"No Negro will come here if he can help it."

"So we're here 'cause we're helpless?"

"Jen, stop twisting my words. We're here by the grace of God. You hear me?"

The girl gave the slightest nod.

"If you were wised up, you'd give thanks every day."

Annie sat beside her daughter, her face to the window. She glanced at Jenny, a lovely child, who she could seldom look at for any length of time.

"You like scary stories?"

"Yes."

"Even if they're true?"

"*Yes.*"

"I will tell you one if you sit still and don't say a word."

Her mother lowered her eyes. She kept her voice down as if some eavesdropper might sidle up near Jen's window, catch her words, and broadcast them through town.

"Years ago, when I carried you inside me, I learned how our men deal with intruders. Sy Clausen, driving into Orville on Route 6, noticed two Negroes fishing on the north shore of the Illinois River. They weren't in town, never crossed that line, but it was sundown and they were near. Well, Sy drove around and spread the news to the taverns. Some of the men had had too much to drink. Later on, your dad told me Will Dempsey and Joe Zeul hatched a plan to scare those Negroes half crazy. A black cat, a stray, used to hang around the trashcans and rubble behind Sonny's Place. Well, after buying a round, Joe sauntered out back, gave the cat a few pets, then snared it. The men—around a dozen—piled into three or four cars. Your daddy stayed at Sonny's, had another drink, but I saw this prank as through a dream. I was riding with Mrs. Sedlak, coming back from our afternoon shopping in Mayville. We came round the bend just as the men started crowding the shore, putting the fear of God in those Negroes. Joe Zeul held the black cat by the nape of its neck. Those darkies were older than your grandpa and twice as bent."

She took a slow, deep breath. "Mrs. Sedlak pulled over and we watched through the open windows. Joe Zeul's long gone, but on that day he stood front and center. Gus's dad was the best-looking guy in town and the meanest, too, after he married Cassie. Those two were bad for each other. Joe was religious, or thought he was. He seldom missed Mass, but on weekends he drank too much, beat up on Cass, and got in fights in the taverns. Anyway, he's the one who dropped the cat in a gunnysack weighted with a brick. I remember him smiling, happy-go-lucky, but then his face scrunched up and he breathed hard and I thought he would cry." She shook her head. "He tied a knot, sealed the cat in its grave, and that poor thing thrashed and cried something awful as Joe whirled it round and round over his head, then sailed it out over the Illinois. The water—I remember it churned a little before the whole river got so still I could've believed it too had drowned. No one spoke for a long while. Those Negroes, heads bowed, reminded me of old men at a wake, quiet and respectful, but I could feel their anger, too, the way it was simmering, boiling up with nowhere to go. When Will called, 'We'll need two more gunnysacks, *big* ones,' those darkies leaned on each other, maybe mumbled something, then moved quiet as ghosts to their pickup. Cane poles, tackle box, bait box, bucket—they left it all. Just got in their heap and rattled off, never looked back. No, Joe and Will and the others wouldn't have hurt those men, but Orville earned its reputation. I'd say every Negro within fifty miles knows of this town."

Jenny held her breath a long time. When it came forth it was like an explosion—small but powerful—that filled the room.

"What was the cat's name?"

"Don't guess he had one."

"I wish I could drown Joe Zeul."

"Well, by now I'd say he's taken care of that himself. Liquor."

"That cat—what'd he ever do to Joe? Or Will Dempsey?"

Her mother held her hand. "Nothing. But it wasn't about a cat. It was . . ."

"What?"

"You're smart enough to figure this out yourself. Don't make a puzzle from something simple."

The girl drew a long breath.

"Jen, I need to hear a promise. We'll never speak of this again, not even to each other."

"But—"

"No buts. I've told you everything you need to know." She squeezed Jen's hand. "Promise?"

"I don't have much choice, do I?"

"Jen, stop wriggling around. Can't we hold hands?"

"You're sweating."

"Never mind the sweat. Do you promise?"

The girl nodded.

"I'm trying to protect you, make things easier."

"I know."

"Well, you *better* know," said Annie. "There's no such thing as a second chance."

Jenny looked out the window at the silver maple that was three or four colors, none of them silver. "Grandma's name starts with GL. Is it Gladys?"

"I wouldn't worry yourself."

"You can't tell me her name?"

"I forgot."

"I don't believe—"

"I wouldn't lie, Jen. I haven't looked at that picture in decades." She released her daughter's hand. "Even a name carved in stone fades with the years. A walk through any old graveyard will tell you the same."

～

Late that night, as her husband and daughter slept, Annie took the picture of her mother from her purse and locked herself in the bathroom. She glanced at it twice before she tore it in strips and dropped it in the toilet. She closed her eyes and pressed the handle. She doubted her mother was sentimental. Anyone wised up would understand that Annie had kept the picture as long as she could, that no good could come of it anymore.

Glenda Baines was her mother's name. Annie didn't know, or wish to know, where she lived, or where, if her time had come, she was buried. *Your mama love you and understand you.* How could the simplest words be unfathomable? Love *who*? Understand *who*? The world was hard, *is* hard. And maybe this was the sum of knowledge she and her mother shared.

Boys in Tandem

On Krapalna Street, on the brow of a hill that extended from St. Roch's Church to the Illinois River, Fenza dared Gus Zeul to perch on the handlebars of his bike. "You got anything better to do?"

"Maybe."

"We'll burn this hill in ten seconds flat."

Down the hill a ways, near the river, Jenny Biel, the prettiest girl in town, and Patricia Lemkey, chubby and broad as Fenza, sat on a dilapidated porch. They rested in maple shade, gossiping, it seemed, or sharing stories, on a stoop that sagged like earth over a forgotten grave.

Fenza clamped his fists on the handlebars. His bike—minus the rust, the scratches—was the color of a flame.

What was Jen doing on that porch? A St. Roch's girl, a cheerleader, but setting on the steps of an old clapboard—raw wood, no paint—a wreck sinking slowly into the earth, a home that was never a home, a place born to be swallowed. It had been around five years since Joe Miller died in that dump (it was a dump even then), and Fenza knew it was haunted. A few months ago, he and Gus and Jimmy Posey crawled through a back window at night, prowled around inside, and though all three heard a small voice under the kitchen floorboards, only Gus heard the words: "Break your backs, throw you in the river." They shot out the side door and never went back after sundown. Now, though, the sun high in July and as bright-hot and fat as it would be all year, maybe it was safe for schoolgirls to linger in the shade.

Chin raised, Fenza perused what lay before him as if he were evaluating a property, considering a purchase. To the west, on a low ridge over the canal and the Illinois River, the Orville Clock Factory, three stories high, lorded over the Five-and-Dime, J. C. Penney's, Mutts Marelli's Tavern, and the Rock Island Depot. The canal, a strip of green and gray fringed by cottonwoods and willows, looked lazy as summer. The Illinois, maybe a half-mile wide here, ran slow and deep between tall trees that framed it like a picture. The boy admired the swamp oaks and box elders, the honey locusts, and the clumps of dogwood in the shade of taller groves. Fenza wished he were rich. If he could point a finger and say, "I'll take these trees and this river and this town and this clock factory," he might also take Jenny and marry her someday.

Fenza gave Gus thirty-five cents to scrabble up on the bars. Gus pocketed the coins, but he would've done this for free. He, too, had an eye on Jenny Biel.

"Hold on," said Fenza.

"What you think I'm doing?"

"You're light as a girl."

"No one asked you."

"You're light as a bag a bones."

Fenza pushed off and at first they coasted. Halfway down Krapalna, he rose from his seat, bumped a knee into Gus's back, and churned the pedals with force and fury. The boys flew. Warm wind swooped down the hill and pushed them toward the Illinois River. Fenza's eyes were a kaleidoscope: St. Roch's girls, bright sun, the orange brick of Krapalna, girls again, river again, trees, everything shifting. The bike wobbled on loose wheels. Fenza pedaled faster, steered with one hand, willing to do anything but die to make a lasting impression. Some twenty yards away the girls—Jenny in yellow and white, Pat in blue—blurred, shimmered. Gus clung to the bars. Fenza, who'd never ridden this fast alone or in tandem, tapped the brakes, burned rubber, and shimmied sideways over a curb and into tall grass. Gus took flight. His hands pawed the air, a display of helplessness, a cartoon of failure. Fenza wrestled the bike to the ground. Whooping, a rodeo star overpowering a bull, he rode it down nose first and wouldn't let go of the beaten, half-dead beast even after he'd twisted its horns (those handlebars were long) and rolled it on its side.

Gus, who'd landed in the grass, was dazed but unhurt. "Well," he said, "I just joined the circus," and drew a laugh from Jenny. She and Pat were holding hands.

Fenza crawled free of the bike. Blood oozed from a gash on his right calf. The imprint of the bike chain looked like a tattoo, a quick scribble of jailhouse ink. He poked the wound with a thumb.

"Don't," said Gus. "You'll make it bleed more."

"I'm fine."

Jenny said he didn't look fine.

"It doesn't hurt much."

Pat, in falsetto, her voice breaking, said, "I'm so impressed, I'm so impressed."

"Well, you should be. I set a record."

"Oh?"

"Lit up Krapalna Street in ten seconds flat."

The bike's handlebars were canted at an odd angle. The wheels turned but scraped against bent fenders. Fenza rolled his bike back and forth in front of the girls. "Fix this in no time." He shrugged. "Just need some pliers."

Jenny and Pat, eyes at half mast, did their best to ignore him.

"No bull," said Fenza. "I'll be ready to ride by tomorrow noon."

Gus began to drift away.

"See ya," Fenza said to Jenny, and at least she smiled. "I'll call you later, all right?"

The smile faded.

"Or I'll call you tomorrow if you like."

Head down, trailing Gus Zeul, he limped down Krapalna Street with his crippled bike. Did she like him? If not today, tomorrow? Fenza glanced at the sun silvering the river, greening the trees. Jenny was prettier than Illinois, prettier than summer. Damn. It hurt plenty to need her this bad.

The Den

After Fenza parked his bike in the garage, he asked Gus if he wanted to "see something off-limits." Pop's den, an abode within an abode, was the one place in the house he was forbidden to enter without permission. Invitations were rare. Maybe once a month, after Pop nursed a few drinks in solitude, he allowed his son to sit with him or look at photographs. All important conversations happened in these special times, conversations about hunting and baseball, and best of all, a few words about soldiering, precious few, but words Fenza remembered far better than any lesson learned in school. "A man cannot know who he is until he risks his life . . . He cannot know the world until he knows its cruelty, its danger." If Pop was on a bender, or steering toward one, he mentioned those who fought at his side on Okinawa, the men he loved more dearly than his wife and mother. "It's hard to describe," he once said, "but I wanted to give these guys everything—even my life." He showed his son pictures of his pals: Boomer and Boston, Rat Man, Lucky, a lieutenant called Plato. Fenza wished he too had a nickname and was loved more than Pop's wife and mother. He knew, though, he would never be on par with these men without the gift of a war.

Now he nudged Gus and said, "Seems nobody's home. You don't yet know how lucky you are."

~

The boys entered the den in silence. On a long desk, under a sheet of glass, Pop displayed important photographs, World War II memorabilia. Fighter planes strafed lush tree lines; B-29s rained bombs across a valley, a bridge, a river; two Marines, wounded and wrapped like mummies, shrouded by smoke, leaned on each other and shared a cigarette; the American flag flew over a battle-scarred hill that had just become the property of the United States Marines. Pop had clipped these images from history books and *Life* magazine. His personal pictures, though less dramatic, revealed his youth and exuberance. Behind the desk, on a mantel under a mirror, was a framed portrait that his son considered the second-best picture in the world.

Fenza led Gus to the alcove behind the desk. "You see this guy?"

Gus looked at a Marine Corps sergeant cradling a rifle to his belly.

"That's Pop," said Fenza, "on Okinawa." He pointed to the sun in the picture, the smoke over a distant tree line. "He's headed straight for those trees."

Gus had a hard time seeing Fenza's father in the image. This young man, stout and strong, had a dare in his eye, and he was smiling as if he'd arrived at a party rather than a war. Fenza Sr., the man Gus knew, was a door three-fourths shut on good days, closed and bolted on others. He didn't speak much, or smile. Maybe the only time he relaxed was at the neighborhood bars.

"Doesn't look like your old man," said Gus.

"But it damn sure is. That's how he looked in World War II."

Now Fenza spoke as his father would speak, somber and slow. "Okinawa," he told Gus, "was worse than Iwo Jima. Survivors call it Typhoon of Steel, or Steel Wind." He nudged Gus. "You ever hear of the Japanese Imperial Army?"

"No."

"Pop calls them 'an elite force,'" said Fenza. "They were all over the island, in bunkers and tunnels, and hunkered down where they could wreak the most havoc."

"I suppose."

"Suppose?" said Fenza. "Suppose *what?*"

"I don't know."

"Hey, this was no Sunday stroll in Pulaski Park. Pop's lucky he didn't get his head blown off!"

Gus lacked two things—awe and respect. He stared at the portrait, seemed to notice details, but did he care? Fenza had seen more reverence in his friend when they were altar boys at St. Roch's, Gus determined that each gesture, each step, match the piety of Father Janecek. Fenza doubted the sanctity of the priest. He would have given ten-to-one odds that old age, fatigue, the feebleness of limbs, forced Father to move with such slowness that he sometimes appeared meditative, even sacred. But what's more holy? thought Fenza. The early Mass at St. Roch's? The old ritual repeated each day? Or the wild calmness that enters a man as he battles for his life?

"Your dad looks happy," said Gus.

"Not exactly."

"What, then?"

"Lock and load," said Fenza. "Flip the safety to *off*."

Fenza had never shown anyone Pop's den, and Gus—too dreamy to recognize privilege—ruined the unveiling. Everything within these walls was ready for inspection. Pop was a Marine. His desk, solid oak, drawers full, must have weighed two hundred pounds. The glass that protected his portrait and the photographs on his desk was dusted and polished daily. A pad of paper was to the right of a black phone. Fenza had never found written messages, only clean sheets, a hundred or so as clean as the desk, as spotless as the black leather chair, the beige carpet, the mirror above the mantel. The boy knew his mom kept the room tidy, made it her priority. But without Pop nothing—no picture, no object—meant anything at all.

He knew where Pop hid dozens of pictures—a desk drawer, bottom left—and the best one, X-rated, deserved its own envelope. Fenza first discovered it on June 14, Flag Day. Since then, whenever he had the house to himself, he was free to open the envelope marked Luz Marie, remove the picture from a white handkerchief, and find the girl as she always was—half-naked. Fenza often thought of her as *the girl*, sometimes his girl, but she was old, in her twenties, he guessed, and lived halfway around the world, in the Philippines. Had Pop taken the photograph? Had he touched her? It was signed on the back—*Love & kisses from Manila, Luz Marie*.

"Pop has one picture you'll like," said Fenza, "but you can't have it."

"I don't want it."

"You will," said Fenza. "Just keep your hands to yourself."

Minutes later, after teasing Gus about being scared of girls, Fenza removed a handkerchief from the envelope marked Luz Marie. His thick fingers, made more to scuffle than caress, turned soft now, and always did as he peeled back the pleats to reveal the girl he shared with his father. After Okinawa, after the war, Pop had gone to the Philippines. He had a camera, or one of his pals had a camera, and they found this girl. She wore blue jeans, nothing else, and was smiling. Slim in the waist, full in the chest—the beautiful Luz Marie.

Gus struggled to breathe.

"You like her?" said Fenza. "Is she too much for you?"

He poked Gus in the ribs.

"Luz Marie of Manila. She was Pop's hussy after the war."

Her breasts were more beautiful than any Gus could have imagined. They were reddish-brown, sunlit, with nipples as dark as the skin of figs. He stared at a round face a shade darker than breasts, and soft eyes that confused him. Luz Marie seemed shy, as if any second she might raise her arms to cover herself, but she also seemed proud of her beauty. The top button of her pants was open. Her hands rested on her hips.

Fenza said, "St. Augie, you still want to be a priest?"

Gus closed his eyes.

"Soldiering's more fun," said Fenza. "If you survive long enough, you can sail into some port and have any girl you want."

You can also sail straight to hell, thought Gus. You can begin to sample the agony that is deathless. A battle, however horrible, comes to an end, but the fires of hell endure. Forever is not merely a word. Sister Damien had taught Gus that "infinity, whether in God's realm or Satan's realm, has nothing to do with duration." There are, for example, no minutes in hell, no hours, no days, no years. There is no way to measure time or suffering amid fires that have neither beginning nor end.

But Gus looked at the girl once more. He'd probably get away with it, live long enough to go to confession. A sexual sin, in thought or in deed, was a mortal sin. Sister Damien had taught him this, as had Father Janecek. Both suggested that Gus consider the priesthood. Sister once called him "her hope," and warned him to stay away from Fenza. "He'll lead you the wrong way," she said, and of course he had.

Fenza wrapped Luz Marie in the handkerchief and returned her to the envelope. He said, "Shame on you, St. Augie," and poked Gus beneath the belt.

Priest

Gus was a sinner. At morning recess, while his pals hurried across Krapalna Street to Pulaski Park, he had to remain in class with Sister Damien. She dragged a chair to a low window, ordered him to sit, and stood motionless at his side. All morning he'd struggled with impure thoughts, but how could Sister know that he'd pictured Luz Marie naked, that he'd walked with her to the shore of the Illinois River, or that he had a crush on Pat Lemkey because she wore red nail polish and a black leather jacket? He feared Sister saw through him, counted his sins, found him irredeemable. He drummed his hands on his knees till she ordered him to stop.

The questions came fast.

"What is the date?"

"November 2, Sister."

"And which Feast Day are we obliged to observe?"

"All Souls' Day."

"And how will you observe this day from morning till eve?"

"I will pray for the dead."

"Which dead?"

"Those in Purgatory, Sister. The sufferers."

"And?"

"They must have a vision of heaven to leave Purgatory on All Souls' Day. I will pray they succeed."

"And if they fail?"

"They may double their suffering. They will need more prayers and gifts of grace."

She gave a reluctant nod. "Your answers are satisfactory."

"Thank you, Sister."

"Today is a day of prayer, but will our efforts lead those in Purgatory to experience visions of heaven?"

His hands rose from his lap, palms open. "If God wills it."

"Yes, but what exactly *is* His will? Can we fathom it? Can we *know* it?"

"Perhaps through grace, Sister. All we can do is pray that His will be served."

Her eyes softened. "I appreciate your diligence."

He almost made the mistake of smiling.

"Can you tell me the two additional names for All Souls' Day?"

"The Feast of All Souls, the Commemoration of the Faithful Departed."

"The Commemoration of *All* the Faithful Departed. Each word is essential."

He chided himself till she interrupted.

"One mistake is acceptable. I only wish your classmates were as knowledgeable as you."

She asked that he look outside now. "Go on," she said. "You've earned the privilege."

"Thank you."

"Do your classmates bore you? Do you find them amusing?"

Gus looked toward the playground, the boys and girls. He thought it might be wrong to insult anyone, even Fenza, so he said his classmates were amusing.

She folded her arms to her chest. "Is that so? Everyone's amusing?"

"Well, maybe not everyone."

"I ask that you observe your classmates and contemplate a simple question: How long will they live?"

He touched a hand to his chest. He'd anticipated her previous questions, but this one was truly difficult. He knew it was a sin to want Fenza to live forever. Look at the brute enjoying his freedom. Whooping, jogging through Pulaski Park, he flung a football at a covey of crows perched in the crown of a maple. "Beat it!" he said, his voice deeper and wilder than the black-winged birds issuing complaints in mid-flight. Fenza ran forward to retrieve the ball, said, "Think fast!" and threw a bullet-pass to Jimmy Posey. "Yeah, you're jerkin' it," he said, when Jimmy juggled the ball, then let it slip through his fingers. "Give it here," he said, and Jimmy threw him a pass that he caught one-handed on the fly.

A red spark, a cardinal, rose over a sycamore and vanished. Massive clouds hung low and gray.

Pat Lemkey and Jenny Biel, arm in arm, were the last girls to reach the playground. They dawdled, seemed to want nothing to do with anyone else, and Gus wished he could eavesdrop. Like other girls, Pat wore a plaid skirt that fell to mid-calf, a white blouse buttoned to the throat, but she distinguished herself with a black leather jacket. She looked pretty in hoodlum garb, a boy's jacket, open at the collar. The other girls wore bulky coats the color of November clouds.

He wanted them to live forever, especially Pat. It was a black sin to hope Sister Damien would die.

"Do you miss your friends?" she asked. "Would you like to join them?"

He hesitated, then lied. "No, Sister."

"Your classmates are incapable of serious study. Are you aware of this?"

He responded with a solemn nod.

"Father Janecek sees little potential in average boys, little or none."

He believed he was below average, so he apologized.

"No, your grades are excellent, and your aspirations may soon extend well beyond scholarship."

He drummed his fingers on his knees.

"But you must stop fidgeting. Can you sit still?"

He could, except for barely visible tremors.

"Father believes you have a calling and asked me to speak with you."

"Yes, Sister."

"Do you know how rare it is to have a calling?"

He said he did.

"One boy in a thousand, or perhaps ten thousand, walks through a wilderness and into the arms of God."

Well, Gus knew wilderness, the sensual kind, but where was eternity? Where were the arms of the Almighty? He saw sprigs of white hair on Sister's chin. Why did she smell of vinegar, and something as dour and plain as the roots of radishes grown in a cellar? In black robes, tall and angular, she lent to his life a shadow surpassed in length only by the memory of his father. She was the second most difficult person in the world.

He leaned toward the window, the playground, the boys and girls who would one day die. Fenza stood near Jimmy Posey and his other pals, the football in the crook of his right arm. Hot-blooded, he'd left his coat in school, but his cohorts were bundled for winter, layer upon layer over dark blue pants and white shirts with starched collars. At present, they were closing in on Fenza, setting up to play Bull in the Ring. In this game, a favorite at St. Roch's, boys encircled the beast, the one with the ball. At the call of *Go* they would tackle the brute, pile on, rip the ball from his grasp, and the boy who snatched it and leaped to the center and yawped and bellowed would be the next Bull in the Ring.

"Do you enjoy this game?"

"I never have, Sister."

"You're sure?"

He paused. "The one with the ball . . . the one with the ball gets creamed."

"Do you like to watch? Is it fun?"

"No, Sister."

"But what if I instruct you to watch? Can you do that?"

He blinked.

"Is it possible that every life depends on careful observance? The stripping away of imagination?"

"Yes, Sister."

"Then ask yourself if anything beyond this window may be called your own."

Gus squinted. The bare sycamores and maples appeared dead, beyond hope of resurrection. In a way, they belonged to him, as did the grass, dull and stiff, ready for winter. He watched Pat and Jenny push the merry-go-round, then sit and whirl through the uniform grayness of Pulaski Park. Gus liked these girls, especially Pat, though she didn't seem to know he existed. Only when he saw Fenza, the swaggering brute, did he nod at the one thing he still had in this world—a friend. "Fenza," he whispered, and to himself, in silence, The Bull in the Ring.

The other boys, a bit cautious about closing in on the Bull, repositioned themselves while Fenza prodded them with insults. "No need for jockstraps, pussies, but don't forget your makeup! Anybody got a mirror? Don't forget to powder your nose!"

Sister's nostrils flared. White hairs poked out. She exhaled and the smell of vinegar grew stronger. "You call this one your friend? Fenza Ryczhik Jr.?"

Gus swallowed. "Well, I'm not sure he's a friend. I guess he's more like a neighbor. We've known each other a long time."

"Maybe too long."

"He's a troublemaker, but . . ."

"What?"

"He saved my life once. I didn't know how to swim and Fenza pulled me from the river."

"Oh? And this makes him your Savior?"

"No, it's just—"

"But he *is* your friend, your companion. Do you contradict me?"

He hesitated. "No, Sister."

"So let's think about this boy, let's think hard. How long will he live? Can you guess the years?"

Gus gaped.

"Do you see any girls in the park? Do they interest you?"

He thought he should reply that he saw them with disinterest.

"Are you sure?"

"Yes, Sister."

"No temptations? No urges at night?"

He bit down on his lower lip. "Sometimes."

"And how do you manage these urges? What happens?"

"I ignore them."

"You can do this?"

His shoulders bunched. "I try."

"You must touch yourself solely for the purpose of washing. Do you hear me?"

He closed his eyes. "Yes, Sister."

"What is the antidote for lust? What is the antidote for most feelings?"

"Prayer."

"Yes, how easy to say and hard to accomplish. You must pray with your whole heart if you wish to be a priest."

His forehead was warm and dry. His hands dripped sweat. He opened his eyes. Everything was a blur.

"Is there something else you wish to be?"

"No, Sister."

"You don't wish to marry, raise children? Become the head of a family?"

He could barely imagine what this involved.

"One day every girl you know will be dead. Do you understand?"

He tried to swallow.

"You too will die one day, the sun will die. Do you hear me?"

"Yes."

"Is there anyone beyond this window who can help?"

He knew the answer. He had no one, nothing, ashes to ashes, yet he eyed the playground. Sister had asked if he touched himself, but it was the world that touched him, that drew him toward colors and shapes, that engendered a response. Could anything other than the soul exist without a curve, a spiral, a blush of color? The trunk of an oak, a tree that had probably stood in Pulaski Park for a century, thrust straight up for some twenty feet, then opened in a web of lines, an elaborate design beneath a gunmetal sky. The curves and spirals of a tree, a girl, a cloud—how could he not admire them? The world lacked one thing: a refuge. Even St. Roch's, its very mortar blessed by God, was a tower of curves, pillars, and its substance was its beauty. Stone, flesh, earth, oak—why so pretty? Every inch of this world could lead to sin.

And now Fenza was ready. Head down, The Bull in the Ring roared as he lunged forward, sent two boys sprawling, then toppled and rolled and railed as three more jumped on his back and others piled on, a whirl of arms and legs like those of insects snared in a web. Nothing beyond this window—St. Roch's boys, St. Roch's girls, the sun above clouds—could save Gus Zeul. The wise learn to observe skeletons rather than flesh, and foresee the not-so-distant day when bones become dust. The sun would shine for eons, but Sister was right—it would die. She wished to escort him to eternity, some lofty, bloodless place free of lusty boys.

He breathed in. "I want to be a priest."

"Are you sure?"

"Yes, Sister."

"Not as the world giveth give I unto you. Do you understand?"

He did not.

"If you are sincere, you have the blessings of Father Janecek, the blessings of the Church."

Gus bobbed his head. He said he was grateful.

"You no longer need the comforts of the world, the countless distractions."

"Yes, Sister."

"You will renounce all pleasures but the utmost—the ineffable grace of God."

He would try, but just now Pat was speaking with Jenny, a hand on her friend's arm. The merry-go-round was still. Jimmy Posey was the new Bull in the Ring.

"Do you wish to join your friends? Fenza and the others?"

"No, Sister."

"Then come," she whispered. "We will say our prayers in the church."

~

Old St. Roch's, its fortress of walls three feet wide, reduced the light of mid-morning to candles of devotion. The boy, the initiate, and Sister, a bride of Jesus, knelt at the communion rail. Only the crucifix above the altar was bathed in light. In the vaults, in the pews among pillars, around statues of saints, the only color came from candles in glass jars—yellow, gold, red, blue. Gus looked to the cross and pretended to pray. Before Resurrection there had to be Death, a crown of thorns, a white face rivered with blood. He restrained himself from using the communion rail as a drum. Beyond the altar and the cross, the vaults and pillars, came the picayune sounds of children. Recess, what did it mean? Noise and fiddle-faddle. Puerile games. And yet he wished nonetheless—or perhaps more—to strike out, hit something. Drum. Stand. Wail. Protest. Stomp. Turn the altar on its side. Was it possible that a boy as boisterous as Fenza and a girl as ornery as Pat Lemkey would one day enter this church in coffins? Yes, not only possible, inevitable. Good as done. Fare thee well. He guessed it was a venial sin to want Fenza to live forever, and a most grievous sin to want the same for a girl. How could he be a priest if he wished in his heart that the boy who invented Bull in the Ring and the girl in black leather live in happiness beyond the end of time?

"Pray for strength," Sister whispered. "Pray for unrelenting purity of heart."

~

Late that night, unable to sleep, Sister Damien knelt at her bedside to ask for forgiveness. She feared that Gus suffered as she once suffered. Her memory of boys, her wish to be loved, made her cringe with shame even now. In high school, at night, she often knelt at her bedside till her knees were numb. *Jesus mercy, Jesus mercy* . . . She remembered a night when her prayers failed, her desires increased, and she scratched her thighs till they bled.

She shared a room in the back of the priory with Sister Walburga, an overweight nun who slept easily and snored like a man. Decades ago, Sister Damien had heard her father's snore, a sonorous baritone that sometimes kept her and her mother awake. Then and now, she tried to accept the disturbance as her penance. What is suffering but an invitation to pray?

Sister wondered if Gus lay awake, if he too asked for forgiveness. The torment that she faced as a girl, that Gus faced now, could not be avoided. What keeps us from heaven? Is it not the body, the pleasures of the body, the pleasures of the world? Today she'd invited Gus to look out the window of his classroom at the girls and boys in Pulaski Park. She heard again, unwillingly, the tenor of her voice, callous, even cruel: "One day every girl you know will be dead . . . You too will die one day, the sun will die." Sister pressed a hand to her sternum. It felt wrong to hurt Gus, yet there was no other way. Those who led her to her vocation had been persistent, merciless, while at the same time they bestowed the greatest blessing, the knowledge that one must choose between heaven and hell. As a girl, when her body was still her friend, she was beautiful. She knew this herself long before a boy—Tommy Lanik—told her so. She spurned him. She spurned everyone else she might have loved, so all her sinning occurred in her mind. Never a kiss, never a dance. Never a walk by the river. After all these years, two questions still haunted Sister Damien: What if I'd let Tommy touch me? What if I'd let someone touch me? Maybe she would be subject to doubts, temptations, barely controllable urges, until the day she died. Does anyone become holy without great suffering? A sinner who begs for mercy may be better served by indifference, even wrath. If one reached heaven along an easy path, saints would be as numerous as weeds.

Mrs. Dempsey

Early Saturday morning, three weeks before Christmas, the town was so quiet Fenza wanted to bust through a door and jump in some St. Roch's girl's bed and kiss her hard enough to suck the oxygen from her lungs and right out of the house, the town, the sky. Instead, he and Jimmy Posey threw stones at a garbage can near Sonny's tavern. They shared a Lucky Strike, talked trouble, and Fenza claimed Jenny Biel already liked him. "She's not mine yet," he admitted, "but she will be by Christmas. She'd tell you this herself."

Gus Zeul, head down, threw no stones and told no stories. He turned away when Fenza called Jenny "the hottest girl from here to Sells Landing. No lie," said Fenza. "She just pretends to be good the way most girls do."

Fenza ran down Krapalna Street and kicked the garbage can, sent it spinning and rolling. Orange peels spilled out, fishbones, sanitary napkins, and he jumped the rattling can and took off running, Jimmy and Gus at his heels. They ducked in the corner grocery of Tony Rehn, bought licorice whips two feet long for a nickel, and outside Fenza and Jimmy name-called and hooted and raced through yards and jumped hedges and whipped each other like jockeys whipping horses. Gus, a flagellant, followed at a distance, and whipped his own thighs. Fenza slowed to a trot as he and Jimmy approached the drawn shades of a sleepy white house. Frost sparked the grass. It was 8:13. A Christmas wreath hung from Jenny's door.

Fenza crept into her yard. He knelt, dropped his red licorice in the grass, and curved it into a heart. In frost, he wrote his initials, then hers, and he asked the sun not to melt any letters before she woke.

They cut through her backyard and ran down an alley behind Moshnik's Garage to Canal Street. They smelled the river now, and in winter she smelled more like clean ice than belly-up catfish or carp. They broke a sweat as they passed Marelli's Tavern, zigzagged across the street and burst over the footbridge above the canal, their winter boots and cleats ringing the metal slats like ball-peen hammers. Fenza, heavier than his pals, fell behind and said, "First one to the river's a moron!" Long-legged Jimmy won the race to the shore.

A yellow-cabined barge plowed the currents at mid-river. Fenza, catching his breath, picked up a stone and hurled it as high and far as he could. It plopped down shy of the barge's payload, a mountain of coal that made the Illinois River look bright as a gold ribbon. After a rest, he almost struck the barge at the waterline with a skipping stone. Two men huddled in the cabin, the taller one at the wheel. "Hey!" Fenza hollered. "Hey motherfuckers! You fuck corn cobs too?" His hunting-horn voice spanned the Illinois, but the barge rolled on, the river rolled, and it seemed to Fenza that he and his pals were the last chumps in the world stuck in Orville, Illinois. Those river-wanderers, bargemen rough as winter, probably knew girls in big cities, and they captained the Illinois for a hundred miles.

He shouted more insults, Jimmy too, and they threw stones at the barge and the river and the sky. Jimmy mostly did what Fenza did. On his own he was shy, forlorn, but with Fenza he became a hoodlum. Gus, uncomfortable in their midst, averted his eyes, paced the shore, and gave himself to contemplation. Several weeks ago, he'd promised Sister Damien he would be a priest. Yesterday, in a fever, he upped the ante and told her he would be a saint. Father Janecek had assigned her to mentor the boy, and she often made him stay in class during lunch hour and recess. At present, the memory of her most recent lesson made his head spin. How could he be a saint if all he could think about was death and pretty girls?

Yesterday, at lunch hour, Sister told him of a ditch-digger who loved the most beautiful woman in Europe. Everyone else loved her too, including Louis XIV, le Roi Soleil, the Sun King who ruled France for seventy-two years. The ditch-digger? Well, he never dared to speak with her, nor she with him, but his love for her was greater than his love for the Sun King and for France, and even greater than his love for his Lord and Savior. Not only was he taken by her elegance and physical perfection, but by a flowery scent she exuded with no help from perfume. "Sweeter than jasmine," Sister told Gus, "on a summer night."

Even the Sun King wept when she unexpectedly succumbed to a fever on the longest day of the year—the solstice of 1674. Thousands gathered in Paris, the ditch-digger among them. He helped dig her grave, perfect in its precision, and he tossed a handful of earth on the white coffin. The rain of dirt on marble—was there a more terrible sound? After the Sun King and the other mourners had left, the ditch-digger knelt with his shovel. Night came. He saw heat lightning in the heavens, then darkness, then a star. He quaked and howled as he rose with his shovel. Driving the blade into the earth, he begged Jesus or Lucifer or any god or demon to trump grim-faced Lazarus and wrest beauty from the grave.

He was a man of extraordinary strength. Gus imagined Fenza a few years from now, a brutish fellow with thick hands and a wide back, his arms churning like pistons as he shoveled black earth and tossed it in the face of God. Yes, the ditch-digger hurled dirt at the heavens, tried to eclipse the entire firmament. "And with a strength born of rage," said Sister, "he scraped every speck of earth out of the grave faster than you can say— 'Beware of Satan!'" He stood on the coffin and dug footholds to either side. Then, straddling his beloved, he opened the lid, grasped her beneath her arms, and brought her face to his lips. Her filth sprang forth like a beast. Dead but a few days, she was host to worms and rot; her face rippled with maggots. Yet horror and loss were salvation in that even a common man understood the fate of the body. "Maggots devour us," said Sister, "or if not maggots—fire." She startled Gus by touching the inner side of his wrist, soft and sensitive. "Remember," she whispered, "that all mortal beings share the same fate."

She claimed the rest of the story was deductive. "If you pause for a moment, you know what the ditch-digger did next: he vomited. Then, moaning and shivering, he crawled from the grave, her smell still on him, and fled to the forest. 'Forgive me,' he beseeched Jesus, 'forgive me my delusion.'" Gus assumed he wept for all of us: the living, the dead, and those lost in the swiftness and swirl of the in-between. Alone in the forest, the ditch-digger vowed to become a saint.

Gus squinted at the gold shine of the river. He'd forgotten one thing—the saint's name. Racho? Raulus? Had Sister concocted the story, or was it true?

He must quit hanging out with Fenza. By dropping Fenza, he would also drop Jimmy Posey and every other hood at St. Roch's School. He whispered,

"Cut him cold," but how could he? Fenza was a bully, a lout, yet who was a better pal? Who was more loyal? Gus shivered at the thought that he was worse than Fenza because of gross hypocrisy, blatant lies. In Sister Damien's classroom, head bowed, he vowed to be a saint, to follow the example of the ditch-digger and give himself fully to Jesus. The vow seemed genuine when he made it, but Gus lived a double life and despised himself for his weakness. Over and over, he sinned and hung out with hoods and thought of girls and how lovely they would look if they took off their clothes. On Judgment Day, he had little chance of meeting St. Peter and St. Racho or Raulus at the gates of heaven. No, he was on track to spend eternity with Fenza and Jimmy and the ten million louts of the netherworld.

Something drifted near shore. At first Gus thought it was a fish, a giant carp, though he'd never seen one this size. It fluttered, pale and wide, and one side of it—a starfish shape—poked the surface. He removed a mitten, almost touched it, then pulled back. He saw a hand, blue veins above knuckles, and now an arm, a length of cloth, a robe spread open in the waves. A heartbeat later he saw a woman, blinked and saw her again. A woman. She was white and blue and gray and black and she was dead, dead, dead.

He blinked and looked, blinked and looked. A wound like a canyon split her from heart to navel. The river splayed her open, revealed her sex, revealed everything. Gus tried to look away, but he couldn't. Her eye sockets were black. Her hair was an undone nest, whitish-gray. Her lips curled, opened; her mouth spewed bubbles. The river, unsure of what to do with her, dragged her out a ways before nudging her shoreward. She lolled, almost motionless, till an up-swell arched her shoulders, lifted her face. *Ruth Dempsey. Crazy Ruth. Mrs. Dempsey.* Somebody must've murdered her with a cleaver or an axe.

The yellow-cabined barge was receding round a bend. Fenza was telling Jimmy how to take it out with a deer rifle, lace some holes at her waterline so she'd sink before she reached Sells Landing. Gus, moaning, unable to speak, pointed to Mrs. Dempsey. He came between Jimmy and Fenza and pushed them apart. Jimmy kept chewing licorice, so Gus grabbed what remained of the red rope and flicked it aside. "Hey," said Jimmy, "hey," but Gus shook him by the shoulders. He was strong enough now that he could've hurled him to the ground.

Fenza said, "Okay, Augie. You got something to show us?"

A nod.

"This better be good or your ass is kicked."

Fenza had never seen a corpse, except those prettied and plumed for funerals. At first glance, Mrs. Dempsey played a trick. A swimmer, he thought, alive, because the river sashayed her this way and that. Gus surprised him when he took her left hand. He tried to steady her, but she kept sloshing around, slipping back in the shallows. Crazy Ruth wrestled the river. Fenza had to look hard to see she was dead.

Gus tugged at her hand, but she was heavy, waterlogged, and he was sick to his stomach. Seven years ago he'd almost drowned on this stretch of river, and just now he wished he had. There was one good thing, though: The near-naked body of Ruth Dempsey elicited no desire. She scared him, was all, and yet he couldn't run up the beach and over the footbridge and leave her alone. The issue was less moral than scientific, something like metal to magnet. He held her left hand, or she his, and now Fenza took hold of her right. They dragged her face-up, legs splayed, onto the frozen shore.

Gus took one side of her robe, Fenza the other, and they covered her breasts and wound and sex and thighs. Jimmy helped, too, lifting her feet and bringing her heels together to close her legs. She was decent now, dead but decent. Now what? Some blank time passed before Fenza and Jimmy caught a breath and ran up to Marelli's Tavern and told the Saturday morning drinkers Ruth Dempsey was dead and murdered and call the police and come look at her lying on the Illinois shore in nothing but a robe and no she was not alone because Gus would stay with her till the police or the undertaker came to carry her away.

~

She was blind. If carp and catfish hadn't eaten away her eyes, a murderer had scooped them out by their roots. Gus stared at empty spaces, black holes. No sun in any season could have brightened her eyes.

~

For two weeks, the *Illinois Valley Gazette* featured stories of the murder. Will Dempsey, after three rounds of interrogation, confessed that he killed his wife in self-defense, rowed her to mid-river a mile east of town on the night of December 1, and sank her by shoving stones down the pockets of her robe. The river, the currents, must have shucked the stones and washed her into town like a chunk of driftwood. Will said he dumped his wife's body in the river for one reason: he feared the authorities would question his assertion that he killed her in self-defense.

In taverns, in the shops on Canal Street, in every kitchen and bedroom, the sole topic was the murder and madness of Ruth Dempsey. Beware the strength of the insane. Beware a woman angry at her husband, her town, a white cloud passing too low in the sky, a star too small or far away, a steeple too tall, a cross that fits the notch in her shoulder, a universe of imagined enemies haunting her day and night. Against the advice of his attorney, Will invited three reporters (longtime acquaintances) to the Orville County Jail so he could tell his story in his own words. "What would you do?" he asked. "What would you do if every night for six weeks you woke in your bed to find someone standing over you with a cleaver?" A veteran of World War II, Mr. Dempsey slept—if he slept at all—in fits and starts, and if not for his insomnia his wife would've butchered him "as easily as butchering a chicken." On the night of December 1, she swung the cleaver and nicked his left shoulder. He lay stunned, confused, but when he felt his blood ooze out, the hot sting of it, he rose and howled and fought for the one thing no man should surrender to anyone but God—his life. "I wrested the cleaver from her hand," he said, "but she took it back. We fell on the floor by the bed. I rolled, got on top of her, and when I saw the cleaver coming straight for my throat, I leaned back, somehow got hold of her hands, and when the cleaver came down—both of us driving the weight of it—she split open like a dry apple." Will admitted bashing her again, then a third time, only because he was terrified and in shock. He hadn't been this close to meeting his Maker since he was a nineteen-year-old PFC on Omaha Beach.

In hindsight, he realized his mistake: He should have taken his wife to the state hospital and had her locked up years ago. "Dumb of me not to," he said, "but I kept hoping Ruth would get better, revert to the woman I married. It's hard for me to give up on anyone. Ruth and I had some good times our first few years. After that, something inside her went haywire, something no one could fix or fathom." He shook his head. "I could never figure out what she wanted from me. Out of the blue, she'd be docile one moment, furious the next." He wrung his hands, as though to clean them. "I never threatened Ruth, never raised a hand till I had to save my own life."

Will was savvy enough to know his alibi only needed to be somewhat tenable. The case would not proceed to trial if the district attorney concluded no jury of his peers would convict him of murder. Will had a robust presence in the community. Few in this town could imagine that a man who fought bravely on Omaha Beach, who served as a deacon at St. Roch's, a foreman at the clock factory, would murder his wife without justification. The *Gazette* published Will's story, "In His Own Words," on the front page. Three days later, the district attorney dropped the charge of second-degree murder. No one came forth to contradict Will's account of the night in question. No witnesses, no complications. He would never again speak of his wife or even mention her name, except to himself.

In exchange for pleading guilty to one crime—concealment of a corpse—Will was sentenced to time served and six months' probation. On the morning of his release, December 21, he made one detour before returning to his home. The deputy sheriff gave him a ride to St. Roch's Church, where he received communion and helped Father Janecek administer the Eucharist at eight o'clock Mass.

~

The town largely believed Will's alibi, but there were doubters, including Gus and his mother. Cassie Zeul brought up the matter on a Friday evening as she walked home from work with Eddie Tapusko. They were nearing Marelli's Tavern on Canal Street when she stopped, karate-chopped the air, the edge of her hand the blade of a cleaver. "How drunk was Will Dempsey on the night of December 1? Did anyone ask?"

Eddie guessed someone had.

"Drunk enough to butcher his wife and dump her in the river."

Eddie shrugged. "Self-defense, Cass. We read the story in the paper."

"You believe that trash?"

"I've known Will since I was six years old. Don't paint him as a monster."

"Well, how *should* I paint him? As a harmless drunk? A hero of the Big War?"

"He *is* a hero, Cass. You might not remember much history, but you surely heard of Omaha Beach."

"Will wouldn't let anyone in town forget."

"Go easy, Cass. You don't know what the man went through."

"No, but maybe I know what Ruth went through."

"Not a chance. You'd have to be schizophrenic."

"I once had a husband, Eddie. He threatened my life before he vanished. He may still wonder why he spared me."

"That's got nothing to do with Will."

"Hell it doesn't. Two plus two. Do the math."

But Cassie was a woman of unpredictable equations. She surprised Eddie when she sauntered into the Canal Street tavern and sat at a front table. He followed happy as a pup, and Iseppa, Mutts Marelli's sister-in-law, served them draft beers, Old Style, plus a whiskey chaser for Eddie. Every barstool was occupied. The after-work crowd, friends and neighbors, talked sports and weather, and then Sy Clausen, a fixture at this watering hole, toasted Will Dempsey, the only man in town who could be nowhere in sight but seem present. Eddie drank to Will, praised him under his breath, then let his mind wander. He squinted at a calendar picture of the Virgin Mary tacked to the front door. In her robes, amid swirls of cigarette and cigar smoke, she was pale, ethereal, adrift amid the clouds.

He told Cassie not to judge Will too soon or too harshly.

"Okay, then, he's a saint. Saint William of Orville."

"You're lovely when you're mad."

"Eddie—"

"All I'm saying is don't judge my friend before you know him. Will deserves better."

"Easy for you to say."

"Not really. I have dreams."

"Oh?"

"A woman coming at me with a knife. A woman chasing me down a hall."

"You have that one after you pass out drunk."

"Not always. Maybe once a month."

She sipped her beer.

"Eddie," she said, "you are so full of shit."

Cassie would stay longer, nurse another drink, if she had someone to talk to. It was payday. It was Happy Hour. The problem was Eddie, his lack of moxie, plus his tendency to drink himself silly. While sober, he was smart enough to doubt his friend's innocence, but doubts made him queasy. Will Dempsey, a hero of World War II, a foreman at the factory, a deacon at St. Roch's, had every man in town guarding his back.

"See you, Eddie."

"Did I forget to shower? Wrong toothpaste?"

"Grow up a little."

He winced into his shot glass, drank.

"I'd say I'm grown. I measure six feet tall."

She glared at him.

"What did I do, huh? Unforgivable sins?"

"Tell them to Father Janecek."

"Christ, lighten up a bit. It's Friday."

"I'm light."

"Then why fly down on me like a hawk from the blue?"

Cassie slipped on her overcoat and stepped back from the table.

"I don't know what I was thinking coming in here."

"You needed a drink."

"That's right, a drink. Maybe two. But you'll keep going till you fall off your chair."

Eddie smiled and shrugged.

"Hell's bells. Is a man innocent till they hang him?"

"Ask someone else about innocence. I won't be around when you have your bad dream."

Cassie took her beer, licked the foam, and on her way out slammed the half-empty glass on the polished bar.

$\sim$

She walked east on Canal Street, her arms folded to her chest. The last sun left cold gray streaks on swells that rose from the Illinois like flexed muscles. Will Dempsey had rowed his wife to mid-river and cast her from his boat, her pockets filled with stones. A more sober deacon would have devised a way to sink her and keep her sunk, a vanished woman. The river was the sole witness and brought forth what it could—the body. Something had to make up for the blind eye of God.

December 24

A light snow came down in the early evening. Cassie had cookies in the oven and was brewing coffee when her mother, Olga Renh, in a white coat and with a babushka pulled tight under her chin, came through the kitchen door and called, "Merry Christmas!" She carried in her arms a Santa-sack filled with presents. Tony Renh, sucking on an unlit cigar, followed her inside, his favorite roasting pot a black circle in his arms.

"Smells like Christmas," said Olga, and to Cassie it had before her parents arrived. Her father didn't need to lift the lid of his pot for her to recognize the smell, *kiszka*, blood sausage, a Slovenian delicacy she hadn't sampled in years.

"So where's Gus?" said Olga.

"In his room."

"When's he not in his room?"

"When he's an altar boy, or hanging out with Fenza."

"That Fenza . . . he's always into something."

"Not tonight. He and Gus will be altar boys at Midnight Mass."

Olga hesitated. "Fenza?"

"Gus says he's filling in for Jim Banik."

"What's wrong with Jim?"

"Pneumonia."

"Good Lord. Can't St. Roch's do better than Fenza?"

Cassie shrugged. "Why fret over a child when Will Dempsey's the deacon?"

"Cassie, please. Let's not speak of this unfortunate man on Christmas Eve."

"You'll see him at Mass."

"Yes, and the last thing I'll do is point an accusing finger, especially on the holiest night of the year."

Before Cassie could disturb the Christmas spirit any further, Olga carried her grandson's gifts to the living room. Arranging red-and-white striped packages beneath the tree, she thanked the Lord that Gus was easier to get along with than his mother. Her grandson was a jewel. Several weeks ago, before this whole mess with Will and Ruth Dempsey began to haunt the town, Father Janecek told Olga that Gus had a calling. "A priest," he had said, "a priest in the making, and perhaps one of our finest." But God works in mysterious ways. Why had Gus, of all people, found that insane half-naked woman washed up on the shore of the Illinois?

～

Gus turned off the light in his room. He lay in bed, slipped under a quilt, and rested his hands on his sternum. How much had Mrs. Dempsey suffered? The thick bone between his ribs sounded hollow when he knocked. This is where the blade went through, but maybe it hurt only for a moment. Maybe she felt nothing and died at once.

He remembered the night he rode with her and Will Dempsey in a brand-new Chevy Impala. The deacon's car was white as milk, and the chrome and everything else, inside and out, was polished to a shine. In the light of an oncoming car, Gus saw bruises on Ruth's right forearm, a black-and-blue mark on her neck. Maybe Will had hit his wife, or maybe she'd hit herself. Maybe he'd tried for years to stop her from shaming them both with her bursts of song on summer eves. Maybe her infatuation with Indians and Blacks and tits made him dizzy with rage.

Then it happened. On the night of December 1, Will chopped that woman the way Grandpa Tony would chop a pig before he hung it from a hook in the cold room of his grocery. Just chopping, chopping, horrible and routine, his hands red and thick, blood on his apron, an unlit cigar stub in the corner of his mouth. The boy tried to see butchery as natural, or at least familiar, but all of it—the animal slaughter, the human slaughter—made him shiver. Perhaps he and his mother were the only ones in town who'd been fond of Ruth Dempsey. Her husband hated her enough to butcher her like a hog.

Gus switched on the lamp on his nightstand. How much did she suffer? How much? If Ruth Dempsey wasn't in heaven by now, everything was wrong.

～

Grandma Olga entered without knocking.

"So quiet," she said. "I thought you were sleeping."

Gus sat up. The bedside lamp wavered like a flame.

"Are you going to join us for Christmas? Your mom and your grandpa and me?"

He nodded.

"Can't happen too soon," said Olga. "We don't like you being alone here."

"I'm okay."

She sat beside him on the bed. "You're not sick, are you? Don't tell me you're—"

"I'm not sick."

"Well, come on then. I'd say supper's about ready." She patted his shoulder. "You could use some meat on your bones."

～

Gus had the appetite of a penitent. He picked at *kiszka*, mashed potatoes, honey-glazed carrots, and refused to drink his eggnog.

"You want to play football?" said Tony. "Be a linebacker like your grandpa?"

"I think so."

"Then you'd better clean your plate and reach for seconds. A top-notch linebacker weighs two hundred pounds."

Gus couldn't force down more than a few mouthfuls. "Sorry," he said. "Maybe I'll be hungrier later on."

～

After supper, they moved to the living room and gathered near the tree. Tony sat in the recliner and lit a cigar. Olga and Cassie hovered near Gus as he opened his gifts.

The ladies oohed and ahhed over ice skates, a hockey stick, a football, a Chicago Bears sweatshirt. "There's one more thing," said Olga, "and it won't need any wrapping." She handed him a black rosary blessed by Father Janecek. "He blessed it twice," she said, "when I told him it was for you."

Cassie was about to put on a record when someone knocked at the front door. Fenza called, "Gus, hey Gus! We brought you a lump of coal!"

The snow, flurries earlier, came down thick and hard now, and a wave of cold swept into the house when Cassie opened the door. Fenza barged in, followed by Jimmy Posey. "Merry Christmas," said the big boy, his cheeks as flushed as a Christmas-card Santa. He came in without wiping his feet on the mat.

Cassie went to the kitchen and returned with cookies and cake that Fenza and Jimmy gobbled. The boys dripped snow on the carpet. "Take off your boots," said Cassie, "and make yourselves at home."

Fenza said he and Gus had better skedaddle. Father Janecek wanted to talk with them about their "responsibilities at Midnight Mass."

Cassie looked at him. "At ten o'clock?"

"A special Mass, Mrs. Zeul. He asked me to bring Gus to the rectory two hours early."

Gus hadn't heard of this, though it seemed plausible.

"Special instructions," said Fenza. "Things to practice."

"Like what?" said Cassie.

"We'll find out soon, Mrs. Zeul. Father said Midnight Mass is the most important Mass of the year."

Cassie smelled mischief, but she wasn't about to call the rectory and check Fenza's story. Father Janecek was almost as onerous as Will Dempsey. She kept as much distance from these men as the town allowed.

She bundled her boy for the weather. Wool sweater, pea coat, scarf, stocking cap, mittens. His arms, loose as a rag doll's, suddenly turned hard and stiff as pokers. No one—not even Sister Damien—could wind Gus any tighter. He had Mrs. Dempsey to remember, to keep in his heart, and he believed he had a vocation. This morning at breakfast he told her for around the twelfth time of his vow to be a priest. She knew he liked girls, though, which meant there was a battle in progress: Catholicism versus puberty. Cassie rooted for the latter, though it was fraught with complications. Teens who abandoned the Church often turned wild, traded in piety for kicks. There was a name for this when Cassie was at St. Roch's— *Catholic crazy*. And the boys tended to be a little crazier than the girls.

"Be careful," she said. "And remember I love you."

He stepped back.

She reached for his hand.

"I'll be here when you get home."

~

Fenza led the way along Canal Street, up Krapalna, and stopped before a dilapidated house. Old Joe Miller, deceased, once lived in this haunt, which Fenza referred to as Dead Man's Digs.

"Fetch my pack," he told Jimmy. "You remember where you put it?"

"Under the stairs."

"Then haul it out and recheck our supplies."

Gus asked Fenza about the meeting with Father.

"What meeting?"

"You said—"

"Never mind what I told your momma and granny. We don't need to be at the rectory till eleven forty-five."

Jimmy ducked into the crawl space beneath the front steps, rustled around, and emerged with Fenza's backpack. He pulled out a half empty bottle and whistled. "Hand it over," said Fenza. "I might need a bracer before I climb the tower."

Gus glanced at a nearby streetlight, a swirl of snow. "What tower?"

"You'll see."

"Maybe not. You can pull whatever stunt you want, but I'm telling Father."

"Hell you are."

"You lied to—"

"Venial sin," said Fenza. "Maybe not even that."

"A *big* sin," said Gus. "You lied about a priest."

Fenza shrugged. "Everyone in town knows Father's busy. Nursing his brandy about now, mixing it with eggnog."

"You don't know this."

"Know it sure as I know Jenny'll be mine tomorrow."

"Jenny? She doesn't even like you."

"Wrong again," said Fenza. "You're too dumb to know anything about a girl."

Gus stood near the curb beneath white trees. About six inches of snow had fallen. It kept swirling from the heavens, flakes the size of nickels burying the world's sins. He prayed for purity, but his mind drifted to Pat Lemkey, her black leather jacket, red nail polish, and then to Ruth Dempsey, her unspeakable fate. Neither one, the living or the dead, cared about a white Christmas. *I like Indians, I like Blacks* . . . This wanton refrain kept shooing away his prayers.

Fenza bent over his backpack. He took off his gloves, poked around, and grabbed a paintbrush by its bristles. "All set," he said, and put it back. He did the same with a wooden slat and a one-gallon can.

Fenza described his plan in whispers. Before Midnight Mass, before his altar boy stint, he would climb the water tower north of St. Roch's Church and paint Jenny's name and his initials in capital letters. "*Big* letters," he said, "high as my arms can reach. And a heart the size of a Cadillac." He tried to convince his friends that Jenny would see his overture from Krapalna Street on Christmas morning, love him back, or at least like him. Gus heard in his whisperings the most unanswerable prayer in the world.

"Jimmy," said Fenza, "you remember what I told you?"

"I'm your sentry."

"Would be good to have *two* sentries," said Fenza. "Watch for nosy neighbors."

Gus said, "Ask Butch Yansik."

"I'm not asking Butch. I'm asking *you*."

"Tough luck."

"All I need is ten minutes to get the job done."

Gus said he'd tell Father Janecek, Sister Damien, and Sister Walburga.

"You do and I'll drown you. I'll throw you in the Illinois River."

"You and whose army?"

Fenza grinned. "Such a clever line."

"Shut up."

"Have a Merry Christmas, Saint Augie. Bend over and search for your balls."

Why did he follow these heathens up the hill to Pulaski Park? Why did he loiter near a tavern, Sonny's Place, and half-wish he were dead? St. Roch's Church stood across from the tavern. The pitched roof was white, the steeple too, and the north wall—streaked with snow—loomed like a mountain. The crèche, lit with gold lamps, lay in the churchyard. Squinting through snow, Gus saw Jesus and Mary and Joseph, the Three Wise Men looking on, and the animals who had witnessed the Birth from a white knoll. A thatch roof sheltered the Holy Family and the Wise Men, but the beasts stood exposed to the storm. The rectory, Father's home, stood a few paces from the crèche. A porch light was on; a yellow lamp shone in the front window. Perhaps Father was rehearsing his sermon for Midnight Mass.

Gus said, "Let's go see Father. Let's ask him if you should climb a tower for a girl."

"You want to die?" said Fenza.

In a state of grace, thought Gus.

"Don't cross me," said Fenza, and shoved him. "One word to Father and I'll toss you in the goddamn river and feed you to the fish."

And with that Fenza walked point through Pulaski Park, Jimmy at his heels. Gus wished he could pray. He watched his friends blur and soften in snow, their silhouettes as tender as gauze before they disappeared.

He tried to believe in his innocence. On Christmas Eve, or any eve, would he climb a tower that rivaled the height of St. Roch's and risk his life for a girl? "No," he told himself, "never," before a truer voice slipped his guard: "Why in hell *not*?" Fenza, in love, would climb a ladder into the sky and the storm for a good girl, Jenny Biel, whereas Gus, if he climbed, would do so for Pat Lemkey. Everything about her was desirable and dangerous: the leather jacket, the painted nails, the cigarettes, the defiance. Wouldn't Ruth Dempsey admire a girl whom Sister Damien had failed to intimidate? Yes, Ruth, if she could, would bang her tin pan and lead a sing-along: *I like Indians, I like Blacks* . . . He could almost imagine these hellcats spouting this in Sister's face.

He sidled past Sonny's Place, ran across the street, and lingered near St. Roch's Church. The crèche was set in a hollow, a sort of nest between the church and the rectory. Two lamps suspended from the beams of a stable cast gold halos on Mother and Child. The Virgin was the size of a grown woman, the Wise Men were as broad as the fathers who attended Mass or frequented Sonny's Place, and the animals on the periphery recalled those Gus had seen on farms. The Baby Jesus was pure, His face as white as His Mother's, His eyes blue and amazed. Gus wished he had a statue of Ruth Dempsey to place near the manger. A woman in a colorless robe, blind, bleeding, forsaken. A demon, or something untamed in him, longed to wash the Lord's face in her blood.

Head down, he stood beside a statue of a donkey. By now Fenza was climbing the water tower, rising over the town, the valley. The cross atop the steeple might soon be level with his eye. Gus glanced toward the church, then lifted the donkey in his arms. The beast was heavy, but he carried it a ways, then dragged it, and set it beside the cradle. He lowered a shoulder to an ox, the largest of the menagerie, and shoved it till it was closer to the Savior than the Wise Men. Year after year, Gus had admired these Men, their regal countenance, their pride, but tonight they struck him as arrogant. He saw them as Ruth Dempsey might have seen them: tall, imperious, unkind. He felt more affection for the animals who seemed to sense one thing—the stirrings of a mystery. So Gus demoted the Men by moving three donkeys and four oxen closer to the Babe.

He whispered Ruth Dempsey's song: "I like Indians, I like Blacks, I like tits." He turned from the crèche, leaned a shoulder into a Wise Man, and knocked him on his side. Father's door swung open and a voice boomed: "Who's there?" Gus, running and sliding, lighted through the churchyard and up Krapalna Street toward the water tower. "Ruth Dempsey!" he called over his shoulder. "Try and catch her!" His throat burned with snow. The voice seemed too thunderous to be his own.

Huffing, out of breath, he found Jimmy patrolling back and forth near the tower. He looked up the ladder, ten rungs or so, but where was Fenza? A Christmas Eve Jack in the Beanstalk, he seemed to have disappeared in the sky.

"He up there?" he asked Jimmy. "All the way?"

"A mile high without a parachute."

Gus squinted into the snow. "Dumb," he said, "crazy. But I'd better help him out."

He saw how Fenza had climbed to the first rung of the ladder. Earlier, before the hoods came knocking on his door, Fenza and Jimmy must have made this snowball that stood some five feet high. Now Gus clambered onto it, stood, and wrapped his mittens over the first rung of the ladder. He pulled himself up and began his ascent.

"Hey," called Jimmy. "You're supposed to be a sentry, not a paratrooper."

I like Indians. I like Blacks . . .

"Fenza!" said Jimmy. "You up there?"

They heard a muffled voice through the snow, something about being near the top.

"Here comes Gus," said Jimmy. "He's on his way up."

Gus rose in a fury. Snow stuck to his pea coat, made him shine. Near the summit, he looked over his shoulder to the town and the river valley muted in white, the dim glow of stained glass windows one block south, the beams of a car pulling up to the curb at Sonny's Place, and spots of color—red, green, gold—from Christmas trees in Krapalna Street windows. The town was mostly white, the earth too, but Gus liked Indians and Blacks and tits. He looked south toward the river. It would be winding its way toward St. Louis, a black snake too deep and fast to freeze, but tonight it lay hidden in the blur of wind and falling snow.

~

Fenza, standing on tiptoes, then crouching, painted a red heart on the water tower. Horizontally, there was little limitation; he gave it the width of a Cadillac. He paused when he saw Gus scoot onto the railed catwalk that circled the tower.

"Numb nuts," said Fenza. "What you doing here?"

Gus shrugged.

"Guess you didn't tell Father Janecek."

"You knew I wouldn't."

"Yeah, but I thought you'd help Jimmy keep an eye on the street."

Gus watched him work. Fenza painted Jenny's name, then his initials, and drew Cupid's arrow—poinsettia red—coming out the sides of the heart. His derring-do would fail to impress a St. Roch's girl as virtuous as Jenny Biel. Try Pat Lemkey, thought Gus. She might share a cigarette with you, or a kiss in Pulaski Park.

Fenza stood aside to observe his handiwork. "Needs more paint," he said. "These letters need to be seen from the ground on Christmas Day."

He slopped on the paint so that each line of each letter was about a foot wide. "Think she'll see it well enough?"

"If she looks up."

"The cops won't know it's me because I'm just leaving my initials."

They'll know, thought Gus.

"They might suspect Frankie Reardon. He's crazy enough."

So are you.

"But Jenny will know," said Fenza. "There's no way she'll think of anyone but me."

Minutes later, they appraised Fenza's work, judged it satisfactory, and then Gus took the brush. Fenza had lugged a gallon of paint in his pack, and there was enough left for another heart and two names—Pat S. & Gus Zeul. Fenza said, "Dummy, just write your initials," but Gus ignored him.

He used broad strokes, slopped on the paint and watched it drip from the letters like red icicles. "Cops'll fry your ass," said Fenza. "You're writing your own ticket to a Christmas in jail."

Gus didn't care where he spent Christmas. He stretched to make the heart large, the letters tall. Fenza's heart had more height, but Gus's was wider. Pat Lemkey should be able to see it from three blocks away on Christmas Day.

Finished, he crouched on the catwalk. "Pat," he said, and his breath smoked. There was still some paint in the can.

"Come on," said Fenza. "We been up here too long."

"I need more time."

"Well, you can stay till the cops come. You wrote your whole name, so they'll meet you here or at home."

"Here's fine."

"Just don't tell on me. I'll kill you."

Gus waved a hand to dismiss the concern.

"See you," said Fenza. "Be careful going down."

Gus, once a model of self-restraint, held still a final moment before he began shaking and moaning, muttering at the sky, the earth, and at God, whether or not He had ears. Paintbrush in hand, the boy beat on the tower with all his might. The metal boomed, echoed, and sent peals of thunder into the clouds. Maybe this tower, this water-filled oval of steel, was the largest drum in the world. When Fenza growled, "Hornets in hell," Gus thought, No, Ruth Dempsey's tom-tom! He wished he could make it boom with lightning bolts rather than this small brush and a whip for an arm.

Fenza said, "Well, piss on the party then," and started down the ladder. It was too late to stop Gus from carrying on because he'd already made enough racket to alert the neighbors. Mr. and Mrs. Ciernik, busybodies, would've called the police by now. Gus, panting and moaning, hammered on the tower as if to sculpt a new shape or knock it to the ground. Crazy, thought Fenza. Little fucker's gone ballistic. Before Fenza could monkey his way back to earth, Gus blared at the top of his lungs—"I like Indians! I like Blacks! I like tits!" He wailed, chanted, drummed, and made more noise than the sirens now blaring up Krapalna Street toward St. Roch's Church and the tower. Wake the dead, thought Fenza, and while you're at it—the living! He swooped down the ladder two rungs at a time and leaped the last seven or eight feet into the snow.

"Fly!" he said, and he and Jimmy lit out down a privet-lined alley behind the tower. He let Jimmy go first so he could cover their tracks. Half-running, half-shuffling, Fenza destroyed potential evidence. He left in his wake no clear prints that could be identified by a cop or a vigilant neighbor, or by Father Janecek and the Sisters. The snow might soon erase everything, but why take chances? The holy ones were always the worst snoops.

~

Gus stopped drumming long enough to leave one more message: REMEM-BER RUTH DEMPSEY! If the sun shone on Christmas morning, this taunt —wider than the heart he had drawn—could be read by anyone who walked up Krapalna Street to St. Roch's Church.

He greeted the police and firemen with drumming and chanting. As several firemen spread a net beneath the tower, he called, "Take it away, I won't need it." This happened to be true. Some ten minutes later, he quieted, dropped the paintbrush in the can, and flitted down the rungs of the ladder with the ease of a wild crow flying from branch to branch.

~

At 11:35 he was in the custody of Officer Krupovich. In the back seat of the squad car, hands cuffed, he made his confession. "I did it all," he lied. "The hearts, the names, the initials. And the tribute to Ruth Dempsey."

Krupovich, in the driver's seat, aimed the car's beacon at the hearts on the tower. "Well, Merry Christmas. I suppose you're proud of yourself."

"I had no choice, sir."

"Who's F.R.? Fenza Ryczhik?"

"No, that's my alias. Frank Robinson."

Krupovich eyed him in the rear-view mirror. "I hope you're smart enough to know you're in trouble."

Gus nodded.

"Aren't you one of Father's altar boys? Midnight Mass?"

"I was, sir."

"You're headed for juvie," said the officer. "But first we'll have to tell Father or the Sisters to find another boy."

He flashed the beacon on REMEMBER RUTH DEMPSEY. "No," he muttered, "let's not," and turned off the light.

He drove down Krapalna and parked in front of the rectory. All the lights were on at Father's home, and Will Dempsey was scattering salt on the steps of St. Roch's. Sister Damien and Sister Walburga stood near the Nativity. They gave orders to Butch Yansik, whose job was to drag the animals, the donkeys and oxen, behind the Three Wise Men. Gus slumped down to escape the quick eyes of the Sisters. He was no longer afraid of them, but he preferred his own company to that of nuns.

Krupovich lit a cigarette. "Topsy-turvy," he said. "Even the Nativity's a mess."

Gus watched Will Dempsey. He wore a tweed overcoat, a dark hat, a muffler—all speckled with snow. He scattered salt the way a farmer would scatter grain on fresh-plowed earth. He appeared as wholesome as any man. He finished his work, climbed the stairs, and disappeared in St. Roch's Church.

Krupovich went out to speak with the Sisters. He wished them a Merry Christmas, then told them about "Gus Zeul's rampage."

Sister Damien had a hard time accepting the truth. She said Gus Zeul was a good boy, not a bad boy. She suggested that Krupovich or other authorities had nabbed the wrong boy.

Krupovich said, "Every cop and fireman in this town will tell you the same: We caught Gus Zeul red-handed."

Sister Walburga said, "Well, I certainly heard the commotion. Who didn't?"

Krupovich grunted.

"But that's not like Gus," said Sister Damien. "You're sure he did this?"

The officer nodded.

"I thought of Fenza when I heard obscenities, wild cursing and shouting and drumming."

"A good guess," said Krupovich, and flicked the ash from his cigarette. "But that was none other than Augie Zeul."

He led the nuns to his car, the lights still flashing. "Here he is," he said, "if you want a look. Your good boy painted our water tower, gizzied it up with hearts and names and initials. Plus a little something for Ruth Dempsey."

"Oh my," said Sister Walburga.

"And for who knows how long?—you heard him—he banged that tower like a giant drum."

Sister Damien, her face ghostly, snow sprinkled on her habit, peered through the window. Gus waved to her with cuffed hands.

"We'll need another boy," said Sister Walburga, "for Midnight Mass."

Krupovich glanced at his watch. "That's why I came by, Sister. So you'll have a few minutes to sort things out."

Sister Walburga called to Butch Yansik, who still needed to move two donkeys to their proper places. "Leave them where they are," she said. "Sister Damien and I will finish. Go ask Father if you can serve as his altar boy at Midnight Mass."

"Yes, Sister."

She glanced across the street to Pulaski Park, the shadows of trees.

"And remind Father that Fenza will be his other altar boy if he gets here on time."

Fenza arrived at St. Roch's after Krupovich and his squad car vanished. Sister Walburga and Sister Damien were struggling with the last of the donkeys, so he stepped in, wished them a Merry Christmas, and dragged it back where it belonged. "Good," said Sister Walburga, "we're all set. Now go and see Father and prepare for Midnight Mass."

Fenza

By daybreak, the snow had stopped and gale winds scoured the valley. Fence-high drifts swept down Krapalna Street and the Highway Patrol closed Route 6, the road that led east and west from Orville. The local radio station announced that Father Janecek would still offer two Christmas Masses at Saint Roch's Church, and the town's taverns would remain open as long as they had patrons. "Temperatures plummeting," said the weatherman, "so light a fire, pull up a chair, or gather in the warmth of your neighborhood bar."

Fenza Ryczhik Jr. had lain awake through most of the night. Curled beside the radio on his nightstand, he'd listened to Christmas songs, Ave Marias, weather reports, and—at the top of each hour—state and local news. At 7 a.m., he punched his pillow at the mention of "a St. Roch's boy who climbed the Orville water tower before Midnight Mass. A big hullabaloo," said the announcer, "with no rhyme or reason, only a major headache for our police and firemen. According to Officer Krupovich, one teenager acted alone, smeared red paint all over the tower, shouted and drummed, and turned Christmas Eve into a carnival. We've been asked to withhold the identity of the perpetrator because he's a minor." Fenza, smiling in the dark, said, "Augie Zeul, my secret agent." His pal had come around. Gus often worried Fenza with his religious sentiments, his kindness, but he would never—in any season—stoop so low as to be a snitch.

⌇

He called the Zeul residence—no answer—but Cassie picked up a few minutes later. "I just got back from Juvenile Hall," she said. "The roads were so bad I had to get a ride from the sheriff."

"Juvie? But why—?"

"Fenza," she said, "you *know* why. I'm in no mood to listen to a spiel."

She told him Gus confessed to three crimes—trespassing, vandalism, and disturbing the peace—but what might rob her of sleep for nights on end was that he climbed a 188-foot water tower during the biggest snowstorm of the year. "I almost lost him," said Cassie. "One misstep, one gust of wind, and he would've been gone for good."

Fenza cleared his throat. "I'm sorry, Mrs. Zeul."

"And you were with him, weren't you? He claims you weren't, but why would he write your initials?"

"You'll have to ask him."

"And Jimmy was there too. Maybe not on the tower, but he was part of it."

Fenza chewed his lower lip.

"No more stunts," said Cassie. "I can't bear the thought of losing any of you boys. You hear me?"

"Yes, ma'am."

"That *yes* better mean something, Fenza."

"It does."

"You boys are so young you don't know you can die."

Her motherly concerns were more intricate than she could reveal. Sister Damien and Father Janecek had groomed Gus for the priesthood, but he escaped their grasp by climbing halfway to heaven on Christmas Eve. So the priesthood was gone, au revoir. Gus was a different kind of holy with a tower as a pulpit, with an admonishment for the church and the town—REMEMBER RUTH DEMPSEY! Rather than endangering his life, Cassie wished he'd splashed red letters across the facade of City Hall or the Court House. No, he had to climb the tower, taunt death, taunt the town, and where would this lead? No one was more reckless than a thirteen-year-old boy.

"I need to tell you," she said to Fenza, "what I told my son. Nothing any of us can do will make up for what happened to Ruth Dempsey."

Fenza shrugged. "I guess you're right."

"In a few days they'll whitewash the tower, the mention of Ruth, the hearts and names and initials, and the town will seem normal."

"I know, Mrs. Zeul."

"The heart you painted for Jenny may be gone before she sees it."

"I never—"

"So no more stunts," said Cassie. "I'm sure you can find other ways to impress a girl."

Like what? thought Fenza. Should I scale St. Roch's steeple and let out a cry? Wave a flag with Jenny's name? Fenza had not lost hope that his gallantry on Christmas Eve would pay rich dividends. Yes, the tower would be whitewashed, everything painted over. But all Jenny needed was a split second on Christmas Day to fancy Fenza's work.

"The sheriff told me Gus would be on probation for at least a year."

"I don't think that's fair."

"I see no reason to tell the police you were involved, but your mother and father should know you climbed the water tower in a near blizzard."

"But Mrs. Zeul—"

"Are they awake? Can you call them?"

"They're late sleepers."

"Fenza, this is not the time to try my patience. Stalling won't help."

Might help a little, he thought as he set the phone in its cradle, unplugged the jack, and sprang from a chair.

He put on a wool sweater and his lumberjack boots, stuffed some cookies in the pocket of a sheepskin coat, and slipped out the back door. Jimmy's house was four blocks south. Fenza could hear snowplows clearing the street near Sonny's Place and St. Roch's Church, but near the river he had to plunge through drifts like a fullback bulling his way to a first down. The sun edged over the trees. Drifting snow—bright as the flash of a knife—made his eyes tear. Christmas Day shone sharp as a blade.

Jimmy's house was a three-room clapboard with a sagging roof. Fenza went around to the south side, kicked through a drift, and knocked on the bedroom window. One swell thing about Jimmy—he'd follow you, a good soldier, before you told him where you were going. Fenza took off his gloves and banged and rattled the pane till Jimmy came to the window. "You deaf?" said Fenza. "Get some clothes on. We're going for a walk."

Jimmy, in astronaut pajamas, stars and planets, nodded a sleepy Yes. A blond cowlick curled like a horn.

He cracked open the window. "Where's Gus? He in jail?"

"Never mind. Your parents asleep?"

Jimmy nodded.

"Then throw on some clothes, shake a leg. Hurry the hell up before they wake."

～

67

Shoulder-to-shoulder, they plowed their way through alleys, then cut over to Krapalna Street and the water tower. They looked over the night's work, the hearts and names and initials—what Fenza would later call "the best graffiti in Illinois." Just now, though, it bothered him that Gus's heart was wider, and the name of his girl—PAT LEMKEY—was easier to read. REMEMBER RUTH DEMPSEY! was better, too. In crooked red letters like a stop sign gone berserk.

The glare of sun and snow almost blinded him. He strained to see Jenny's name, his initials, and the oval of the heart. The letters were fuzzy as Braille, probably easier to feel than to read. Hope returned when he shaded his brow and saw her name, tall as a soldier and red as blood.

Dust devils of snow blew down Krapalna Street. Bent over, the boys passed St. Roch's Church, then flitted across the street to Pulaski Park. Fenza led the way to a grove of maples. Last night their branches gleamed with snow, but they were naked bones now, swept clean by the wind, and a few of the weaker appendages had been tossed to the drifts. Fenza slammed a fist into a frozen trunk, then shook the hurt from his hand. Maybe nothing could soften this day but a well-honed scheme.

He gave Jimmy the low-down. Before eight o'clock Mass, he would meet in private with Jenny Biel, face-to-face and close enough to kiss. "Your job," he said, "is to waylay her parents, find a way to distract them." He jabbed the tree again, but with his other hand. "If they lose sight of Jenny for thirty seconds, I'm good as gold."

Jimmy looked around. "Okay, but where's Jenny? Where's her parents?"

"They'll be here."

"When?"

"Fifteen minutes, maybe twenty."

"You're sure?"

"They're always early for eight o'clock Mass."

Fenza said he'd give Jimmy a silver dollar if he waylaid her parents a full minute.

"Before you said thirty seconds."

"I'm upping the ante, winner take all."

Jimmy shivered. "But I can't stand anyone's parents. I hardly talk to my own."

"Yeah, so where's the problem? The trick's to distract them, not like them. Just say Merry Christmas and start jabbering about how goddamn pretty the snow is."

"Aw, Fenza."

"And shake their hands, make a show of it, before you charm them with a story."

"What story?"

"Whatever slips into your mind . . . Maybe your mom wet her drawers because she won at bingo last Thursday. She's giving half the money to St. Roch's Church this Christmas morning, and the other half will help fund new uniforms for the basketball team."

Jimmy squinted in concentration. He tried to remember the lies.

"And keep going back to how goddamn pretty the snow is. No harm in repeating yourself."

"I don't know, Fenza."

"One minute with Jen. That's all I ask."

"But—"

"Save the butts and smoke 'em. Just imagine your life hangs on this."

Jimmy sighed. "Christ, Fenza."

"And leave Him out of this. It's me, not Him, telling you how to play."

~

The sky was brilliant and blue and the sun lit the snow and the white street and the parishioners were trudging up Krapalna toward St. Roch's Church as on any Christmas morning. Fenza wished he had black grease beneath his eyes to deflect the glare. Ballplayers had it, soldiers too, especially snipers. Only Negroes didn't need war paint to fight the sun.

Jimmy said, "What if Jen's already in church? What if we missed her?"

"Not likely," said Fenza. "But if she is inside, we'll hang tight and wait till she leaves."

Jimmy hugged his arms to his chest and thought, Come on, Jen, *hurry*. He might soon have a choice—abandon his friend or suffer frostbite. Fenza was tougher than winter. Or maybe he was too crazy to feel the cold.

The big boy saw her first. A red coat, a Christmas coat, made Jenny look wooly and wide. He nudged Jimmy and said, "Showtime, run the reel." So they kicked through snow, crossed Krapalna Street, and made a beeline for the girl.

A few steps away—*in range* was how Fenza framed it—he hung back and let Jimmy take charge. Jen walked on her parents' left. Jimmy wormed his way between her and her folks, said, "Merry Christmas," and started shaking hands. Pump the old man's hand, then the old lady's, and jabber away about the hundred-sixty dollars his mom won at bingo, how she was giving half of it to Saint Roch's Church this Christmas morning, how the other half would help fund new uniforms for the basketball team. He surprised himself by garnishing fiction with fact: He was leading the team in scoring. "But how 'bout this Christmas?" he said. "Isn't it pretty?" He sounded sincere enough to draw a smile from Jen's mom. The old man said, "Merry Christmas, Jimmy," then peeled back the sleeve of his overcoat to frown at his watch.

Fenza blocked Jenny's path. She stopped and glared at him, then tried to walk around.

"Wait," he said. "I have something to tell you."

"I don't care to hear it."

He grabbed her gloved hands and whispered, "Meet me at the water tower after Mass. Look high, Jenny. Your name and my initials. Halfway to the sun."

"Let go of me."

"I will."

"Dad."

"Easy now."

"Dad!"

"Can't you just—"

"Let go of me!"

"I haven't got any cooties, not a one."

"Yes, you do."

"No, I don't."

"You're nuts."

"Meet me at the water tower after Mass."

Mr. Biel, tall and rude, stepped between them. But Fenza had already said some of what he needed to say.

～

After Jimmy headed for home, Fenza went to the tower and waited. He ate the sweets he'd brought along, big Santa Claus cookies, and he could've devoured a dozen. He stamped his feet and walked around to try and keep warm. Now and then he spoke his thoughts aloud: "Come on, Jen, give me a chance. Don't be a loser." Fenza continued to walk in circles after Mass was over and the church bells tolled the hour—nine o'clock. Maybe Jen would make her way to the tower after she ditched her parents. What if she was too shy to admit she liked him a little? Shyness is a disease, but curable. A kiss or two and it disappears.

His face was a frozen slab, his feet numb. Defeat was impossible to accept. Fenza whispered her name, a one-word prayer, and he waited. It was almost nine thirty when he glared at the tower, the sun, the sky, and he raised his arms and railed at the girl and the town and the whole spinning world that ground to dust his intrigues and hopes and desires— "Fuck yourselves blue, you dumb fuckers! Fuck yourselves *blue!*" He bellowed this in the blur of wind and light. The neighbors had to hear him: old Mrs. Janes, Mr. and Mrs. Ciernik, Mrs. Plesko—her moose-fanny wide as her front door—and all the other dupes who knew nothing about nothing. And after he carried on awhile, his throat raw, he wondered if Jenny, four blocks away and shuttered in her home, heard some measure of her comfort drift away in the violence of his voice.

He tried to hate her, but the old feelings of love crept into his heart. Fenza cried on the way home. Bitter tears. Frost. The ice of love wiped away with fists.

～

Gus was released from Juvenile Hall on December 27. Cassie spoke with Fenza's parents first, then Jimmy's, and the boys were grounded during Christmas vacation. In mid-January, after days of discussion, the mothers agreed their sons could see one another after school and on weekends if they stayed out of trouble. Mrs. Ryczhik, who believed Gus and Jimmy were spoiling her Fenza, gave her consent upon one condition. "We must provide our boys a meeting place," she said, "so they won't be traipsing around town searching for mischief. What they've been lacking—Gus and Jimmy especially—is supervision, *adult* supervision. One of us, or our husbands" —she looked askance at Cassie, who probably had lovers—"need to chaperone the boys."

～

The Ryczhik home had a basement. Fenza's mom ordered him to clean it up, make a clubroom for his pals, and Gus and Jimmy helped. One corner of the basement had a shed-sized room with a door. Fenza's father kept his tools here, plus certain books about World War II, but there was enough space for a card table and three chairs. A poster of the Chicago Bears fullback Rick Casares was taped to a wall. This annoyed Fenza because a real men's club would have calendar pictures of naked girls.

So after school one day, the boys huddled around the card table, and Fenza gave their club a name—The Moose Brotherhood. He asked Jimmy and Gus, "Did you ever fuck a moose? Did you ever?" When Jimmy bragged, "Every day but Sunday," Fenza lunged forward and got him in a headlock. "Wrong answer," said Fenza. "I *hate* wrong answers." He coached Jimmy to moan and say, "Don't ever, don't ever." This coded response signaled membership in the club.

They loved music. On a Saturday night in late January, a sleepover, Gus played drums on the card table, Jimmy pounded an empty paint can with chisels, and Fenza sang "Duke of Earl." The lyrics were outstanding, especially the part about the Duke and his girl and nobody big enough to stop them. Fenza pretended his fist was a microphone. He keened and crooned, and the sounds swelled from his chest with the authority of a testament. Jimmy, basso buffo, sang accompaniment. He put down the chisels and banged the can with his fists.

Fenza ended the song on a high note. "Moose brothers," he said, "I think we got the makings of a big-time band."

Hoodlum Girl

At morning recess, she jaywalked across Krapalna Street to Pulaski Park. She quickened her pace when Gus Zeul called, "Hey, Pat, wait a second! Can I ask you something?" She heard him catching up, the horselike clomp of winter boots. She couldn't outrun him, so she turned, chin up, eyes cold, a practiced gesture that froze him in mid-stride, his mouth open, his left hand raised in a failed greeting. A moment later Jimmy sidled up beside Gus, then Fenza, and the latter incited a three-way shoving match across from St. Roch's Church. Pat was pleased to see them occupied. The one thing wrong with Gus would never change: he was a boy.

But St. Roch's girls were a weary lot. Wives-in-training, they mostly hung in cliques, and whiled away their recess and after-school hours palavering in shrill voices about this boy or that, a covey of sparrows vying for crumbs. One reason Pat was drawn to Jenny Biel was that she spoke rather than twittered. She liked the sweetness in Jenny, and the way her friend tended to confide in her when confused or lonely. "Why's Fenza still after me? I just wish he would go away."

To play the devil but appear normal, Pat had a boyfriend—Frankie Reardon. He was a public-school creep, a bad boy, or at least he liked to think so. Touring the town with Frankie, walking hand in hand down Krapalna Street, Pat would interrupt his stories, ignore his jokes, but for Jenny Biel she behaved. She hung on her friend's least word, her most nuanced gesture. Once, on the playground, she almost took Jenny in her arms. They stood near the merry-go-round during morning recess. Pat, her arms half-open, turned, but then she got scared and called, "Chase me, I dare you!" and they ran toward the swings. The grass, glazed with frost, made every step a gamble. Pat sprang ahead, then grabbed Jen's arm to keep from fall-ing. They reached the swings in the same stride. "Okay," said Pat, "one more dare. Chase me to the sky!" The girls began to sway back and forth on the red swings. They gathered momentum, kicked their legs high, feet to the sky, then crimp-kneed and earthbound, heels skimming the packed dirt, and then up again, a longer arc, and nothing to stop them save the length of the chains. Okay, thought Pat, chase me till I'm yours! Last November, three days shy of Thanksgiving, she knew when to hush. A few words at the wrong time might scare her friend away.

∽

Now Gus said to Fenza and Jimmy, "So long, saps," and ran till he reached the baseball diamond, home plate. Pat Lemkey, some thirty yards ahead, sauntered toward the swing set. She glanced back as if expecting someone to join her. Probably not me, thought Gus, but who knows? Although Pat never saw her name scrawled on the water tower before workers smothered it in white paint, she knew his sentiments. In Orville County, one thing traveled faster than light: gossip. The moment Gus was jailed for vandalism and disturbing the peace on Christmas Eve, the entire Illinois Valley learned of his love for this girl.

Gus checked his watch—eight minutes before the schoolhouse bell would signal the end of recess. Christmas Eve was a month ago, yet he still didn't know how to approach Pat, what exactly to say. He trotted around the bases, touched home for luck, then walked slow and steady toward the swing set. The air was misty, a gray blanket, but something flashed in his field of vision. A cardinal had lighted in a sycamore tree. What Gus felt inside was this color, this winter red more beautiful than any flower. He imitated the sweet, twittering sounds of the cardinal. Did the bird hear him? He gleamed an eye at Gus, then gave the torch of his feathers a shake.

Pat was eyeing Jenny Biel. She didn't see him as he neared, as he gathered what he could of his breath and his courage. Three inches of snow had fallen in the night. Jenny, a cheerleader, was practicing jumps on a cleared path-way near the merry-go-round. Four other girls were with her, four jumpers, but Pat seemed to see no one but Jen. Maybe she, too, wished she could jump high, bound like a deer. A few weeks back, she gave Fenza a shiner when he called her a moose. Gus, when he was alone with his friend, said, "Serves you right, dumbo. She's not fat, she's *chubby*." Pat certainly could fill out a sweater, and no other Orville girl wore a leather jacket. She smoked, too, Lucky Strikes, same as Fenza and Jimmy. She was secretive, she was pretty. And no other girl would ever lead Gus to take such a terrible risk.

He had to step in front of her to cut her eyes from Jenny.

"Hey Pat," he said. "How's it going?"

She flicked a hand into her jacket and brought out a cigarette.

He said it was cold today, but spring was near.

She shrugged.

He wanted to say something about the red bird, but he felt dull in comparison. The cardinal perched in the sycamore was brighter than the heart he had painted on the tower.

He mumbled about school, how boring it was. It took a while to speak clearly and come to the point.

"I know Frankie Reardon. You're better than he is."

"You think so?"

"Way better. It's not even close."

She glanced around for nuns. Sister Mary Margaret and Sister Walburga were keeping an eye on the boys, Fenza and some others, so she lit a cigarette. She was almost ornery enough to blow smoke in Gus's face.

"What do you want?"

"Nothing."

"You're never getting a kiss. You know that?"

"Well—"

"You want to know if you have a chance with me? Is that it?"

He nodded.

"Not much chance," she said. "I wouldn't even try."

He looked down.

"You can go now."

His feet were stuck.

"You're okay," said Pat. "Or at least nicer than Frankie."

He didn't know what to say to this.

"If I wanted a St. Roch's boy, I might try you."

He didn't know what to say to that either.

"Here," she said, and handed him her Lucky. "Remember I'm not the only girl, okay?"

He puffed and coughed.

She said, "Maybe I can be your friend."

His feet came unstuck and he shifted his weight. He looked at the sky, the gray sweep now barren of birds. Bye, he said, and darted off toward Krapalna Street and the school. He searched the sycamore and other trees for the cardinal, but maybe it had flown toward the river. That's where Gus would fly if he were a bird—south to the river. And he would disappear in the willows and cottonwoods till the leaves turned green in summer light and the water shone bright enough to hurt his eyes and chase him to shady woods.

~

The bell rang and Sister Walburga led the kids across Krapalna Street and past St. Roch's Church and the rectory and the nuns' house adjacent to the school. The latter, a cinder-block fortress three stories high, was the color of the winter sky, and topped by a brick tower where a nun always stood sentry when the children returned from recess. Gus saw it was Sister Damien this time, and for some reason he waved. She must have seen him, she could have waved back, but she didn't. He had a notion to yell at her and the other nuns wrapped in robes, "I like Indians, I like Blacks, I like tits!" He restrained himself, dug his hands in his pockets, and found himself shivering. His chest, his arms, pulsed and quaked as if hooked to high voltage. He took off running, passed Jenny and the cheerleaders, but he backed off when he saw Fenza and Jimmy near the nuns' house. If his friends asked about Pat, he might wink and smile and sing an old Slovenian song: "I don't want her, you can have her, she's too fat for me." He might even dance, hop about, take Fenza as his partner. He could fool his friends, but then what? The bright sheen in his eyes, the rawness and soreness in his throat, told the hard truth, the only truth: Gus loved her too much to be her friend.

~

A few days later, in Pulaski Park, he approached Jenny at recess. He didn't care to be her boyfriend. He went up to her because she was watching the girl he still loved a little, Pat Lemkey, swinging on a swing, an unlit cigarette like a piece of chalk in a corner of her mouth. Jenny stood near the merry-go-round. Those two girls kept glancing back and forth, as if awaiting a signal. They seemed to share something illicit, some secret knowledge of each other, but what? Maybe he'd ask Jenny if he still had an outside chance with Pat, or maybe not. Snow showers made the air fuzzy. He walked up to her, held out a hand, and watched the bright dust disappear in his palm. More snow came. She shook off a glove, touched his hand, and the flakes—the size of freckles—melted. Gus could never have grasped what made him do this—catch snow—nor what made a pretty girl help him melt it. Crouched to her height, shaking a little, he said, "Well, I guess we'll never build a snowman. What are we doing?" She said they were wasting time, but she kept touching his hand to turn snow into water. They were magicians. They understood heat and cold. They knew chemistry. They knew how to change one thing into another. Jenny didn't want to like him, but she did. He was the first and last boy to give her something soft from the sky.

Fenza

On Valentine's Day he had no sweetheart. He walked home alone after school, moped around in his room, then went out back and played with his jackknife. Whatever caught his eye was a target. Sparrows were too quick, he missed them, but he didn't miss tree trunks. He liked the sharp, clean sound of the blade shunting through bark and the way the handle quivered, then stilled. The sky was pale blue, the air crisp, the trees brittle with winter. He remembered Pop telling him he was "good with a knife, maybe better than good." He wished the old man were here right now to offer some tips, or demonstrate. If Pop were sober, he might be quick enough to pin a sparrow's wings to a frozen limb.

The boy looked down the alley. The houses, mostly clapboard, had a crumpled look, and if spring didn't come soon, winter might flatten them to the ground. Fenza sometimes felt ashamed of his neighborhood. The houses were small, better suited for pigeons than people, but there were trees in the yards and the tallest—an oak—stood near his bedroom window. Thank God he didn't live in a damn clapboard, the paint peeled back to bare wood. Fenza's home, a stout pebbledash, its walls speckled with pebbles and stones, might survive a century of winters. What pleased him most, though, were the trees, the oaks and maples, La Harpe Street's only splendor. Bare and gray, they weren't as dead as they looked. Maybe just drowsy is all, half-asleep. He could wake any one of them with the blade of his knife.

He went up to the big oak tree and cut it. It would've been easier to carve his name once spring softened the bark, but he was short on patience. Stabbing and chiseling, he made his marks—FENZA. Maybe his name would be part of this tree for a hundred years.

The late sun leaked its yellow light over the rooftop of a neighbor. Katie Flannery, a widow, lived next door, in the only other pebbledash home within a quarter mile. Pushing eighty, she was deaf enough that she might not hear Fenza if he scooted up her TV antenna and stomped on her roof. He wanted a vantage point from which he could peer down at the setting sun, the glint in his eye the equal of any star at its zenith. The antenna seemed too slight to hold him, though, and he might bring it down with a crash. The sun might not hold him, either, if he could grab on somehow. There was no telling how many things Fenza could bring down with his bull shoulders and broken heart.

This morning at recess, Jimmy Posey told him he spied Gus kissing Jenny behind some chokecherry bushes in Pulaski Park. "Just took her and kissed her," he whispered. "She didn't seem to mind."

Fenza kept quiet. Lover Boy Gus, he thought. He wouldn't kiss her so well if he lost his teeth.

He leaned on the tree that bore his name. There was no heart and no Jenny, nothing more to carve. The winter sun shone no brighter than a matchstick. Maybe he was done with pretty girls.

~

Gus came up the alley at twilight. He had a book-bag strapped to his shoulders, so maybe he'd told his mom he was coming over to study. Fenza ducked behind the oak tree. He cocked his right arm and thought, Step it up, Romeo, you're almost in range. A phrase found a niche in his mind, a shell in a chamber—*killing zone*. He'd learned this from Pop, and he remembered reading a story about three Marines luring nine Japanese soldiers into a ravine and killing the whole bunch in one burst of fire. Fenza didn't want Gus dead, but a hint of death might sweeten his day. He pictured his knife piercing the ground inches from Lover Boy's feet.

Blackbirds lighted in high branches. Gus, at a stroll, passed between the giant tree and the backside of the house, the entry to the cellar and the clubroom on his right. He didn't pause to notice the name carved in the trunk—FENZA. Blackbirds bickered, flew up and resettled. Lover Boy glanced sidewise at the tree, the noise, the sky.

Fenza let the knife fly straight out. He aimed well, but the blade ricocheted off a stone or the frozen ground and came up fast. The knife stuck in Gus's right calf. Fenza could feel more than see the blade quiver a split second before it fell.

At first the shock deadened the pain, except for a slight pinch. Gus bent down and poked a finger through his torn pant leg. A bullet would have made a similar mark.

"Fenza?" he said.

Silence.

"You get dumber every day."

Fenza heard the whoosh of his heart in his ears. He emerged from hiding, his eyes downcast, his shoulders hunched. Gus rolled up his pant leg. A steady stream of blood trickled down his calf and into his sock.

Fenza recovered enough to feign indifference. "It's just a scratch. You can stop whining."

"Who's whining?"

Fenza glanced toward the kitchen window. "Don't tell my mom. We'll both get in trouble."

"Moron."

"If our parents find out, they'll break up our club."

Gus was in a daze. "Club?"

"Moose Brothers. The only club we have."

"Who gives a damn?"

"Someday you will."

"I'm bleeding."

"Just a flesh wound."

"You put a hole in my leg."

Gus shook his head, as though to clear it. Everything was light and bright and swaying. The trees were huge, monstrous. His fingers looked strange against his white leg, and the blood felt like someone else's. He squinted to see things better. The neat hole, the blood staining a white sock. "Fenza," he said, "no one cares about the club."

Fenza draped Gus's right arm over his shoulders. "Come on," he said. "You know I wasn't meaning to stick you."

"You're an asshole."

"All I wanted was a little scare."

He helped Gus along the backside of the house, past the shrubs under the eave, and lifted him down the steps and through the doorway of the cellar. He'd always liked the smell here, rooty and moist, but now it brought no comfort. What did bring comfort was to envision a hill, a field of battle, a flag going up over Iwo Jima. He would never forget the photograph on Pop's desk, a bunch of GIs raising Old Glory over a dead landscape. The lowliest survivor was forever changed.

Fenza led his friend through the cellar to a small partition—the clubroom. He switched on the overhead lamp, nudged Gus into a folding chair, and examined the wound. "Don't act like you're dying," he said. "This is like a little scrape in the schoolyard."

"Oh?"

"A nickel-dime wound, or maybe a penny."

"Fuck you, Fenza."

"A few days off and you'll be back with the pack."

He told Gus to sit still and hurried upstairs for a bandage. He found a roll of gauze in the medicine cabinet in the bathroom, but there was no tape. On a field of battle, a corpsman sometimes ran out of supplies. No bandages. No tape. No morphine. Sometimes the dead outnumbered the living and a corpsman used his hands to staunch wounds.

He ducked into the kitchen where his mom was preparing supper. He smelled meat loaf in the oven, boiled cabbage on the stove, and his appetite surprised him. He wondered if Pop, during the war, ever ate a full meal after one of his friends was wounded. And what about the corpsmen who had to deal with amputations, spilled guts, piles of dead bodies? Hungry or not, they eventually had to eat.

His mom wore an apron with a lavender imprint—CAPITAL OF HOME COOKIN'! She and her Betty Crocker kitchen threatened his mood.

"Can Gus have supper with us?"

She glanced at him. "He's coming over on a school night?"

"He's already here. In the clubroom."

"And what about your homework?"

"Mine's finished. I need to help Gus with his math assignment. He has a lot of trouble with math."

~

In the cellar Gus was moaning. Fenza knelt in front of him and told him to quit whining like a baby. The wound—from what Fenza could tell—was about an inch deep. "Flesh wound," he said, "Minor. The knife hit you at a glance."

"Minor?" said Gus. "Why don't you stick a knife in your own leg? See how it feels."

"I might."

"Go on. Who's stopping you?"

"No one."

"You're dumb enough to do any dumb thing in the world."

Fenza wrapped the wound in layers of gauze and secured the bandage with a knot. "You got some tape at your place?"

"I don't know."

"You need some tape to keep the bandage from slipping."

"Thanks, Dr. Fuckup."

"Shut up."

"You're really a big help."

Gus looked at him. "So why'd you throw at me?"

"No reason."

"You mad about Jenny?"

Fenza shrugged. "She's yours if you want her that bad."

"Jimmy said you'd try something. I should've listened."

"I meant to scare you, is all."

"Because of Jenny?"

Fenza swallowed. The ache in his throat surprised him. "I hear you kissed her."

"Who said?"

"Jimmy."

"He's half blind," said Gus. "She kissed *me*."

Fenza shivered. "Well, I already said you can have her." He bent down and looked his friend in the eye. "She's yours," he said. "Gus Zeul and Jenny Biel from this day on."

Gus wondered if he meant it. "Don't throw any more knives at me."

"I won't."

"Promise?"

Fenza nodded. "The knife was supposed to land beside you, stick in the ground."

"I might believe you tomorrow."

"It hit a damn rock or something, bounced up. Honest."

"The rock's fault?"

"No, my fault. But once I saw a guy at a carnival stick a knife near a lady's ear."

He sank his hands in his pockets. Fenza always carried his knife, but there was no knife now. In haste, he had disregarded a primary rule of combat—never abandon a weapon on the field of battle. "Be right back," he said, "stay put. I owe you something good."

Gus didn't care what Fenza owed him. His wound hurt now, he needed a painkiller, so he remembered the way Jenny kissed him in Pulaski Park. Sometimes his heart felt like the noisiest drum in town. Jen must've heard the boom and shine of it because she held an ear to his chest and said, "You're the loudest quiet boy I'll ever know."

∼

Fenza, jackknife in hand, came back down the cellar, pulled up a chair in front of Gus, and rolled up his right pant leg. "This'll make us even," he said. "Blood brothers."

"I'd rather be unrelated."

"I didn't mean to hurt you. I got one way to prove it."

"Put the knife away."

"I will," said Fenza. "In a moment's time."

He pushed the blade about a half inch into his right calf. Gritting his teeth and moaning, he jerked it out and wiped the blood on his pant leg. "There," he said, "blood brothers. Now we'll each have a scar."

Gus needed time to catch his breath. "Fenza," he said, "you're worse than stupid."

"Semper fi."

"I ought to just let you bleed."

But he leaned over and pressed his right hand to the wound to staunch the flow.

"Blood brothers," said Fenza.

"Shut up."

"I knew this would happen someday."

Gus untied his bandage, unwrapped a foot or so of gauze, and used Fenza's knife to cut it. He secured his bandage again, then attended to Fenza. He folded the loose strip of gauze and pressed it tight to the wound.

Fenza grimaced with pleasure. "You're my corpsman, my ace in the hole."

"I'd rather be an Oscar Meyer wiener."

"No, you're my main man, my battle buddy. This wound is deep enough to scar."

And the pain, too, at least for a few minutes, was a kind of blessing. Fenza tried to convince himself he was free of Jenny Biel. There were hundreds of girls in Orville, so why get stuck on one? Why not shake the dice, play some new numbers? What's to lose? Fenza offered himself sound advice, but he still suffered. Would he like Jenny so much if she liked him back? He should have gone deeper with the knife.

PART 2

The Boys and Girls of St. Iggy's

(1964–1966)

I'll take heaven for the weather, hell for the company.

—MARK TWAIN

Poetry

The Catholic high school, St. Ignatius, St. Iggy's, was on the west side of town, a short walk from the river. Gus, once groomed to be a priest, began to cut school his freshman year, as did Fenza and Jimmy. Sunny days drew them to the river. They dallied away the hours in willow groves, and if they got fidgety or bored they dug up some night crawlers and caught a few fish, none of which they kept. At three o'clock, when their classmates began to hurry down halls and out schoolhouse doors, they stashed their fishing poles in the willows and sauntered up Krapalna Street to Fenza's cellar, their faces flushed with good weather, their packs laden with books never opened. Fenza made up stories of hitchhiking to neighboring towns to rendezvous with prostitutes who liked him so much they never charged him a penny. Only Gus could boast of a sweetheart, Jenny Biel, but they all agreed she would be a virgin till her honeymoon.

At Fenza's urging, they formed a band called Don't Ever. In the cellar, their "studio," Gus used empty paint cans for drums, but for his birthday in mid-March, his mother, who thought music might keep him sane, ordered a bongo set from a retailer in South Chicago. Fenza polished a rusty harmonica till it shone, and Jimmy spent his paper-route money on a used guitar. By refusing to play on the freshman basketball team, Jimmy, a talented player, roused the wrath of his father. Fenza and Gus also lost interest in sports. The life they loved most was the life of hoods.

St. Iggy's was like St. Roch's. The nuns were strict, Father Janecek had his say, but there was one difference. In April of '64, Sister Damien, who taught at both schools, took sick and was replaced by Sister Clair. In religion class, the new Sister abandoned the text of the archdiocese, *Catholicism and Youth*, and taught the course through poetry and gospel. She instructed her students to write haiku. "Keep it simple," she said, and printed on the board:

"Sparrow singing—
its tiny mouth
open."
—Buson

"Hearing," said Sister Clair, "seeing—that's all this poem is about. If you experience or witness the present moment, you have a chance to write haiku."

Fenza, in the last row, wrote, "Jack be nimble, Jack be quick. Jack jumps over the candlestick and burns his asshole black!" He showed this jingle to Jimmy, then passed Jimmy a note: "Sir, did you ever fuck a moose in springtime? You goddamn pervert—DON'T EVER!" Catholic boys knew how to suppress laughter. Shoulders jiggling, arms drawn in, they seemed to ward off seizures.

Sister Clair said, "Do you boys need some help?"

They shook their heads and were ready to burst.

But there was one kid who wanted to be a poet. Weeks later, on a form on which each student was to choose from a list his or her future vocation, Gus wrote in the margin in capital letters: I NEED TO BE TWO THINGS AT ONCE—A DRUMMER AND A POET. MAYBE YOU CAN ADD THESE TO YOUR LIST.

The students survived the fall and winter of their freshman year, and they did better than survive after Sister Clair arrived from Montgomery, Alabama. Accustomed to rules, the tedium of rote learning, they soon came to the conclusion that Sister lived beyond the Church and made her own rules. Stout, energetic, she performed all tasks with urgency and interest. She loved Jesus most "for the qualities He combined—love and defiance." According to Sister, the Lord's utmost virtue was His refusal to be tethered by any man or institution, regardless of how powerful. Gus asked what *tethered* meant. "Bound up," she said, "made mild. Restrained." She motioned to the window. "You can know the opposite of tethered if you look outside."

The sun was climbing the sky over St. Iggy's schoolyard, shining on a strip of earth as black as Sister's robes. Blue sky and black earth. Sycamores so green Gus squinted so some of the light would bounce off his eyelids and back to the trees. The boy began to wonder about the mettlesome Saint who refused to be tethered. What did He want? What did He really *want*? Gus drummed his desktop, shuffled his feet. There was joy in the sky, the earth, the trees, the body. Maybe all He ever wanted was to gather it in and give it away.

～

On a morning in May, after a week of soft rain, Sister said to her religion class, "Do you believe in the miracle of the loaves and fishes?" She raised her arms. "Did the Lord feed multitudes? Did fish leap from the sea?"

Fenza, slouched at his desk, said, "I doubt it."

"Well, I see no reason to believe what we can't know. What matters now is to ask each of you, to ask myself, how do we share our gifts? What do we do with our lives?" She rubbed her chin. "Please take a moment before you respond."

Fenza and Jimmy needed less than a moment. They said they'd join the Marines the day they turned eighteen. Jimmy, who'd flunked fifth grade, who was almost fifteen, had less time to wait.

Sister asked what they knew about the Marines.

"Plenty," said Fenza. "My dad's a Marine. He's a combat veteran of World War II."

Marge Biersten said she wanted to stay in this town and be a mother, a homemaker.

Jenny Biel, less enthusiastic, said, "It's not easy being a mom, but if I have a family I want four kids—two boys and two girls."

Pat Lemkey spoke her best thoughts to herself. Maybe the Lord multiplied loaves and fishes, but He never dropped no kids from a womb and neither will I. She looked cross-eyed at Jenny. You want four babies? You might be better off joining the Marines.

Sister Clair said, "Ho-hum." She turned to the board, took a piece of chalk, and wrote in a scrawl:

"Insects on a bough
floating downriver,
still singing."
—Issa

89

She tossed the chalk and caught it. "Stay awake," she said. "And do your best to sing an original song."

Fenza began to hum "Moon River."

"That's enough," said Sister. "Truth or myth, here is the Gospel of John."

She opened the big book and read of the miracle of five loaves and two fish that fed thousands. Gus listened to the silence that cradled the sounds. The Lord cobbled His gifts from earth and sea, the clang and color of His voice, the beauty of stillness. Words and their flesh arose from silence, multiplied, and to silence returned. Gus made a drum of his desktop. He eased into a slip-slide rhythm, the cadence of gospel words, and now he paused till the silence told him—*Make some noise*. His feet joined the jive, played a riff off buckled linoleum. Any other nun would have stopped him, but not Sister Clair. Gus, St. Iggy's drummer boy, shared a gift—prayer and percussion. He married these rivals in a gospel song.

He gave Jenny a sidelong glance. All winter and spring they'd had trouble being near each other and trouble staying apart. They'd break up a few days, then Gus would call her, and they'd agree again to be boyfriend and girlfriend. Last night by the river, she led him to the dark of a willow grove and kissed him hard. He kissed her back before she hurried off toward Canal Street. Maybe she loved him a little, or maybe not. She often seemed to be waiting for someone else.

Sister Clair handed out mimeographed copies of a poem by Langston Hughes. She asked Fenza to stand and read it aloud, but when he eyed the title—"The Negro Speaks of Rivers"—he balked. "Sister," he said, "I think Jimmy should read this. His mama's part Negro."

Jimmy hiccupped. "No way. She's whiter than you."

"She ain't *my* mama."

"Boys—"

"Sorry, Sister," said Fenza, but he was aping a grin, savoring the disruption. "You won't find any Negroes in this town."

In a way, he was the teacher and Sister Clair the student. This upstart nun should know by now she was a long way from Montgomery, Alabama. She'd plunked herself down in Orville, Illinois, a sundown town where any Negro, if he dared show his face during the day, vanished with the setting sun.

Jenny Biel turned to the window. Shoulders hunched, hands knuckled in her lap, she searched for distractions. A squirrel flew from one oak tree to another, its fur the color of her face in a flash of sun.

Gus's hand shot up. "Can I read, Sister? I know rivers."

Several boys chuckled.

"Hey, that's no bull," said Gus. "A long time ago I almost drowned."

Fenza fidgeted with his pencil, then snapped it in two. "Biggest mistake of my life," he said. "I pulled this runt from the Illinois."

Sister, after restoring some semblance of order, invited Gus to the front of the class, where he stood straight and proud. Because he was almost a man, because his voice had changed, he offered the poem in a deep and emotional pitch, as a priest might offer a sermon. Pausing after each phrase, his eyes shifted from the words that made rivers, from Langston's miracle to a greater miracle—Jenny Biel. This girl was stubborn as a root that refused to suck water. She met his glance once, then looked long and hard at something outside.

> "I've known rivers:
> I've known rivers ancient as the world and
> Older than the flow of human blood in human veins.
> My soul has grown deep like the rivers . . ."

She didn't seem to care about rivers or blood, but she let him walk her home from school that day. Gus had a poem tucked in a back pocket, and when they approached Canal Street, he took it out and held it in both hands. He could out-sweat anyone, and he was sweating hard on the brick walkway in the bright sun. Just water, he thought, the same thing rivers are made of. They stood alone on a corner near J. C. Penney's. He tried to calm himself before he recited the poem for his girl.

"I wrote this last night," he said, "when I couldn't sleep."

The water ran down his fingers and onto the paper.

"It's short," he said, "so listen."

"Sure."

"This is my poem for you and Illinois."

Gus held up hands shiny as fishes. He cleared his throat, then lowered his voice to meet the near silence of the words.

> *"River and Stars*
>
> My long back on the waves,
> drifting with leaves and light,
> I love all that goes beyond me.

I look out on the stars,
the stars look inward.
I close my eyes and
hear the silence of the earth."

He waited for Jenny to say something.

"Your back's not long."

He thought about this. "Sometimes it is."

"But the poem's nice," she said. "I sort of like it."

He handed it to her.

"Well, I guess this makes you a poet, whatever that means."

"Thanks."

"I wouldn't know how to write a poem."

They drifted along Canal Street, passed Marelli's Tavern, and then she turned to the river. "You want to go down by the willows? Just for a minute?"

She took his breath away.

"You can walk me home after we kiss."

~

The trees were in a cove by the train station. Humpbacked willows that rose to the height of a man, then swept down to a weed-strewn earth. Jenny parted a curtain of willow wands, reached for a sweaty palm, and the boy followed. The light under the trees was a dusky green.

They knelt and faced each other but kept their hands to themselves. Gus peered through a gap between boughs at a tugboat pushing a barge upriver. "Maybe going to St. Louis," he said, "or Sells Landing."

"No, that would be downriver," said Jenny. "Don't poets know geography?"

"I better learn."

"Probably just going to Mayville," she said. "It doesn't have much of a load."

Jenny leaned the side of her face on Gus's shoulder. "Maybe you can tell me another poem."

He looked at the barge. His hands were sweating real good now, so he told her his hands were rivers. "This one," he said, raising his left, "is the Illinois. And this fat one," he said, raising his right, fingers splayed, "is the Mississippi." He hoped Jenny would hear this as a poem because he had no other. She liked it enough to kiss him. She liked it enough to lean into him and push his Mississippi hand to the center of her chest.

Fenza said some girls padded their bras with cotton to make their breasts look round. Jenny did no such thing. Gus held one breast, then another, and they were true as earth.

He began to tremble and moan and she had to stop him before they went too far. "Don't," she said, "please," and then his hands held the air around her. Her breasts were already a memory. "I have to go," she said. "Sorry." She didn't even hold his Mississippi hand when he followed her from the willow dark to the light of day.

Caution

Jenny sat in the passenger seat, her hands in her lap. She and her mom inched out of town in a '55 Nash Rambler, graveyard gray, Annie Biel's favorite color. If Jenny were old enough and rich enough, she would buy a yellow Thunderbird or a red Corvette. Her mom, after eyeing a hundred or more vehicles in a used car lot in Sells Landing, had goaded her dad into shelling out hard cash for the Rambler. She called it "a family car," but to Jenny it looked as stiff and rectangular as a coffin. The girl wondered why it had a speedometer. Gus and Fenza rode faster on rusty bikes.

The Rambler crept along a riverfront road a quarter mile west of Orville. Jenny's dad had gone golfing with Will Dempsey and Eddie Tapusko. Her mom, earlier, after Jenny finished the breakfast dishes, said, "Let's make this a ladies' day. How about if you and me go for a ride?"

Jenny distrusted her enthusiasm. "Where?"

"Nowhere special. I just want to get out in this weather. We might go all summer and not see a more beautiful day."

Well, Jenny knew the sunny skies of mid-June had nothing to do with this jaunt in a Nash Rambler. As always, her mother proceeded with caution. Annie Biel had no sun in her, no clear skies. No hint of summer. The only paths she walked narrowed into tightropes. She seldom blinked an eye before considering the risk.

"You won't get a ticket for speeding, but you may get one for poking."

"I'm going the speed limit."

"The speed limit's thirty."

"It should be twenty on this curve."

Annie Biel took the curve at fifteen miles an hour. It was almost too straight to be called a curve, but she clenched the wheel in her fists and leaned into it. She put on her blinker, stretched her left arm out the window, and pulled into Dead Cat's Cove. Near the shore the river had dredged a channel, kicked up sand and muck, a beach the shape of a crescent. Annie parked in the shade of a swamp oak and turned off the ignition. The river went nowhere in a hurry on this windless morning. The currents that braided the channel welled into waves, none of them tall enough to break silver on the shore.

Jenny started to get out and stretch her legs.

"Not yet."

She left the door half-open.

"Close it," said her mother. "Maybe later you can roam."

They looked to the river. Jenny could feel her mother straining for a way to begin, a way to reveal something sensitive. On this blue morning, Annie wore beige slacks and a long-sleeved blouse, a wide-brimmed hat the soft brown of her skin. Rain or shine, in any season, she kept herself covered. Jenny found it curious that the sun could reveal secrets. "A tan," her mother once said, "is pretty till it's dog brown and dingy." She often berated Jenny for parading around hatless and in shorts.

They glanced at each other, then returned their gaze to the river.

"You know what the old folks call this place?"

Jenny shrugged.

"Dead Cat's Cove," said Annie. "I told you some time ago how it got its name."

Jenny swallowed. "Joe Zeul drowned a cat here. You told me this story when—"

"I know when I told it and why. You left me no choice."

Jenny sulked. "So it's my fault?"

"Well, you'd been rummaging through my purse, but you're forgiven."

Christian generosity, thought Jenny.

"I'm thankful you haven't told anyone, nor nagged me with questions."

"What's the use? I stopped asking things a long time ago because you won't answer."

Her mother sighed. "Silence is a blessing. Sometimes it's our sole comfort."

Comfort? thought Jenny.

"I told you all I could the day you found your grandma's picture."

I don't think so.

"You needed to get older and smarter before I could tell you more."

Jenny, after watching the river a short while, said, "Can I see grandma's picture again?"

"That won't be possible."

"Where is it?"

"Have you been rummaging through my purse again?"

"Just once. It's not there."

"Or anywhere."

"You mean it's gone?"

"Afraid so. Some roads don't fork."

"What's that mean?"

"They go straight ahead."

Annie gripped the steering wheel. Her daughter was so pretty it hurt to look at her. The boys of St. Ignatius would pine for her all the more if they knew she was colored, and a few might have their way with her before their fathers drove she and Jen far from this river valley and its sundown towns that stretched from here to St. Louis. Annie knew white folks better than they knew themselves. Her father, as a teen, craved something sweet and forbidden, so he fled to West Rockford, the wrong side of the Rock River, and ravished the girl who became her mother. Nothing original in Daddy's story. The worst boys, as if stricken by fever, craved colored girls whether or not they knew any, maybe because they could do as they pleased and go unpunished. Annie deplored cursing, but whenever her mind separated from her will, she could match anyone in a barroom. Just now she heard a familiar voice in her head: "Lord, this damn town, this hillbilly hell— you can shove it where the sun don't shine!" Damn was often the first word in a litany, the one that beat down the door to every foul invective. It was beyond shame to kneel each week in Father Janecek's confessional and admit her mind was as vile and ill-tempered as that of a drunkard pounding his fists into mush on a barroom table. Annie failed to improve, though Father always imposed a stiff penance. Her spoken words were kind, even virtuous. But she feared the vileness inside her was her truest tongue.

Jenny would turn fifteen in a week. How long could Annie protect her? One week? Nine days? The time it took to pray a novena? Nine was the magic number, nine days of prayer, but Annie might kneel for nine years and still lose her daughter. She could feel Jen slipping away, abandoning her mother to age-old curses, age-old fears. Annie wished she could brand her daughter with religion. A girl determined to be a nun might never be fondled by a boy.

"Jen," she said, "I watch you get prettier every day."

Her daughter fluttered her eyes in mockery.

"Next week you'll turn fifteen. That's not the easiest age for a girl."

Jen figured it was easier than being old and bitter.

"Are you and Gus serious?"

The girl tilted her chin and smirked.

"Answer me, Jen. Are you serious? Has Gus—"

"He's more a friend than a boyfriend."

"You're sure?"

Jenny remembered the willow grove, his wet hands, his strained breathing. "Don't worry," she said. "I'm sure we want different things."

A motorboat pulling a skier cut inward toward the cove. Jenny needed a moment to recognize Sal Salenski in a yellow bikini, her skis plowing the water, slicing up silver sheets of it, her hair blowing like a veil. Jen's mom would never in a million let her ski the Illinois in a two-piece suit. She believed in modesty, in masks, and she hated the sun.

"Jen, are you listening?"

"I'm still here."

"Important matters are hard to put into words. Have you noticed?"

The girl looked straight ahead. "You never tell me anything."

"That's not true. I told you about your grandma."

"Only because I found her picture and you had to."

"Well, I did my best. Believe it or not, I still do."

"You got rid of her picture."

Annie nodded. "A precaution. What did I just say about roads that don't fork?"

Jenny squirmed in her seat. "Okay, you trashed her picture because you had no choice."

"That's a mean way to put."

"Fine. How would *you* put it?"

Annie paused. "I refuse to be sentimental."

"Did you burn it? Tear it up?"

"That's enough, Jen. I won't be distracted by small talk."

"Small? I'm just—"

"That picture was old and of no use."

"You set it on fire, didn't you?"

"Well, it wouldn't matter if I did. That day's gone and this one's upon us." Annie sipped a long breath as through a straw. "A girl your age has hungers she hardly knows."

Jenny gave her a blank look.

"You're sure you and Gus aren't serious?"

"I already told you."

"And Fenza Ryczhik?"

"I can't stand him."

"Well, at least I can sing one hallelujah."

"Go ahead."

"Not before I ask a question. Are you aware you can get in trouble without being serious with a boy?"

Jenny crossed her eyes and the river blurred.

"You know what trouble I'm talking about?"

"I could guess."

"Well, I'm not fond of guessing. A girl can ruin her life in less time than it takes to say *pregnant*."

"Mom!"

"*Pregnant.* You can say it in a second."

"Okay, then. *Preg*nant!"

"Not so loud."

A bare whisper: "Pregnant, pregnant."

"Did someone give you permission to mock your mother?"

Jenny, gripping the handle of the door, said, "No, I'm trying to be serious. I love your Nash Rambler. I won't get pregnant."

"Will you stop it, Jen?"

"Nash can't make babies—"

"*Stop* it!"

"—because all he can do is fifteen miles an hour."

Annie hugged her arms to her breasts. Her mind was saying, Goddamn, goddamn, goddamn, can't someone make this easier? The Lord might at least tell Jenny her mom was on her side and always would be. A second of carelessness, maybe less, could ruin her child forever. The devil would sing his hosannas and whisper amen.

"Remember when you used to beg me for a sister, a brother?"

"I really just wanted a sister."

"Well, I figured as much. But I couldn't give you one."

Jenny sat still, her right hand still firm on the handle.

"I'm high yellow and you're lighter. We gambled twice and came out winners."

Jenny tensed.

"People can play long odds a short while, then it's over."

"Mom, please."

"Lots of women have families without giving birth. Someday, if you really want a child, there are thousands of kids with nobody. Not even a cousin."

Jenny shivered. "Mr. Nash—"

"Give that nonsense a rest. You'll never have a sister, Jen. I made sure of it."

"You mean—?"

"You know what I mean. I did what had to be done."

The girl looked to the river. She distrusted the wide stretches that appeared serene, a harmony of sun and water. A tumbling waterfall would've made more sense.

"So whatever you do, don't get pregnant. We cannot take that chance."

We? Are we in the same body?

"You hear me?"

The girl shut her mouth and eyes.

"I'm not saying you can't get married someday."

See if I care.

"I don't believe in what I did, but I had no choice. I went to a clinic in West Rockford when you were six weeks old."

Jen opened her eyes to the river lit with sun. Another boat sped by, another skier, a boy. The box elders and swamp oaks on the far shore looked like the careless squiggles of a green crayon. God was messy with summer, messy with everything. Or maybe He was anywhere but *here*.

"So where was Dad when you made sure you were done with babies?"

"At home," said Annie, "taking caring of you."

Jenny squinted. "If I was six weeks old, this was late summer."

"That's right."

"So how'd you get away? You make up a story?"

"Well, I wouldn't put it that way, nor should you. I told your dad I was going to Rockford to visit your Grandma Sophie and Grandpa Luke." She shrugged. "The truth is, I *did* visit them, took a cab to their place after my surgery. I told them I was sick as a dog, needed to be alone, and they set me up in my old bedroom. Sophie called your dad and told him I'd be spending the night in Rockford. The next day was complicated. I'd left the car at the west side clinic, and I was scared it might be vandalized. I told your grandpa it broke down, overheated or something, and he gave me a ride over the bridge. He didn't seem to notice the clinic, didn't ask questions. He opened the hood and I started the engine. We had an old Chevy then, but it ran real smooth."

Jenny held her knees close together. "Dad doesn't know anything?"

"You know he doesn't."

"And Grandpa Luke?"

"He works hard to keep things simple."

Jenny twirled a hand. "You and Dad could adopt a girl."

"Oh, Jen. He still thinks our situation could change. He keeps trying."

"I don't need to hear this."

"Nor do I," said Annie. "You have no idea how difficult this is."

The girl squeezed her legs together, knee bone to knee bone. She wanted to crack them the way Fenza cracked his knuckles when he interrupted class at St. Iggy's, the *scrunch* so abrupt the older nuns flinched, struggled to breathe. Squeeze and twist, no luck. Just a little bruise maybe, plus the awkward silence. Her tongue went limp. Her bones wouldn't talk. Life would be easier as a blustery boy.

"Let me just say your dad's a gentleman. He never blames me."

Jenny was sweating and shivering.

"I didn't choose my life, never had the privilege. I make do with what I'm given."

Oh, the road again. It won't fork.

"You wouldn't hate me if you knew me."

Jenny found a scrap of her voice, a whisper. "And Dad? Would he—?"

"No, he wouldn't hate me for a minute. But knowing another person, the kind of knowing I'm talking about, is all but impossible in this world."

They watched the river a long while. A barge heaped with coal inched its way around a bend. No speedboats and skiers now. If the barge and the river moved any slower, they'd come to a halt. Jenny didn't know if one day she'd want her own baby, but she wanted the choice. No point saying this aloud, because she knew what Annie would say. "That's just natural, the same thing any girl would feel. What's important is to see the difference between what's natural and what's needed. Only God can fashion this world any way He likes."

Annie folded her hands in her lap.

Pat Lemkey

She was the last tomboy in the Illinois Valley, if not the world. She could still roll a cigarette, shimmy a tree, sass the sun, but life had become complicated. At lunch hour, she stood alone in the playground outside the cafeteria and brooded on a question. Would anyone miss me if I vanished from the earth?

She wondered if John Maylor, the town's architect and industrialist, designed St. Iggy's cafeteria. Sunk in a basement, with window slats at ground level, it would've made a superb bunker had he buried it a foot deeper. Pat, squatting in tall grass, winked down at the cheerleaders' table, and then at the adjacent table where noisy Glee Club girls nibbled fish sticks that tasted like fried paste. No witchery was needed to augur the future. In the coming years, the prettiest and the ugliest and the in-betweens would join the assembly lines at the clock factory, marry Orville boys, have babies, pay monthly dues to the Women's Auxiliary of the Altar and Rosary Society, attend Mass on Sundays and Holy Days, organize bingo games, bake sales, chicken dinners, and all because of a tired notion that the Church speaks for God and boys are pretty. Well, thought Pat, maybe God has a more mysterious voice, a keener eye. Maybe nobody in this town knows Him too well.

She eyed Jenny Biel through a paint-flecked window. The sweetest girl at St. Iggy's was sitting with four cheerleaders and the secretary of the Student Council. They were slender, delicate, and it seemed strange to Pat that they would want anything to do with boys. Sister Clair, presiding over the cafeteria, walked up and down the aisles with a book in her hands. On this last day of school, humid and hot, the boys were demons. Fenza dolloped a spoon of creamed peas into his right palm and shook Gus's hand. The big boy roared, danced a jig around a table, and Gus gave chase. Pat tried to ignore the fact that she had three more years at this school. How did boys manage to get dumber as they got older? Was it just Orville boys who were dumb, or had a pandemic circled the globe?

Sister Clair said, "Fenza! Gus! Go to the restroom and wash your hands!"

Pat turned and looked out beyond the baseball field to a green valley parted by a stream. Early June now and she was hot enough to roll in her own sweat, to stretch out on the earth and sleep till sundown. She made her way to center field, her back to the school. No clouds in the sky, the sun too bright for more than a glimpse. The land, softened by snowmelt in April, rain in May, was now as fertile as any Myrtle. Pat could poke a seed in the ground, *any* seed, and after a few cycles of bright days and dark nights it would burst with roots, a stem, small leaves. Never mind the Lord's loaves and fishes, His miraculous walk upon water. One inch of earth is the cape of a magician. God runs out of numbers when He counts seeds in Illinois.

She heard Sister Clair calling, "Honey? Pat? . . . Are you okay?"

The nun stood outside the cafeteria. "You haven't eaten," she said. "Can I bring you something?"

"No thank you, Sister."

"The fish sticks won't help, but what about an apple?"

Pat shrugged.

"Wait here," said Sister. "I'll bring you something good."

She hurried inside and returned with an apple. "Best one in the bushel," she said, and polished it on her sleeve before handing it to Pat.

The girl sat cross-legged in the grass. Sister glanced toward St. Iggy's, then knelt beside her. Pat had never seen a nun touch her robes to the earth.

They faced the valley and the stream. Pat watched three starlings spiral over a sycamore. Their blackness pleased her more than the blue of the sky.

She ate half the apple.

"I hope you're not trying to lose weight."

The remark caught Pat off-guard. "I don't think so."

"Forget about being skinny. There's nothing wrong with you."

Pat shrugged.

"*Nothing*," said Sister. "You understand?"

"I'm trying."

"I'll tell you a secret. I suffer with any student who is not generous to herself."

Pure kindness knows nothing of guile or subterfuge. Pat trusted this nun, yet there was little to say.

"Grade school was easier, wasn't it?"

"Yes, Sister."

"For me as well. I had few close friends in high school. By my sophomore year, I was something of a loner."

"Is that why you became a nun?"

"No, I was influenced by a priest. Daniel Berrigan."

"Who?"

"Father Berrigan, a poet-priest."

Pat shrugged.

"An *inspired* priest. Can you imagine?"

"No."

"Well, I wish he'd visit Orville."

"Me, too."

"He taught me that a religious person can have a useful and poetic life."

Pat, stretching her legs in front of her, said she had no ambition, no wish to be anything.

Sister smiled. "Enjoy the sun. You've got a swell spot here."

"You're a nun and I'm nothing."

"Oh, come now."

"But it's true," said the girl. "I have no ambition at all."

This was a lie. She wanted to be Jenny Biel's confidante, her lover. She wanted midnight rendezvous, trysts, illicit joy. Pat remembered a line from a poem Sister Clair brought to religion class last week: *I want to be with those who know secret things or else alone.* At least her solitude was comprehensible. At St. Iggy's, as at St. Roch's, she might always be alone.

~

School let out on the ninth of June. By week's end, kids had drifted into the ease of summer lives: girls working on tans, swimming and sunbathing at Dell's Cove, fisher-boys pulling up carp and roasting them on beaches, getting into fights over girls and sports and cars, playing ball at St. Iggy's and making bets in late innings. The nights were as predictable as the days.

Boys too restless to sleep would slip free of their homes in the wee hours, sidle down Krapalna Street or gather in the dark of trees, or race through the yards of pretty girls and lark their way to the shores of the Illinois River. At a distance, in a farmhouse twelve miles away, Pat could imagine it all, the gyrations of a new summer. She, too, knew the river, the beaches, the town, the boys, the girls, but they seemed to be made for everyone but her.

For human company she had parents, and for something more she had milk cows, Sadie and Beth, a gray mutt named Spencer, an assortment of ducks and chickens, a pond with a ramshackle landing called the Minnie Docks, and the farm itself, three hundred acres of corn and beans, a wide pasture, a barn with a hayloft, and a dozen paths that spider-webbed through thick woods. Here, and nowhere else, she relaxed. Sadie and Beth didn't care if she was St. Iggy's lone lesbian. Her dog didn't care, nor the chickens, the ducks, and as for the land, the sun, the sky—they were the margins of home. Sister Clair said, "There's nothing wrong with you," but this didn't mean Pat was normal. Did anyone in town trust some old mutt, his nose in the wind, more than Father Janecek? Did anyone wonder if a paw of black earth was holier than Sunday's sermon? No, Orville was as straight and dry as a schoolhouse ruler. Girls longed for boys, boys for girls, and made no reach beyond the human. Maybe one had to live apart from one's own kind to belong to something as vast and lovely as the world.

But the farm couldn't satisfy every need. On a morning in late June, after she finished her chores, she sat under a tall oak, lit a cigarette, and hung her head. She told herself Jenny Biel meant nothing to her, never would. Her dog lay beside her in the grass. She could see the cows in the distance, beyond a picket fence, their heads bowed to the green pasture. Shouldn't this be enough? The farm in summer? The animals and the land more alive than anyone in town? Pat puffed on a Lucky, whispered, "Bye, Jen," and blew smoke at the undersides of leaves. A human being should be made of something more durable than flesh. Thorns. Barbed wire. Cement. A block of wood . . . She got up fast, kicked the tree, and the grackles perched in its crown rose toward the sun. Pat moaned, hopped around on one foot. A stubbed toe gave her mind a rest. Spencer, dazed and skittish, whimpered with human pain, *her* pain. She would've kicked the tree again if not for that dog.

~

On the first of July, she took the noonday bus to Orville. There were only three other passengers, but Pat made her way to the last seat and sat in a corner. She hadn't talked to someone her age since the last day of school when she and Jenny parroted each other—"Have a nice vacation." In eighth grade, Jen called her almost every night, they'd talk for hours, but now the phone never rang. At this point, what could they prattle about, over the wire or in person? Boys? Suntans? A new movie at the drive-in? Pat looked toward the fields, soybeans on one side of the road and hip-high corn on the other. If it was green, she trusted it, or if it had four legs, or two wings. She trusted the red of the tractor coming toward her along a pathway between fields of corn. She might be unwise to trust the farmer, his face invisible beneath the brim of his cap.

The bus driver let Pat off in front of J. C. Penney's. Pausing to window-shop, she did her best to picture Jenny in bright-red heels, or these black ones, stilettos. No housewife in Orville County would wear either pair in public. These were the kind of shoes a woman might wear for her husband behind closed doors.

Stilettos.

Jenny would look like she was six feet tall.

Beyond the bridge over the canal, two paths led to Dell's Cove. Pat chose Snake Path, the narrow one, and risked poison ivy. The bushes and trees—willows, cottonwoods, swamp oaks—hid her from view. She paused and considered turning around when she heard the racket of boys. Aimless shouting, hooting. Someone banging on a drum. She inched forward and peeked out from behind a cottonwood. She saw five girls among the boys, including the one she loved.

Jenny sat on the beach on a pink towel. She'd come with her cheerleader friends, Marge and Becky, Daisy and Sal, and they made a sweet picture. Girls lazy in the sun, shoulders and legs shining with Coppertone, voices small except for Marge, who spoke in high-pitched twitters. Fenza was trying to sing. He knew the words to "Be My Baby," but he sounded nothing like the Ronettes who sweetened this song twelve times a day on every radio in the Illinois Valley. Gus punished his bongo drum with arrhythmic slaps. Jimmy, in dark glasses, head dipping and rising with the non-music, seemed to have no more intelligence than what allowed him to moan. Pat looked back and forth from the boys to the girls. She felt like an exotic animal, a being so rare that perhaps no others of her kind could be found anywhere on earth.

She watched Jimmy. The way he sat with his shoulders bent toward his chest, the way he cowered. If he ever had the gumption to rise and stand to his full height, he'd tower over every girl in Orville, seniors included. He and Fenza couldn't wait to join the Marines, but would the Marines take Jimmy with that crooked spine? He was an oversized chameleon, eager to vanish in the glare of water and sun.

What if she liked a boy long enough to seem normal? In eighth grade, when Pat pretended to like Frankie Reardon for three months and six days, she got her wish—the camaraderie of girls. It was Jenny who told her Frankie talked bad about her, who warned her to stay away from every Orville boy who thought she was hot. Well, the farthest Frankie got was to slip his tongue in her mouth. Had Pat known he would French her, she would've bit down and sent him away yelping and whining and calling her a bitch.

Now Fenza spotted her and let out a whistle. "Hey," he said, "hey Pat," and then he said something about "an Illinois moose" that made Jimmy blush and snigger. Pat looked at the skyline above the trees on the far side of the river. The tilt of her chin said, "I don't hear you, Fenza. Have you noticed you don't exist?" Jenny waved and called her name. Pat moved toward the girls with her usual facade of languor and ease.

Jenny asked her where she'd been all summer.

"Yeah," said Fenza, "I got the same question. I been missin' you since school let out."

Pat rolled her eyes.

"No lie," said Fenza, and Jimmy sniggered again. "I was about to take the afternoon bus and visit you on the farm."

Gus tapped his bongo and grinned. Pat had a brief urge to dazzle these boys, lead them on before brushing them aside. She should've worn a sexy bathing suit rather than a baggy T-shirt, knee-length shorts. She had big breasts, a big fanny, which might explain Fenza's musings about a moose. Pat wished she were larger than the animal of his puerile imagination. She longed to loom over him like a dinosaur, or an old cottonwood throwing an acre of shade, her trunk too wide and gnarly for the arms of a boy.

Jenny said she missed her, but was it true? She was prim, well mannered, as were the other girls. Jenny asked why Pat had stayed away all summer, never joined in the fun. The farm girl had no better answer than to claim she was busy with chores.

She sat in the sand between Jenny and Marge. Gus love-tapped his drum, then took Jenny's hand. Fenza wanted to arm wrestle, "to take on anyone and his brother." Jimmy, his voice the lean side of a whisper, proved he could speak by saying he was tired. Well, thought Pat, maybe we're cousins. Sometimes I'm so weary I could faint.

She rested a while, then waded out in the shallows to escape the heat. She turned, waved to Jenny, but who sprang to his feet? Fenza Ryczhik Jr. He whooped, jackknifed his knees to his chest, and cannon-balled into the river. A geyser rocked Pat onto her heels. Fenza rose smiling and spitting, hawking river muck. "Pat," he said, "you look pretty as lights."

She hugged her chest, but he'd already seen some of what he wished to see. Her wet T-shirt and bra were transparent as gossamer. Fenza, she thought, maybe you can stare at the sun till you're blind.

The moron followed her from the river. After she shooed him away, he sat between the other stooges, Gus and Jimmy, and she sat with the girls. There was no way to win Jen's love any time soon. There might be a way to stay near her, though, a way to join her clique—a fake boyfriend. Pat eyed Jimmy. His sitting posture—legs crossed at the ankles, chin near his chest—copied the curves of a question mark. What was wrong with him? What had happened? Jimmy was sad the way the river was sometimes sad. He was like a nameless weed choked and buried in the flow.

Fenza.

All Pat had to do was keep his chubby hands off her body. If she hung with a clique, Jenny's clique, time with Fenza would be communal time. Fenza and his stooges, the three of them, and Jenny and her cheerleaders and Glee Club girls, the rah-rah spirit of St. Iggy's. Fenza was no worse than Frankie Reardon. Pat felt wily enough to fight off his advances for at least one summer, maybe more.

~

The 3:20 bus took her back to the country. Spencer, loping out from the shadows of the barn, followed her down a tractor path to the pond and the Minnie Docks. Sunburned, baked, she slipped free of her sandals, her T-shirt and bra, and in she went.

Her body was like fresh bread, the crust starting to cool, the insides warm enough to melt butter. Spencer flopped in and swam beside her. Pat heard his muffled yelp when she dove for bottom. Mosses and weeds tugged at her hands, her wrists. She rose for air and wished she were a boy.

There were times when she wanted to hug a stone and drown, but not now. Her mind turned toward another season, the winter of eighth grade. Gus had a crush on her then, too bad for him, and on Christmas Eve, after he and Fenza climbed the Orville water tower in a snowstorm, Gus painted her name near clouds. Now she pulled herself onto the dock and shook with giggles. Yes, she had something in common with the imp—irrepressible urges. That riotous Christmas Eve seemed eons ago, but what Gus shouted into the night—*I like Indians, I like Blacks, I like tits*—was the echo of a ghost. Everyone in town heard him carrying on, and everyone on the farms heard about it later. Ruth Dempsey was in a grave, but Gus sang her song over and over. He made Orville blush, stained a white Christmas, and none too soon.

Pat admired his nerve and envied his privilege. If she, on a whim, had climbed the tower and wailed and drummed and painted a sloppy, red heart and two names, *Jenny & Pat*, the punishment would have been greater than a night in Juvenile Hall and a year's probation. There were her parents to consider. Her father might have rushed her to the nearest asylum, or he might have imitated Will Dempsey and locked her in his house. One outburst would have marked Pat for life, made her a pariah. No girl in these parts could desecrate the holiest night of the year and slip free of the shackles that had probably been here for a hundred years.

She sat on the dock, her feet in the water. She petted her dog and whispered, "I like Indians, I like . . ." She closed her eyes. "Don't tell Dad, though. Don't even tell Jenny Biel."

~

Jenny didn't call her that night, but Fenza did. His voice, burbling with tension and hope, was halfway poignant. He rambled on about things Pat would never care about. A three-boy band, for instance, Don't Ever, Fenza and Gus and Jimmy, and wouldn't she like to hear them? She said she'd heard them on the beach that afternoon, but he said, "No, that was just a warm-up, a way to cut loose. You haven't heard the real band." He said he'd left his harmonica at home, and Jimmy hadn't brought his guitar because "sand and sun can ruin good instruments in the blink of an eye. We can play," he said, "honest. And I can sing a whole lot better than what you heard today."

Pat was afraid he would sing now. "Some other time," she said. "You and your band can invite me and Jenny to a party."

"Sure, just say when."

"I'll get back to you after I speak with Jenny. If she's ready for a party, so am I."

Fenza cleared his throat. "Hey, what about the Fourth of July? Saturday?"

"We'll see."

"You can take the bus into town, meet us by the river."

"If I have my chores done."

"Let me come out and help. I'm good at farm work."

"No thanks."

"Fine, then. I won't argue. But don't hang up before I ask you something else."

His next words, though soft, came quick as gun bursts. "Tell me, just tell me. Will you be my girl, Pat? Will you?"

A fake girl? she translated. Your pretend sweetie? Pat almost felt sorry for Fenza when she said, "Yes, maybe yes, one summer. But I hope you don't expect too much."

She lowered the phone to its cradle and hugged her arms to her chest.

Holiday

Gus sprinkled sawdust on the stained floor near his grandpa's butcher block. The Fourth of July, almost time to lower the shades and count the cash, but Mrs. Moshnik kept searching for bargains. Ceiling fans pushed warm air over tubs of sauerkraut, trays of *kiszka*, a meat-jelly grandpa called headcheese, pork loins smeared with barbecue sauce, buckets of fried chicken. Mrs. Moshnik said all her family was in town for the fireworks. "My strudel could feed an army," she told Gus's grandpa, "but I may need some *kiszka* and kraut."

The old lady wheedled for dimes, then dollars, bargain basement discounts for *kiszka* and headcheese and kraut, plus three cases of Star Model Beer. Grandpa told Gus to set aside the pail of sawdust and carry the order to Mrs. Moshnik's Buick. Cooped up all afternoon, he sauntered outside and into the weather, the late sun still bullish and bright, the sky the color of jade. Gus set a jumbo box of *kiszka* and kraut and headcheese on the back seat, then returned for the beer and loaded it in the trunk.

"Here," said Mrs. Moshnik, and slipped him a nickel. "Go buy yourself something sweet."

She drove away at a snail's pace. He was about to go back in the store when he heard a whoop and a whistle. Fenza and Jimmy came zigzagging down Krapalna Street, riding fast on rattletrap bikes.

"Careful!" said Fenza. "Here comes a moose!"

Mrs. Moshnik passed them going the other way.

Fenza fishtailed his bike up and over the curb in front of Tony Renh's Grocery. Jimmy, his guitar strapped over his left shoulder, turned in on a gravel driveway and coasted to a halt.

They leaned their bikes on a fence and followed Gus into Tony Renh's. The old man, perched on a stool behind the butcher block, told his grandson to lower the shades.

Fenza said, "Can you spare a box, Mr. Renh? My mom needs to put some things in storage."

Tony wiped his hands on a blood-stained apron and lit a cigar. "Boxes are in back," he said. "Help yourself."

Fenza winked at Jimmy, then came around the meat counter. The open door behind the butcher shop led to the storage room. Cases of beer and canned goods lined the shelves, and empty boxes were stacked in a corner. Fenza filled a Rinso box with Star Model Beer. This was too easy, like shooting fish in a barrel. He vowed to give himself a more formidable challenge if he robbed another store.

Fenza sauntered out of the storage room. "Many thanks, Mr. Renh, and Happy Fourth!" He was strong enough to cradle the box in one arm and wave farewell.

Jimmy swung open the side door.

Fenza called to Gus, "Later, alley-gator. Bring your drum and meet us in the willow grove."

～

Gus stopped at home for his drum, then made his way to the beach and the willows.

His hoodlum friends, hidden beneath the skirts of trees, made no sound, but he knew where they were. Seven willows grew so close together they looked like one wild tree. Gus ducked through a tangle of fronds to find his pals squatting over beer cans. They'd dragged their bikes under the trees, left them on the ground, and Jimmy had propped his guitar on a wide trunk. In lieu of a greeting, Fenza belched, slurped down the dregs of a Star Model Beer, then scrunched the can in his fists.

He said to Gus, "Stay down. We can't have the girls knowing we're here."

"Girls?"

"Iggy girls," said Fenza. "They'll be here soon enough."

Gus set his drum on the ground.

"So where'd you get the beer?"

"Never mind," said Fenza. "Just punch one open."

"You steal from your dad again?"

Fenza paused. "Maybe I did."

"We got beer," said Jimmy, "plus some hard stuff. Wild Turkey."

He held up an official Marine Corps canteen.

"Happy hour," said Fenza, and handed Gus a can and a church key. "Punch it," he said, "chug-a-lug. You got some catching up to do."

After they were all a little woozy, Fenza said, "Let's practice." He got out his harmonica, Jimmy picked his way through "Freight Train Blues," and Gus sat on his haunches and listened. Fenza used the harp sparingly, relied mostly on vocals. He sang with a Hank Williams twang, a melancholy brought on by whiskey and sorrow and losses too large to bear. Gus approved the rendition. Fenza might never match Hank for down-and-out gut wrench, but he crooned with enough misery to chase a screech owl from a nearby cottonwood and into the sky.

Fenza said, "That's right, boys. Drop that dime in a juke box." He sipped from the canteen, gargled with whiskey, then set forth his plan with whispers and winks.

"When the girls come by, we'll let them pass before we start playing. When they hear the music, they'll turn and say, 'Where's the band? Where's the band?' but we'll hang tight and keep playing." He punched open another can of Star Model. "Iggy girls will think Hank Williams is in here, no shit. Or maybe they'll think somebody's got a transistor sister and is camping out in these willows on the Fourth of July."

Gus said he didn't get it.

"That's 'cause you're dumb."

"Hank Williams? There's no way—"

"Fuck you and your loved ones," said Fenza. "I might even steal Jenny before the night is done."

The boys passed around the Wild Turkey, Dirty Bird Bourbon, and washed it down with sips of Star Model. As from a private hedge, they watched Fourth of July revelers cross the footbridge over the canal and parade down to the beach. Men plucked bottles of beer from iced buckets. The Moshnik clan, sitting in folding chairs and on blankets, ate *kiszka* and kraut and fat pickles and headcheese from paper plates.

St. Iggy's girls came across the footbridge at sundown. Fenza saw them first: Jenny and Pat, Marge and Sal, and others not worth naming. Except for Pat, they wore Bermuda shorts, and Jenny's came to mid-thigh. Pat was the odd one out in black cutoffs, a T-shirt, and high-top sneakers that would've looked better on a boy. Fenza eyed her as through the crosshairs of a rifle. A few nights earlier, over the phone, she almost agreed to be his summer girl. Pat hung up on him, but not before saying, "Yes, maybe yes, one summer." Why the maybe? he thought. If she's got to tease me, I'll tease her right back with a Dixie song.

He did just that the moment she and the other girls passed the willow grove. Fenza sang of his hobo life, poverty and bad luck, and he added a new wrinkle, claimed he wandered this whole busted-up world with three pennies in his pocket and songs in his heart. The girls stopped, looked around, and Pat said, "Sounds to me like a cat's concert." Jimmy hummed and strummed while Fenza kept wailing. Gus rap-tapped his bongo, then paused. This was not a great song for an African drum.

Fenza's voice cracked. He wondered if Hank's did, too, on nights when he was drunk and nervous for a girl. He shucked the lyrics he knew by heart and made up his own: "Girls, come follow me 'long the rails; I'm ready to roll. This town makes us tired, oh Lordy. So we'll shake away the blues with our wanderin' shoes."

Pat, her hands at her hips, said, "That's just Fenza." His heart skipped a beat. *Just Fenza?* Did he matter to anyone? His summer girl, his maybe girl, was backing away, so he edged out from the willow curtain, a harmonica in one hand, a can of Star Model in the other. Jimmy, a cringe in every step, emerged with the canteen of Wild Turkey and his Gibson guitar.

Fenza shooed him back in. "You forgot the beer. These girls might be thirsty."

"We're not," said Jenny.

"Don't know till you try some," said Fenza. "This local brew is sweeter than lemonade."

Now Gus came out, his drum cradled to his belly. He felt awkward, as if he held a baby in his arms.

The girls had no appetite for beer, except for Pat, who sampled Fenza's. She let him hold her hand for seven breaths—she counted, she endured. The girls had blankets and paper cups and a jug of orange Kool-Aid. Fenza followed them to a grassy hummock above the beach. Jimmy and Gus lagged behind.

Pat let Fenza put his arm around her when the fireworks began. A burst of red, a delicate spray of silver, and then boom, boom, boom, the sky flashing and sparking and the river a moving mirror, a kaleidoscope of color. She pushed him away when he started to moan. He smelled boozy, sweaty, and she almost told him to jump in the river and bathe. Fenza was so ornery, though, he might say, "Sure, come on," and grab her hand. Every thought of this boy came uninvited. She pictured him stripping down and jumping buck-naked and whooping into the Illinois and dragging her down under a wave.

❧

After the last colors faded from the sky and the night turned quiet and dark, Fenza listened to frogs and girls and crickets. July 4 was far from over. Jenny was hosting a sleepover for seven girls.

Marge had left her toothbrush at home.

Jenny said they could share.

Fenza keened his ears to hear voices quieter than crickets.

Sorry, he thought. I forgot my nightie. May I borrow one?

He held his breath to keep from laughing.

My favorite color is white.

Pat turned away when he reached for her hand. Would she sleep in Jenny's bed tonight, or in a sleeping bag on the living room floor? Maybe all these Iggy girls would snuggle together in one big nest until a knock at the window made their blood run cold.

❧

Almost midnight. While Gus and Jimmy were at home, probably shining their shanks with Vaseline, Fenza prowled the garden of a widow. Mrs. Novacek, bless her heart, had lovely flowers—roses, violets, hollyhocks—so he used his pocketknife to borrow her best blooms and make a bouquet. A waning moon, a yellow haze, gave all the light he needed. The flashlight in his back pocket would come in handy later on.

Bent over, he wove his way up Krapalna. In peasant's hands, fingers chubby as cigars, Fenza held blossoms. Humming "Freight Train Blues," sometimes moaning, he made a crooked path to Jenny's. Seven girls in a clapboard home, iceberg girls, chastity belt champs, and he had a notion to blow the place up, trade flowers for high explosives, flatten the walls, blow these babes clear out of their jammies. He swaggered, puffed out his chest, but his hands trembled. Girls, even a homely one like Pat, always shook him somehow.

115

"Goddamn," he muttered. "Remember you're the son of a Marine."

A fist for a vase, he marched into Jenny's yard, chin up, and stood tall at her living room window. Seven girls, he thought, so he tapped the window seven times. Two sweeties might be curled like lesbos in Jenny's bed, but the others would be on the living room floor in sleeping bags, and maybe one would be sacked out on the sofa. He counted seven more taps, each a bit louder. He backed off and waited for the curtains to part.

Flashlight in one hand, flowers in the other, Fenza took center stage. A girl—he couldn't see which one, just a dark blob of a head—came to the window. Flash. The light silhouetted the bouquet stolen from the widow's garden. Roses yellow and white, hollyhocks whorehouse red and purple and pink, and violets peeking out between larger blooms. He wanted the girl to see his damaged right hand, the work of roses. "Thorns," he whispered, "*thorns*." He hoped he was speaking to Jenny or Pat.

He heard, "Oh my God, oh my God," and then the curtains closed. A moment later a light came on in the living room. Girls muttered his name—"Fenza, Fenza"—with wonder and dread. Well, this was his signal to vanish, but not before leaving the bouquet at the front door. Roses, hollyhocks, violets, blood. Pat would know the bouquet was for her.

~

A little before midnight, Pat had been lying wide-awake on the sofa. Jenny and Marge had Jenny's bed, Jenny's bedroom, and four other girls curled side by side in sleeping bags on the living room carpet. Pat? She had a pillow and a purple blanket and this damn lump of a sofa. Marge rated tops, cheerleader Marge, Pep Club Marge, with cheerleader Jenny in Jenny's bed. Maybe they didn't have urgent feelings for each other, but they were as near as lovers. The living room girls, minus Pat, slept like pups in a pile, and oozed soft, sweet snores. Pat was alone because she hadn't brought her sleeping bag. She'd gambled on Jenny's bed and should have known she would lose.

Somehow those taps on the window didn't surprise her. Peeking out and seeing Fenza didn't surprise her either, but the flowers did. Nothing as delicate as blossoms belonged in those hands.

The girls woke and someone turned on the light and they were all a-jabber. You saw *what*? Fenza and flowers? Jenny and Marge heard the racket and came out sleepy-eyed, frowsy. Marge, after Pat told her and Jenny what had happened, said, "Maybe we should call the cops."

Jenny's parents straggled out of their bedroom in robes. Mr. Biel, on hearing Fenza's name, said, "You wake me if he comes around again. I don't want him anywhere near you girls."

Mrs. Biel chimed in with a lecture. She gave the impression she knew everything worth knowing about Illinois boys on midnight prowls. "Never answer a knock on a window," she said, "especially at this hour." She ordered the girls to stay clear of Fenza and others like him. "Out of every hundred boys at St. Ignatius," she said, "you're lucky to find one you can trust. And this one and only—I assure you—won't be wandering our streets at such an ungodly hour."

This made Pat want to stay up all night, and she did. The other girls went back to sleep after Mrs. Biel's admonition. She stayed up to conjure a better world, at least in her mind. She pictured Jenny and herself slipping out the side door. Hand-in-hand, free of parents and boys and chatty girls, they crept down Orville streets and back alleys, stole kisses now and then, invisible as bats in the nightshade of trees. Maybe Orville was safe only as it slept. Iggy boys, weary of pranks and prowls, might rest their desires, drag themselves home, and pass out in their beds. Black folks might slip by, unhurried, unseen. In the quietest hour Jenny and Pat could roam from tree to tree, shadow to shadow. The unheard of became possible, though not for long. Two girls could draw near each other before the town woke to the normalcy and light of another day.

Girls

Jenny and Pat and Sal and Marge came out of Marylou's with Neapolitan ice cream cones and a clear path down Krapalna Street past St. Roch's Church. No boys in sight, so walk fast and lick fast, slurp the sugar and melting cream—strawberry, chocolate, vanilla. Oh, it was good the way summer was good. Ice cream wouldn't taste this rich after the regimen of classes and homework once more defined their days. Tomorrow the girls would be sophomores, as would Fenza and Gus and Jimmy. Tired of boys, they'd saved the last day of summer for themselves.

Marge said, "We'll have Sister Damien for catechism this fall. Sister Clair will teach literature to seniors."

Sal said, "Fenza fed us another lie. Sister Damien didn't have brain cancer last spring. My Aunt Eli said it was a case of nerves."

"I believe your aunt," said Marge. "Remember when Sister kept all the girls after class to remind us to wait till marriage before . . . you know."

Marge and Sal broke into giggles.

"And Sister blushed," said Sal. "She was shaking all over."

"I felt sorry for her," said Marge, "except it was sort of funny."

"Well, nerves or cancer," said Pat, "let's forget Sister Damien till tomorrow."

"And forget Fenza," said Jenny. "He'll be telling us taller tales soon enough."

Jen skipped ahead. It was her idea that they treat themselves to ice cream, then gather at her home. She had nail polish, a selection of colors, and they could paint each other, take turns. The last day of summer should be a day of indulgence. Any day free of boys was Armistice Day.

❦

Cones finished, finger licks too, they barged into the Biel home. Jen thought they'd paint each other's nails in the living room, but her dad was watching baseball, the Cubs and Cards, and couldn't be disturbed. The girls filed out the side door and into a backyard of just-cut grass and trimmed hedges. Clumps of goldenrod bloomed under the eaves.

They sat in the shade of a silver maple. Jen had four colors for four girls: plum, lavender, carmine, jade. She set the polish in the grass, then named partners. "How's this?" she said. "Me and Pat can paint each other's nails, and Marge—you're with Sal. We got all day to do as we please."

Pat asked Jenny what color she liked.

"Anything but plum."

Pat, kneeling beside her, touched one bottle, then another. "Carmine?"

Jenny hesitated, then sighed. "My mom won't like it, so go right ahead."

Jen lay back in the grass, eyes closed. She heard Sal and Marge discussing colors, then other things, and then she drifted. She felt Pat's hands on her left foot, a soft tug, and then her foot and calf nestled in Pat's lap. Pat rubbed the sole, made it tingle. Jenny, new to pleasure, almost asked her to stop.

Pat said, "Your feet are cute."

Jenny opened one eye. "They're just feet, these things I walk around on."

"Yeah, but . . ." Pat rubbed the arch of the foot. "Does this tickle?"

Jenny lolled in the grass. "It feels nice."

Pat pressed a bit harder. "Just let me know if it hurts."

Jenny turned her head to the side. Sal, bent down near Marge's left foot, splashed some jade on a big toenail. Marge lay in the grass with one hand over her eyes, the other behind her neck as a pillow. Don't start in on boys, thought Jenny. Don't say a word. She got her wish because all Marge and Sal whispered about was complementary colors. Jade for the toes, lavender for the hands. "But jade's a secret," said Sal. "We won't walk barefoot on the beach till some time next June."

Jenny welcomed the silence that followed. Pat held her foot just so and painted just so, as if she had all day to complete ten miniature canvases. No boy could touch her this way, relax enough to feel the happiness of toes, nails, foot, calf. Jenny looked up between the high branches of the maple to a fat cloud and a gold sun, one beside the other. Were they as happy as they appeared? They made each other pretty with no effort at all.

What if Pat knew she was Negro? Would this change anything? Would she keep a secret, or would she tell?

The day lingered. The other foot, now the hands, the nails. *You choose the color, Pat. Yes, carmine again. Please. My mother's favorite color is graveyard gray.* And then Jenny painted Pat, fingernails, toenails—carmine, carmine, twenty more times. Frame this with a few words, but remember how time slowed; remember how nothing became fully pretty till the clocks clicked to a halt. Marge and Sal, busybodies, finished too soon. They gossiped about other girls, then ran in the house and came back with plastic cups and a pitcher of orange Kool-Aid. No, no thanks. Jenny and Pat lacked nothing. They lay under the tree and watched the fat cloud grow rounder and shinier as it passed beneath the sun.

Autumn

Fenza snapped a card on the table.

Ace of spades.

Gus drew a nine of hearts, Bad Luck Jimmy a deuce of diamonds.

Jimmy slid Fenza a nickel.

"I'm tired," he said. "Even my cards are tired."

"Save the sad song," said Fenza. "Luck can change."

Gus sipped his drink and wondered what Jenny was doing.

"Hey," he said. "There are still three aces in the deck."

They'd holed up in their speakeasy, Fenza's cellar, to sip stolen booze from Mason jars and turn cards for nickels. Fenza, the bartender, dispensed Red Hook Rye and Pepsi-Cola. He had a pile of nickels in front of him. If these were dollars, he could get on a plane and go somewhere.

An hour later they stopped gambling because it seemed nobody was winning. Bored with cards, bum nickels, they drank and groused over cold weather, cold girls, a town so dead Jesus couldn't have raised it even in His prime. "No lie," said Fenza, "forget Lazarus. This town never sucked a breath."

But then he remembered a rumor he heard somewhere, or was it a fact? After another drink, he was sure he heard it, though he couldn't recall the source. He told Gus and Jimmy a Negro girl had come all the way from Peoria to dance one night in Orville. They could see her perform at 9:30 at the Cloverleaf Palace, the forbidden dance club west of the Rock Island Depot. "Let me know," he added, "if you scatterbrains have something better to do."

Jimmy said Negroes stayed clear of Orville, day and night.

"Ninety-nine percent true," said Fenza. "But this one has permission to do her routine at the Palace and slip back home on the late-night train."

He rooted around in his father's cabinets till he found a chisel.

Jimmy asked what it was for.

"You'll see," said Fenza. "Let's down a few more drinks before the show."

～

At 9:30, they stood across the street from the Cloverleaf Palace. Fenza and Jimmy shared a cigarette, a Lucky Strike, and huddled for warmth. The November night brought freezing rain, gusts of wind, intermittent flurries. Gus shivered with cold and fear and confusion. He'd never seen a naked girl, except in pictures. It must be a joke that the townsmen called this haunt the Cloverleaf Palace. Gus wanted to peek inside, but the windows were boarded. The building had a slapped-together look—brown brick on two walls, stucco on the others. Drunken carpenters must have improvised, but at least the result was honest: the Palace was a patchwork of sin.

Jimmy said he couldn't imagine a Negro girl in Orville even in broad daylight.

Fenza tried to blow a smoke ring, but the wind dispersed it. "Relax," he said. "You can't strain your imagination if you don't have one."

"I'm just saying—"

"You want to see her, Jimbo? Yes or no?"

"Sure, but—"

"All you got to do is open your eyes."

Gus more or less knew this was another of Fenza's fabrications. He was drunk, though, and hopeful, and willing to be surprised. Gold neon—DANCERS, DANCERS—flashed on and off over the entry to the Palace. Gus counted seven cars on the south side of the building, eight more on the north, so a Negro girl or somebody sweet must be drawing a crowd. He heard faint drumbeats, big band sounds whittled to whispers, trumpets that segued to tenor sax, alto sax, a dozen or more horns, plus a drummer, all jamming together. Thick walls and boarded windows muted the music. Who knows? Maybe a Negro girl was shimmying and swaying and slipping free of her clothes.

Fenza took the last drag of the Lucky Strike and flicked the butt in the street.

"Gus Zeul," he said. "You with us?"

A shrug, then a nod.

Fenza looked both ways. No cops. No oncoming cars.

"Okay," he said, "here's the deal. Stay behind me and don't say a word."

Hunched over, Fenza led the way to the north wall of the Palace and stopped beside a boarded window. He took his dad's chisel from the inner pocket of his coat, and in the time it takes to say *Peep, peep, peep* he removed the window cover and tossed it to the ground. Jukebox music, unbound, rushed outside, Glenn Miller's "In the Mood," and a red-hot light flashed off and on. The boys huddled shoulder to shoulder at the narrow window. A white woman was dancing, preening, and they saw her breasts, her hips before—abracadabra—she vanished. A strobe light made her a magician, appearing, disappearing, a chimera of desire. "Christ sake," Fenza whispered. "Blaze the lights so I can *see*."

But they all saw—in flickering visions—red tassels dancing like kites from long nipples, red pigtails like horns, hips wide as Mrs. Moshnik's (Fenza noted this later, in retrospect), and love handles, rolls of fat over pink panties. A near-naked woman didn't need to be dark or pretty to win their attention. Their breaths steamed the window. They pressed their foreheads to the glass.

Gus thought her red hair too bright. A wig?

Fenza said it matched her tassels.

A Negro from Peoria? I bet she lives on Krapalna Street.

Shut up.

She's probably your neighbor.

Shut up or die.

She's white as a glass of milk.

Gus was bug-eyed, dizzy. The strobe teased him the way Jenny teased him. A glimpse, a glimmer, and then nothing to grasp. *A light shineth in darkness and the darkness comprehendeth it not.* For the first time this passage from Scripture made sense. Red tassels, pink breasts, pink panties— here and gone, here and gone. *The darkness comprehendeth it not.*

The game was eternal. The stripper played hide and seek, now you see me, now you don't, light and dark, in the mood, yes, no, sorry. The boys watched with such awe that they failed to notice the squad car pulling up to the curb. Officers Krupovich and Dantley never had such easy prey— just walked over and informed these boys their peeping party was over. Fenza thought he'd run for the river, but Krupovich—quick for a big man—

lurched forward, snatched him by the wrist, and held tight. Jimmy and Gus cringed with shame. The light and dark pulsed off the tops of their heads as the music soared.

Fenza tried to resolve the predicament as Krupovich led him to the squad car. "I'm sorry for the misunderstanding, sir. I was trying to fix that window, get the board back in place."

~

So they were hauled down to the Orville Police Station, cattycorner from St. Iggy's. Phone calls informed three moms of what smut their boys had been involved in, but Mrs. Ryczhik voiced doubts. "How do you know Fenza was part of this? Do you have proof?"

Officer Krupovich leaned back in his swivel chair. "I have proof a-plenty, Mrs. Ryczhik, and so does Officer Dantley. We caught your boy peeping, him and two others. We might let them off with a warning if they make certain promises. For now, though, all I can say is get down here ASAP and pick up your boy."

Farm Girl in Summer

A red-tailed hawk rode the high winds over the pasture. Pat and Jenny, from a back-porch swing, watched clouds veined with light, clouds tall as mountains that crackled and swirled. Pat's dog lay beside her on the swing. When lightning lit the corn and bean fields beyond the pasture, he slunk to the floor, rag-like, and lay still to deceive the sky, play dead. The porch had no screens, no windows. Walls so low they offered scant protection. Jenny, hunched over, wondered if she should join the dog.

Pat leaned over to pet the mutt. "Spencer spooks easy," she told Jenny. "We got plenty of time before the storm reaches the house."

Jenny was ready to bolt. She wanted four walls and a roof, a home, a shelter. A storm was like a boy with too much muscle. Fenza, for instance, wild and dumb, and lucky for her he had his eye on a farm girl. Pat? She didn't seem afraid of him or anyone else. What other girl would pine for a thunderbolt sky, a sky about to fell a tree perhaps, or drown a dog, or electrocute any creature smaller than heaven? What did Pat Lemkey fear? God Almighty? The fires of hell? Sister Damien never found any fear bone to fiddle, nor had Fenza or any boy.

～

A downpour scoured the pasture and washed from sight the pin oaks that bordered the fences, the corn and beans due north. Jenny, in the shelter of the farmhouse, had a bookcase and a wall between herself and the storm. It was one of those sky devils that jump the land, a quick wash and a dozen booms, a brief stirring across the face of all that lives, plus moisture for graves.

Pat stayed on the porch till the rain pelted her and rocked the swing she rose from. Spencer tried to shake himself dry after he led her inside.

Pat hoped her friend wouldn't see her as a freak.

"I forgot to warn you," she said. "Farm girls don't know enough to come out of the rain."

~

In mid-afternoon, the sky patchy with sun and clouds, Pat freed the milk cows from the barn. Spencer, scooting behind the beasts, shooed them from shadows and toward the pasture. Jenny trailed the cows at a safe distance. They seemed docile enough, but she was wary of any creature larger than herself.

Pat jaunted along beside them. "These ladies won't bite," she said.

Jenny gave her a shy glance.

"They're tame as old Spencer. I give you my word."

Pat spoke like a boy sometimes: *I give you my word.* But she'd painted Jenny's nails once, hands and feet, and she didn't touch like a boy. Maybe Pat knew things no Orville boy could imagine. Gus Zeul? The day Jen let him hold her breasts in the willow grove he worked up such a sweat that he hailed one of his hands as the Mississippi River, the other the Illinois. How could he or any town boy summon enough poise to paint a girl's nails?

At a lazy pace, they followed Spencer and the cows through a gate and into the pasture. The cows huddled side by side and munched clover. Pat, resting her back on a fence pole, introduced them by name: Sadie, mostly black with a white chest, white patches on her face, and Beth, a soft brown like coffee double-dosed with cream. Pat fought off the temptation to ask Jenny if she'd like to pet one, or if she thought the farm was beautiful. Spencer began rolling around in a pile of green manure. Yes, manure was green in July, though paler than grass and alfalfa. The rain brought on rich smells, and nothing excited an animal more than smells. Pat started to explain this, then quieted. It would be a shame if this farm with its smells and colors and critters made Jenny long for town.

~

Spencer and the girls came out of the pasture, passed the backside of the barn, and took the tractor path to the pond. A dock that looked too rickety to walk on held Pat's weight with but a few creaks of complaint. She took off her sneakers, sat on the far end, and dipped her toes in green water. "There's catfish here," she said, "and bluegill. Some of the catfish are long as my arms."

Jenny took one step back before she edged out on the planks and sat with her friend.

Pat called this haunt the Minnie Docks. "Straight down," she said, "it's about twelve feet deep. I almost drowned here when I was small. My dad had to jump in and pull me out."

Nerves made Pat tell things that needed no telling. So what if she almost drowned? That was ages ago. She rocked forward now and plunged into the pond. Spencer leaped in after her and stopped whimpering after she rose with a gasp.

She paddled toward Jenny. "Come on in. The water's perfect for swimming."

"Not in my shorts."

"Water won't ruin shorts," said Pat. "I'm *swimming* in shorts."

Jenny shook her head.

"All right," said Pat. "But maybe you can bring your swimsuit next time you come."

Jenny slipped free of her sneakers. She wriggled her toes in the water while Pat dove for bottom and rose with a stone as dark and shiny as polished coal.

∼

Jenny had come for supper, her first visit, and Pat helped her mom with the cooking. Jenny wanted to pitch in, claimed she could cook, but Pat sat her in the parlor with lemonade. The guest soon smelled supper—corn bread, mashed potatoes, fried chicken—smells that reminded her of her mother's kitchen. The lemonade was bittersweet, the way she liked it, and she began to relax. A picture window guided her eye to a grove of trees, giant oaks and maples that survived the storm unscathed. Now and then a car passed by on Ballinger Road. The hiss of tires on wet gravel sounded like rain.

∼

The phone in the parlor rang shortly before supper. Sue Ann, Pat's mom, came out to answer, and at the sound of her husband's voice her face wrinkled with worry. He'd gone to Orville for supplies to repair the tractor, but the storm had washed out a culvert north of town and Ballinger Road would be closed till tomorrow noon. Sue Ann knew from the background noise her husband was at a tavern. "I'll be home soon as I can," he promised. "Be sure to tell Pat to take care of my cows."

Pat always cared for Sadie and Beth, so he was just jabbering. His tongue loosened when he wasn't telling full truths, and Sue Ann wondered when he'd last stripped his words to essentials. The culvert was out, yes, but why couldn't he drive north on Krapalna, west on St. Vincent's, and come in the back way while putting no more than ten additional miles on the odometer? Well, he wanted his Saturday night in the taverns, that's why. He'd drink till closing time at one joint or other, then make a pass or two at some spinster like Cassie Zeul. If no woman took him home, warmed her sheets for him, he'd wind up at his sister Sharon's and sleep till noon.

He had a big voice, so Jenny knew Mr. Lemkey wouldn't be giving her a ride home after supper. Sue Ann hung up the phone and turned to her. "Well, are you ready for your first night on the farm?"

Jenny smiled. "I think so."

"Then call your parents and ask permission. Tell them there's a culvert washed out and my husband can't drive you back into town till tomorrow afternoon."

Pat heard all this from the kitchen. In silence, setting a jug of milk on the table, she pictured herself jumping like a cheerleader after a hometown win, legs flared, arms raised, clenched fists shaking pom-poms at the sky.

∼

After supper, Sue Ann complained of a headache, left the cleanup for the girls, and retired to her room. She was grateful for one thing: no town boys had visited the farm, only girls, and they were as sweet and light as cotton candy. Her daughter couldn't have a nicer friend than Jenny Biel. On the other hand, if Fenza Jr., who sometimes called Pat on the phone at night, ever showed up here, Sue Ann would have to chaperone, keep those two away from the barn, the fields, the acres of corn where kids could disappear in the dark, pay their dues to the devil. Regarding boys, she relied on a refrain her daughter had heard umpteen times: "They got no conscience when they're excited." In her mind, never aloud, Sue Ann would sprinkle a forbidden spice: "A hard *dick* got no conscience!" Because this was too racy to whisper to a child, she relied on warnings as plain as the recurrent notes of a broken record. Her daughter had been hearing about the lack of conscience of the male race since the day she began to bleed.

~

At dusk, the girls sat in the parlor with Spencer. The storm had ushered in cool weather, so Pat draped a shawl over her friend's shoulders. She and Spencer ensconced themselves at the opposite end of the sofa. A pickup toting a cattle trailer rattled by on Ballinger Road.

Jenny brought up her ongoing problem with Gus Zeul. Sure, the boy was sweet on her, but did he love her? "He thinks I'm cute," she said, "but so what? I'd be a fool to imagine we're in love."

Pat nodded. "A boy's after just one thing."

"I suppose."

"Iggy boys are notorious. Not a one of them knows how large a girl is."

Jenny seemed to be wondering—large as *what*? Well, large as a church, thought Pat. Large as a barn or a pasture, or a covey of trees with roots halfway to China. But then Pat knew these words were false for they gave the impression that large trumps small, that a girl should cast a shadow as broad as St. Roch's Church. No, she thought, I'm sweeter than Gus because I take as much interest in a spear of grass as the hair on your arms, as much interest in the valleys of rivers as the shade of thighs. No Iggy boy will ever see you this way.

Jenny said, "You think you'll marry Fenza someday?"

Pat's mouth came open. "*Me?*"

"Well, he likes you. You've known this for a while."

Pat crossed her legs. "No wedding bells for me," she said. "Besides, Fenza plans to join the Marines the day he turns eighteen."

Night arrived. They quieted long enough to hear frogs in the pond out back.

"Croakers," said Pat. "Down by the Minnie Docks."

"There must be a hundred."

"More like a thousand. You want to go down there? Sneak up with a light?"

The picture window framed darkness. "What if it rains?"

129

"It's done raining. No more rain till the next heat wave."

"You're sure?"

"Sure as summer," said Pat. "Come on. The Minnie Docks is beautiful at night."

～

And beautiful it was in itself and in what surrounded it. A pond bordered by bushes and trees, jet black on a moonless night, a thousand or more frogs invisible so that the water and the trees seemed to sing in concert. Pat, flashlight in hand, led the way down a grass-fringed path to the Minnie Docks. She knew how to silence the frogs. "Hey," she said, "*freeze*!" And painted her beam of light across the overgrown shores.

She trailed the light behind her to help Jenny follow her onto the Minnie Docks, a patchwork of two-by-fours buoyed by barrels and moored to land by a metal cable. "Careful," said Pat. "Some planks are missing."

The light blinked off.

"Wait," said Jenny. "Where are you?"

She churned her arms like a slow-motion swimmer till she found her friend's hand.

"Tell you a secret," said Pat. "We'll see better once our eyes adjust to the dark."

The torch had narrowed their vision to a stream of light. They needed the darkness to seep in before they could see clearly the silhouettes of trees, the fields of stars. Pat pointed to Orion, the Big Dipper, the Little Dipper, and she named the trees that circled the pond: box elder, swamp oak, cottonwood, willow. Her parents should have named her for a tree or a constellation. She pointed to Lyra, or Lyre, and its brightest star—Vega. She swept a finger beneath the Milky Way.

Jenny held Pat's hand for balance. "You know all the stars, the trees?"

"Just a few."

"All I know are the Dippers."

They raised their eyes to the little one.

"Are you okay?" said Pat.

"I think so. It's just . . ."

"What?"

"I feel I could slip from this dock and fall down, down, down to who knows where."

Pat rubbed Jenny's hand till it was warm. She started to say something about another constellation, the Northern Cross, but her voice faded. Her eyes shifted from the sky to the water. Silence is difficult to improve.

∽

Midnight.

A bed wide enough for two girls and a dog. Spencer slept on Pat's side, used her feet as a pillow. The bedroom was over the back porch, a good place from which to hear pond frogs, cicadas, and night birds like the occasional owl.

Jenny had a hard time sleeping. These night sounds weren't new, but they were louder than in town, or else farmhouse walls were thinner. She remembered her cheerleader friends, and her best friend, Marge, who often said mean things about Pat behind her back, called her Weirdo or Mutant or "our friend from outer space." Jen would have defended Pat if she knew how. Pat *was* weird. She spoke different, acted different, dressed different, so the names sort of fit. Pat loved thunderheads and rain. She loved an old mutt who rolled in green manure. The makeshift landing called the Minnie Docks—maybe she loved that, too. Today Pat tumbled from the Docks and into the pond and in went her dog and maybe came out a bit cleaner. Now Jen shared a bed with this pair who smelled neither good nor bad, just *farmy*. Maybe by morning she would smell of dog and cows and manure and pasture and pond and Pat. Weirdo? Mutant? Well, the names fit Jen, too, for various reasons. One thing for sure—Pat was never boring. Marge rarely said or did anything that came as a surprise anymore.

At last, Jen curled on her side and slept. A hand moved to Pat's abdomen, the roundness beneath the navel. Her breathing, erratic at first, became calm and measured. Her hand was warm as oven bread.

Pat lay awake a long while. A clock ticked on the nightstand, its cadence slower than her heart. She heard the rustling of prowlers, the raccoons that visited nightly, in the crawlspace beneath the back porch. She placed a hand lightly on Jenny's. She understood the affection—the entire evening—was incidental. A burst of rain, a culvert washed out. Two girls stranded on a farm. Jenny didn't love her, not yet. Pat figured she had one advantage over Gus Zeul or any Orville boy: she had long ago learned to wait.

Zhongzheng, Zhongzheng

Recruiters for the Army and Marine Corps set up tables outside St. Iggy's cafeteria every Wednesday and Friday. Fenza and Jimmy befriended a middle-aged Marine, Sergeant Peterson, a massive, red-faced fellow who walked with a limp. Fenza, certain the sergeant had suffered a war wound, asked numerous questions and received blunt answers. "Talk is cheap," said the sergeant. "You'll learn about wounds soon enough."

Yet little by little, in the month of October, Fenza transformed fragments of personal information into a story. The Korean War almost became a world war. The Chinese sent troops into Korea. A soldier in the People's Volunteer Army (PVA) shot Sergeant Peterson with a Zhongzheng rifle, also called a Chiang Kai-shek rifle, on December 8, 1951. The sergeant, instead of nursing his wound, fired back, wounded the man who shot him, then crawled up and finished him with his knife, a Ka-bar. "I'm telling you this," said the Marine, "because you have potential. I expect you to join the Corps as soon as you come of age."

I *am* of age, thought Fenza. I could be a Marine today.

~

In catechism class, Fenza jotted the details in a spiral notebook:

Korea—almost World War III!
Sergeant Peterson shot by Zhongzheng rifle
Ignored pain, fought back in trenches
Made soup of PVA soldier, semper fi

~

It was difficult to pronounce Zhongzheng, but he enjoyed trying. Zhong-zheng, Zhongzheng. The syllables were sexier than anything in English, even the honky-tonk yammering of hit songs. Fenza wanted to whisper in Pat Lemkey's ear, "Zhongzheng, Zhongzheng," but she never came near enough. He hardly believed her anymore when she told him over the phone she was still his girl.

The Willows in Winter

Christmas Eve

Pat rubbed her mittens together, then rapped on Jenny's door. Someone was home because she heard the radio, the last verse of "Little Drummer Boy," and then the announcer came on "to wish one and all a Merry Christmas and Happy New Year." She removed a mitten and knocked hard enough to redden her fist.

Jenny opened the door a smidge, then swung it wide.

"Pat, when'd you get in town?"

"Maybe a minute ago."

"Well, come on in. You're my best surprise all day."

In the entryway Pat kept her coat on.

"You want to go window-shopping at J. C. Penney's?"

"Now?"

"Yeah, I only have about an hour. My dad's at Sonny's with his friends. I'm supposed to meet him at four and head back to the farm."

Jenny said, "Wait a sec. Let me grab my coat and things." She skipped through the living room to the kitchen. "Mom, Pat's here. We're going window-shopping at Penney's."

"So I heard. But not so fancy free."

"Huh?"

"I don't want you staying out for long."

The house smelled of sweet bread and cookies. Mrs. Biel, wiping her hands on her apron, came out of the kitchen to wish Pat a Merry Christmas. "You girls have a nice time," she said, "but don't linger. I'd say one hour is more than enough."

~

The girls followed the wind down Krapalna Street. Flurries dusted rooftops, trees, St. Roch's steeple. A black cat watched them from the alley behind Moshnik's Garage.

Pat paused at the entrance to J. C. Penney's to point out the black stilettos in the window. "They been on display since July," she said. "I don't guess they're church shoes."

Jenny giggled.

"Stilettos," said Pat. "I've never seen anyone in Orville wear such shoes."

They would sure look fine on Jenny, though, with a long black gown. Never mind Christmas with its shiny trees and tinsel. Jenny in black would be drop-dead gorgeous any day of the year.

⁓

Nothing else in J. C.'s was black. Up and down the aisles, the girls drifted past displays of scarves, hats, jewelry, lingerie, and paused before a mannequin in a green sweater. Pat said, "Wouldn't it be nice if the one who could best use something *owned* it? You'd look better in this sweater than any girl in town."

She had her weekly allowance—seven dollars, one a day. This green sweater was warm and wooly and $13.99.

Jenny pointed to a red dress. "You'd look swell in that one."

"Yeah, I'd wear it when I milk cows."

Jenny laughed.

"I'd wear it when I walk the fields."

They browsed this world of women's things: blouses, bracelets, shoes, cosmetics, a green hat with a black veil. They ran their hands over fabrics and jewels, checked prices, teased about who would look prettier in this or that. Arrangements of wreaths and holly decorated the glass counters. Pat searched for something she could afford.

She bought a bottle of nail polish—called "Poinsettia" for Christmas. "Here," she said, and gave the paper bag and receipt to Jenny. "This is the brightest red in town."

⁓

Leaving the store, Pat checked her watch. She still had twelve minutes before she had to meet her dad.

They walked up Canal Street toward the Rock Island Depot. The snow, a bit more than flurries now, drove horizontally across the river. Pat looked toward the cottonwoods on the far shore, their limbs charcoal in the blur of snow.

"I'm cold," said Jenny.

"Me, too."

"How much time you got?"

"A few minutes."

"You too cold to stay out?"

"Not really."

"I know a place where there won't be much wind."

Jenny would never tell a soul about the spring afternoon when Gus Zeul touched her breasts in the willow grove. It had been dusky and dark, soft green, and the shadows all green. Nobody eased down in the willows now, in December. Their green skirts were gone, stripped of leaves. Maybe, though, the umbrella of boughs would shield them from the wind.

Jenny said, "Come on. We can huddle in some trees."

~

The willows nested in a hollow near the train station. Jenny slipped between the boughs, then Pat, and they squatted side by side. No river traffic on Christmas Eve, no barges. And just now no cars on Canal Street and no sound but the wind and a few fidgeting sparrows. The birds, in twos and threes, flitted in and out of the cottonwoods and swamp oaks east of Dell's Cove.

The high-arching boughs left room to stand. The willows secluded them, and eased the wind, the cold. The Rock Island Depot was closed for business. Orville had shut down except for J. C. Penney's, the five-and-dime, and the neighborhood bars.

Jenny could not recall turning her head. She must have turned to Pat, lifted her arms, and then their faces merged. They kissed each other's cheeks, lips, ears, chin, throat, hair. Soon the willows held a measure of their warmth.

New snow sheathed the trees. Maybe the light of the earth and the light of the body are the same light. Two girls might never be prettier, or more holy. But Jenny had never been more afraid.

~

The tryst ended as abruptly as it began. Jenny pulled back, her mittens near her face, and said, "I didn't mean . . . Oh my God."

She brushed through the boughs and ran till she reached Canal Street.

"Jenny," called Pat, "Jenny. I think it's okay."

Jenny half-turned. What's okay? she thought. Being colored and queer? Wanting to kiss you? Wanting you more than a boy? This town might drown me if it knew.

She darted ahead when Pat came near enough to touch. The second they came out from those willows they'd crossed a line and entered the town. Jenny wiped away a tear, then walked faster. She wouldn't cry again for wonder or shame till she was alone in her room after Midnight Mass.

～

It didn't matter that Pat was late. Her dad was drinking boilermakers, shots and beers, and had lost track of time. He gave her a silver dollar, a Christmas present, and let her sit with him and Frank Moshnik at a back table. Eddie Tapusko and Will Dempsey and some others leaned against the bar. She watched Will toss down a jigger of JD and shut his eyes. She wished his dead wife were here to rouse him with a song—"I like Indians, I like Blacks . . ." Pat wanted to say something to hurt Will, hurt her dad too, but she sat straight and held her tongue.

Her dad said, "That silver dollar's in mint condition. My advice is to wrap it in cotton, stash it away, and let some years go by. It'll be worth decent money if you wait long enough."

The Photographer
December 29

Cassie Zeul basked in the warmth of her tub. She'd left the bathroom door half-open so she could hear the stereo in the next room, John Coltrane's "Naima," delicate and drowsy, a tenderness she could trust. A cocktail glass set on the edge of the tub. Whiskey and water, a long bath, a song with wide margins (Trane could play this for a wound or a resurrection) were her best date in ages. The aches in her body were beginning to ease.

She heard someone knocking on the front door. Gus was spending the night at Fenza's. At half-past nine, she expected no one, wanted no one, but the knocks grew louder than the music. She rose, patted herself dry, and put on a frayed silk robe, a long-ago gift from Eddie. She no longer desired him and never would. She guessed right that he was the one raising Cain, trying to shake sawdust from the oak door.

Cassie turned off the music. The one window in this house that lacked a curtain framed Eddie's face. At least he'd cleaned himself up, donned a new hat, a Homburg, the brim turned up all the way around. He winked, rocked back on his heels, and said, "Hope I'm not interrupting anything."

"You are."

His eyes strayed across her breasts, her throat.

"Well, I wouldn't just swing by here on a whim. I stole something for you."

"You *what?*"

"Read all about it. I snatched a letter off the bar at Sonny's because it's from your ex."

Tomorrow, Cassie told herself, or tonight, I'll snuff this window with a towel, a rag—anything. A temporary solution till I can run down to J. C. Penney's for drapes.

Eddie held up a white envelope.

"You want this or not?"

"Keep it."

He tapped a corner of the envelope on the glass.

"Joe Zeul always has something to say."

"You trying to scare me?"

"No, I'm trying to help. Is that hard to believe?"

"Yes."

"You might want me around after you read this."

"Not a chance."

"I'm your canary in the mineshaft, your one and only."

"Spare me."

"Joe hasn't gotten any saner over the years."

He was drunk if he thought this clumsy ploy would tempt her to open the door. Joe Zeul, Cassie's vanished husband, had been gone eight years, and she'd count herself lucky if he stayed gone the rest of his life.

Eddie hugged himself to stop shivering.

"Can't you let me in, Cass? I'm freezing."

"Beat it before I call the cops."

"They're my friends, not yours."

She clenched her fists.

"Go ahead and call. See where it gets you."

"You break down this door and I'll bust your head."

Eddie steamed the glass with his breath. "Well, Happy New Year to you, too. Am I a louse just for delivering a letter?"

"It's not for me."

"Not me either," said Eddie. "Joe sent this letter to the guys at Sonny's. He's been sending us cards and letters for years."

Cassie shrugged.

"He scribbles things like, '*Don't tell Cass I'm down south because I got no money for child support and she and that boy don't deserve anything but a sack of coal and slug nickels.*'"

"You trying to impress me, Eddie?"

"No, just trying to be neighborly." He pressed the letter against the glass. "You need to read this, Cass. Can't you open up?"

"Not a chance."

"He's not the same Joe. He's gotten worse."

She wagged a fist near the window. "You're in the same club, Eddie. You're a creep."

"I'd be less creepy if I weren't cold."

"Stay cold. *Freeze.*"

She turned off the living room light and disappeared.

Eddie rattled the door. "Judas priest, can't you open up? This letter from Joe is front-page news."

Cassie retreated to the bathroom, closed the door, and switched off the light. She couldn't tolerate Eddie's touch, nor the sight of him, since the murder of Ruth Dempsey. Eddie still drank with Deacon Dempsey in the taverns, and still believed—or pretended to believe—the deacon killed his wife in self-defense. She wished this room had a lock. She had little faith, but she prayed to someone, anyone, "Just make him go away, or at least make him harmless." Eddie mostly was harmless, a good-natured drunk, but sometimes he scared her. Crouched in the dark, she listened for movement. If he was drunk but not too drunk, he might jimmy the lock and let himself in.

"Eddie," she prayed, "go stick it in the deacon's ear."

She heard what sounded like a soft-soled shoe dragged across the floor. A light swish-swash sound that seemed to come from inside the house. She waited for the next step, but none came. Maybe he was standing still.

"Cass?" said Eddie.

The muffled voice meant he was still outside.

"No hard feelings, all right?"

She closed her eyes.

"I'm on your side," he said, "always was."

He was more loyal to Deacon Dempsey.

"Joe Zeul's a loser."

You too, Eddie.

"He was never anything but a bum."

She heard retreating footsteps, then nothing. Three inches of snow had fallen in the afternoon. If Eddie came around to the south side of the house, her bedroom window, she would hear the scrunch of his steps. Every moment of stillness gave her more hope that he was gone. He'd probably drifted back to Sonny's and anchored himself on his usual stool at the front of the bar.

She stayed in the bathroom until the silence felt safe. A half hour, maybe more, before she tiptoed to the living room and glanced outside. The nearest streetlamp lit bare trees, a windrow of snow piled along the curb. No one was about. Orville, or what she could see of it, had turned in for the night. She stepped on something that made a shushing sound. Almost no sound at all but she gasped, jumped aside. She groped her way to the kitchen and returned with a flashlight. Eddie had slipped the envelope beneath the door.

Swish-swash. A lisp from hell, a letter from Joe Zeul. A letter addressed to *All My Friends & Foes at Sonny's Place.* Cassie groaned as she stooped down to retrieve the envelope. Her greatest fear was that Joe would return.

She sat on the edge of the sofa. Bent over, her knees pressed together, she read the letter twice.

~

December 22, 1965
Dear Sonny & the Guys,

Just a note for Auld Lang Syne. I'm still down here in Macon, Georgia, working road construction for the county, no complaints. I won't say life's a bowl of cherries, but everything's a peck easier in the South. I've mostly forgot about Cassie & the old scars have begun to fade. The loss of my boy still riles me, but at least I wasn't fool enough to name him Joe Junior. Deep down he's fickle as his mom.

You want my opinion, the South's got more going for it than the North. No sundown towns in Georgia, or none that I know of. Negroes live in their own neighborhoods, keep a respectful distance, but they also work for us, do most of the tasks we choose to avoid. Negro cooks, maids, nannies—they're common as bunch-weed. No need to give them the boot at sundown if they're useful at night, too. In Orville, I can't recall seeing a Negro even drive through town in the wee hours. Here's a little secret from the South—some sweeties do more than dishes at night. You can take this thought where you want, maybe straight to confession with Father J.

I feel like I belong here. Just the thought of coming back north makes me sweat, so don't expect me to waltz into that bar & buy a round any time soon. Let me say, though, I miss you guys & all the times we had. I know I got ornery, pushed my weight around, but that's over. These past few years, I got some health problems crimping my style. Doctors tell me I've pickled my liver, varnished my own coffin. I plan to work till I die, though, & say I'm sorry only in confession. Cassie & Gus—I won't see the likes of them in heaven. With some luck, though, I'll share a round in the hereafter with some of you guys.

Raise a cup for me! Merry Christmas one & all!

Joe Zeul

~

Cassie set the letter on fire in her kitchen sink. There was no return address on the envelope, just a smudged postmark—Macon, Georgia. She poked the fire with a knife. The flames brightened before they crumbled to ash.

She held a towel over the window of the front door and secured it with tacks. Sleep would be merciful, but it wouldn't come any time soon. Cassie drained the tepid water in the tub and filled it up again, warm enough to steam. She eased in and felt a bit cleaner and safer. Joe was down south, and if all went well that's where he'd die.

How would she ever again make love to a man? In Orville this dizzy word—*Love*—should be driven out before sundown. Eddie had told Cassie he loved her at least a hundred times. Joe Zeul staggered into the thousands before switching to *I hate you, I hate every whore*, in their last year as a couple. Nowadays, maybe he crooned his *I love yous* to some Negro in Macon before he screwed her, then whispered his black sin in a confessional booth on Saturday afternoon. Joe was pious and horny, a dangerous combination. She began to understand this on their honeymoon.

They'd taken the Saturday afternoon train to Chicago. Cassie saw Black and Brown people for the first time, and at night, half-lost, she and Joe wandered into a jazz club in The Loop. *This is music?* That's what her husband said halfway through a piece called "A Night in Tunisia." Joe shut his ears, drank Old Crow with beer chasers, while Cassie thrilled to sounds she had never heard. What did she know of Tunisia? What did she know of jazz? Nothing. Which meant—she knew this now—she was wide open for everything. Some music had to be made and had to be played. Something like blood ran through it, plus rhythms and winds as keen as heartbeat and breath. A wild beauty came alive, said, *Catch me if you can, hear me shine. Hear your own self.* Joe heard nothing and saw nothing. She should've known right then her marriage would fail.

Cassie first took off her clothes for her husband in a rented room near Union Station. He said, "Hon, leave the lights on," and she obeyed. Fully clothed, his trousers bulging—she thought this was cute at the time—he took what he called their "private pictures." He had Cassie kneel on the bed and bend forward so her breasts were pendulous, her nipples engorged. She posed on her side and let him take close-ups of her hips, her breasts, her throat. He moved behind her and photographed her ass. She wanted him to notice her face, or the shape of a hand, a toe, an ankle, but Joe kept shooting the same shots. Cassie was aroused when she stripped for him, but soon her nakedness felt obscene.

"Joe," she said, "can we just hold each other? Start sort of slow?"

He didn't answer.

"Joe?"

She heard the snap of the shutter.

"Turn around."

Afraid, Cassie turned to face him, mouth open.

"Perfect," he said. "Hold still."

She felt battered before he pinned her to the bed.

~

Cassie still had his camera. Around midnight, she rose from the tub, dried herself, and walked naked to a small office. The camera was in the bottom drawer of a file cabinet, a twenty-four-shot roll in its innards, nine shots left. Cassie turned on the overhead lamp, then lay face-up on the cot where she sometimes napped after work. Joe had married her for her beauty, or his idea of beauty. Tits and ass.

She raised her left knee near her chest, took several breaths, adjusted the focus, and pressed the button. In the reflected light, her knee—seen separately from the rest of her—resembled a bright globe, the caution light of a semaphore. She raised her head and photographed her left nipple. If she lost track of what this was, if she was just wakeful and curious, she might see a strawberry—pink, not yet ripe—or the lip of a volcano, the glow of a fire. Cassie sat up and used her right hand to photograph her left. Such a complicated and beautiful form could be anything. The lines of her palm reminded her of a picture in *Life* magazine, the meandering paths of a river delta, the smoothness of sunlit plains. A photograph from space.

She turned her hand slightly and took another shot. Everything looked at carefully slips free of itself, becomes something else. Tit. Erase the word and maybe you'll see one. The roundness she beheld could be a grapefruit pin-stuck with a rose. Could be the warp of half the planet. Men see *tit* in their minds so many times they'd be better off stricken by hallucinations. To at last *see* one they would first have to confuse themselves and discover something to behold.

She looked at the back of her left hand, arched her fingers upward, and took a picture of four thin bones and the declivities between. She hummed the first bars of "Naima," then something of her own, a song sultry in one moment, raspy in the next. She looked at her left hand, the light on her fingers. Happiness—where it strikes—erases the known world. No Orville man could sense something as complicated as a hand, blood vessels, a breath, a song. Illicit pleasures, secret pleasures. These were the kind a woman could trust.

Farm Girl in Spring

Pat swung her legs over the side of her bed. She heard raccoons beneath the porch, and night birds in the oaks and maples. Her dog stretched and yawned, then lay beside her. His ears perked when an owl called.

The old boards creaked with her weight. Pat went to the window and yanked a cord to open the curtains to the moon. The floor took on the shine of an ice-skating rink.

Spencer slid from the bed and tickled her toes with his tongue. "Sweet of you," she said, and stooped to scratch his ears and whiskers. Insomnia, chronic in recent weeks, had given Pat a nightlife. She slipped on her robe and raised the window. The moon, one rib shy of a circle, would be full tomorrow. She had become a keen observer of the moon.

Pat dragged a straight-back chair to the window. She lifted a corner of her mattress, grabbed a notebook, an eraser, a pencil, and set them on the sill. She sat in the chair with the notebook in her lap. She opened to a fresh page, licked the tip of her pencil, and began to write.

~

Dear Jenny,

Big moon tonight. I don't know what to do with all this light. Spencer just enjoys it. If he seems simple, an old farm dog, look again. I say he's wiser than a girl.

I wish I could show you the farm now. You know a plant called Blue-Eyed Mary? On each flower you'll find three blue petals & two white ones. We could gather them in the hollows near Tomahawk Creek.

Two redbuds are showing their colors on the south side of the barn. These are the first trees to bloom in spring, their flowers a purplish-red like a bruise, but I promise you they're pretty. I invite you to pick buttercups & bluebells on your way to the Minnie Docks. Is it possible to give a flower or anything a perfect name? The buttercups are brighter than butter. Right now they are brighter than anything on the farm.

I am curious. I know the names of flowers & trees, a few stars, too, & I wouldn't be snide or sassy to sit quiet & wonder, Do they know mine? Jen, we haven't talked in ages. I can part with the words, or most of them, but I miss the feelings. In the willows in winter, I recall the silence. Christmas Eve, Jen, but it seems like a long-lost century. I sometimes wish we'd never kissed. I wish we'd saved everything we wanted for some night so far off in the future that it couldn't scare us yet.

I have questions for St. Roch's & St. Iggy's & the world. What if it were a sin to love buttercups but not rosebuds? Or what if it were a sin to love bean fields more than corn, or night more than day? What if laws set in stone told us to love certain shades of green but detest others? What if the most grievous sin was to love everything? What if all laws & creeds said, Pat Lemkey, you can love Fenza, or at least marry him, have his kids, a whole litter of Fenzas, but you take one look at Jenny & you'll be an outlaw for life.

Orville has no exit. Sometimes I still pretend I'm Fenza's girl so no one will despise me except myself. Jen, will you marry Gus one day, settle in town & have two boys & two girls? Maybe you can order a white house with a picket fence, too, & some smoke curling up from a red chimney in a J. C. Penney's catalog. I hope you'll forgive my sarcasm, plus a few unavoidable questions. When Gus kisses you, is it better? Cleaner? Less of a sin? Or even a blessing? Do you miss the girl in the willows? Do you remember her name?

P-A-T spells PAT.

~

The next morning she nodded off in English class. Maybe Pat had it in her to care about Beowulf, or at least Grendel, the outcast, but fatigue overwhelmed her. Sister Mary Margaret kept trying to impose a religious theme. "If Beowulf is indeed a hero, as contemporary scholars lead us to assume, he slays Grendel and Grendel's mother not for his own gain, or even his survival, but to uphold the most fundamental Christian laws."

Fine, thought Pat, call me Grendel. Drink to my death.

Soon she slept with a hand braced on her forehead, her elbow on her desk. A thread of drool slid from her mouth and made a pool on *Thy Father's combat feud enkindled* of the open book.

∼

Her last class of the day, Catholic Values and Traditions in the twentieth century, took a pleasant turn. Sister Clair walked in and told the class she was filling in for Sister Damien, who was ill. "I've arranged for a presentation," she said, "that will hopefully keep us awake."

She ordered Fenza to take his assigned seat in the front row. The other students, free to choose their seats, gathered in cliques or pairs. Pat, in a back corner, half-asleep, watched Gus scribble a note, pass it to Jenny, and a moment later his sweetie whispered something, then smiled. Was this the way of love? Maybe Pat should also write a note, something provocative and romantic, say a question or two appropriate to the season: *What if it were a sin to love buttercups but not rosebuds? Or what if it were a sin to love bean fields more than corn, or night more than day?* Perhaps Pat was more of a pariah than Grendel. Every question led to others that were off-limits, obscene. Grendel at least had his mother, another monster, for whom nothing was taboo.

Jimmy Posey, who could've chosen any seat, plunked himself down beside Fenza. Such a sweet couple, thought Pat. They should share hot kisses in the willow grove.

∼

The presentation came from Mr. John Runyan of Sells Landing. He wore bellbottom jeans, an orange sweater, but Sister Clair introduced him as a veteran who recently returned from Viet Nam. The young man paced back and forth in front of her desk. He was tall, stooped, and walked with a cane.

Fenza spoke his thoughts aloud: "War wound, sir? A little skirmish?"

The veteran nodded.

"Booby-trap? Mortar? Bullet wound?"

"Fenza," said Sister Clair, "dispense with the chatter. This is Mr. Runyan's presentation and he has yet to begin."

Fenza guessed the veteran was nineteen or twenty. He was pale, drawn, a bit wizened from—Fenza was hoping—the effects of combat. No one would

147

best Mr. Runyan in a staring contest. He seemed to fear he might miss something if he blinked.

He stopped pacing and leaned on Sister's desk. He ignored the girls, narrowed an eye at Fenza, then other boys, and dismissed them with a shrug. "I doubt I can help," he began, "but Sister asked me to have a word with you." He looked out the window, then back to the boys. "My story's no more original than the numbers on my dog-tags. My wounds are no more original than yours will be."

He said he played football in high school. "Quarterback for Sells Landing," he shrugged, "if that means anything. I remember we played Orville my senior year."

"Beat us," said Fenza. "Always do."

"Yeah," said Mr. Runyan. "But this time it went down to the wire."

He said he had a girl back then, and a red-and-white '57 Chevy. "Jill," he said, "was the girl's name. She was our Homecoming Queen."

"But then you joined the Corps?"

"Fenza," said Sister Clair, "this is a presentation, not a dialogue."

"Yes, Sister."

"All we need to hear for the next twenty minutes is Mr. Runyan's voice."

So the veteran spoke of high school, what he called his "halfway normal years," and then he spoke of military service. "It's not what you think," he said. "There's no peg on which to hang such a thing."

Mr. Runyan horrified every girl and even a few boys by marching in place and bellowing a drill song from basic training. At first, he had seemed detached, half-alive in his shadow, but now his voice shook the students awake, blared through the open windows and across the lawns, and returned as an echo down St. Iggy's halls:

"I went to the market where the women shop.
I took out my machete and . . . chop, chop, chop.
I went to the park where the children play.
I took out my machine-gun and . . . spray, spray, spray."

Fenza, nodding, pen poised, said, "Run this by me again, from start to finish."

The veteran looked at the ceiling.

"Fenza," said Sister Clair, "have I wasted my breath?"

"I hope not."

"This young man's trying to tell us something."

"I noticed."

"You've interrupted him several times."

Fenza, a puzzled smile on his face, raised his left hand.

"Hey," he said, "just one thing. Don't I get any slack?"

"No."

"I always like poems that rhyme."

Pat let her head roll back. This was her beau, her fake boyfriend? She'd dumped Fenza on Valentine's Day, but in the past month she'd let him hold her hand and walk with her to the bus stop after school. This had to end. No more masquerades, no more puppet-shows with Fenza. She'd bop him upside the head if he ever tried to come near her again.

The veteran cut his presentation short. "Sorry," he told Fenza, "but I'm no jukebox. Maybe you can find your entertainment through someone else."

~

Filing out of St. Iggy's after the last period, Fenza and Jimmy followed a short distance behind the girls. The sun was still high, the sky cloudless. Fenza heard the marching song rise to a roar inside his head.

I went to the park where the children play . . .

He whistled at Pat. "Hey, can I ask you something?"

She was the last girl, the only one with nobody at her side.

"Fenza," she said, "go tell your troubles to a frog."

She ran ahead to catch up with Jenny and the other girls. Fenza heard whispers, keened his ears, but couldn't make head or tail of what they were saying. He more or less knew he didn't have a girlfriend anymore. He said to Jimmy, "I'm pretty sure I know that marching song by heart."

~

For the first time in months, Pat walked at Jenny's side. Marge and Sal, a few strides ahead, were whispering about Fenza, how impossible he was, how disgusting, how the mere sight of him was sometimes enough to make them retch.

"More than enough," said Pat. "I had to be crazy to ever be his girl."

Marge expressed sympathy, Jenny too.

"No more," said Pat. "I wouldn't hold that boy's hand for a million bucks."

Jenny said she might be breaking up with Gus.

"For the ninth time?" said Marge.

"No, the *fourth*," said Jenny, a stickler for facts. "It just bothers me that Fenza's his best friend. That marching song . . ." She pressed her binder and books to her bosom, a makeshift shield. "I don't get it. Why are boys crazy? I mean, what *is* it?"

Pat shrugged. "Each Iggy boy's got one oar in the water."

"Huh?"

"He works like a devil to spin himself round and round."

In a few minutes, the bus to the country would be pulling up at the south gate of St. Iggy's. Pat had no objection. She felt awkward chatting with girls after months of solitude. The farm, with its three hundred acres, its sky unbroken by spires, a steeple, would always feel more welcoming than Orville or any town.

～

Jenny called her after supper. Pat was upstairs in her room, staring out the window at a fox ambling along the tractor path toward the Minnie Docks. When her mom called up the stairs, "Phone, hon," she knew it was Jenny. The fox accelerated, leaped a fence, and disappeared.

Pat galumphed down the stairs two at a time. In the parlor, she grabbed the phone and carried it to the sofa. "Hello?" Big heartbeats, small voice. Pat suspected her face was redder than the fox.

Jenny sat cross-legged on her bed, the cord of the phone cinched tight as a fishing line that snagged bottom. She hadn't called her friend in almost four months. At St. Iggy's, she'd avoided Pat and tried to forget the willows, the pleasure of kisses, plus the previous pleasure of painting each other's nails. She admitted tonight that she'd missed Pat, missed talking to her at school and on the phone. She complained about Gus, how he was sweeter than most boys but not sweet enough. She said, "He's a thousand times nicer than Fenza, but I still don't think he's the one."

Pat wondered if Jenny heard her heart. "It was good to see Sister Clair today."

"It always is."

"I felt sorry for the veteran, though. If Fenza had any manners, he would've kept quiet and listened."

"But that's not Fenza."

"No, and never will be. He can't go two minutes without making a scene."

The silence felt awkward at first. Pat began to say something more about Fenza, then said, "Never mind. Let's give him a rest." She remembered the letter she wrote last night, the letter to Jenny in the notebook beneath her mattress. The silence made her think of it, though in some ways the letter was loud. *When Gus kisses you, is it better? Cleaner? Less of a sin? Or even a blessing?* Pat wondered if she would ever show Jenny her secret writings. Maybe yes, maybe no. Her face softened as she kissed Jenny in silence over the phone.

Underwater

Former inmates of St. Iggy's crowded Dell's Cove on the first day of summer vacation. Jenny and Pat planned to meet some other girls on the beach, but they had time to dally. They window-shopped at J. C. Penney's, then drifted up Canal Street toward the willow grove and the Rock Island Depot. A wave of noise jounced after them, a transistor radio tuned to rock & roll, the cove so jammed with boys and girls it seemed about to erupt. Fenza sang along with the radio, Roger Miller's "King of the Road," and Gus banged out slick beats on his bongo. Jimmy Posey, the third member of the trio, plucked his guitar too softly to be heard.

"Gus takes that drum everywhere," said Jenny. "It's like his new sweetheart."

Pat glanced at her.

"He's gotten better, though, don't you think?"

"I guess so."

"Fenza still sings like a wounded beast."

Pat preferred silence to boy talk. Jen was gorgeous in white slacks and a blouse sheer enough to reveal the pink swimsuit she wore underneath. At home, Pat had tried on her bathing suit and posed before a full-length mirror. She was chubby, needed to shed a few pounds, so she'd tucked in her stomach. Now she wore that one-piece suit beneath knee-length shorts and a yellow T-shirt. She carried her sandals in one hand and walked barefoot on the brick road.

They hadn't come this way together since Christmas Eve. Pat was surprised Jenny trusted her, or had she forgotten? On Christmas Eve, after they browsed the aisles at J. C. Penney's, Jenny led the way to the willow grove near the Rock Island Depot. Hidden from the town, sheltered from wind, they kissed till they were warm, then ran from that haunt like scared kittens. Jenny remained Gus Zeul's girl till mid-May, when she broke up with him for the fourth time and hopefully for good.

Today the Rock Island station was in full swing at high noon. People milled about on the landing, and gathered in the coolness beneath the eaves. The train for Chicago would arrive at 12:18. The stationmaster had his radio tuned to a ball game, the Sox and Yankees in New York City. Pat half-listened to the nonstop banter of the announcer, then turned toward the willows. Thinking about kissing was almost like kissing. If for one second this town held its breath, shut off its radios, buttoned its lips, she might hear her own heart and Jenny's too.

Pat eyed the station. "We should go to Chicago someday. You know I've never been there?"

"Me either."

"But I doubt it's prettier than here."

She kept glancing toward the willows. She wanted to kiss Jenny once more, just once, and then she knew she was lying. She wanted to kiss her all summer and into the fall, all winter and into the spring. Jenny's lips were soft as pillows, thick as thumbs. Pat remembered they were warm, too, even on Christmas Eve.

Jen went up to the station and pretended to read the schedule stenciled to the window. She was so light-headed the numbers meant nothing. If she liked Pat Lemkey more than Gus Zeul, what did this mean? Before Pat could step beside her, confuse her any further, she said, "Marge and Sal are waiting, come on. I'll race you to the cove!"

Pat fell behind. Still holding her sandals in one hand, she felt clumsy at first, but then her strength, plus the intangibles—desire, the fear of being alone—quickened her stride. Maybe Jen let her catch up, pass her by, or maybe Pat had learned to run. Racing across the footbridge over the canal, she decelerated, let Jen come even, and they glided side by side to Dell's Cove.

~

They joined Marge and Sal and other girls on the west side of the beach. There were some boys nearby, but Fenza and Gus were a good distance away, Fenza wailing a song from last summer, "Wooly Bully," and Gus slapping his bongo to a rhythm of his own making. Neither girl had brought a towel, so they sat cross-legged in the sand.

The boys who came by to flirt had no chance whatsoever. Go talk to the river, thought Pat. Talk to the birds in the sky. Talk to the fields. If they answer, I might believe you have something to say.

After the boys wandered off, tried their luck elsewhere, Jenny and Pat stripped down to their swimsuits and eased into the river. Warm currents hugged the shore, then swept outward. The girls followed the pathway of the river. They waded in belly-deep, breast-deep, and kept going. Jenny was two inches taller, so she stopped and hunched down when Pat was up to her neck in the Illinois.

The water was murky enough that she and Pat could touch hands, then hold hands, without anyone knowing. Maybe a hundred kids on the beach and in the shallows, but not a one could see their hands underwater. Jenny shook with the thrill of it, Pat too, and then they turned, switched hands and faced the far shore, the trees a brilliant green a half mile across the river. The train for Chicago blew its whistle as it approached the station. The earth moved, and the riverbed, in small tremors. This train was on time. The long line of passenger cars rattled and rolled and the wheels screeched before they stilled.

Fuses

They awaited the five o'clock whistle that would release some of them to their homes, others to taverns. Will Dempsey, foreman and junior manager, needed a stiff drink to calm his nerves, but first he had to conclude his presentation to thirty-one workers, Cassie Zeul among them. In the conference room, a lectern between himself and his audience, he lauded the local boys who'd joined the war effort, and he bowed his head when he spoke of Donny Zorich and Joe Selbst—"young men cut down in the prime of life who made the ultimate sacrifice for our freedom." He ignored Cassie when she shifted in her seat and raised her hand.

"As I said earlier, you'll earn an extra thirty-seven cents an hour, and in a two-week pay period—do the math—this adds up to almost thirty dollars. Mr. John Maylor, the founder of this plant, has combined his concern for his employees with his love for his country. The result is a rare opportunity to do important work."

Cassie Zeul, restless and rude, rose to her feet.

Will said, "Stay seated, please," but she stood there, arms akimbo, as if she were in charge.

"Let me conclude this presentation with a promise. Beginning tomorrow, your finished products will be far more essential than the wristwatches and alarm clocks boxed in warehouses and shipped to Chicago and Boston and New York City. The Department of Defense, thanks to Mr. Maylor's efforts, has awarded the Orville Clock Factory a contract that will remain in effect for eighteen months or until the war's won—whichever comes first." He glanced at his watch. "Because I have other business to attend, I ask that you save your questions for tomorrow. Orientation will begin in this room at eight o'clock sharp."

Only one woman could make Will sweat in the cool of autumn. Cassie Zeul, maiden name Renh, but was she ever a maiden? She stood pert and pretty, waved her left arm, snapped her fingers. "One question, Mr. Dempsey. Just one that won't wait for morning."

"Ma'am?"

"This new job is about making fuses, right? Fuses for bombs?"

"Well, yes. That's the gist of it."

She brushed an unruly strand of hair from her brow. "If you don't mind, sir, I'd rather keep making watches and alarm clocks. I know my job inside out."

"Yes, but you've been reassigned. You'll hear the details at orientation."

She shook her head. "I won't need an orientation."

"Oh?"

"This new job doesn't suit me. I don't know anyone I'd care to bomb."

Her coworkers needed a few moments before they could register their surprise. The women whispered, fidgeted with their hands; the men gawked and grumbled. Will Dempsey said, "Let's hold on here, let's keep our focus." He informed Miss Zeul his intention was to present a few facts rather than invite commentary or discussion. "The situation couldn't be simpler," he said. "You'll do the job you're assigned and do it well or you won't have a job at all."

～

Every assembly line worker except Cassie filed from the room after the five o'clock whistle. A rectangular room, white and clean. As orderly as the cell of a monk. The sole adornment—photographs of the factory in black and white—were identical in size, and hung from the walls at equal intervals. Only one rose above eye level, a close-up of John Maylor displaying a blueprint of assembly line renovations. Sharp clean angles, geometry. Everything but the man designed by a draftsman. Cassie gave him a wink he would never see. A sighting of Maylor (other than in photographs) was like sighting a rare bird, though he sometimes cruised Krapalna Street in a souped-up Buick Riviera. He was out of town often, on business or leisure. His son Dave, a supervisor at the plant, spent long hours driving the old man's pride through town and along the river. Mr. Maylor's show car was cherry red with a white top. Boys and even grown men would follow the Riviera with their eyes the same way they would follow a fine-looking woman walking down a street.

Will gathered his notes in a manila folder. This woman was bent on crowding him, pressuring him, erasing his formality. He leaned over the lectern and pretended to read.

"Am I fired?"

He looked up. "Not if you do as you're told."

"But what about my old job? Doesn't nine years—"

"I've been here twenty-one years. Your old job is history."

"Well, that's nice to know. Do or die is the rule here."

"I wouldn't put it that way."

"How *would* you put it?"

He looked past her. "I've made everything very clear."

What in hell would she know about do or die? Will reminded himself he was in charge here, a honcho with the power to hire and fire, and what's more he'd seen more of this rude world than Miss Zeul could fathom. He was a veteran of combat, and in this town and most towns this was hard currency, sort of like being a star athlete. He didn't want to think of his wife, what he'd done to her, but this too was in the arena of combat. Except for Miss Zeul, the town respected him, even admired him. If insolence were a virtue, this woman might attain the sanctity of a saint.

Will straightened his posture. "Everyone else is eager to perform the work I described."

"Fuses?"

"Yes, fuses. And why not? Our boys in Viet Nam, those from our own town, our church—they need our support and need it directly."

"I'm for those boys."

"Well, that's wise of you. Your own son may soon be among them."

"I hope not."

"Let me tell you something that may come as a surprise."

"I'd rather—"

"I wouldn't be alive if it weren't for pilots, planes, factories, and men like John Maylor who make things happen."

She sighed as if the spiel were familiar.

"You may see this as some sort of game, but it isn't."

"You're sure?"

"No, *do or die* is more than a figure of speech."

"You would know."

"Yes, I *would*," said Will, and wiped his moist hands on his trousers. "Any veteran will tell you the same: the best reason to make these fuses is to help our boys survive."

He turned toward the window that faced the river, the sky cold and gray. Late October was whiskey weather, barstool weather. Praise the season. Only Miss Zeul stood between Will and the nearest tavern. She'd never trusted him, never liked him. She might be the only woman in Orville who believed he murdered his wife in cold blood.

"Do you have Mr. Maylor's number?"

"I'm not at liberty—"

"Oh, Christ—*liberty*. You can lick that syrup without choking?"

"Cassie—"

"I'm fired, so what do I care?"

"You might care when the rent's due."

She shrugged.

"You made a choice," he said, "so you'll live with it."

"You too, Will."

His left hand flew between them like a startled bird.

"Enough," he said. "You have no right to speak to me like this."

He dared to look at her. In her uniform, a dark blouse, dark-blue slacks, stubby black shoes, she still blossomed. She was the prettiest woman in Orville, but he hated her from toe to crown, and back down through her heart and innards. Will always had the feeling she saw through him, or worse, *into* him, and maybe she was well acquainted with every part of him crooked or cruel or mangled. She had the nerve to ask again for Mr. Maylor's number. "Private info," he said. "And besides, you'd waste your time begging for your job."

She took one step forward and shook her head. "I don't beg, Will, never have. No one but me could tell Mr. Maylor he's on an express train to hell."

She walked off snapping her heels on concrete.

Will flinched as if shots were fired.

⁓

Gus Zeul, home from school, heard the music before he opened the front door. Max Roach, jazz drummer, drove a beat through the season, shook the leaves from the trees. "Ezz-thetic"—he'd heard this piece a hundred times and wanted to hear it a hundred more. Max Roach whacked the drums. Sonny Rollins and Kenny Dorham blew their horns and rode the sounds the way rodeo stars rode broncos. Gus found the beat, his hands warm on his thighs. Music is always a flame.

He was happy to be home. His mom sat on the sofa, legs crossed, her left ankle twitching to keep time with the song. A drum solo left her in its wake. She couldn't match the backbeats and sprints, the tempo that seemed to morph into something new no matter how many times they'd listened. She balanced a cocktail glass on the arm of the sofa. Her work clothes were wrinkled, so maybe she'd just risen from a nap. He smelled whiskey and water, a dash of lemon. She rarely drank before the sun went down. He asked her what was wrong.

She got up to lift the needle from the turntable.

"A little of everything," she said. "Everything but you."

She took his left hand and led him to the sofa. Sitting at her side, he looked through the front window at a bare maple as she spoke of fuses, bombs, assembly lines, Mr. Maylor and his new angle for increasing profits. "Instead of making clocks and watches," she said, "some workers will make fuses for bombs, but I am not among them." She sipped her drink. "This means I'll be looking for another way to pay the rent, fill the fridge, but this is my problem, not yours." She rubbed his shoulders. "Don't worry," she said. "I'll find a way to keep us in this home."

He glanced at the stereo. "Can I put the record back on?"

Cassie winced. "You hear what I just said?"

He nodded.

"I wish you'd listen to me as well as you listen to Max Roach."

He looked into her eyes. "I heard you."

"Are you sure?"

"Yeah, it's fine with me if you don't make fuses for bombs."

More often than not, he appreciated her surprises. In some ways, she was a little like Max Roach and Sonny Rollins in those dizzying numbers like "Ezz-thetic," "Dr. Free-zee," and "Kids Know." It seemed to Gus these jazzmen loved nothing more than springing a surprise, neither one knowing too well what would come next—what sound, what riff, what combo of noise and color. The boy heard lots of red in Max Roach's drums, and brilliant blues and yellows from Sonny and his sax. The idea about color would be hard to explain, even to his mother. He was pleased, though, because she squeezed his hand and said, "All right, let's play some music. After we give this album its due, I'll go see your grandpa about working at the store."

And these were the best of times—listening to Max Roach on drums, Sonny Rollins and Kenny Dorham blowing their horns, George Morrow on bass, Ray Bryant on piano. His mom had ordered maybe a hundred albums through the mail from—among other places—South Chicago and New York City. Sometimes they both decided what to order after listening to DJ Al Benson on WGES radio from Chicago. Earlier today, she turned her back on a steady job, bread and butter, but now they were listening to "Just One of Those Things." Her color was high, her eyes bright, and he sat with her on the green sofa at the center of the world. The turntable—she'd ordered that through the mail too—was a Crosby Traveler, a Stack-O-Matic that let them stack records and listen for hours. The stereo fit into a tan suitcase. Gus had a hunch they'd go traveling someday, maybe South Chi first, then New York City. The day he turned twenty-one, or sooner if he had a fake ID, they'd let him in the clubs.

∾

Tony Renh's Grocery, at Third and Krapalna, was open past closing time because Mrs. Sedlak was searching for the perfect head of iceberg lettuce as she listened to Cassie Zeul ask for work. Tony Renh kept shaking his head and telling his daughter to keep the job she had. "I can't," said Cassie. "Don't you hear a word I'm saying?" She'd already told him she was "done with the factory, done with Mr. Maylor and his schemes, done with all of it." She refused to stand on an assembly line and make fuses for bombs.

It seemed to Mrs. Sedlak that Cassie herself was a bomb, or at least a lit fuse. She failed to recall when she'd last seen this woman in church, or when she wasn't fuming at this, that, or the other. Make a scene, stir the pot—that was Cassie. She didn't have a single friend in this town, though she probably had lovers. Lushes like Eddie Tapusko followed her around.

Tony stood behind his meat case, his daughter at his side. He said, "You can't just quit, Cass, you *can't*." Tony told her what everyone in town already knew: He'd lost most of his business to the A&P; he barely had enough work for himself, let alone another person. "If not for special orders for *kiszka* and kraut," he said, "I wouldn't make any money at all."

But Cassie seemed deaf to the facts. She offered to make deliveries on Saturday mornings. She offered to stock shelves, sweep and mop, shine windows, dust light fixtures, arrange produce, do the books, add and subtract the numbers. Mrs. Sedlak hoped he'd let her dust the fixtures, for the light in this store was dreary, almost unclean. Tony reminded Cassie that her own son stocked shelves and swept and mopped on Saturday mornings for thirty-five cents. "Pocket change," he said, "plus some licorice." He picked up a cigar stub from the butcher block and lit it with a wooden match.

Mrs. Sedlak inched closer and began poking through cabbage. Cassie tried to tell her father she wouldn't need a car to make deliveries on Saturday mornings. No, she'd save him gas by carrying sacks of goods up Krapalna Street to their few remaining customers, including Father Janecek and the nuns. Cassie, who hadn't been to church in ages, would be a sight knocking on the door of the rectory. Mrs. Sedlak fondled cabbages and grunted. She pictured Cassie in a tight skirt, a red blouse. A sack brimming with milk and butter and *kiszka* cradled in her arms.

Mrs. Sedlak strained to hear whispers.

"You been drinkin', Cas. Hauling groceries up Krapalna—that's out of the question. The whole town would think I'm so busted I can't put gas in the Chevy."

"I doubt they'd notice."

"Oh, they'd notice. What *don't* they notice?" He sucked his cigar and blew the stink toward his daughter. "Your only option is to keep the job you have."

The old man had been pushed to his limit.

"Mrs. Sedlak," he said, "I'm sorry but I need to close now."

"No," she countered. "Let me be the one to apologize."

He looked at her.

"I've kept you here past normal hours," she said. "You've been kind not to turn me away."

He sucked his cigar, brightened the embers. A lit fuse, thought Mrs. Sedlak, a replica of his daughter. He'd probably give Cassie the verbal whipping of her life the moment there was no one to eavesdrop. Mrs. Sedlak wanted to stay for the fireworks, but the best she could do was pay for her lettuce and cabbage and imagine the show on her way home. Maybe Tony Renh would stomp and curse, shake the floorboards, and give his daughter an ultimatum: "Keep your job at the clock factory or never set foot in my store as long as you live."

∼

Four days later, after school, Sister Clair stood at Cassie's front door. She heard horns and drums, a jazz piano, and worried her knock might interrupt a party. She didn't hear anyone dancing, though, or talking, just this music she couldn't quite place. In the South, in her work in the civil rights movement, she'd gone to gatherings in Montgomery and heard jazz recordings of Chet Baker and Ornette Coleman. She'd heard something called "Walkin'," too, by Miles Davis, but what she heard now gathered more steam. The melody warmed her because it reminded her of the South.

Cassie opened the door an eye width. "Sister?"

"I hope I'm not disturbing you."

Cassie shrugged. The entire town was a disturbance.

"Maybe I should've called before rattling your door."

"Maybe you should've."

"But can you spare a minute? Is that possible?"

"If you're here to lecture or preach—"

"Oh, heavens no. A lecture or a sermon is the last thing we need."

Cassie opened the door wide enough for the music to slip out onto Canal Street and for Sister to slip inside. Then she shut the door and let the music come home.

"I should turn off this stereo."

"No, I'd rather you keep it on if you don't mind. It reminds me of home."

Cassie looked at her quizzically.

"Mobile," said Sister, "Montgomery. I was born in one and raised in the other."

"I didn't know. I guess you left your southern accent behind."

"No, never had one. My parents are transplanted New Englanders."

"I see."

"They were too snobby to let me speak with a southern drawl."

She approached the stereo. "What are we listening to?"

"'Cousin Mary,'" said Cassie. "Have you heard of John Coltrane?"

"The name's familiar."

"My boy idolizes Max Roach, a drummer. He dreams of being a jazz drummer."

"And a poet," said Sister. "He told me so his freshman year."

Cassie noticed two envelopes in Sister's left hand. "Please," she said, and motioned the nun toward the sofa. "Is Gus in trouble at school? Has something happened?"

"Oh, no. Your son's doing well."

"He's at Fenza's, but I'll call and tell him to come home if there's a problem."

"There's no problem with Gus."

Cassie stood back. "May I ask why you're here, Sister?"

"Of course. I dare say I've come to admire you."

"*What?*"

"I admire you," Sister repeated, and sat on the sofa, the envelopes in her lap.

Cassie lowered the music to a hush. "Excuse me," she said. "I may need a moment to get my bearings."

"By all means."

"I'll heat up some coffee and be right back."

Sister was pleased to find her alone, for they had much in common and much to discuss. Mrs. Sedlak, a main branch in the town's grapevine of gossip, had told the nuns and Father Janecek—and by now the entire parish—that Cassie Zeul quit her job in protest because the Orville Clock Factory was making fuses for bombs. "Or maybe Mr. Dempsey fired her on the spot," she'd said. "Either way, she's got no job, nothing. Everyone else is eager to make fuses, help win the war, bring our boys home, but not Cassie. The gall of that woman, the foolish pride. Can you imagine?" Sister Clair had confused her by saying, "I am sometimes an admirer of gall."

Cassie served coffee in her best cups, robin's-egg blue, with matching saucers. Sister sat on one end of the green sofa, Cassie on the other. "Do you take sugar? Cream?"

"No," said Sister. "This suits me just fine."

She noticed the turntable, the suitcase it rested in, though perhaps rest was the wrong word. The music, quiet now, reduced to background noise, still gyrated with energy, vim, and the drummer and saxophonist played in antiphon, a secular conversation. Sister leaned an ear to the music and recalled a night in Montgomery. She was one of three white people amid hundreds of Negroes in a church hall in December of '55.

"I once met Rosa Parks," she said.

"Who?"

"Oh, you know. The woman who refused to move to the back of a bus in Montgomery."

Cassie stared into her coffee.

"A Negro," said Sister. "She wouldn't give up her seat to a white man."

"Good for her."

"It was in the news, though perhaps not in Orville."

"Surely not."

"The Chicago radio stations and newspapers would have filed reports, but this was years ago, 1955."

Cassie calculated. "Gus would've been six."

"Yes, and I was a young woman, just finishing my training at St. Mary's Convent."

"In the South?"

"Yes, Montgomery."

"So who sent you to Orville? Your church?"

"Yes, you could say that. Some of my superiors approved of my work in the civil rights movement, but a few important exceptions disagreed."

Cassie sighed. "I'm sorry you had to come here."

"No, c'est la vie," said Sister, and winked. "They are confident I'll cause less trouble in a small northern town."

Cassie awaited an announcement. The envelopes were conspicuous in Sister's lap. Whatever they contained would explain the purpose of this visit. Sister's voice rose a few decibels above the music. Cassie caught every word, but the praise showered on her, the unlikely adjectives—"conscientious, ethical, wise"—made her laugh. Sister laughed, too, and almost spilled her coffee. "Oh, I suppose I go on a bit," she acknowledged. "But that's because I know it took some courage to walk away from that job."

Cassie said she hadn't given it much thought.

"Oh, but you did," said Sister. "A decision of this magnitude comes from all the years of one's life."

She opened one of the envelopes. "A letter," she said, "from a young man who's in prison. I met him in Montgomery eight years ago, and I know his family. He was drafted into the army the day he turned eighteen."

Sister handed the letter to Cassie. "Dr. King wrote to us from the Birmingham City Jail. His letter is famous, deservedly so, and this one is equally important."

Cassie glanced at the salutation. "Should I read this now?"

"Please," said Sister. "It will explain in full why I knocked on your door."

◡

October 12, 1966

Viet Nam

Dear Sister Clair,

Here I am at LBJ, Long Binh Jail, nine thousand miles from Montgomery. Me and Marvyn, this other brother, been cleaning the honey buckets most days, dousing them in diesel, lighting them up, and trying to stay upwind of the smoke and stench. My daddy used to have a outhouse, no plumbing, but the yards all around smelled as good as a dog's paws. Smelled like grass, I mean, or moist straw, or sometimes like the soil after an all-day rain. A dog's paws smell like the places he loves. Our hands would smell this way if we walked on them through yards and gardens and fields.

Honey buckets are raw sewage mixed with fuel and flames. Don't blame the Vietnamese. Don't blame their country. We exported the worst of ourselves. We left the good smells in the gardens back home.

Nine days ago, Sister, I sat down on a rice berm and refused to carry a weapon. Is No the bravest word in the world? Rosa Parks said No. MLK said No. Malcolm said, NO, NO, NO. So why'd it take me all my life to love this word?

I am a veteran of 83 combat missions. The Vietnamese call our choppers dragonflies. High flyers, loud as hell, they carried me up over the clouds and set me down on the earth 83 times. I've looked out from the wild blue at the bombed forests and fields, the villages in shades of gray, ash and rubble, and I whispered No in my heart 83 times before I mustered the strength to push this word from my mouth. All I can do, Sister, is hint at what I've seen. Gunships that "put a bullet in every square inch of a football field in less than a minute." Bombers, B-52s, blowing apart rice fields, sugar palms, birds, bees, water buffalo, fish, grass, leaves—whatever conceals or sustains the "enemy." I don't sleep much, Sister, and late at night I tend to wonder, in the relative quiet, how America can sleep. LBJ's a Black jail with white guards, and I wish America could tune us in on TV, or better, meet us at night in the cellblock. America needs some dark dreams to survive her dumb innocence. She needs—excuse the language, Sister—honey buckets, shit & fuel & fire, plus the courage to breathe.

Sister, I want to visit you when and if I leave this place. Some brothers here are from Chicago, and one of them says that town you're in—Orville, Illinois—is a Sundown Town. No Negros after dark, right? And I bet you don't see any even at high noon. Sister, I'm sure you're trying to love everyone, and that's nice. Don't be down on me, though, if I visit Orville some moonless midnight and knock on a few windows. I just don't have many fears anymore, which may explain why they locked me up. I trust you, Sister, the same way I trust my mama and daddy. And maybe some night you and me will walk side by side through the heart of Sundown Town.

With love from LBJ,

Kenny Jefferson

P.S. Anybody in Orville say no to the war? Seems unlikely, but I always like to hear of a surprise.

～

Cassie whispered the young man's name. "Kenny's mother must be worried."

"She is."

"Can you make a copy of his letter?"

"Of course."

"I need to show it to my son."

Her eyes were red. She touched the letter to her chest before she returned it to Sister.

"Would it be all right if I write to Kenny?"

"Please do."

"I will thank him for saying No."

～

At the door, Sister Clair pressed a sealed envelope into Cassie's hands. "A gift," she said. "Please open this after I leave."

A cyclist passed. A small wind louder than her voice.

"I'll bring a copy of Kenny's letter tomorrow."

"I'll be here."

"I'll stop by before school."

～

Cassie sipped lukewarm coffee at her kitchen table. She opened the envelope and money spilled out.

~

October 30, 1966

Dear Cassie,

I pray you will accept this gift, which comes from my heart and the generosity of my family. My grandparents left me a trust that allows me to sprinkle a bit of money where it is most needed. As a nun, my own needs—food, shelter, clothing—are provided. I can offer a gift of the same amount ($240) every two weeks. I am fortunate to know you and your son, for courage is contagious. Please know you can count on me for friendship and support.

In solidarity and peace,

Sister Clair

Riviera

The world would change at 9:26 p.m. Fenza swore by it, hour and minute, but kept further details private. He would soon join the Marines, and he already knew a few things about military operations. A colonel, for instance, or even a lieutenant, discussed strategies and objectives only among equals. Fenza diverted Gus and Jimmy with braggadocio and booze.

They sipped a blend of Old Crow and Wild Turkey from a one-quart canteen. Fenza pilfered the booze from his father's liquor cabinet, but he called it "Dirty Bird Double" and claimed he brewed it at home. In Pulaski Park, in the nightshade of a sycamore, the boys huddled, passed the canteen, and awaited the new world. St. Roch's Church stood some thirty yards away.

Fenza pressed Jimmy to drink. "Don't be shy," he said. "Flay your guts." Jimmy drank and coughed, drank and trembled.

"Hail Mary full of moonshine," said Fenza. "Don't die on me, Jimbo. You're almost a Marine."

Over the sycamore a claw of moon and clouds delicate as lace. Girlie shapes, enticing. And as untouchable as Pat Lemkey and the girls of St. Iggy's. On November 2, All Souls' Eve, the ground lay frozen, already sealed in winter, and clouds drifted. Only Fenza could devise a scheme to salvage the night.

On Krapalna Street, cattycorner from St. Roch's Church, Mr. Ciernik burned yard debris in a barrel. A stiff wind blew north to south, so the boys breathed fine smells: wood smoke and whiskey, charred leaves, the sting of autumn. Fenza led a few toasts, then slipped his canteen in an olive drab knapsack. "Come on," he said, "zip your zippers. We need to be down on Canal Street to meet the westbound train."

He wouldn't say why. On point, he led his cronies through the park and down Krapalna Street toward the Illinois River and the Rock Island Line. A Chevy sedan wheezed by going the other way.

Fenza glanced over his shoulder at receding taillights. "Jimmy," he said, "I'd tie you in knots if I had a minute to spare."

Jimmy threw a shadow-punch. "What for?"

"For besting me," said Fenza. "You'll be the first to leave this town and all its stupid girls."

Two weeks earlier, on his birthday, Jimmy turned eighteen and joined the Marine Corps. He would leave for basic training at Parris Island on December 3, his personal D-Day. Farewell St. Iggy's girls. Farewell Orville and good riddance. Fenza, his mentor, had given Jimmy two quarts of Star Model Beer, plus some knowledge, for his birthday. "One thing for sure," he said. "Boot camp will squeeze the shit right out of you, blow everything soft to high heaven. You'll have three months—maybe four—before they send you to Viet Nam."

Now he and Jimmy began jabbering about handguns, the virtues of the German Luger, the Colt .45, and the Nambu, a semiautomatic pistol used by the Japanese Imperial Army in World War II. Gus Zeul listened. If his pals weren't pining for girls, they were pining for weapons. A couple chumps, he said to himself. I'd trade any weapon in the world for a set of drums.

The trio passed Tony Renh's Grocery, then Old Joe Miller's shack with its swayback tarpaper roof and boarded windows. Gus, lagging behind, shuffled his hands over his thighs. He thought of Jenny Biel, the sweetie who'd dumped him four times, and then he thought of the music his mother had ordered through the mail, the 1956 studio recordings of Max Roach and Sonny Rollins in New York City. Over and over, Gus had studied the beats Max Roach put out in "Ezz-thetic," "Mr. X," "Dr. Free-zee," and "Just One of Those Things." A talented drummer had a choice—keep time with the beat, or *make* time. The keeping bore no risk, merely followed a set pattern. But Max Roach? thought Gus. "Dr. Free-zee?" He *makes* time, he *is* time. A good drumbeat is the heart of the world.

Krapalna met Canal Street at the base of the hill. Fenza led Jimmy to Moshnik's Garage, the staging area, or so thought Fenza. They ducked behind a heap of discarded tires as Gus breezed by whirling his arms, whacking his thighs. "Hand Job," said Fenza, "you care to join us?"

Gus turned in a half circle.

"Surprise me," said Fenza. "*Find* us."

And drew him with whispers to the dark.

The tires were piled beside the garage and had spilled onto the gravel drive near a red gas pump. They'd been there for years, crumpled and rotting, a small mountain. Fenza and Jimmy hid behind the tallest stack, but Gus had to be told—by Fenza, of course— "Get down, get down. We can't have anyone knowing we're here."

Moshnik's Garage looked ready to be condemned. A flat-roofed stucco, ash-colored, with a yellow sign—Penzoil—taped to a cracked window. For over a year now, since Fenza turned sixteen, he'd worked for Frank Moshnik, doing tune-ups and lubes and oil changes, plus running errands. He'd never borrowed a car left overnight, mainly because most cars trusted to Frank would soon be carted to the junkyard. Tonight, though, tuned and ready to roar, was a '51 Buick Riviera, cherry red with a white top, and with a flash of chrome teeth, *fangs*, he called them, a foot long over the front bumper. This souped-up machine was more menacing than on the first day it rolled out of a Motown factory and down the highways and byways of the Great Midwest.

The home nearest the garage belonged to Mrs. Sedlak, the receptionist of St. Roch's rectory. Nosy, upright, she would think borrowing a car was stealing, and she would call the police if she heard so much as a faint step or a stray word drift her way with no appointment. If she heard a garage door open, a car starting up, her nose would part pale curtains. The other home, dark tonight, often dark, belonged to Mrs. Novacek, a widow. She went to bed with the birds.

Gus Zeul felt the train before he heard it. A shiver in the earth, a slight movement to accommodate the swaying weight of a freighter two miles long, two or three miles away. Fenza, squatting, felt it too, and gave an order. "Gus," he said, "close the garage door after I back the car out."

"Car?"

"A Riviera," said Fenza. "We can borrow it a while."

Jimmy grinned. "A Riviera?"

"That's right, jarhead. But if Mrs. Sedlak sees the garage door open, she'll mess up our plans."

And on came the train, a storm on wheels. Fenza hustled a key out of his coat pocket and scuttled to the garage. He cut a look at Sedlak's house (curtains closed, porch light on), then opened a door that—like the 9:26

freighter—slid along rails. The rusted chains that hung from each side must have rattled, but all Fenza heard was the mad clackety-clack of the train, the wheels spitting sparks, metal on metal. He plucked the key to the Riviera from a hook near the cash register. The freighter would take almost four minutes to pass (he'd timed it the night before), and he used maybe thirty seconds to back the car onto Canal Street. Jimmy, breathing hard, rushed for the front seat, the passenger side, and Gus pulled on a metal chain to close the garage door. "Come on," Fenza whispered, "step it up." Gus poked along like someone at the tail end of a funeral march.

The freighter clanged and blew through Orville. Fenza wondered if the horn of the Riviera could match the scream of the whistle, but this was not the time for research. He hit the gas hard after Gus lollygagged into the back seat.

"You can't move any faster, dick lick?"

"I'm here."

"This ain't no Sunday afternoon."

Gus was smiling because a car this fine would have a radio. "Turn on some tunes," he said. "See how fast you can turn the dial."

They cruised along Canal Street, parallel to the train. Gus wanted a jazz station, but Fenza tuned in WLS, the rock-and-roll hit parade straight from Chicago. This classic car—among other things—had custom seats, white leather as soft as the skin at a girl's wrist. Fenza proved himself a prophet. The world changed at 9:26 and placed him at its center. The sumptuousness of the Riviera eased his angst a little while.

Jimmy said, "This is John Maylor's car."

Fenza pretended not to hear. "*Whose?* Is some monkey in the peanut gallery?"

"Everyone knows this car," said Jimmy, "and who owns it."

"Maylor the sailor?"

Jimmy giggled. "Oh, man. He'd piss blood if he saw us."

"Poor Maylor."

"Rich prick thinks his car's in the garage."

The wheel had strips of leather to cushion Fenza's hands, provide the feel of gloves. This was a Roadster Supreme, a show car, and tonight it was his. John Maylor? He was a fancy-assed financier who owned everything in Orville but St. Roch's Church. He'd never spoken to Fenza, and he'd ignored Frank Moshnik, too, till his son Dave knocked up Moshnik's daughter and married her against his wishes. Yesterday afternoon, Dave brought in the Riviera for servicing, and made the mistake of leaving it with Fenza. The car was in top shape, but Fenza told him he would need a few days "to work out the kinks. Don't worry," said the junior mechanic. "I'll make this car *better* than new."

Fenza shot a haughty glance at Marelli's Tavern, J. C. Penney's, and the drab houses on the hillside. He cruised by the Cloverleaf Palace and the Rock Island Depot, then gunned the engine till he reached the parking lot of the clock factory, a dead end. He made a U-turn and checked his watch—9:34. He had more than an hour to ride this beautiful beast through Orville. On Saturdays, Fenza and Gus had an eleven o'clock curfew. Jimmy, soon to leave Orville for Parris Island, had to be in by 11:30 or call home if he stayed at Fenza's. The 10:48 eastbound freighter was well timed. Fenza could nose the Riviera into Moshnik's Garage under the cover of sound, and then the three hoods could hustle home through back alleys. Thank you, Lord Jesus, for nightly freighters. And thank the Rock Island Line for the infernal noise.

Fenza turned up the radio and helped Johnny Rivers sing his number-one song—"Poor Side of Town." Soon Jimmy joined in while Gus jigged and jammed, a hustle of hands over bony knees, thin thighs. Eastward they rode in a muscle car, a priceless machine, but by 10:48 they'd be poor again. Fenza gripped the wheel in his fists. He sang as though pitching lifelines, and Jimmy sang, and they had rhythm. Gus played drums on his knees, his thighs, and jitterbugged his feet across the plush carpet. The boys moaned in unison. Fenza added his own words, and stretched his neck, his vocal cords, to hit the high notes—"All my life's for you, girl." He and Jimmy and Johnny Rivers sang the truth: Nothing came easy on the "Poor Side of Town."

The Riviera—the muscle, the shine—was too much for Fenza. He wondered how fast it would go, how it handled. Approaching Marelli's Tavern and J. C. Penney's, he jammed the accelerator to the floor. "Indy 500," said Fenza, but then he teased the tempest, hit the brakes, and shivered the long lines of the Riviera from front fender to tail.

He skidded sideways into a turn. Up Krapalna now, up the hill, the engine roaring. He accelerated as he approached Pulaski Park and St. Roch's Church. The speedometer flirted with fifty, then sixty. Fenza felt invulnerable as he flew past the church.

He pumped the brakes and came to a halt near Mary Lou's Ice Creamery. Another song came on the radio, "Good Golly Miss Molly." Fenza, singing along with Mitch Ryder and the Detroit Wheels, made a U-turn and headed back down Krapalna. He coasted, let the car glide, toward St. Roch's Church.

Jimmy asked about the size of the engine.

"Jarhead," said Fenza, "we've got enough horsepower under the hood to blow through this town before you suck another breath."

He hit the gas. One hand on the wheel, he fishtailed, and the church—through the windshield and coming on fast—looked like the wavering wall of a cordillera, its drunken spires tilted toward stars. Fenza let out a hoot. A car this fine, if you knew how to handle her, said nothing but *Go*.

At Sixth and Krapalna, a wide intersection, he jammed the brakes, cut the wheel, and spun into a donut turn. Rubber scorched the orange brick. Fenza left his marks, or call it a signature, but he shot too fast and hard out of the turn and lost control. The car jumped the curb across from St. Roch's and spun sideways into a stout sycamore. Another song came on, "Sunny," but not for long. The engine died, the radio blinked off, and they heard nothing for a few moments but the rush of their breaths.

Fenza tried to start the car. "Gee-sus," he said. "*Gee-*sus!" Blood ran down his forehead, into his eyes. He tried the ignition again, then pummeled the wheel with his fists.

Jimmy touched himself, his chest—some soreness there—and his left knee began to throb. He turned to Fenza. "Hey," he said, "you're bleeding."

Fenza groaned.

"If I had a bandage—"

"Shut up. You don't have shit."

Gus had been thrown sideways across the backseat and against the opposite door. By midnight, he'd wear a shiner, black as war paint, under his left eye.

"Fenza?" he said.

"Yeah?"

"You may as well take a bow."

Up and down Krapalna Street, lights flared from porches. Fenza tried to bull his way out of the Riviera, but his door wouldn't budge, nor could he roll down the window. "Open your door!" he said to Jimmy. "Open the damn door and get out of my way!"

Jimmy, dazed, took nearly a minute to pull up on a handle and stumble into the grass. By then, Mr. Ciernik and other neighbors had surrounded the car. Father Janecek, in a long black coat, hurried from the rectory, Sister Clair from the nunnery, and the siren of Officer Krupovich's squad car was a swift arrow headed for its mark.

Slouched near the ruined vehicle, his hands in his pockets, Fenza apologized to Father Janecek, Sister Clair, and a dozen or more neighbors. "Some things just don't turn out," he said, "but we had permission to borrow this car. We didn't steal it."

"Mr. Maylor's car?" said Father.

"As I understand——"

"Don't try and tell me he loaned you his Riviera."

"He did, Father."

"Fenza Ryczhik?"

"Yes, Father."

"You can only worsen your trouble with lies."

Sister Clair wore her habit, her black robe, but her head was bare, dappled with blond hair. She held out a hanky to Fenza. "Here," she said. "Press this to your forehead, press hard. Don't let up."

She looked at Gus.

"Are you hurt?"

"No, Sister."

"And you?" she said to Jimmy.

He flicked a hand, shook his head.

"But you need a physician," she said. "You must be examined."

"Examined by the *police*," said Father. "And perhaps a psychiatrist."

Sister took a quick breath through her nostrils.

"Since when do eyes serve as X-ray machines, Father? These boys may have serious injuries."

"Oh come, Sister. The car is the only casualty. *Look* at it. They may as well have pushed the thing off a cliff."

The hood had popped open. The radiator hissed, smoked. The panels on the driver's side resembled the bellows of an accordion. Father brought his hands together and pronounced the requiem. "*Mrtev*," he said, "kaput." He shook his head in disgust.

Mr. Ciernik, stout and stolid in overalls, a feed cap covering his baldness, said to Fenza, "So you stole this honey of a car, huh? And now you'll answer to Mr. Maylor."

"They *all* will," said Father, "they *all* will. And that—I promise you—is an undeniable fact."

The church, too, was undeniable. Fenza couldn't help noticing it in the background, its largeness and grandeur a mockery to petty verbiage. He'd cut his head, banged it off the windshield, but the wound was so small it embarrassed him. He winked at the Riviera, a show car in ruins, and resisted the urge to kick off the fancy tires and diminish it further. He turned to Father and Mr. Ciernik. "An accident," he said, "a mechanical problem." He shook his head and sighed. "But I'll pay Mr. Maylor back even if I have to work like a slave till the day I die."

Fuck Maylor, he was thinking. He could buy a brand-new car before they haul me to jail.

Officer Krupovich pulled up across from the church and got out with his deputy. Handcuffs jangling from belts, they hustled up a slight incline. No siren now, but the light on the roof of their car spun round and round, the color of a wound. Swaths of light painted the facade of St. Roch's, the playground and trees of Pulaski Park, the swing set and merry-go-round. And now a red mist swept over the ball field from which Fenza used to pick up a stick and drive balls through the crowns of trees.

Jesus Christmas, he said to himself. I am up Shit Creek.

Father Janecek briefed the police officers as they approached the crime scene. "Stolen vehicle," he said, "Mr. Maylor's show car." He nodded toward the smoking heap, then sneered at the boys. "Fenza, Gus, and Jimmy," he said. "Three hooligans who belong in jail."

Fenza hung his head when Officer Krupovich cuffed him. "A steering problem," he said. "That's what caused the accident."

"Tell it to the judge."

"I will," said Fenza. "I'll swear on a Bible."

"I wouldn't bother."

"No, listen," said Fenza. "I'd be crazy to tell anything but the truth."

The officer gave Fenza a soft shove to shut him up and get him moving. "You know the way," he said, and herded the big boy to the car.

PART 3

Changes

(1967)

A wild patience has taken me this far.

—ADRIENNE RICH

One True Sound

Four hours late for confession, Will Dempsey wobbled drunk into Pulaski Park. He sat on a bench, the playground on his left beyond some choke-cherry bushes and silver maples, the church before him, its spires and steeple, and on high the white cross of the Lord, His wounds visible to an angel or a hawk. No one but Jesus knew today was Will's birthday. He winked at the cross and thought, "Light a candle, Lord, and save me a seat at the Last Supper." Right hand raised, forefinger curled and twitching, he proceeded with a lesson. "Be grateful for the fall of Judas, for You can't die without him. The equation is one You know well: no Judas, no cross; 1−1=0." He shrugged. "I'm just a small-town deacon, Lord, but I am a Judas. Take away sinners like me and You're nothing at all."

He eyed the rectory. There was one problem with Father Janecek: he knew nothing about confession. A mere listing of sins (I lie, I kill, I betray) worked well for a man never called upon to struggle for his survival. Will needed a confessor who understood nuances, conditions. A soldier saint with old wounds, invisible scars. Will, at forty-three, was now a decade older than Christ at His crucifixion. The Savior, in His glory, was forever a Saint, never a soldier. The Son of God lacked knowledge of half the world.

∾

Will got into his car and rode. He circled the block—St. Roch's Church, Pulaski Park, Sonny's Place—and almost stopped for a drink. Eddie Tapusko and Fenza Ryczhik Sr. were at the bar, other lushes at tables, but everything seemed out of sync. A sickly sun hung over oaks and maples, a pale orange wound.

July 1.
Will's birthday.
Jesus, where's Your bandage for the sun?

∽

Sipping from a flask, he drove down Krapalna past Tony Renh's Grocery, then west on Canal. He almost pulled over at Cassie Zeul's. She and that renegade nun, Sister Clair, were sitting in lawn chairs in the shade of a maple, drinking something cool from glasses, probably whiskey on ice for Cassie, lemonade for the nun. They seemed copasetic, at home with each other, a bride of the Lord and a floozy. Sister Clair waved at Will as he idled by at five miles an hour. Cassie played a child's trick: she closed her eyes to make the man disappear.

Will cursed her in silence. He rolled up the windows, turned on the air-con, and the cool air slid up his bare arms and under his sleeves. He shut his eyes for the count of ten, then opened them. He'd driven blind for a stretch, at no risk whatsoever. The Chevy ran as on tracks straight down the center of the road.

He slid back in his seat, one hand on the wheel. He drove past Mutts Marelli's Tavern, J. C. Penney's, the Cloverleaf Palace, and pulled into the parking lot of the Rock Island Depot. Will's best memory was of his first train ride. He stopped near the entry, let the car idle, and flicked on the radio. A tired announcer gave the time, 8:15, the Cubs score, the Sox score. Two losses, no surprises. On Will's left, down a green slope fringed with trees, was the river. He swilled Jameson whiskey from a flask.

He cut the ignition and drank in silence. A tree in front of the depot had caught his eye. A jungly overgrown giant with heart-shaped leaves and lime-green tassels longer and thinner than Panatela cigars. Will's dad, twelve years dead, had called this the cigar tree. The prettiest thing in Orville, it hinted of the tropics, had a sugary name, catalpa, and Will loved it as much as he loved anything, its umbrella of shade in fresh-clipped grass, the green halo of its crown. He began to relax till Gus Zeul and Fenza Ryczhik Jr. coasted by on bicycles. A minute later, having reached the dead end behind the clock factory and ridden back up Canal Street, they paused for a breather between the catalpa tree and his car. They might have taken their pit stop elsewhere had they seen Will slouched behind the wheel.

He said, "You boys planning to steal any cars tonight?"

The Zeul boy jumped.

"Well, just thought I should mention Mr. Maylor's got a red Corvette now."

Fenza spat. "He can have it."

"Yeah, I suppose he can, if he keeps an eye on it. If he keeps it somewhere besides Moshnik's Garage."

"I don't work there anymore."

"I gathered that."

"I don't work for anybody now."

Will eyed a long cloud the shape of a sickle. "I hear you boys are headed for the Army. If I recall the story correctly, Judge Bencek gave you no choice in the matter."

"You recall half of it," said Fenza. "I'm going to the Marines, Gus to the Army." He shook his head. "The Army's got no use for me; the feeling's mutual."

Will grinned.

"Jimmy, though. He's the lucky one."

"How's that?"

"He's already in Viet Nam."

That car wreck eight months back turned out to be a boon, at least for Fenza and Jimmy. A few phone calls from court officials to the Marine Corps recruiter and the Army recruiter sealed the boys' fate. Jimmy, who had already joined the Corps, was sent to Parris Island on schedule, nine days after Thanksgiving. Fenza would become a Marine on July 30, his eighteenth birthday, and Gus would report to the U.S. Army on the sixth of September. For their first thirteen months of service, their pay would be diverted to the court, which would allot most of it to pay damages to the plaintiff, Mr. John Maylor. The day the decision became official, Fenza, in high spirits, huddled with Gus and Jimmy in the foyer of the courthouse. "Who needs money?" he whispered. "As far as I can tell, Viet Nam is free."

Will got out of his Chevy and stretched his legs. The last sun was on the river. If his wife were here, she might rattle a tin pan and wail her nightly anthem: "I like Indians, I like Blacks . . ." Too bad Ruth didn't lose her faculties *before* he married her, not after. She was pretty in a delicate way till the devil caught hold of her and made her his twin.

Will stood in the deep shadows of the tree. He felt uncomfortable with these boys, but lately he felt uncomfortable everywhere, even in bars. Fenza and Gus wore cutoffs, T-shirts, Keds. Will? He never left home without the proper creases in his slacks, some starch in his shirt, and shoes shiny enough to serve as mirrors. His late wife, when he courted her, wore fine dresses and skirts, satin blouses, a blush on her cheeks, paint on her lips, but never too bright or vulgar. Ruth seemed to be his type, but this was wishful thinking. Will never had a type, in this town or any other. Ruth be damned—she was a nightmare, a tour guide of hell. Yet he thought he loved her in the spring of '45 when he returned from the war.

He glanced at Fenza and Gus, then lowered his eyes.

"I wish you boys well," he said. "If I had a four-leaf clover, or two of them, I'd hand them over."

They eyed him with suspicion.

"Once you boys are in the service—the Marines, the Army, whichever—you'll have a clean slate. No black marks on your name. Nothing to scare away your pride."

Fenza shrugged.

"So stand tall," said the old man, "or try to." He shuffled from foot to foot, edging closer. "Times aren't what they used to be. I remember when this town knew how to send boys off with something more than a prayer."

His voice sounded odd now. A bit high in pitch, almost feminine. He informed the boys the best day of his life was June 3, 1943. "Ninety-one of us right here," he said. "Ninety-one Orville boys, either joining up or being drafted, marching down Krapalna and across Canal to the Rock Island Depot." He gestured toward the catalpa. "I'd say this tree was a green sprout back then. And me? I was eighteen years old, almost nineteen, but I felt like a man." He turned to Fenza. "Your dad was a fine-looking Marine, all spit and shine even in street clothes. On the morning of June 3, he was ready and willing, same as all of us. I was Army, he called me a doughboy, but no matter. Your dad and me walked side by side through the heart of town."

Fenza, chewing Blackjack gum, blew a bubble, then popped it with his teeth.

"Always liked your old man," said Will. "Thought the world of him. Still do."

Fenza zapped another bubble.

"A straight shooter," said Will. "What you see is what you get."

The Zeul boy had been tapping the handlebars of his bike, catching the cadence of Will's words. He quit drumming when Will quit talking. He seemed to know in advance not only what Will would say but how he would say it. A ventriloquist of sorts, he used Will as a puppet. If this boy were a few years younger, Will would take him over his knee and whack him till he wailed.

But he told Gus and Fenza about June 3, or part of it, because they were here and he was drunk. At nine in the morning, the troops gathered in front of St. Roch's Church to receive a blessing from Father Bacar, Father Janecek's predecessor. Will spoke in plain terms, but the Zeul boy kept mocking him, rap-tapping the rhythms of words on handlebars speckled with rust. Will, straining to keep his composure, looked toward the river. A pleasure boat drifted near shore, sidewise to the currents. A young lady propped her bare legs on the dash. Will waved and almost called howdy when she lifted a hand, but she was merely removing her straw hat now that the sun was gone.

He told the boys the whole town and every farmer in Orville County came out for its soldiers. "You had to see it to believe it," he said. "The throngs lined up three or four deep along Krapalna Street and Canal, our route-of-march, and hundreds more waited for us at the Rock Island Depot."

Fenza shrugged. "A hundred years ago."

"Nineteen forty-three," said Will. "Don't they teach math at St. Ignatius?"

Fenza waved a hand.

"Sunny and clear," said Will. "We couldn't have asked for better weather."

Will coughed and the Zeul boy banged his handlebars with a stiff hand.

"Now what's that about? You making fun of me?"

"No, sir. Just listening."

"Then listen for all you're worth," said Will, and jabbed a finger at Gus, then Fenza. "Otherwise, you'll be gone from this town before you've learned anything at all."

But he couldn't say the rest because it did seem like a hundred years ago, or a thousand. The troops marched from St. Roch's Church to the Rock Island Depot with the ease and dignity of departing gods. In a way, they *were* gods, and anything they asked for would be given. Girls tossed bouquets into their arms. Daisies and daffodils, tulips. And there was music. One thing came back to Will now, and maybe it was the only thing worthy of reminiscence. At the depot, the Orville High School Band played Sousa marches, then broke into "The Star-Spangled Banner" as the troops began boarding the train. Will took a window seat in the first car. Moments before the train pulled away, Ray Yellich, his next-door neighbor, banged a cymbal, and the tuba player—Will had forgotten his name—unstrapped the instrument from around his neck and raised it to Will. "Blow," said the boy. "Dang you, just gather some air and *blow!*" Will blew into that tuba and the sound—wilder than the caw of a crow, keener than the Rock Island whistle—was the truest sound he'd ever made. In the beginning was the word and the word made flesh. Maybe God played the tuba, blew the world from the gold of a horn. Will had never heard a more powerful or cantankerous sound.

Fenza said, "See ya," his voice no more respectful than if he were addressing a child. Will stiffened, his hands clasped at his waist. Fenza dug up the grass as his tires spun and he shot out toward Canal Street, the Zeul boy on his tail. A man was foolish to try to tell these ne'er-do-wells anything. Hooligans, thieves—this town didn't need them and never would.

~

One true sound, one more, might have been enough to live on, or at least soften his hate. Will would despise those boys till he died. Years back, they and Jimmy Posey found his wife washed up on the nearby shore. Will told his story to local reporters, told this town what it needed to believe—he'd killed his wife in self-defense. He never felt dear to anyone, but he garnered respect for his war record, his service as a deacon at St. Roch's Church, and his position of authority at the clock factory. By and large, the town welcomed his alibi, except for a few misfits who had funny ways of seeing. Gus and Cassie Zeul, Fenza Ryczhik Jr.—he hated them with his heart. Did he kill his wife in cold blood? Did he kill Germans in cold blood in World War II? Ruth might have become the woman he described, a maniac swinging a cleaver over his half-asleep form in the dark of a bedroom. No, Will didn't kill her in cold blood; he never killed anyone in cold blood. It was infinitely more complicated than any misfit could conceive.

He strolled out from under the catalpa, his hands clasped behind his back. The river had turned the color of pewter, a blade unpolished. *Ruth had no reason to live.* Will knew this, so why did the thought of her still prey on him, especially at night? Because he killed her at night? Or was it wrong to search for logic and imagine it had anything to do with Ruth? In her last hour, she spoke of giving birth to "a child of song." She sat up in bed and began fussing with a blanket. She plucked some lint, rolled it between forefinger and thumb, set it in her lap, searched for more, plucked it, rolled it, set it in her lap, all the while palavering about "a child of song, diffi-cult and dark, with no wounds on her body, no glass in her voice, and you can't tame her, she's strong, she's ten of you, and she won't back down, won't listen, so you best give up and shut up, amen and hallelujah, praise Jesus and His child . . ." She rattled on as Will, drink in hand, slouched in the doorway. She didn't notice him, but when he retreated to the kitchen and returned with a weapon, she glanced from him to the window, curtains closed. In the next while there was silence. Did Ruth know she was almost dead? Did *he* know? She might have lived had she kept quiet. Instead, she went back to fidgeting with her blanket and blathering about her "child of song, difficult and dark, with no wounds on her body, no glass in her voice," and on and on. She might still be dreaming out loud and playing with lint if Will hadn't stopped her. Everything seemed to happen without volition, or with no more effort than pressing a button. He made a lake of her, blood all over the bedroom, his clothes, then his car, his boat, the shore of the river. It never felt like murder. It felt like necessity, a nightmare near-ing its completion. Had Ruth pined for a child and plucked lint one min-ute more, he himself might have perished. That's how Will saw it, how he *had* to see it. Me or you. Not so different than the war. A very small battle, yes. But the lines were clear.

Will looked to the far shore, the trees dark above the river. Was Ruth better off dead? Better off tucked down in the earth's shadow? *And what about me? Am I better off without her after three and a half years? Do I have a future somewhat brighter than the present? If so, where's it at, Lord? Under what damn rock did You hide it? I mean, what exactly do You want from me? A few words of guidance would be better than none.*

The deacon watched the sky above the river. The silence always hurt more as night drew near.

∽

At home, after another whiskey, Will lay on his sofa bed and waited for sleep. He never went into that back room anymore. The old bed and headboard, the dresser, Ruth's colorless robes, blouses—he'd hauled it all to the dump himself. The back room was bare, as it should be. A maid—the same lady who cleaned St. Roch's Church on Saturday mornings—put Will's home in order twice monthly. But the door to the back room stayed shut even to her.

Will tried to coax himself to sleep in the light of a muted TV. A lullaby light—that's what he'd called it for years. Was it odd that a man who'd seen war and the world falling apart should need a hint of softness at night? A pulled plug, a blackout—Will wasn't sure he could take it. The notion that a soldier who'd faced death over and over could endure anything was counterfeit. This same man was likely to shiver a bit every time the sun went down.

The war Will remembered was both unimaginable and predictable. In the first moments of combat, he learned what most soldiers learn: he would do anything to survive. *Anything*—now there's a word with some blood inside. A man could paint the world red with such a word. Will survived Omaha Beach and other battles and returned home and married Ruth and she became sick and he stood by her for eighteen years before he killed her. More exactly, he put her out of her misery. There was no trial, nor should there have been. So why did this prey on him? Why couldn't he sleep? It maddened Will that what he wished to believe, what would justify his life— *I'm no better or worse than any man*—might not be enough.

There had to be a reckoning. From his sofa bed, nightly, Will held mock trials, presented evidence, argued with an imaginary jury, and he would have argued with God or Satan or even Ruth had any of the interested parties mustered the courage to appear. *I tolerated my wife for how many years? Eighteen, plus a few months and days as extra penance. Find me one Orville man who could've stood her this long. Go ahead. Knock on every door, search every cellar. Keep accurate records, you sons of bitches. Cross off names till you come to me!*

Will often reminded the jury he was a veteran of combat, a recipient of the Bronze Star for Valor. Was it easier to be brave in a world war than in some backwater town on the Illinois River? The jury didn't know and Will didn't either. Nobody was clean, he knew that much. Maybe he would've been luckier to die on Omaha Beach, or—best of all—to die onboard the war-bound train before it left the Orville station in June of '43. When and where the Lord decides to take a man home or even birth him to begin with is the mystery of mysteries. The jury? The best they could do was scratch a fingernail across the surface. No honest man would try to see beyond the glaze.

My closing argument is my only argument. On June 3, 1943, I blew through a tuba, made one true sound. Yurrraaaaaaaaaaaaaggghhhh! Something like that, but beyond letters, beyond words or hints of words, and surely beyond what a jury of my peers is capable of hearing. So help me God, it was glorious! This was the only time in my life I delighted myself. I keep trying to remember the sound exactly, but I can't. It's mainly an idea by now. A shadow in the fog. A tongueless man trying to sing beyond the clouds.

He did remember his wife on the night of December 1, 1964. Ruth fought him at first, thrashed and wailed, but her last sound was a whimper almost impossible to interpret. Darkness and sadness and thank you all in one utterance. No, this was a lie. Will was making it up. There was no thank you in a woman who kept trying to live for no reason. Her squirming reminded him of a worm trying to slip free of a hook. Each time Will struck her, he was praying, yes praying, *Please be still. Please.*

The nineteen-year-old soldier who would do anything to survive now wanted nothing more than the comfort of sleep. Such a strange and lovely vanishing act—sleep. But did the world ever completely go away?

Will tried to induce a dream, even a nightmare. His fingers crawled across his belly, the inner sides of this thighs, and teased the stump of his penis. No help, almost no sensation. The body was a shell. He might as well trail his fingers through a sterile wind.

All Will could do was join one hand to the other and hold hands. *Ruth, how's this for a reckoning? You hear me?* No response. He didn't expect one. He separated his hands—the touch felt wrong. *Okay, then, I'll go this alone. No touch, no prayer, no curse, no sound. But it all makes a man wonder why in tarnation he was ever born.*

⁓

On the sixth of July, west of Dead Cat's Cove, Will drained a flask of Jameson and eased into the river. Late at night, he waded in knee-deep, then chest-deep, before he slipped from a ledge and into the channel. He hoped for nothing: no heaven or hell, light or dark, good or evil. Eternal sleep? That's just a phrase best left alone.

On the seventh of July, Father Janecek filed a missing person report with local authorities and the Highway Patrol. The next afternoon, humid and hot, Will's body washed up a mile east of Sells Landing. He'd drifted in belly up, bloated, and was beginning to rot, spoiling a sandy stretch of beach. His eyes, the lids eaten away, stared blind at whatever came near: clouds, trees, birds, the surge of waves. The deacon had known common words, common meanings, almost nothing of God. In forty-three years, this reticent man made one true sound.

~

The Orville County coroner needed less than seventy-two hours to determine William Dempsey's death was accidental. Everyone in the taverns had already assumed he drank himself into a stupor, fell in the river, and was carried away.

Cowgirls

Maybe the storm predicted for the early evening would stray beyond the fence lines. The heat lightning in the west might mean rain in the west. The massive clouds on the horizon might set sail for another county. Pat hoped for a spell of dry weather as she and Jenny tracked Sadie, a pregnant cow, along a creek choked with willows and poison ivy. They batted mosquitoes that made more noise than whispers. Night would come in an hour. The rain might come sooner, or not at all.

Some twenty feet ahead, Sadie, blacker than willow shade, sniffed the air and lowed. Of the milk cows, she was Miss Affectionate, always fond of a pet, a kind word, but tonight, about to give birth, she was half wild, half tame. Wide-eyed, she arched her neck, shook her head, her flanks, and bawled. A sound as sonorous as a foghorn swept down the creek and through the trees. Pat said, "She can't wait much longer to birth this calf."

But the cow moved deeper into the willows. Given a chance, she might disappear and birth her calf in one of the few niches of wilderness unclaimed by the gridded order of the farm. Pat, hunched to half her height, inched forward, Jenny at her heels. Heat lightning stuttered like a strobe. The thunder was too far away to hear.

They parted willow wands, blackberry vines, and skirted patches of poison ivy. Pat stopped when she saw the white polka dots of Sadie's face, the gleam of her eye. Jenny knelt on one knee beside Pat. No wind now. No rustling of vines or willow wands. No sound but mosquitoes and the hum of Tomahawk Creek and now the black cow snorting and blowing, the bellows of her chest swelling and falling. Sadie had backed up beneath some willows. "Any minute," said Pat, "any second." She brushed a hand to shoo a mosquito from Jenny's face.

Quiet as heat lightning, the girls watched the calf's feet and forelegs emerge from its mother. A snout appeared, a scrunched face, closed eyes, and then there was a pause. Sadie grunted and blew and strained till the shoulders came forth and a short gasp later the calf plopped to the earth, a stiff package slick with mucous. The creature lay on the ground a long while. At last it wobbled to its feet, sniffed, and nudged Sadie's udder with a pink mouth. The cow let her calf suckle, then stepped aside to lick it clean. The tongue made a window-wipe sound: "Shwoosh-shwoosh-shwoosh." The willows made a margin, a sort of chancel, around Sadie and her child.

Pat whispered to Jenny, "I better get up there, but don't follow. I have some work to do."

Pat had to make sure the mother was sound, the afterbirth flushed out, and she had to check the calf. By nightfall, she hoped to shoo these creatures to the shelter of the barn.

Sadie, a stern eye on the girls, lowed and shied, then stood her ground. Closing in, Pat made cooing sounds, whispery sounds, and let Sadie sniff her hands, her wrists. The calf let go of a teat and teetered, almost fell. It leaned against Pat, who reached over its back to cradle the sides of its face and turn its head one way, then the other. She checked the legs, the underbelly, the flanks, the sex (female), then set it free.

The calf stumbled, blinked, grunted, sniffed. The world beyond her mother's body was everywhere. She canted to the left, now the right, and swayed. Her mother, after Pat checked her, stepped to the side and made for her calf a roof. Huffing and snorting, Sadie was big and black and blowing heat. Her calf raised its mouth to a teat and closed its eyes.

～

At dusk, after Sadie and her child were sheltered in the barn, soft rain began to fall. Pat said, "I think these two will get along fine without us. Maybe we should go inside."

But the quiet of the barn and the new creature and its mother held them a while longer. Side by side, elbows propped on a paint-flecked rail, they watched Sadie nurse her calf. The snuffling and slurping of the newborn almost smothered the sound of rain on the metal roof.

～

Earlier that day, Pat had invited Jenny and Marge and Sal to be farm girls for a night and perhaps have the good fortune of witnessing the birth of a calf. She was pleased, though, that Marge had to baby-sit her sister and Sal was a Saturday night waitress at Marylou's Ice Creamery. Pat invited them only because she felt she had to. Jenny, in her last summer before leaving for college, seldom went anywhere without her cheerleader friends.

Pat's parents trundled off to bed at 9:30. She and Jenny had the parlor to themselves now, and they wondered aloud what to name the calf. Maybe Willow because it was born beneath willows. Or Dusk because of the hushed light of the sky. Or Miracle because there was no hard word, no measure or frame, to describe being born. The calf, like her mother, was black, but sported a white bib. Jenny noted that the colors, mixed together, made dusk. "Maybe we have a name," said Pat. "Dusk has a softness that suits this calf."

The rain had let up, but every so often the wind shook some water from the trees. The girls sat side by side on the sofa, their hands almost joined. Pat, thinking of herself, said, "That calf's both ugly and beautiful."

"No," said Jenny, "she's just beautiful. I bet by now she and Sadie are asleep."

~

It was almost midnight when Pat led her friend up a creaky stairway and down a hall lit by a nightlight. Pat's room had the same light, a little wink of a thing beneath a plastic star. She opened the top drawer of her dresser and chose her best nightgown, pink with white and blue flowers at the breast. She took her time getting out of her farm clothes. Her fingers trembled with the buckle of her jeans.

Jenny set her overnight bag on the floor near an open window. She'd watched out the corner of her eye as Pat undressed, left her T-shirt and bra and jeans in a pile near the wall. Pat was no "moose girl," as Fenza once claimed. No, she was strong and solid, pretty all over, though this was hard to admit. Jen shuddered at the thought that Pat was perfect compared to Orville boys, especially Fenza. Can't make a baby with a girl, she told herself. Can't get in trouble even if you try. She'd just seen a calf being born, but she had no urge to lay with a boy, love him up, take a chance at having his baby. Black baby, white baby, high yellow baby—Orville would note the color. Jen undressed and slipped on her nightgown. Her yearnings—where did they come from? She fussed with her gown till it drew tight across her hips.

She closed the shades. On a blue bedspread, the girls lay side by side, face up. The calf had a name, Dusk, and now Jen wondered if she, too, deserved a new name. In alternate moments she felt happy, confused, calm, hateful, ebullient, overjoyed. What name did she deserve? Dizzy? Dingbat? Loopy? She chased her desires with insults, but then she got brave.

She slipped her hand beneath Pat's, palm to palm. She began to say something, hushed, lay still, and prayed for more courage. The nightlight was fainter than a candle. The ceiling, some ten feet over the bed, appeared dark enough to hold rain. No atheists in foxholes, no atheists in beds. She began a silent Hail Mary and made it to the word *grace*. What Jen wanted was a sin. She felt herself breaking, splintering, and if she didn't stop soon, she would never again reclaim the shards of herself and piece them back where they belonged. She tried to remember who she was: an Orville girl, a cheerleader at St. Ignatius; a girl on her way to college in the town of Normal, Illinois State; a girl who would marry and adopt children. She let out a moan. Her life, like her mother's, was a lie, and always would be unless she surprised herself. Maybe she would stay in Orville, skip college. Be a farm girl's secret lover. The townsfolk would harbor no hatred for either of them unless they discovered the truth.

But resistance was a habit. She stared at the ceiling and said, "Now what? I don't even know who I am anymore."

Pat closed her eyes. "That's how it is sometimes."

"No mercy."

"Not yet."

"What should we do?"

"Wait."

Jen sighed. "I'm good at that."

"We both are."

"Maybe too good. Jesus mercy."

"I doubt He cares, Jen."

"Why would He?"

"He can't be as good as they say."

"Let's hope not."

"If JC stopped in Orville, hopped off a train, He'd bang a tin pan and walk through town singing, 'I like Indians, I like Blacks . . .'"

Jen shivered.

"I'm sorry. I don't mean to be glib."

"You're not."

"I was remembering Mrs. Dempsey."

"I know."

"I never spoke with her, but I missed her when she was gone."

I like Indians, I like Blacks, I like tits. Mrs. Dempsey was dead. Jen had always seen her as the town's crazy lady, but now she and Pat had inherited the song. *Pat, I like your tits. Mine are three shades darker. No one's supposed to know.* This was Jen's life, a sin and a secret. She was just another Orville girl till mercy made her brave.

So she turned and kissed Pat's hair, her cheeks, her nose, the tips of her fingers. "You're pretty," she said. "You're pretty all over."

Pat blushed. "*Me?*"

"Yes."

"Pretty?"

"*Yes.*"

"I . . ."

"What?"

"I seldom see myself this way."

Jenny kissed her lips, her throat. She kissed the bone between her breasts. She kissed her stomach through the silk of her nightgown. She kissed Pat soft, then hard. "You believe me?" said Jen. "You believe me now?"

A mouth may open to let a word in, not out. Pat arched her neck and felt this one—pretty—in her throat, her chest, her stomach, her calves. It was as if a word had struck a nerve and begun to travel the maps of her body. *Pretty? Yes, I believe you, Jen, I believe you.* By now the word was in her toes.

⁓

The morning sky was cloudless, pale yellow. After a cup of coffee, after the sun warmed the grass, the girls walked barefoot to the barn. The calf was now ten hours old. Nursing in the shadows between Sadie's hind legs, she snorted and slurped and blew, her voice wetter and happier than last night's rain. Jenny, in a corner of her mind, said, She's blacker than spades.

The girls stood outside the stall. Jen leaned over the rail, closed her eyes, and said, "I may as well spit this out while I can."

"What?"

"I'm not who you think. I'm part Black, I mean Negro."

Pat squinted. "Jen?"

"I got some shadows in me, same as my mom."

Jenny held her breath as if she were underwater. She remembered the black cat Joe Zeul stuffed in a gunnysack and drowned in the Illinois River. Her mother's stories, even when told in whispers, were insistent as shouts. According to Annie, a tale worth telling and hearing did one thing: teach you to survive.

"I hope this won't change anything."

"Jen, you could be a coal mine and it wouldn't matter."

"I promised my mom I wouldn't tell."

"I can keep a secret."

Jenny breathed in. "Did you know I was colored? Could you *see* it?"

Pat smiled a while. "I always liked your big lips."

"That's sweet, but did you know?"

"I never gave it a glimmer."

"The plan seems to have worked, then."

"What plan?"

"The silence."

"I suppose."

"I won't tell anyone else. Or at least no one in Orville."

"They don't deserve to know anything."

"But it's still going to be hard to look my mother in the eye."

Pat kissed her left hand, front and back, and the inner side of her wrist. "Maybe you don't have to."

"I sort of feel like a fake, a pretender."

"I know the feeling."

"Orville . . . I've seen enough of it."

"Me too. But other places might be worse."

"Not San Francisco."

"We haven't been there. It's just a name."

"We could hop a freight tomorrow."

Pat kissed her hand again. "We could."

"So what's stopping us?"

"I'm not ready."

"No? Well, tell me why."

"I can't leave the farm, Jen."

"Okay."

"It's a friendly place, except for my parents."

"Mine would kill me."

"Mine too."

Jenny shrugged. "I like your cows well enough."

"They're nicer than parents."

"And your dog, Spencer, he's sweeter than anyone in town."

"And don't forget the fields, Jen. The corn was hip-high on the Fourth of July. It'll be over our heads in August."

"I will trust your corn when it's tall enough to disappear in."

"And the nights are prettier than in town. You can see constellations."

Jenny leaned closer. "Can I tell you one more secret?"

"Yes."

"I like the dark between the stars more than the stars."

"That's most of the sky."

"I like that it has no name."

Pat nodded. "Incognito."

"That's not its name. No one looks at the dark and says, 'There's Incognito.'"

"I won't argue."

"Almost no one knows it's there."

Fight

The night before Fenza left for basic training, his dad invited him and Gus Zeul into his den. He dispensed drinks, Old Crow on ice, and led toasts to the Marine Corps, the Army, and the war in Southeast Asia that might last long enough to turn juvenile delinquents into men. As a rule, the old man drank alone in this room. Tonight he huddled with boys only because they were vulnerable, about to be tested. Compared to World War II, Viet Nam was a nuisance, a gnat in the eye of a giant, yet Americans were dying. So Fenza Sr. spoke of strategies, campaigns, the light at the end of the tunnel. Eager to counsel these boys, he ordered them to sit in the straight-backed chairs across from his desk.

Gus twirled a finger in his drink. The den smelled of linseed oil and whiskey. The desk, the length of a fishing boat, was polished to a shine. Fenza Sr. had clipped photographs of World War II from *Life* magazine. At the center of his desk, where a woman might place flowers or knickknacks, he'd made a collage and sealed the images beneath a plate of glass. B-29s let loose a necklace of bombs on a green valley. Smaller planes swooped over a village, roofs gold and yellow in sun and flames. Two Marines, wounded, sat shoulder to shoulder in a ditch, the tall one bending down to share a cigarette, the smoking butt as soothing as a tit on his buddy's lips. Gus, sipping whiskey on an empty stomach, saw blurs of color and shape, a war like a fucking flower. He arranged a bouquet at the center of the desk.

Mr. Ryczhik sat in a leather chair with armrests. His voice—sonorous, spry—reminded Gus of Father Janecek imparting a personal touch to a Sunday sermon. "You boys are like I once was," he said. "The only world you know is in these few square miles called Orville, Illinois." He lifted his glass. "I'm not saying this is bad, mind you. I'm just saying this hayseed town is your whole world." He downed his drink. "You boys have pulled some stunts, tried my patience time and again, but I'm still proud of you. Every sin of your lives, large or small—stealing Mr. Maylor's car, screwing up in school—will be forgiven and forgotten the day you are sent to war."

He filled his son's tumbler halfway, then his own, then a tad more for Gus. "Tomorrow," he said to Fenza, "you'll be dealt a new hand of cards. You'll catch the morning train for Chicago, take your oath and join the Corps, and be on your way to Parris Island by noon Thursday."

"Can't happen too soon."

"Yeah, you're hale and hardy. But I hope you've considered the fact that you're about to get your ass whipped."

Fenza cocked his head.

"Let me put it this way: training's a preview of hell, and war's the main feature."

Fenza sat straighter. "I know, Dad."

"If the Corps sends you to Viet Nam, if you see combat and survive, I can make one promise and no other: You will never be the same."

Gus watched Fenza suck his whiskey and smile. Tomorrow he would leave this town in its well-worn ruts, board the morning train, and never look back with anything less than militant condescension. *Never be the same, never.* There was no war yet, only the promise. Maybe Fenza was living the happiest day of his life.

The old man spoke of character, the need to build some before it was too late, the need to toss childhood in a box and bury it deep, and then he glanced at his watch. He had a 7:15 euchre date at Sonny's Place. He promised Gus and his son that when they returned from Viet Nam, whether or not they were twenty-one, he would give them a personal tour of the town's watering holes. No veteran of combat was underage, not in his book or any book in the Illinois Valley. He invited the boys to polish off the bottle of booze. "Take your time," he said. "This room rarely has visitors, but tonight it's yours."

They only stayed a few minutes because they had permission.

Fenza said, "Let's get the fuck out of here. I need some air."

~

197

The river awaited them at twilight. Woozy with whiskey, stray desires, they sauntered down Krapalna Street, cut west on Canal, and quickened their stride at the sight of water. Gus picked up a scent, a mix of things difficult to define. A warm wound—this was the river in summer, or what he could name. Baked all day in July heat, it reeked of growth and decay, birthing and dying, a million or more changes. Frogs made a racket in shoreline thickets and trees, locusts too. Bats flicked by, seen but not heard, like good children. He smelled reeds, moss, mud, fish. No one had names for most things alive or dead in the air of a summer eve or the heat of a moving river. This one-horse town was richer than it seemed.

Gus patted his back pocket to make sure he still had a copy of Kenny Jefferson's letter to Sister Clair. He'd almost shown it to Fenza in the den after his dad left, but they lit out of that haunt before he could spring his surprise.

The boys crossed the footbridge over the canal and ambled to the cove. The fallen trunk of a cottonwood served as their bench. The sun had slipped free of town, save for a band of light on St. Roch's steeple. Gus took Kenny's letter and ruffled the pages to draw attention. He had no way to prepare Fenza to meet a Negro prisoner in the Long Binh Jail on the other side of the world. "Here," he said, "for you," and nested the two-page letter in Fenza's hands.

Fenza read the salutation and looked up.

"This letter's for Sister Clair. You break in the nunnery and steal it?"

"No, she gave me and my mom a copy."

"What for?"

"Just read it," said Gus. "It's from a guy who's in jail in Viet Nam."

Fenza fanned his face with the pages.

"Okay," he said, "but this better be good."

Dear Sister Clair, Here I am at LBJ, Long Binh Jail, some nine-thousand miles from Montgomery. Me and Marvyn, this other brother, been cleaning the honey buckets most days, dousing them in diesel, lighting them up, and try-ing to stay upwind of the smoke and stench. Fenza, eyes narrow, moved his lips over these words a second time. A dumb jig in jail, he surmised, but he kept reading. *Honey buckets. Eighty-three combat missions. Dragonflies. Ash and rubble.* He perked up at the mention of *bombers, B-52s, blowing apart rice fields, sugar palms, birds, bees, water buffalo, fish, grass, leaves—whatever conceals or sustains the "enemy."* The colored boy's handwriting was choppy, maybe because of bad nerves, jittery fingers. *I don't sleep much, Sister, and late at night I tend to wonder, in the relative quiet, how America can sleep. LBJ's a Black jail with white guards, and I wish America could tune us in on TV, or better, meet us at night in the cellblock. America needs some dark dreams to survive her dumb innocence. She needs—excuse the language, Sister—honey buckets, shit & fuel & fire, plus the courage to breathe.*

Fenza paused when the Negro said he might visit Orville on some moonless night and knock on a few windows. He would do no such thing even if Sister Clair held his paw and prayed a novena. The guys in the bars would gather in the streets, a crowd of hellions. The boy might discover a town no less dangerous than the jungles and prisons of Viet Nam.

"Why'd you give me this?"

Gus shrugged. "I don't know. I just thought you should see it."

Fenza glanced at the letter. "This boy's a goner if he shows up here after sundown."

"Maybe not."

"He best eat his last supper before he arrives. Fried chicken and watermelon. Skip the trimmings."

"Fenza, you're so dumb I can't even—"

"Then why'd you give me this letter? How dumb is that?"

"What's your hat size?"

"No, let's take my question first. Why'd you give me this letter?"

"I'm not going to Viet Nam."

Fenza froze.

"Three weeks after you leave, my mom and me will pack our bags and scram."

"Like hell you will."

"Sister Clair has friends in Buffalo, New York. My mom's going to work as a receptionist for a dentist. She'll settle there a few years, but she'll visit me in Toronto."

"Toronto?"

"There's some good music there, or at least that's the rumor."

Fenza, glowering and groaning, said, "You must be kidding."

"I'm not."

"Then I'll have to fuck up your plans by stopping by the police station on my way home."

Gus knew he was bluffing. Fenza could threaten to tell the cops, but to snitch on a friend—or even an enemy—went against every principle he held dear. "Go on," Gus taunted. "Tell the cops, tell the town. What are you waiting for?"

"Just this," said Fenza. "Watch." He ripped the letter in pieces and tossed the scraps to the river. "Only mud bass will eat this sort of shit."

Fenza missed when he tried to end Gus's night with a sucker punch. "I forgot to ask if you've made funeral arrangements."

"For you, Fenza."

"You got one more minute to live."

They faced off on the strip of beach between the cottonwood trunk and the shallows. Fenza, fists raised, said, "You afraid of the war? Is that it?"

"Not really."

"Forget about Viet Nam. You're about to die right here."

Gus glided around him in a slow circle. "You ever hear of Muhammad Ali?"

"Another jig with a loose screw."

Gus connected with a jab.

"And what's that? A warm breeze on the verandah?"

Gus struck again, harder.

"Son of a bitch," said Fenza. "This is your night to die."

He missed with a roundhouse, but then he lunged, gathered his friend in his arms, and the two toppled and squirmed, legs sliding down in the shallows, torsos mired in muck and sand. Fenza whacked Gus upside the head. "And how's that?" he said. "How's that for starters?" Gus answered with a jab that caught Fenza mid-face and rang his ears.

The big boy rolled off him and retreated. He threw some shadow punches and promised August Theodore Zeul a ticket to St. Roch's Cemetery, a cheap coffin. "Toronto?" said Fenza. "You ain't ever leaving this town."

Ragged, wet to the waist, the boys clambered up the shore. Fenza took a glancing blow to the chin, the side of his head, then another. "Motherfucker," he said, "try that again." Gus flicked his left fist and this time Fenza caught it with both hands. The big boy squeezed, tried to break bones, but Gus, slippery little bastard, wriggled free and struck Fenza mid-face with another jab.

Minutes later, they were saved by a siren. Tired but still tousling, half-holding each other, half-fighting, they pried themselves apart and slunk toward the swamp oaks and thickets west of the cove. By the time Officer Krupovich parked his vehicle near the footbridge and painted his spotlight back and forth along the shore, the boys lay as still as the shadows under the arms of an oak.

Gino Marelli, from the doorway of his tavern, said, "They're out there somewhere, Krup, Fenza and the Zeul boy raising Cain again. I swear they were about to tear each other apart."

So Krupovich, on his megaphone, called, "The show's over, boys, and the encore too." His words carried over the shore and across the water. "If you come in on your own steam, I'll let you off with a warning and call it a night."

He froze his searchlight on a dense thicket beneath a swamp oak. He guessed they were backed up in those shadows, and if he went after them they'd take refuge in more thickets, a nest of willows, a haven for mosquitoes. Like everyone in Orville, the officer knew Fenza was scheduled to leave town tomorrow morning, the Zeul boy soon after. Eddie Tapusko, sitting on the steps in front of Marelli's, advised the officer "to come over and have a drink. The fight's over," he said. "And those boys, wherever they are, won't show their faces till you're gone."

He was right on this. Face-down, the boys lay side by side, legs and arms flexed, ready to spring. A quarter acre of jungle, a hint of night, was all they needed to fend off Officer Krupovich or any adult. Fenza, sucking a bloody lip, touched his friend's hand for an instant. Gus Zeul, he thought, you ain't so bad a fighter. He wished his best friend were coming with him to the Marine Corps, the same unit. He wished they could fight side by side till the war was won.

"Gus," he whispered.

"Huh?"

"You're a damn nuisance. You know that?"

Gus was smiling. "And you?"

"Only a bigger war could keep me from this one."

"Careful what you pray for."

"Rodger-dodger. Hail Mary full of moonshine. Semper fi."

They kept lying there in the thicket after Officer Krupovich joined Eddie Tapusko at the tavern. Gus listened to Fenza fetch deep breaths, fill his chest, and he almost confessed he would miss his pal in the same way that he would miss the river. He guarded this thought, its tenderness, but it was safe to admit he missed Jimmy because Jimmy was gone and might never come back and most likely couldn't rag on him now or ever. "Jimmy," he said, and ran his fingers through the grass, a light rustle like the wings of hoppers. "I never knew I'd miss him, but I do."

Fenza, with a shrug, repeated his father's line: Jimmy, who by now had experienced combat, would "never be the same."

Gus murmured his agreement, then quieted. Frogs hidden in snags and willow swamps called back and forth, no two voices the same. He heard a rattling riff, a tap, a series of clicks. The sounds were sibilant and seductive, as if someone shook a castanet under a wave.

"I'm changed forever too," he whispered, "because I refuse to kill anyone."

"I have a hunch it's easy."

"That's not the point."

"You ain't got a point."

"Just one, and it's real quiet."

"I don't hear you."

"No, listen. I don't want to kill anyone."

"You already told me."

"Yeah, but I mean nobody, nobody, *no*body." He shook his head. "Not even you."

Fenza smiled in the dark. He still wished they were going together to the war in Viet Nam.

PART 4

Christmas Eve

(1967)

I'm Dreaming of a White Christmas.

—IRVING BERLIN

Orville

Fenza, home on leave, due to celebrate the New Year in Viet Nam, cruised Krapalna Street in his father's '53 Chevy. In dress blues, the Marine Corps version of a tuxedo, he sat tall at the wheel, shoulders back, chin up, and wondered how he might claim the attention of this penny-ante town one last time. Approaching St. Roch's, he used the horn as a punching bag, made more racket than the pigeons rising from the bell tower, circling the steeple. Butch Yansik, shoveling snow from the top step, turned, dropped his shovel, and called, "Fenza! Hey Fenza!" The Marine, as if he were an officer, acknowledged his friend's existence with a curt nod.

Fenza fishtailed the car toward the river. Early this morning, six inches of snow had blanketed the town. Now, at midday, the wind a curse from the north, drifting snow erased curbs and painted tree trunks and fences. Fenza wished he were sliding down Krapalna Street with his pals, Gus and Jimmy. More than anything, though, he wished for a girl of his own, one who would write to him if he was wounded and remember him if he died.

He drove to Jenny's house and pulled over. The Christmas tree in the front window shone with lights and tinsel, but not for him. Fenza punched the horn and drove off down Krapalna Street. The old car knew the way past Tony Renh's Grocery, then west on Canal to the Illinois River. Fenza punched the horn again as he approached Mutts Marelli's Tavern. The bums sitting at the front windows looked up from their drinks. Losers, thought Fenza, overgrown children. Except for the few who'd survived what his father called "the crucible of war."

Fenza made a U-turn at the Orville Clock Factory and headed back the way he'd come. He turned on the radio to a holiday favorite—"I'll Be Home for Christmas." Fenza sang along with Bing Crosby as he cruised over Canal Street and up Krapalna at ten miles an hour. His father, reasoning there was nowhere to go, had loaned out his Chevy for a half hour. Fair enough, the town was dead, call the morticians, but Fenza knew Pop didn't trust him even now when he was a Marine with orders for Viet Nam. Home for Christmas? It was like opening gifts, peeling away shiny paper and ribbons, to find nothing inside.

He punched the horn again as he passed St. Roch's Church and Butch Yansik. Were those the same dumb birds rising from the bell tower? Was Butch shoveling the same snow? If, a year from now, in the aftermath of war, Fenza revisited this scene, he might discover that nothing but his character had changed.

He continued up Krapalna Street and into the country. To hell with the old man and his demand to run this heap back home in thirty minutes. Fenza needed at least an hour to surprise Pat Lemkey, pull up at her farm, knock on her door, give her something to fret about. He wondered if she'd let him in and rated his chances at fifty-fifty. Jenny Biel? She'd shun Fenza till he died, but he and Pat were once boyfriend and girlfriend. She was the only Iggy girl who let him hold her dumb hand a few times. Today, with any luck, she'd learn to respect him. The uniform should help, plus the correct posture and bearing. It seemed a sin to leave this town without at least talking to a girl.

The Chevy chugged along a narrow road through winter fields. The reaper had come and gone. Here and there, the stubble of corn jutted above drifting snow. Fenza struggled to grasp the ironies. He was bound for a place hot as Hades, but first he'd be dipped in ice. He had no confidence in Pat Lemkey. He had no confidence in any girl within a hundred miles.

But the Lemkey farm would have made a nice Christmas card. The stately grove of trees, the oaks and maples dusted with snow, the two-story farmhouse white and clean, the barn the color of wine, the color of Canal Street bricks. Fenza surprised himself by praying: "Won't you please let her open the door, Lord? Won't you please?" He tried to ignore the hammer in his heart, the ringing in his ears. He was going to war a virgin and might die a virgin. Shouldn't *that* be a sin? Shouldn't someone hang? He glided down a snowy drive under tall, dark trees.

The porch light was on, but not for Fenza. On a stairway glazed with snow, he slipped, barked a shin, and fell to one knee. The Lemkeys were so damn ignorant they didn't know enough to sprinkle salt on the steps! Fenza grabbed the banister, pulled himself up, and limped onto the landing. He already knew the law of the land: covet a girl and suffer a wound.

He paused to catch his breath and gather courage. He straightened a cap already straight, then the collar of his tunic. He looked forward to the day when he could adorn his dress blues with medals—a Silver Star for Valor, a Purple Heart. At present, Fenza had a Marksman Badge, plus two blood-striped chevrons on his sleeve to signify his rank, Private First Class. Blood stripes graced his trousers, too, and his tunic, including a stripe that split his chest down the middle and stopped a thumb's width above his groin.

When the doorbell sang, "Cocka-doodle, cocka-doodle," he grimaced. A tinny twang, an imitation rooster—to hell with that. Fenza banged the door with his fists. How hard would he need to strike to pop the hinges from the frame?

He was set to experiment when the door opened a crack. He saw nothing but a dark eye, a bronze button on bib overalls. Pat was stingy with that door, opened it just enough for a lean mouse to slip through. He heard the prattle of ladies from beyond the parlor. Maybe she was cautious because there was no man in the house.

Fenza stood to his full height. "Sorry if I'm interrupting," he said. "Just happened to drive by and saw the light on the porch."

"I thought—"

"Yeah, you thought right. I'll be in Viet Nam for the New Year. The Corps gave me a little furlough, though, sent me home for Christmas. A few more days and I'll be leaving this town for good."

The door opened to the half-light of the parlor. Pat Lemkey, in overalls and a green sweater, looked almost pretty. Fenza smelled cookies, cakes, Christmas. He took off his cap (the Marines call it a cover) as he crossed the portal. Maybe she let him in because it was daylight and her mom was home and he was going to war and might die soon. Who knows what she was thinking? Facts colder than Christmas might have opened the door.

Fenza followed her through the parlor to a bright kitchen. No surprise to see Mrs. Lemkey at her oven, but the sight of Jenny Biel made him gasp. "Hey," he said, "I was just thinking of you and here you *are*." The tremor in his voice shamed him. "Well," he said, "Merry Christmas," and sat at a Formica table before trays of reindeer cookies, red-and-white Santas, red and green stars. Mrs. Lemkey, leaning over the stove, applied frosting to a Christmas cake.

Jenny edged closer to Pat. A Marine, an Iggy boy—is there a difference? No, she thought, Fenza is Fenza. He might have hammered the door off its hinges had no one let him in.

Mrs. Lemkey told him he looked nice in his uniform. "That's quite an outfit," she said.

"Thanks."

"You won't find a nicer suit coat anywhere in town."

Jenny watched him cringe. No one joined the Marines to look "nice" for someone's mother. Fenza might have swaggered a step or two had she called him dashing or devilish. In truth, dress blues did nothing to improve his appearance. The Marines had draped their finery on a boulder. Thick bones and bulges, bull shoulders, a stout trunk—this was Fenza. He would never be more elegant than an uncut stone.

Mrs. Lemkey served Fenza Santa Claus cookies and eggnog. He knew she disliked him, always had, but he was a Marine now, and he told her he was leaving for Viet Nam on December 28. "Well," she replied, "we'll remember you in our prayers. People around here—we're good at praying. Especially in times of need."

We? thought Fenza. Will the girls pray, too? He dared a glance at Jenny. Dust off your rosary, darling. Polish a bead and whisper my name.

Fenza told them about the most recent letter he received from Jimmy. "I wrote to him my first week in boot camp," he said, "but it took him maybe two months to write back. He said the Marines own the daylight hours, the yellow man owns the night." He leaned forward, his forearms on the table. "Jimmy says every morning he sees the sun is an answered prayer."

The quiet was delicate, so he chomped a cookie, slurped eggnog, and looked out the window. Flurries like fairies now, tender and girlish. He snuffed the urge to bang the table with a fist.

Mrs. Lemkey said she'd pray for Jimmy, too, and all our boys in harm's way. "This war's taking too long," she said, "and we've already buried some of our best." She named the local boys who'd paid the ultimate price: Joe Selbst, Donny Zorich, and just last week Dale Erben. "I went to their funerals," she said, "and so did my husband. I cried with the mothers as if I'd lost my own sons."

Jenny and Pat seemed to take no interest in Viet Nam. Fenza knew the score: They didn't care if he lived or died, might prefer the latter, but he had no one else he needed to say goodbye to. He asked Jenny about school, life at the university, Illinois State. "That school's in a town called Normal, right?"

She nodded.

"I can't help asking what you and your classmates do for fun."

He didn't care about Jenny's response any more than she cared about Viet Nam. Talking to her was an excuse to size her up in her hip-hugger jeans, a red Christmas sweater, a silver necklace, a shiny cross in the valley of her breasts.

"I'm still living at home," she said. "I decided to hold off on school, at least for now."

Fenza leaned forward. "Why's that?"

"No special reason. I'm just doing what feels right."

Mrs. Lemkey filled in the gaps. Jenny had a job at J. C. Penney's. She'd saved some money and would be moving out of her parents' home on New Year's Day. "You know that place a quarter mile from here? That little log cabin off Ballinger Road?"

Fenza said he did.

"Jenny already has her name on the mailbox. I'd say she's a bit impatient."

Fenza saw Jenny and Pat exchange nervous smiles.

"Well, that's the big news," said Mrs. Lemkey. "You kids are growing up fast. I see Jenny's parents at church on Sundays, and of course they'd rather she stay at home under their wing until she leaves for college."

Fenza, without enthusiasm, said, "They're good parents."

"Yes, and good parents do their share of worrying. Mrs. Biel keeps asking me to keep an eye on her girl."

Pat, at the stove, face flushed, said, "Mom, have you had too much coffee?"

"Three cups," said Mrs. Lemkey, "weak as water. I see no harm in sharing our news, especially since this young man's on his way to the war."

Fenza winked. "No harm, Mrs. Lemkey."

"I've already grown fond of Jenny, and who wouldn't?"

"Mom, please."

"She spends so much time on the farm she's almost like one of my own."

Jenny let her eyes close partway. She and Pat had a secret name for themselves—*The Unthinkables*. They hid in plain view because no one considered the possibility of two Orville girls falling in love. If she and Pat were to hold hands or embrace right now, the affection—if noticed at all—would be no more memorable than the affection of kittens. *The Unthinkables* enjoyed certain freedoms. They'd been careful in their first months of love, but then they discovered they could walk hand-in-hand down Krapalna Street, past St. Roch's Church and Sonny's Place, and on down to Canal Street and the river, their closeness and happiness perceived as nothing more than the amity of girls. They sometimes spoke of flight, a trip to San Francisco, but the discussion always came back to the farm, the land, the animals, the way of life that for Pat—and more and more for Jenny—was too familiar to abandon. There was no reason for haste. Maybe they could be farm girls for years, decades, their love invisible. They were in no danger while living among the blind.

Fenza, after a pause, called Jenny a pioneer. "You'll soon be living in a log cabin," he said, "same as Abe Lincoln and Daniel Boone."

There was still some baking to do. Mrs. Lemkey explained that the cakes and most of the cookies would be delivered to the rectory in the early evening. "I'm going to Midnight Mass with the girls," she said, "but the sweets are reserved for tomorrow, the Christmas Day Social. Me and Mrs. Moshnik are in charge of desserts."

Fenza didn't care if they were in charge of the Vatican. While Mrs. Lemkey blathered, sipped coffee, leaned on the stove, Pat and Jenny began mixing batter at the kitchen counter. Wooden spoons shlurp-shlurped through cookie mush, rattled the sides of metal bowls. Fenza, a sightseer with a sniper's eye, homed in on girls in bright sweaters, red and green, in a kitchen as snug and warm as a fireplace stocking. Why had they grown more attractive in his absence? Jenny, having gained a bit of weight, looked homier, more womanly, and Pat, her every gesture, hinted at satisfaction and ease. Something had blessed these girls, but what? Contentment? Fenza railed at the possibility. Contentment, mystery of mysteries, was maddening, because he felt cursed by its opposite: unrequited desire.

But he promised them he'd changed for the better. "I didn't know it," he said, "but what I needed all along was a strong dose of discipline." He shook his head. "The kid you recall, the hell-raiser treating his town like it's a carnival and he's got tickets for all the rides . . . well, I can hardly believe that was me." He scowled at the memory of his younger self. "The good news is that I've put those days behind me. I've got a lot to be thankful for now that I'm a Marine."

Jenny used the heels of her hands to flatten strips of dough on a tray. Fenza wished she'd touch him this way, knead him all over, or at least say something to let him know she wanted him to survive.

Now she used a cookie cutter, a star, and asked if he'd written to Gus.

"Me?" said Fenza. "All I know is he's hiding out in Canada."

"Toronto," said Jenny. "I bet he'd like to hear from you."

"I hope not."

"Sister Clair told me he's playing music and has a job washing dishes."

"She would know."

"The whole town knows," said Mrs. Lemkey. "Gus Zeul is the only Orville boy to ever refuse a war."

She poured herself a fresh cup of coffee and sat across from Fenza, her back to the stove. "I blame two people," she said. "Cassie Zeul didn't know how to raise her son alone. Gus had no father, no discipline, and all he cared about was making noise on a drum. Maybe he would've straightened out if Sister Clair hadn't come along and shown him some letter from a boy who refused to fight in Viet Nam."

Fenza feigned ignorance. "A boy from around here?"

"No, you know better. A Negro from the South, a boy who's in jail in Viet Nam."

"He's probably scared to fight."

"Scared of all sorts of things, especially his shadow."

Fenza squinted. "You mean Sister Clair showed you his letter?"

"No, but she had the gall to show it to her classes this fall, nearly a hundred students. After complaints were filed, the whole town found out she was using St. Ignatius High to peddle propaganda."

"A good thing they stopped her."

"Yes, and none too soon. Sister never apologized. She admitted to Father Janecek that she first showed the colored boy's letter to Cassie Zeul, then made a copy for Gus." She shook her head. "It seems Father called the archdiocese that same day. To make a long story short, Sister's no longer welcome in our town, our parish, and whatever rights and responsibilities she enjoys as a nun will soon be stripped away by the authority of the bishop."

"Serves her right."

"I haven't seen the boy's letter, but I've heard plenty."

"I bet."

"The latest word is that Sister will be gone in a month, maybe sooner."
She slurped her coffee. "Maybe she'll join Cassie in Buffalo, New York, or
Gus in Toronto. You ask me, the whole bunch belongs in jail."

Fenza had heard as much scuttlebutt as he could stand. He wanted to
hate Gus and Cassie, Sister Clair, too, but his heart betrayed him. "Well, I
better be off," he said, and rose from the table. "I hope to see all of you at
Midnight Mass."

"If I go," said Pat.

"No, you're going," said Mrs. Lemkey, "and Jen, too. That's our agreement if she plans to sleep in this house on Christmas Eve."

Pat blushed.

"You'll see us at midnight," Mrs. Lemkey told Fenza. "Plus my husband."

"I'm grateful."

"That's the last thing in this dizzy world I can guarantee."

~

Back home, after Pop bawled him out for being late and left for the taverns, Fenza made his way down Krapalna Street to the nunnery. He'd never
had any reason to come here. There was no doorbell, nor need for one,
since nuns rarely had callers. A two-story clapboard—spotless, refrigerator
white—shone brighter than Christmas snow.

Minutes passed before Sister Damien answered his knocks. "Fenza," she
said. "What on earth—?"

"Merry Christmas, Sister."

"Yes, Merry Christmas. But—"

"Is Sister Clair at home? May I speak with her?"

She tilted her head. "For what purpose?"

"Just to ask her something," said Fenza. "One question and I'll be on
my way."

She had him wait outside. He was trembling with cold and angst by the
time Sister Clair came to the door. "Fenza!" she said. "My heavens!" The
joy in her voice almost coaxed him to smile.

He refused her invitation to come inside.

"All I need is Gus's phone number," he said. "If you have it."

"You don't need to warm up?"

"I need the phone number, Sister. If you can jot—"

"Yes, yes, of course. But may I ask how you're doing?"

He ironed a hand along the front of his tunic. There were no wrinkles.

"I see," she said. "You're doing well."

He shivered when Sister told him she'd spoken with Gus this morning. "They still let me make one call a week from the rectory," she said. "I also spoke with his mother."

Fenza hesitated. "I thought she's in Buffalo."

"Yes, that's her new home, but she's visiting Gus for the holidays."

Fenza grunted. "Merry Xmas to Canada."

"Gus couldn't stop talking about you. He said, 'Toronto has rivers, Sister, but where's Fenza? How can I get in trouble?'"

She laughed.

Fenza bit his lower lip to edit a smile.

"You and Gus and Jimmy—you were a threesome."

"The phone number, Sister."

"Yes, yes. Just give me a minute. Gus will be so happy to hear your voice."

She told him to wait inside while she fetched the number.

"Please," she said. "It might feel good to come in out of the cold."

Fenza remained on the landing. He was fond of this nun but refused to reveal any trace of affection. He looked toward Pulaski Park, the winter trees, and almost smiled when he remembered roaring down Krapalna Street with Gus and Jimmy in a rich man's Buick. That stout sycamore across from St. Roch's ended their first and last joyride. By now Fenza felt—at most—mild amusement. None of it meant much compared to what he would see in Viet Nam.

The Marine wavered when Sister held out a slip of paper with Gus's number.

"I doubt I'll call him," he said. "I doubt I'll call anyone before I leave this town."

She pushed the paper into his hand.

"Just in case," she said. "Keep it just in case."

Gus

He was learning the sounds of a new instrument in his cellar apartment in Toronto on Christmas Eve. *Le guira*, they call it, and this one arrived from Haiti three years earlier in the suitcase of Dany Lavalliere. A shiny steel tube poked with holes, a tube the length of Dany's forearm, the circumference of a young woman's thigh. "My uncle Evens is right," he told Gus. "A good story needs music more than words."

In the small room, his crest of black hair inches from the ceiling, the young man held the silver tube to his chest. He gripped its wooden handle in his left hand, a kitchen fork in his right. He swayed, relaxed his grip on the fork, and then he made of his music and story a roundelay, a back-and-forth journey from Haiti to here.

Gus, in a straight-back chair, his bongo silent between his knees, watched and listened. The rap-a-tap-tap of a kitchen fork blurred like the wings of a hummingbird. Dany's shirt was red, his music something brighter. Was this a Haitian serenade? The sounds were warm enough to draw a girl to a window on a winter night.

His mother, sitting at a card table in a green dress, sipping eggnog spiked with brandy, swayed from side to side. She met every third or fourth beat with the twitch of her shoulders and the jiggle of hips.

After Dany, his forehead beaded with sweat, sat down and propped the instrument on his knee, Gus asked if the song had a title.

"'A Walk with Mariselle,'" his friend replied. "She was tall and—what's the word?—gorgeous."

"I already knew."

"She was never my girl, but I liked her."

Gus nodded.

"I once walked her home from church on Christmas Eve."

Cassie asked if he could play another song.

"I'll try," said Dany. "Let me see if I can change the mood."

He dipped a hand into a cloth sack full of rags. Faded colors, rainbows gone mild—red to pink, sapphire to soft blue—scraps of old dresses no longer fit for dances. Red was Mariselle's favorite color, but she was gone now. The scraps were his sister's discards, and he stuffed them down the hollow tube of *le guira*. Humming, he swished a blind hand along the bottom of the sack and brought out a short-handled wooden spoon.

"This," he said, "is like the bow of a violin."

He rubbed the instrument with the spoon as if to knead its muscles, locate the softness in steel. Gus, leaning forward, heard shushing sounds, hints of rain. Lonesome, he thought. *Le guira* in gray and blue.

Cassie applauded when Dany set down his instrument. "Nicely done," she said. "Does your song have a name?"

"'Farewell at Sundown.'"

"For Mariselle?"

"No, I play this one for Manman."

"Another pretty girl?"

"Oh, no," he grimaced. "This is a farewell song for my mother."

Cassie reddened. "I'm sorry."

"Please don't be. One day soon she will come from Ayiti to live with my sister and me."

His words and his smile forgave her. She'd driven up from Buffalo this morning, and this was her first encounter with another people, another country. Her son, with the help of Sister Clair, had this little place in the Old City, a job as a dishwasher, and his neighbors were Haitian, Chinese, Liberian, Lithuanian, Jamaican, Portuguese, Venezuelan, Puerto Rican, Malaysian, Ethiopian, Armenian, and so on. Dany, the janitor of this tenement, lived upstairs with his nineteen-year-old sister. Nadine was her name, and Cassie knew Gus was sweet on her. Before Dany came down to play *le guira*, her son told her about his new friend and "his sister who couldn't be nicer. She once brought me cinnamon rice pudding," he said. "It was like home-made ice cream, but better. She sprinkled cane sugar to make it sweet."

Now Gus asked Dany when his sister would arrive.

"When she finishes her cooking. I won't tell you what she's making because she wants you to be surprised."

Cassie, crossing her legs and easing back in her chair, had seldom felt more at home. In the dim light of the cellar, sitting with musicians, nothing was amiss. Her son's studio was smaller than a rich man's closet: the kitchen wedged on one side, the bathroom on the other, the living space in between. Furniture? Gus had shoved a thrift-store couch under a window whose sill was level with the street. He had a card table, three chairs. A cot for a bed. A sleeping bag for a blanket. And there was one more thing to warm this cellar on Christmas Eve.

Cassie had brought for him the best gifts possible, the Stackomatic turntable and their records. The turntable, silent now, rested on a milk crate in a corner. She'd worried that her son would be lost here, that he would disappear in the speed and vastness of a foreign city. No, Gus already had a friend, another musician, and a girl to at least dream about. His few possessions were plenty. What Toronto lacked—a draft, a sundown law—was also a gift.

"Oh," said Gus, and "oh" again, when he heard a light tap on the door. He jumped to his feet and flew the few steps to the entry. Nadine had arrived.

Her hair was black and braided, her blouse yellow, her skirt pink. She held a white coat in one arm, a blue casserole dish in the crook of the other. Nadine Lavalliere seemed to be made of sparks, spirals, colors. On Christmas Eve she was yellow-black-pink-white-blue.

Gus wanted to compliment her beauty, but this was impossible in the presence of his mother. He introduced her to Cassie, took her coat, and the two women gravitated to the nook that served as a kitchen. Nadine set the blue dish on the back of the stove.

"May I look?" said Cassie.

"Oh, yes. Please."

Nadine lifted the foil from the dish.

"The smell makes me hungry."

"You must try some."

"I will," said Cassie. "Let me find a plate and a fork."

Banane pesee, twice-fried plantain. Round and crisp at the edges, pancake-flat along the bottoms and tops. Cassie savored the slight sweetness. This Haitian dish went well with eggnog and brandy. A drop of honey on the tongue.

Cassie said she needed to make a batch of Slovenian donuts. "My mother calls them *krofi*," she said, "and they are another kind of Christmas treat."

Gus picked up Dany's rag-filled *guira* and scraped it with a spoon. He watched Nadine's pink skirt, her yellow blouse, and he played for her. His mother poured oil in a hot skillet. The sizzling sound was brighter than his scraping, so he sought imitation. Oil popping off an iron disc, a wooden spoon tap-tapping a steel tube. He doubted Nadine heard him well, so he removed the rags that muffled the music. Yes, now he was set. He'd slip-slide into a beat, then play it hot and hard as oil popping off a pan.

Cassie gave each uncooked donut a twist, sprinkled it with sugar, and tossed it in the skillet. "I learned this from my mother," she said, "when I was eight years old."

She asked Gus to tone down the music. "No need to shake the walls," she said. "We hear you quite well."

~

Minutes later, the women at the settee, the musicians at the card table, they feasted on Slovenian donuts and *banane pesee*. Gus kept glancing at Nadine, her hand dark and delicate under a cracked plate, her lips pink inside when she opened her mouth. She's prettier than Jenny Biel, he thought, prettier than Brigitte Bardot. He was saying this to himself when the phone rang and he lurched to his feet.

He went to the kitchen, picked up, and heard someone breathing. "Hello?" he said. "Hello?"

He heard one more breath before the line went dead.

The moment he set down the receiver the phone rang again. Gus glanced over his shoulder at Nadine. "Sorry," he said. "I don't know who this could be."

He heard the breathing again, heavier, and then a low grumble.

"Who's calling?" said Gus. "Who *is* this?"

"Oh, hell and hallelujah. I'm the dumbest jarhead in the world to call you on Christmas Eve."

"Fenza!"

"Yeah, I'm a million miles away."

"Where you at, man? Parris Island?"

"No, back in Orville. I wish they'd just sent me to the Nam 'stead of giving me a few days leave. This town's dead as ever, but I saw Jenny today, Pat too."

"How are they?"

"Lousy. They still pack icicles in their drawers."

Gus turned his back to Nadine. "Can't you talk any quieter?"

"I'm the Christmas mouse," said Fenza. "What are you doing today? Anything special?"

"My mom's here. We're sort of having a party."

"You and your mom? You call that—"

"Some friends, too. We're eating donuts and *banane pesee*."

"Banana pussy?"

Gus pressed a palm to the receiver to shield Nadine from Fenza's filth. "Knock it off," he said. "You'll have to talk decent if you want to talk to me at all."

So Fenza whispered, "You have a girl up there?"

Gus stayed quiet.

"A friendly warning," said Fenza. "Don't get syphilis."

"I'm hanging up if you keep on this way."

"All right, then. Merry Xmas and Slappy New Year. I'm leaving for Viet Nam on December 28."

Gus hesitated. "Be careful, okay?"

"I might," said Fenza, "but I doubt they can kill me. They've never fought against anyone like me."

Gus sensed a ray of truth here. The Vietnamese had never seen the likes of Fenza Ryczhik Jr., nor had the world.

Cassie took the phone from her son. She wished Fenza a Merry Christmas, then told him she missed him.

"Everybody's got problems, Mrs. Zeul."

"No, I'm not speaking of problems. There are people who love you."

She could feel him shrug.

"Your parents, for example. Plus Gus and Jimmy."

"Yeah, yeah."

"And then there's me," she said. "Last but not least."

"Thanks, Mrs. Zeul."

"Don't forget us, okay?"

"I'll do my best."

"Take care of yourself and remember what I said."

~

Cassie hadn't been to Midnight Mass in ages. She considered staying in the apartment, listening to records over a quiet drink, but Dany and Nadine begged her to come. "Please," said the girl. "I'm in the choir. We've been practicing for seven weeks."

So nearing the midnight hour, Cassie and Dany led the way toward Portugal Square and Old St. Mary's. Windy and white, harsh and beautiful. Only lovers, or those dreaming of love, could saunter through such cold.

Gus and Nadine lagged behind. The boy might need to embrace her, gather her in, if she lost her footing. The slick walkway made conditions favorable. This light-footed girl both thrilled and disappointed. She seemed capable of walking on anything, even air.

Gus did his best to impress Nadine. Crossing a small bridge, a creek, he told her the Illinois River, the river he came from, was a mile wide in some places, a mile deep in others. "I almost drowned in her," he said proudly, "when I was six years old. I waded out farther than the other kids, got snagged in currents and whirlpools, and down I went." He slipped on the walkway, whirled his arms. Recovered. "Sort of like that," said Gus. "The river started to swallow me, then changed its mind. It was a grave, blacker than I can tell you. But then it cast me up to where I saw my friend Fenza holding a stick over the water and I latched on and let him haul me in like a giant fish."

He shrugged, feigned nonchalance. "I guess I'm lucky to be alive."

Nadine hid her smile behind a gloved hand. Just how big was the "giant fish," how black the water? Was the Illinois River a mile deep? Was it fathomless? She'd begun to like Gus, encourage his affection. A boy who spoke of a river as his origin (I come from here) might one day deserve her love.

Nadine told him her country had an important river, the Riviere Latibonite. "Tonight," she said, "I can't tell you if it's as wide as the Illinois, but it's wider than Toronto's rivers, the Don and Humber, even in spring when they swell with melting snow. The Latibonite pours down from the mountains, muddy and brown, and there are places where it is too deep to dive down and leave a handprint on its bed."

So they had rivers in common, and he saw an opening, a chance to woo her with his knowledge of her country. He'd learned from Dany to call Haiti by its true name, Ayiti, for this was the Indian way of saying Home or Mother of the Earth. Dany had bragged that he and his sister, in their oldest blood, were Zambos, not Haitians. Centuries ago, their ancestors escaped the slavery of Spanish gold mines and fled to Ayiti's most impassable mountains. There, amid peaks filed sharp as swords, a land no European could traverse, they met runaway African slaves called Maroons. The Ayiti and the Maroons had much in common. They mixed, married, and their offspring—of two great lands, two peoples—were called Zambos. Gus failed to mention his source (Dany), but he mimicked his friend's enthusiasm as long as he could. In the end—sober, almost professorial—he said, "The Ayiti and the Maroons share a history largely unknown to the world."

Nadine shook her head and grinned. "And where did you learn this? In your schools in Illinois?"

Gus cleared his throat. "No, not at St. Roch's or St. Iggy's. I learned some things from your brother."

"Dany talks a lot."

"Yes, but I won't tell anyone else what I learned if this is your wish."

Nadine giggled. "Zambos?"

He looked at her.

"Oh, Zambos, Zambos, *mambos!*" She swiveled her hips and laughed. "I hope you don't think you know Ayiti already."

"No, not really."

"You might need a few more years."

So Gus cramped up, silent and stiff, the rest of the way to St. Mary's. He doubted Nadine would walk at his side or ever speak his name if she knew he was born and raised in a sundown town. After dark, the only Black person he'd ever seen in Orville drove an old pickup that broke down on Canal Street. Gus bent his head into a stiff wind. What difference did it make how wide and deep the Illinois River was if a girl as elegant as Nadine, if a young man as musical as Dany, would be unwelcome to walk along its shores on Christmas Eve?

Midnight Mass in Orville

On the morning of December 24, Kenny Jefferson, in a phone booth north of Louisville, Kentucky, called St. Roch's Church. "Merry Christmas," he said. "I hope I've dialed the right number. I'm trying to reach Sister Clair."

Mrs. Sedlak, the receptionist, became addled. "This is the church house," she informed him, "the rectory. The nuns have no phone, but perhaps I can take a message."

Kenny, his voice gentle and bright, said, "Well, nothin' special. Just tell Sister her friend Kenny's bound for Chicago and will stop in Orville for Midnight Mass."

Mrs. Sedlak's heart began to race. "Tonight?"

"Christmas," he said. "Midnight."

"I believe . . ."

"Believe what?"

"It would be better to arrive in the afternoon."

~

She knew by his voice he was Negro, but she relayed the message to Sister Clair. "Your friend sounds peevish," she said. "Like he's got a chip on his shoulder."

Sister Clair stood in the doorway of the priory. "Perhaps he does," she said. "One shoulder may slump lower than the other."

"You're being sarcastic."

"Am I?"

"Your friend has no business in Orville."

Sister winked. "Let the Lord decide."

"More sarcasm?"

"A little."

"You would be wise to ask him to leave the moment he arrives."

Sister Clair, in her letters to Kenny, had never suggested he visit Orville. He was "bound for Chicago," though, and this river-town was more or less on his way. In a recent letter, he said the Army was "cuttin' him loose, just a matter of time," and he mentioned in a previous letter that he might pay her a visit after the war. Kenny had survived combat in Viet Nam, survived the Long Binh Jail, and this Christmas Eve he might survive Orville, Illinois. She remembered Dr. King saying the most dangerous march of his life occurred in Chicago, Kenny's current destination. Maybe Orville would have been no worse.

She stood in the front window of the nunnery and watched sparrows peck beneath the snow for the seeds she scattered at daybreak. "Kenny," she sighed, and shut her eyes to the whiteness. Her young friend knew the South, not the North, and only Orvillians knew Orville. Yet Kenny was clever, intuitive. He might find a way to meet this town on his own terms.

～

He arrived at the nunnery in the late afternoon. She saw him coming up the walk, light snow swirling around him, a hand at his throat to keep the wind from seeping beneath his collar. Here he was with his black coat, black face, black eyes, black hair, black pants, black shoes. She swung open the door and said, "Kenny, oh Kenny. You never cease to surprise."

He grinned and hugged his arms to his chest.

"I surprise my own self," he said. "I'm 'live and well on Christmas Eve."

He was thinner than she remembered, taller too. The impish smile was the same.

He'd parked his '53 Packard on Krapalna Street. At Sonny's Place, two men, beer glasses in hand, were looking out the window. Kenny motioned their way, then winked at Sister. "Let me guess," he said. "These fellows are wonderin' why I'm here."

Kenny knew that men, even white ones in daylight hours, were unwelcome in a nunnery unless they'd come to make repairs or to deliver groceries. "I best not duck inside," he said. "Is there a church hall, a place where we might sit a spell and catch up?"

Sister waved him toward the open door. "This will do."

"You won't get in trouble?"

"Kenny, come in where it's warm. I made some coffee and one of the parishioners brought over a plate of apple strudel. We can sit in the parlor and watch the snow."

An immaculate room, the oak-wood floor as shiny as the silver crucifix on the east wall. Sister served her guest, stirred sugar and cream in his coffee. "This strudel could win a prize," she said, and set him up with a wide wedge of it on a dinner plate.

They sat at a small table. The chairs were hard-backed, cushionless, but the window—wide enough to be called a picture window—looked out on Krapalna Street and the oaks and sycamores of Pulaski Park.

Kenny warmed his hands on his coffee cup, then unbuttoned his coat. "That old car, a gift from my Aunt Alcee, carried me from Montgomery." He shivered. "No heater, no radio. But everything else is sweet."

He kept a half-shut eye on the tavern across from the rectory and the church. Three men at the window now, stiff and still as statues. Sister kept distracting her guest with questions: How was he doing? How was his family? What did it mean to be home, free of LBJ? Why was he en route to Chicago? Did the Windy City hold some promise that Montgomery lacked? Did he have enough support?

Kenny watched the tavern, pondered the questions, and told Sister what he could. His family was well, but he already missed them, and he missed Montgomery. His Viet Nam highlight was saying farewell to LBJ, to Long Binh Jail, dishonorably discharged, a prisoner no more. He had work in Chicago. A blood he was in jail with, a Marine corporal, wrote to a friend who offered Kenny a job in a South-Chi factory. "School desks," he told Sister. "I'll load them on freighters, work the swing shift, plus put in some volunteer time with some veterans who oppose the war." He shrugged. "I start work in three days, but right now I'm just glad to see you." He raised his coffee cup in the gesture of a toast. "So here's to my favorite teacher in Montgomery. You even taught me to like that certain something called a poem."

"Every shut eye ain't asleep."

Kenny leaned back and grinned. "I knew that from day one, but you brought me to Langston and Du Bois and so many others."

"Did you get the books I sent?"

Kenny squinted into his coffee. "What books?"

"The ones I sent to LBJ. Two boxes."

"Maybe the guards are reading them."

"I hope someone is."

"The censors," said Kenny. "They may have a whole armory of books."

Sister Damien, on hearing the voice of a man, came down the hall and peeked into the parlor. One word—"But"—before her heels clacked a fit on the hardwood floor and she hurried outside.

"My colleague," said Sister Clair, "is on her way to the rectory. You may have a chance to meet our priest before Midnight Mass."

He met Father Janecek minutes later. Huffing, the priest hurried over without a coat or a hat. Up the six steps to the porch, one knock, and on into the nunnery. Sister Clair and Kenny rose from their chairs at the window. Father touched for an instant the hand Kenny offered, then turned his attention to the nun.

He reminded Sister she was forbidden to entertain guests in the priory.

"I know, Father. But Kenny has driven all the way from Alabama."

"The length of his trip is not at issue."

"I say it is, Father. An issue almost as important as the fact that he's just returned from Viet Nam."

"A month ago," the young man corrected, half-smiling, eyes closed. "I came up from Montgomery," he said, and cut his eyes a slit to peer at Father. "Me and Sister Clair, we got some history." His smile broadened. "She's known me and my family since 1955."

Father stood stout and somber in black shirt and pants, a white collar.

"I've always honored veterans," he said. "I must ask, however, if you are the young man who refused to fight in Viet Nam."

Kenny shut his eyes. "One of many, Father."

"And you wrote to Sister Clair from jail. Am I right?"

"This is not a court of law," said Sister.

"Nor is it a party," said the priest, "or a coffee club." He turned toward the window, the light of dusk. "Sister, I must speak with you alone."

She followed him into the hall.

"Now what?" he whispered. "Have you lost your senses?" Before Sister could respond, Father issued an ultimatum: "You will inform this boy he must leave this priory and this town at once."

Sister, her eyes blinking as if Father's words were a spattering of stones, said, "I will do no such thing. I believe my friend wishes to attend Midnight Mass."

Father winced. "That would be foolish, even dangerous. I don't need to spell out why."

Kenny moved into the hall and toward the door.

"Wait," said Sister. "We've hardly had a chance to visit."

Kenny winked and waved. "Bad timing," he said. "But maybe we'll meet again at the midnight hour."

Father, after this smart-alecky Negro drove away, promised Sister Clair she would be disciplined for this and other offenses and was in her last days as a nun.

"So be it."

"I must say you're consistent, steady as a compass."

"Is that a compliment?"

"You'll take it as such. You've never brought anything but trouble to this town."

∽

Darkness came. Maybe by now Kenny was on Route 6, halfway to Chicago. Sister Clair found herself trembling. She'd made the mistake of following Father down the hall, leaving Kenny in the parlor. She should have stood at her friend's side, perhaps in silence, until Father gave up and left them alone.

∽

She arrived a few minutes early for Midnight Mass, perhaps her final Mass as a Benedictine nun. She knelt in the last pew, the pew unofficially reserved for latecomers, lapsed Catholics, divorcees, and for tipplers who would wobble out of Sonny's Place at midnight, their eyes too bleary to see the altar or the cross. Sister Clair was the newest member of the Last Pew Club. At other services, she'd knelt near the altar with Sister Damien and Sister Walburga and other nuns, but tonight they could rejoice in her absence. The Mass itself—what could it mean in this church, this town? Sister Clair considered storming out of St. Roch's and wandering in the night till the cold forced her once more to endure the company of humans. The nuns in the front pews, the mucky-mucks, Mr. Maylor and his wife, the members of the Altar and Rosary Society—they were merely staging a show. Sister felt a greater affinity for the animals in Pulaski Park, the squirrels in the hollows of trees, bushy tails for blankets, the screech owls searching the white earth for prey, survival. She looked to the cross and felt nothing. The beads of her rosary, polished from use, felt dry as desert stones.

～

In the last light, Kenny Jefferson drove down Krapalna Street and turned east on Route 6.

Leaving town, he glanced over his shoulder at a sign—ORVILLE, Population 6,830. Well, Kenny knew two of the residents, Sister Clair and the priest. Before the war, he'd never entered nor wished to enter a white man's church in daylight or dark. *You don't want me? Praise the Lord. I want you even less.* Tonight, though, he had a hankering to surprise St. Roch's, cross the front lines of a sundown town. *How close to your altar may I kneel? How will you pray?*

～

Kenny coasted up Route 6 till he found a café and a dark-haired waitress who served him at the front counter. He didn't mind the long wait till the midnight hour. He needed to ease the jangling in his heart and shore up his resolve before he returned to Orville. A Louisville newspaper might help, plus a pamphlet, a Christmas gift from his grandma—Dr. King's "Letter from Birmingham City Jail." Grandma Zora was a lady preacher, though not in the official sense. "My best gift for you," she told him the night before he left for the North, "is wrapped in words. Dr. King, Fannie Lou Hamer, big old me—you feel the wind at your back? So many brave people now it would take all my years to name them. We comin' together, North and South, maybe finally end the Civil War, defiant and holy. And all to watch for at the crossroads is what burns brighter—hatred or love."

Kenny understood the defiance, but little else. The love Grandma Zora so fervently espoused sometimes pressed one's neck to a sharp blade. Dr. King, whom she called "a genius of heart and mind," whom the FBI called "the most dangerous Negro of the future," might as well be on death row. The problem with shining your love on those who don't want it is that you plant your own cross.

He told her all this over coffee at her kitchen table. Old Zora tilted her head and eyed him as if he were a rare specimen. "Well, where you been?" she asked. "You think I'm just born? Don't know a risk from a milk-ripe nipple?" She winked and smiled and waggled a finger at Kenny. "Blood and milk," said Zora. "Don't shy away from either and pretend you're alive."

~

He entered the church in silence at 11:58. An usher, Mr. Ciernik, spotted him first, but he was too stunned to inform this young man he had crossed a line. The Negro, no crimp in him anywhere, walked down the center aisle toward the front of the church. A chorus of murmurs rose from the parishioners. One row turned toward the Negro, then another, another, and onward in a wave to the front of St. Roch's.

Sister Clair had assumed Kenny left for Chicago. She stood, mouth open, as he knelt in the third pew near Sister Damien and Sister Walburga. The first two rows were occupied; Kenny took one of the last available spaces in the front of the nave. Sister Clair made her way to the fourth pew and stood behind Kenny. A five-foot tall guardian was better than none.

Fenza was attending Mass because he knew Jenny and Pat would be here. The girls, flanked by their parents, sat near the center of the church, so he'd chosen the pew behind them. The Marine, in dress blues, took his eye off the girls and for a long minute watched the Negro kneeling up front as if he belonged here, this boy with his black coat and nappy hair, this former soldier who was as tall kneeling down as Sister Clair was standing. Fenza said, "Well, Jesus H," and then this place buzzed with plaints, pleas, quick whisperings, plus enough crackles and coughs to fill an infirmary. Sloe-black—that was the boy's color. He had to be somewhere west of crazy to mosey up the center aisle and kneel near the altar. Sister Damien and Sister Walburga had turned away, heads bowed. Fenza figured they were repeating one prayer over and over: Pick up this colored boy, Lord, and set him down in someone else's church.

The choir sang "Come All Ye Faithful" as Father entered the apse with his altar boys. Sister Damien closed her eyes, but she could still see in her mind Sister Clair's Negro, this young man who'd visited the nunnery earlier, elegant and tall, shiny as a shard of glass, obsidian, and as dignified as any man she had ever seen. Why, at Christmas, must she undergo this trial? Closing her eyes failed to erase him, so now she opened them with a purpose. She glared at the Negro so he might lose his poise, his bearing, and flee from this church. He looked back at her once, twice, then shut his eyes and smiled. *Holy Mary Mother of God, pray for us sinners . . .* Her prayer did nothing to obscure him, nor diminish the power of his presence. Sister looked to the crucifix over the altar. The agony of wounds briefly quelled her desire.

She grew up on the story of the ditch-digger, the story told to her by a nun when she was twelve years old. A common man loved the most elegant woman in Europe. She lived a short while and died, as we all must, but the ditch-digger raged at God, slandered the Creator. He exhumed the woman he loved on a summer eve, pried open her casket, and brought her face to his lips. Maggots, in large numbers, may cause the flesh to quiver. The nun mentioned this with a glint in her eye. She promised Mary Ellen (this was Sister Damien's birth name) that no boy on earth would tempt her if she learned to contemplate the finality of physical death. "A bride of the Lord," she said, "finds solace only in Him."

Kenny Jefferson straightened his spine. Every churchgoer kept glancing his way, but this nun was the most stricken. A face bleached of its blood, a face as white as the alabaster saints and the white Jesus. Defiance had brought him to this pew, so he told her with a firm nod, a calm eye, he would stay till the last hosanna was sung and Mass was over. Discipline, not grace, restrained him from balling his hands into fists.

Christmas Eve Mass, rituals older than the town, the church, descended into chaos. Father Janecek struggled to recall the litany, the precise sequence of sung and spoken prayers. His sermon lacked coherence. He began by speaking of joy, the birth of the Christ Child, the promise of salvation, but the homily drifted. The Negro sitting near the apse—what did he *want*? His mere presence caused the priest to jettison the theme of joy, the crux of a sermon he'd delivered at every Midnight Mass for twenty-nine years. Father lauded our young men in Viet Nam, especially those who made the ultimate sacrifice for our freedom. "Are they not in some ways like our Savior?" he asked. "They gave all of themselves so we may live in safety and deepen our faith in our Lord Jesus Christ."

Kenny, eyes closed, remembered a baby and a terrified mother in a bunker. The bone-thin Mama-san held her child to her breast as if he were alive.

He sat in his pew as others approached the communion rail. He sought solace, strength of mind, solidarity. Four Negro students sat in a communion of silence at a Greensboro lunch counter in 1960. When ordered to leave the premises, F. W. Woolworth's, they perched on those color-blind stools till the store closed. Grandma Zora should've been there to hail them with her preaching: *We comin' together, North and South, maybe finally end the Civil War, defiant and holy*. Well, she sang high praise for defiance and love, a sacred alchemy, but would she sing for her grandson? He could almost see her raise a bent finger, narrow her brow. "Why you sittin' alone in that church? You're nineteen years old and not ready for what's before you." *Same as Viet Nam, granny*. "You lash out now and you're dead for nothin'." *A common death. A Negro death*. "I say muscle up that backbone, bide your time. Maybe a Carolina lunch counter's less trouble than the altar rail of a sundown town."

He sat straight and still. There was no way Kenny Jefferson would kneel for communion while some sundown priest shivered a hand over his mouth and whispered, "Body of Christ." Yes, Father might offer him the Host, wish him dead the same moment. Kenny could accept a refusal, a white Host for everyone but him, but if this cracker's hand rose too close to his mouth, he might chomp it in two. Malcolm, if he were alive, would flash a sharp-toothed grin, but Zora would tremble. Kenny believed neither was wrong. Everything depended on the hour, the predicament. The necessities of those involved.

He stayed in his seat near the grim-faced nun.

∾

After Mass, Sister Clair watched Fenza push through the crowd of parishioners and stop in the foyer. She stepped in front of Kenny and whispered, "Watch out for the Marine, loose cannon." A fragment of a poem came to her: *Give him a blood trail . . . / That's all he wants for Christmas*. "Careful," she said to her friend. "Let me walk point."

Ushers opened the doors to flurries and wind, to Krapalna Street mantled in white, black trees in Pulaski Park, a yellow lamp still on in the front window of Sonny's Place. Fenza stepped outside, then turned to face the parishioners exiting the church. Maybe he wouldn't hurt this Negro, just scare him, watch him squirm. This had to be the boy who wrote to Sister Clair from the Long Binh Jail.

Maybe a dozen parishioners separated Fenza from the Negro. Most drifted past the Marine, but a few paused to shake his hand, wish him well, and Mrs. Lemkey promised to pray daily for his safety. Pat and Jenny lagged behind to walk with Sister Clair and the Negro. Fenza was surprised to see Sister Damien, too, her face a wrinkle of worry. Guardians? he thought.

Peacemakers? He wished he could toss a toy grenade—boom!—and step aside as the nuns and the girls and the Black boy ran from St. Roch's screaming like babies and checking themselves for wounds.

The parishioners who passed Fenza earlier began to assemble on the walkway. Three men emerged from Sonny's Place, drinks in hand. Father Janecek stood in the foyer. No one was going home.

Fenza bounced on his toes on the top step of the church. The boy from LBJ was almost in range.

Sister Clair plowed her way between them. "Fenza," she said, "Merry Christmas."

He winked. "Same to you, Sister."

"If you have a moment, I'd like you to meet a veteran of Viet Nam."

She hoped to disarm Fenza by introducing her friend as a veteran. "Kenny," she said, "this is Fenza Ryczhik. He's on his way to the war you just left."

Kenny offered Fenza his hand.

"So you're the one from LBJ? Long Binh Jail?"

A slow nod.

"Up to me, you'd spend the rest of your life in jail."

Kenny withdrew his hand.

Sister Clair said, "That's enough, Fenza. This young man is our guest and we'll treat him as such."

Kenny grinned, almost chuckled.

"Some guest," said Fenza. "Maybe he can write you another letter from the Orville County Jail."

Sister Damien inched forward. She was near enough that she might have held Kenny's hand, touched the sleeve of his coat, the bend of his elbow. Pat and Jenny flanked Sister Clair. Several men, coatless, stumbled out of Sonny's Place, weaved across Krapalna, and joined the parishioners who had filed past Fenza and now watched the proceedings from the walkway and the curb. Sister Damien began to count them, but they were too many, perhaps the entire congregation. A young couple, three children in tow, walked to their car, then sidled back to observe a spectacle. Sister Damien was shocked by the raw power of her feelings. She would rather offer her life than see this stranger shed one drop of blood on Christmas Eve.

Fenza eyed the Negro. He looked in vain for fear, or some weakness to turn to his advantage. "Tell me something," he said finally. "You know where you are?"

The Black boy answered with a wink, a smile.

"Just what I figured," said Fenza. "You don't know the first damn thing."

Sister Damien bawled him out for cursing. "Do you know where *you* are?" she asked. "You're standing in front of St. Roch's Church on Christmas. And as Sister Clair reminded *all* of us—this young man is our guest."

Fenza tipped his cap to the rubbernecks crowding the stairs, the dark knot along the walkway and curb. He wanted to say something smart, but all that came out was "*Your* guest, not mine." He felt emboldened when he spotted his dad among the spectators at the bottom of the stairs.

Sister Damien saw the makings of a mob, the absence of a congregation. What could a nun do or say or pray to deliver this town from its madness? She remembered the deacon's wife, Mrs. Dempsey, her tin-pan racket and shameless rant—"I like Indians, I like Blacks, I like tits!" Sister Damien regretted her lack of kindness toward this woman. If Mrs. Dempsey could come alive tonight, or appear as a ghost, she would spook Fenza and chase him out of here with a broom.

The Marine glared at Kenny, then turned. Here came his dad wobbling up the stairs.

"What's going on here?"

Fenza butted his chin toward Kenny.

"Yeah, I see, I see. But is there something we need to fix?"

Sister Damien, after scanning the crowd, said, "Yes, there is something that needs our immediate attention. More snow is predicted later this evening. The roads are already hazardous. Our guest needs a place to stay."

The crowd shuffled. Sister heard a murmur in her mind, "I like Indians, I like Blacks . . ." She raised her arms and addressed the multitude. "A *place*," she repeated. "A place of shelter on this auspicious night."

Fenza and his dad looked at each other.

"Beats me," said the old man. "I doubt this town has a place."

Pat Lemkey stepped forward. "There's room at my parents' farmhouse, but it's twelve miles from here."

Mrs. Lemkey grimaced.

"Wait," said Jenny. "My house is just down the street, three blocks away."

The gabble of the crowd made her raise her voice to continue. "I'll be staying with Pat tonight. She's already invited me."

Annie Biel, at the bottom of the stairs, raised a hand, gloved white, and froze.

"My room's nothing fancy," said her daughter, "but I think it'll do."

Eyes turned toward Annie Biel. She lowered her hand in slow motion, then hid her fists in the pockets of her coat. Never had it been so difficult to pretend nothing was wrong. An actress, she relied on skills honed for years, roles she knew better than herself. She would never play a Negro, but she often took the stage as a fat-lipped lady with a thin smile and a voice sweet enough to sing. She said, over the sound of shuffling feet and the bang of her heart, "Why, of course this young man's welcome to stay in our home. I wouldn't have it any other way."

She clutched her husband's arm to steady herself, form a chain. "Well, what's everybody gawking at? I say it's time to go home."

Jenny, pleased with herself, had backed her mother into a corner. Go ahead, Annie. Tell this man he has no place in this town on Christmas Eve or any eve. No, her mother couldn't whisper a word that might tempt her daughter to say something like, *We're Negroes, too, my mom and me.* Annie would accommodate "our guest" rather than risk a revelation. Jenny had tamed her hard-willed mother on Christmas Eve.

Fenza, in a mocking, girlish voice, said, "This young fella can stay in my room, too."

Some of the men hee-hawed. Their wives giggled.

Jenny said, "You think you're funny?"

"No, dead serious. You should know this by now."

Maybe, thought Kenny Jefferson, we're equally serious. Hands clenched, he stood almost as still as the Wise Men in the crèche. No wobble in him anywhere but his lips, a slight spasm that forced him to smile. He stepped aside when the yellow-skinned girl brushed his arm. Her wish to comfort had arrived too late.

Now Jen wished she'd kept her mouth shut. Her invitation would corral Kenny in town. The farmhouse, a safe distance from Orville, would have served as a refuge. The sundown law didn't extend to the fields.

Her mom, forcing a smile, said, "Well, we best be going." She asked the young man if he cared to ride with her and her husband, or if he had his own car and would follow them down the hill?

Fenza rubbed his chin. "Well, I'll be dipped in dung."

Sister Damien ordered him to watch his language.

"No bad words, Sister. Not a one."

"You never have any good ones."

"Well, then, Merry Xmas. Here I am mindin' my business and you act like *I'm* the problem."

"You *are* the problem," she said, "you and your kind." She slashed a hand over the crowd. "Go on home, *all* of you. You heard me. You best mind your business at home."

Sister Clair stared wide-eyed at her colleague.

"Go on," said Sister Damien, and shooed Fenza and his father down a few stairs. "I have half a mind to run you out of here with a broom."

Edging away in the night, his father at his side, Fenza made excuses. *The nuns wouldn't let him fight. Wasn't that Black boy clever to use them as a shield?* The crowd, heads down, dispersed in silence. Fenza had a bad feeling he'd spoiled the party. He brightened, though, when his father invited him to the tavern for a nightcap. "Put away your ID," said the old man. "No one on his way to a war is underage."

At Sonny's Place, slouched over the bar, nursing a whiskey, the old man said, "Don't worry about that Black boy. He'll be gone before the sun comes up."

Toronto

Old St. Mary's, a mountain of stone over Bathurst Street, would have dwarfed St. Roch's. Gus opened the door for Nadine and watched her pass through the foyer and climb the stairs to the choir loft. Dipping his hand in holy water, making the sign of the cross, he wondered if he'd hurt his chances by shooting his mouth off about Zambos. Only someone desperate would take his just-learned history of Ayiti, his slim bright penny of knowledge, and try to impress a girl as smart and pretty as Nadine.

But Old St. Mary's *was* impressive. The vaults and pillars rose toward heaven, and the laity—of every color—must have arrived from every outpost in the world. Gus, with Dany at his side, his mom behind him, moved up the center aisle. The three knelt in a pew near the chancel. Gus felt he was a long way from Orville until the choir sang "Come All Ye Faithful." This was how Midnight Mass at St. Roch's began year after year. The apse of St. Mary's was larger, the Savior darker, His face and body perhaps sculpted from maple. Other details were identical: the thorns, the wounds, the cross of pale wood.

During Mass, during the rendition of every psalm and song, the choir leading, the congregation reciting or singing the refrain, he listened for Nadine. At one point, he was certain he could distinguish her voice from others. He glanced over his shoulder to the choir loft. Yes, she stood in the front row, her voice clear and powerful. She was Zambo, she was Catholic. He might need a century to discover what this means.

～

After Mass, he and this girl walked close together. Gus shivered, not from cold but because everything about her turned him inside-out. He told Nadine she had the voice of an angel. At first this seemed to make no better impression than his earlier chatter about the Zambos of Ayiti amid mountain peaks sharp as swords. Nadine looked beyond him to the low sky, a whirl of flurries. "I can thank my mother," she said. "My earliest memories are of her voice."

So he risked telling her about his first Mass at St. Roch's Church. "I was maybe four years old," he said, "but I can still see the morning light coming through the stained-glass windows, the sun branching like a tree into every color in the world, including its own." He squinted. "Oh, the sun, the glass, the people—they were so alive. The priest came out of the sacristy, his vestments green and red, and his altar boys wore long red gowns, white surplices, shoes shiny and black." His eyes widened. "I was so attentive to the altar, the priest and his boys, the glow of candles, the colors in the windows like pieces of song, that I didn't look back when the choir began to sing. I heard angels, a hundred or more, and I believed they'd arrived from far beyond the walls of the church, the boundaries of the town." He shrugged. "Well, I learned soon enough that angels don't visit St. Roch's Church, but so what? I began to love music. I *had* to have music. I felt like my body, even my hair, was made of sound and light."

Nadine mulled this over. Yes, she thought, even your hair. A body of sound and light has loose margins, always changing. I grow large and shiny when I sing. Does Gus already know?

She remembered her sixteenth birthday and her mother's advice when the party was over. "Don't talk too much to boys," she said, "and don't trust them before they earn your trust."

"I won't."

"Before your father first held me and I him, we'd known each other for many years."

"You already—"

"Yes, but you haven't heard everything, have you? Your father and I once climbed a mountain over our great river, the Latibonite. We sat for hours and watched the sun and the sea, the waves so far off they seemed to break in silence. You are too young to grasp certain things, but you are not too young to listen. We greet our ancestors through love, and nothing and no one is missing if we pay attention. We invite our people to find a home in us, and we invite the mountains, the sea, and no one's grave is alone in the earth. How many boys understand this? If you meet one who takes the time to know you, to learn of your family, he is a strong candidate. You lessen yourself by flirting with boys who are insincere."

Nadine let Gus Zeul hold her hand. Her brother and Cassie walked ahead, and had the courtesy not to look back. She liked the way he touched her, soft but not too soft, and their hands fit well after they removed their gloves. Cars shushed through the snow of Bathurst Street. Now and then a voice rose, Cassie's or Dany's, followed by muffled laughter. Maybe, she thought, I have found a candidate. Nadine understood the joy of her parents' union less through words, lectures, than the strength of her mother's body, the grace of her father's gait. Love brings more love, silence more song. This Illinois boy was pretty. His whole body, even his hair, was made of sound and light.

She kissed Gus Zeul on Bathurst Street. He was the first boy she kissed in Canada. Their tongues, fast but shy, barely passed beyond their lips. She whispered, "Once more, once more."

Orville

The snow came down hard later that night. Kenny Jefferson, in a warm bed under pink blankets, lay awake and listened. The weight of the snow made branches creak. Fresh from LBJ, he lay in a white town in a black bed. The girl and her mama had just enough tar brush to tell him their secret. He doubted the husband knew anything. Like the town, he probably wore blinders that narrowed his vision to a familiar road, no forks or curves, no guardrails, no hazards in the foreseeable future. This made Kenny Jefferson the sole outlaw in Orville. A Black man in a Black girl's bed in a white town on a white Christmas. Could irony, like defiance, be made holy? Grandma Zora would know.

The girl had seemed real sweet till she used him as a bargaining chip. A little rift with her mama, perhaps a chasm, so let's shove this Negro in the center. Why had he let this happen? What was his aim? Defiance had become a habit. Kenny almost hoped the Marine would come by so he could knock him flat a few times before he left for Viet Nam.

~

Sister Damien knelt on a hardwood floor for almost an hour. At her bedside, as Sister Walburga slept and snored behind the partition that divided the room, she asked for forgiveness. How many things in her life had she done right, how many wrong, and what was the balance? Could her defense of the young man be both virtuous and sinful? If his beauty distracted her, she had lost her way. If, however, the stranger brought out in her all the goodness she had hoarded in fifty-one years, she'd at last made some headway into this peculiar intimacy called grace.

She hobbled to her feet. Sister Walburga—how could she snore on such a night, and with such verve? God's will was strange. For eleven years Sister Damien had shared a room with a nun who snored like a truck driver. No, she had no idea how a truck driver snored, but could it be louder or more manly? A wild blowing, a dirge, in baritone and bass. A series of honks and wonks and wheezes that may one night shake the nails from the walls.

Rosary in hand, Sister Damien walked into the hall and toward the parlor. Maybe she could rest her knees now, sit in a chair, and pray her rosary till she was overcome by sleep.

She found Sister Clair standing at the window. No light was on, but the snow lent the room a pale glow. The curtains, normally drawn at dusk, were wide open. The snow swirled to earth in clumps the size of jawbreakers. The metaphor seemed to come from another life. She had not sucked on a piece of candy in more than thirty years.

Sister Clair turned to her. Before tonight, these nuns had shared little or nothing, not even faith.

"I hope I haven't disturbed you," said Sister Damien.

"Not at all."

"I often struggle to sleep."

"Me too."

"Sister Walburga snores like a truck driver."

Sister Clair tilted her head. "A truck driver?"

"Yes, but tonight I'd be awake anyway because of the young man who came to our church." She fidgeted with her rosary. "I was terrified. I had no idea what would happen."

"None of us did."

"Fenza . . . you never know about Fenza."

"God's children are various."

"I was frightened not for myself but for the stranger."

"Yes, me too."

"Somehow he didn't seem afraid. It was as though he'd been through this before."

"Kenny is well versed in bravery."

"Surely more than I," said Sister Damien. "I have now spent twenty-six years in this town."

Sister Clair, after a long silence, said, "This night isn't over. We won't help Kenny by staring out a window."

"What should we do?"

"Make ourselves visible. Patrol the area around the Biel home, especially the alley."

Sister Damien hesitated. "Yes, of course. Everyone in town knows where to find your friend. I wish he'd gone to the Lemkey farm. Jenny was foolish to invite him."

"She may regret it."

"As I regret my own foolish role. I should've let the young man leave Orville, risk being snowbound on Christmas."

Sister Clair sighed. "It was never that simple."

"Snowbound or in town. Which is worse?"

"Well, his car doesn't have a heater."

"Good Lord."

"Besides, he understood the risks before he arrived at St. Roch's."

⌖

Kenny rose from bed, went to the window, and parted the curtains an eye-width. A car—lights off, engine running—had parked in the unlit alley. Falling and drifting snow concealed details. He didn't know the make of the car, or whether either of the two people sitting shoulder-to-shoulder in the front seat was the Marine who confronted him after Mass. He remembered Sister Clair calling the boy by an odd name—Fenza. Well, maybe Fenza had recruited a buddy to do some harm tonight, but would two Orville boys sit as near as lovers? The air was white and bright and fuzzy. There was no clear line to separate one person from another, or earth from sky.

Then something emerged like a stain across the snow. A darkness, edges blurred and rounded, a flicker of shadows coming up the alley. Two figures appeared. Kenny reckoned they were animals—what kind he could not imagine—or ghosts. As they approached the car, he was able to discern human forms, one lumpy and short, the other tall. He wiped the fog of his breath from the glass. Soon he could make out veils, coifs, wimples, the black habits of Benedictine nuns. Well, he said to himself, here come reinforcements. Sister Clair and that other nun, the apparition he'd shared a pew with, the one who'd glared at him inside the church and defended him at its portal, were wading through snow. Someone slipped out of the car and called, "Sisters, Sisters." Kenny recognized the voice of the colored girl who'd invited him to her home.

She swung open the back door of her vehicle and ushered the nuns inside. Kenny needed but a wink to recognize the scheme—they were here to keep vigil. The car's interior light shone bright enough that he could identify another girl, the one who'd invited him to her farm for the night. The colored girl had trumped this by offering Kenny her own room "just down the street." The arrangement seemed sensible, convenient. But the girl must have worried for his safety after offering him her bed.

He gave a low chuckle, then a corny, big-toothed grin they would've seen had they flashed their headlights. Four guardians watched over him: a colored girl, a white girl, and two Benedictine nuns who'd probably brought along their rosaries. Well, Kenny had his squad, but he was not their leader. The house was still. The snow seemed to want to bury this town in a single drift.

~

The phone rang while Annie Biel lay in bed whispering a prayer to St. Jude. He failed her, always did, as did the Father, the Son, and the Holy Ghost. Her attempts at piety were habitual, as were the silent curses that followed. "Damn nigger fool, damn nigger fool. Thank you, Mister Jude. Thank you, Mister Jesus. Let me be the instrument of Your foolery." Muttering, gritting her teeth, she kicked off the blankets and careened toward the hall. Were there any nigger saints? She'd tear into them, curse the halos right off their heads, if she knew their names.

Her husband, putting on his slippers, said, "Don't answer it. Let it ring."

Annie ignored him and picked up the phone.

"Is he awake?"

"Who?"

"Send him outside in ten minutes. Otherwise, you might join him at Dead Cat's Cove."

Click.

She couldn't make out the voice. Fenza? His dad? Sy Clausen? Whoever had called seemed to filter his voice through layers of cotton. A gruff tone, yet dusty with softness. And now she heard the Negro pacing back and forth in Jenny's room.

Her husband crept out from the bedroom.

"We should call the police."

He was sometimes the dumbest man alive.

"There's a car parked out back, engine running."

She nodded. "It's your daughter."

"You sure?"

"Hundred percent."

The phone rang again.

"Don't answer it," said her husband. "It's probably Fenza."

"Or baby Jesus, baby Sambo."

"Huh?"

"Forgive me."

"For what?"

"For being too tired to make sense."

Annie lifted the receiver, returned it to its cradle, then knelt on one knee to unplug the jack.

~

A smiling Sister Clair scrunched beside Sister Damien in the backseat. "Look at us," she said. "The watchwomen of Orville."

Sister Damien spread her rosary across her lap.

"A pleasant surprise," said Sister Claire. "I thought Sister Damien and I would patrol the neighborhood till sunrise."

"You'd freeze," said Pat.

"Might freeze right here," said Jenny. "Look at the gas gauge."

"We'll snuggle up," said Pat.

"We already have."

"Never mind," said Sister Damien. "Cold or warm, we'll maintain our vigil till sunrise."

"Or longer," Sister Clair corrected. "Kenny Jefferson will leave this town when he decides to leave."

Sister Damien listened to an echo in her mind: *Kenny Jefferson, Kenny Jefferson. Lord, let him live in safety one hundred years.*

Jenny turned toward the nuns. "Fenza rode by earlier. He circled the block three times."

"If we're lucky," said Sister Clair, "he's gone home by now."

Jenny shook her head. "I bet he's gathering a posse at Sonny's Place. He was in his dad's car, riding real slow. I could sort of feel him scouting things out."

Sister Damien perched on the edge of the seat. "We'll deal with Fenza the moment he returns. If he or anyone gets out of a car, Sister Clair and I will confront him."

Sister Clair winked. "No one sane messes with Orville nuns. My colleague and I are the Terrible Two."

Sister Damien shuddered. The strangest prayer came unbidden: *Let me be terrible, let me be wretched.* And despite her blasphemy, every fold and suture of her body filled with light.

~

At 3:00 a.m., Jenny turned off the ignition to conserve gas. A half hour later, the car an icebox, she tried to rouse the Chevy from slumber. The car coughed a few times, wheezed and farted, then died a swift death. Nothing to do now but wait for sunrise. The snow had let up, but the clouds hung almost low enough to sweep chimneys. Might not be much sun on Christmas morning. Might just be a blur in the east where the sun teased its way through clouds.

She and Pat sat thigh to thigh. The nuns leaned into each other's arms.

In the last hour of night, three cars circled the block. The sisters, heads turning in unison, noted the pace: ceremonial, funereal. The streets were unplowed. The wind blew down Pulaski Hill from the north. One of the cars—Fenza's father's—smoked and sputtered. Sister Clair, in an effort to lighten the mood, said, "How about a drag race?"

She was the only one who smiled.

Now the last car stopped in front of the Biel home behind Kenny Jefferson's Packard. The others continued, slower than slow, the gradual tightening of a noose. Sister Damien wondered what exactly two girls and two nuns could stop. She recognized Sy Clausen's Corvair when it crept into the alley. The Ryczhik car came around the block and entered the alley from the other side.

Someone emerged from the car parked behind Kenny Jefferson's Packard. Thick-set, roly-poly. Sister Damien recognized the silhouette of the priest.

242

She held her rosary in a fist. "Stay here," she said to her cohorts. "I can dispense with Father on my own."

She scooted from the backseat and into the night.

Sister Clair whispered to the girls, "I'll deal with Fenza. Do your best to distract whoever else is here."

The cars creeping up the alley had turned off their lights.

∽

Kenny Jefferson watched the tall Sister slog through snow toward the front of the house. Head down, she forged a path through knee-high drifts. How could anyone so clumsy, encumbered by robes, appear unstoppable? She had neither roar nor clang nor whistle, yet she called to mind a locomotive gathering speed, determined to be on time.

Sister Clair and the girls were boxed in fender-to-fender. The Marine, the big boy, got out of his vehicle, accompanied by a man Kenny assumed was his daddy. Two more vigilantes stumbled from the other car, weaving and snickering. Churchgoers, impractical jokers. Men drunk enough to saddle the wrong horse, the fear-struck beast who no longer existed. They were fools if they thought Kenny would rear up wild-eyed and fly from this town before the sun came up.

He slipped on his pants, his coat. *They got Negro problems? They want me? Well, where's a rifle when I need one?* He would be less of a pariah, or at least safer at night, in a southern town.

The mother of the house, her husband behind her, parted the curtains to peer outside. Kenny grunted to announce his presence. She jumped as if a viper slid over her feet.

He met the priest at the door. The tall nun was kicking through a drift in the front yard. Father weaved till he had a firm hold on the porch railing. Not much of a porch really, just a stoop. The cold poured into the house.

Father tipped the brim of a black hat. "Young man, I'm concerned for your safety."

Kenny grinned. "Seems we share a concern."

Father wagged a finger. "I don't care for your tone."

"Well, let's improve it," said Kenny, his voice gentler. "Seems we share a concern."

243

"Are you mocking me?"

Kenny shrugged. "Just sharing a concern."

Father huffed a whiskey breath. "Last chance," he said, "take it or leave it. If you get in your car and follow me, I can lead you from this town before you are harmed."

Kenny said to himself, I'll leave with the rising sun, no earlier. I may linger a while if the sun can't shine its way through clouds.

"Route 6 is still open," Father added. "The Highway Patrol has already been informed."

The tall nun, the locomotive, was still gathering steam when she reached the stoop and snatched Father's hand from the railing. "You are so"—she squeezed his hand till he winced—"*rude.*"

"Sister, will you let go of me?"

"I will not permit you to insult this young man."

Kenny remained silent. Behind him he heard footsteps, shuffles, a house haunted by the living. He pictured the Negro mother retreating to her bedroom. Whispers and groans, a soft cry. The click of a closed door. Her husband called, "Annie? Annie?" Her response was wordless. The sound of an animal releasing a portion of her pain.

The nun tossed Father his hand.

"You should be ashamed."

"For trying to protect someone?"

"Don't pretend you're—"

"I'm not pretending anything. I've lived in this town long enough to remember Dead Cat's Cove, how it got its name." He glanced at Kenny. "A drowned cat. A cat stuffed in a gunnysack."

"Father—"

"Some in our parish doubt anyone will miss that boy bad enough to search for him."

The nun shook her head. "But this is ludicrous. You speak as if our guest were not standing before us."

"I've said what needs to be said. I've made his predicament clear."

"Clear? This is *clear?*"

"Sister, lower your voice."

"I won't tolerate this pretense of concern."

"What?"

"This hypocrisy, this rudeness."

Father clung to the railing. "As a priest, my role is to protect and assist, as needed."

"A good shepherd in the field?"

"Careful, Sister."

"Jesus would see you as a bum."

His eyes widened as far as eyes widen. "You," he said finally, his voice breaking, "may soon be gone from this town, this parish. The same as Sister Clair."

~

Out back in the alley, Fenza was holding court. Jenny and Pat and Sister Clair had faced off with him and his dad, then Butch Yansik and Sy Clausen. Now Fenza was saying, "Honest, I don't want to hurt that boy. Just need to draw a line."

"Fenza," said Sister Clair, "you're so drunk you can't even *walk* a line."

"I could balance on one leg."

"Sure. Let's see."

"Maybe later."

Sister stood on one leg. "Can you do this, Fenza?"

"I don't care to."

"I could stand this way till dawn."

He brushed a hand over the ribbons that embellished his uniform. "Sister, you best step aside. I can't let what happened at St. Roch's embarrass me any further."

"Embarrassed? You're em*barr*assed?"

"We all were."

"Well, yes, the whole town. I agree."

Fenza Sr. stumbled forward. "What's all this hemming and hawing? My son already told you we've no plan to hurt that boy. We're just saying he has to leave."

Sister Clair said, "He'll leave when he's ready."

"No, before sun-up. That's what we agreed on."

"Who's we?"

"Everyone at Sonny's Place, plus Father Janecek."

She winced.

"If that boy follows Father out of town, nobody'll ride his tail. His worries will be over."

Sister, still on one leg, folded her hands in mock prayer. "This has a somewhat religious flavor."

"Listen here. You wouldn't be so ornery if you knew what's at stake."

"I know the short and long of it."

"No, you don't know either. That boy's in a world of hurt unless he leaves this town now."

∽

Sister Damien wished she had a long-handled broom. Father, reeking of whiskey, steadied himself with a gloved hand on the porch railing. She could sweep him aside with a single stroke.

"Well?" he said to Kenny. "You ready?"

The young man chuckled. "Almost. But I keep dreaming of a white Christmas."

"You'd best—"

"Never mind," said Sister Damien. "You've no right to tell anyone what's best."

They heard shouting and scuffling in the alley. Lights went on in the nearby homes, the front porches. Dogs barked. Someone moaned. Sister Clair said, "Step aside, Fenza. You're finished here."

"I have a mission."

"Your mission's been scrapped. Tonight *I'm* the barbarian. *I'm* the barbarian."

"*Gee*-sus, Sister. I'm just—"

"Mr. Jefferson will leave this town when he decides to leave."

"Don't make my job difficult."

"I won't. I'll make it impossible."

"You're getting carried away."

"I'm just getting started."

"Relax a while."

"Why did Mr. Jefferson come to our church? You have any idea?"

"He made a wrong turn."

"Only something extreme could begin to save this town."

∽

Kenny sat down on the front step. Sister Clair's voice had boomed louder than a dozen or so harried hounds. Had he come to save this town, or begin to save it? No, he'd come because of the crosscurrents adrift in his own heart: demons, saints, jesters, spooks. He'd almost laughed when Sister Clair called herself "the barbarian." Commendable. Most commendable for a nun at a certain hour.

The other nun, the locomotive, removed her coat and draped it across his shoulders.

"Oh, Sister, that's really not necessary."

"Perhaps not. But I've nothing more to give."

"Well . . ." He smiled up at her, the sincerity in her eyes almost too much to bear. "Okay," he said. "But maybe you and me should go inside."

She trembled and hugged her arms to her chest.

~

At first light, Jenny and Pat and Mister Jefferson sat in the living room. The nuns had joined them a little while, sipped coffee, but now they were guarding Kenny's car. They sat shoulder-to-shoulder to sustain a feather of warmth. A shame this car didn't have a heater. Kenny had announced he would leave for South Chicago with the rising sun. Fenza, so drunk he fell twice in the snow, had left with his dad and Sy Clausen and Butch Yansik. A slurred threat to "burn Kenny and his car, whittle them down to cinders," had seemed a bit empty. Although Fenza was probably asleep by now, the nuns took no chances. Dark habits and headgear loomed in the front seat.

~

The wind died and Christmas turned quiet. Snowplows had cleared a path up Krapalna Street to St. Roch's Church. Father, too drunk to drive, needed assistance to return to the rectory. John Biel taxied the priest three blocks in his Nash Rambler, then returned to a home he barely recognized. Nothing made sense. His wife of twenty-one years, a woman who never cried, suffered moderate outbursts of grief, plus fits of laughter. What to make of it? How to respond? A Negro had come to Midnight Mass, come right down to his home, his daughter's bed, and he was still here at dawn. A wink of sun tried to shine its way through clouds. Was Jesus up there? Was He watching? If so, He had to be shaking His head.

Now he joined his wife in the privacy of their bedroom. He lay beside her, stroked her forehead, and told her he was sorry. "I shouldn't have let that boy come here," he said. "Everything happened too fast."

Annie sniffled. "I'm the one who should apologize."

"For what?"

"Everything," she said, "*everything*. The whole world spinning the wrong way."

He looked at her. "I don't get it."

"You never will. I would need ten lifetimes to explain."

～

Pat fell asleep on the sofa, her head on Jenny's lap. Kenny knew their names now. They were pretty girls. The wakeful one, the Negro, cut him a glance through snake-slit eyes.

A stingy sun this Christmas morning. A cold, gray smear almost smothered by clouds. Kenny gnawed his lower lip, then winked. Jenny smiled and looked straight ahead.

The whole white world would fall to pieces one day, but when? Kenny doubted any of these sundown towns were altogether white. He supposed Jenny's mom came here to give herself and her daughter better odds in life. He was curious about how they landed in Orville, but it would be rude to ask this girl to reveal a secret she and her mom had probably guarded for years.

Kenny took her hand and held it till it matched his own for warmth. "Doubt I'll be back this way," he said, "but I'll remember this town."

Then he winked and waved and was gone in a blink.

～

The nuns came in from the cold a minute later.

"Freezing," Sister Damien told Jenny, "and Mister Jefferson has a long way to go." She brushed flecks of snow from her sleeves. "I offered him my coat to help warm him, but he kept saying he was fine. Well, if that old Packard cooperates, he'll be in Chicago sometime this morning." She turned to Sister Clair. "But what a splendid young man, wouldn't you say?"

"I would."

"And courteous, too. He stopped and waved to us three or four times before he drove down Krapalna and disappeared."

Sister Clair grinned. "I think you miss him already."

"Don't make me blush."

"Too late for that."

Sister Damien concealed her cheeks in pale hands.

"I don't know who misses him more," said Sister Clair, "you or me."

Me, thought Sister Damien.

"Strange how the heart lingers on those who turn our world upside-down."

Sister Damien lowered her hands. "I've learned this well, but must they make us blush?"

"You look quite appealing."

"You flatter me."

"Why not?"

"I admit I miss Kenny."

"I might have guessed."

"I have never met anyone like him in my life."

Sister Damien sat in the rocking chair warmed by the one man she missed. I wish he'd taken my coat, she thought. I won't need it anymore, nor anything else. Good Lord. I could've wrapped that young man in robes and wool. Chicago. I wish that raggedy car of his had a heater to warm him every mile of his way.

Sister Clair stood in the picture window. The sun, what there was of it, leaked slivers of light through clouds. The light inside her burned no brighter. A sputtering votive candle too weak to reflect a color, a prayer. The great mercy of an Orville Christmas was that no one had died.

She looked to the east, the direction of Kenny's travel. She had to see beyond his departure, the fact that he might never be welcome in this town, to find reasons to persevere. Sister Damien, the most disagreeable nun she'd ever known, had become her Christmas Eve accomplice. She joined Sister Clair and two girls to give Kenny a present—messy, unwrapped—but a present nonetheless. Earlier, freezing in Kenny's car, Sister Damien whispered over and over, "If this is the Lord's work, give me more." Sister Clair had let her eyes roll around in her head. What in this world is trickier than a cross? A timely sacrifice may bring down mountains of meaningless suffering, but sometimes—despite efforts to the contrary—Calvary rises a bit higher and becomes harder to climb. On Christmas morning, more than a century after slavery, the most humble, inalienable right still had to be fought for. The day had dawned. The victory, mostly a gesture, meant Kenny Jefferson could ride along riverfront roads without having to glance every two seconds in his rearview mirror. Perhaps the worst that could happen was that Officer Krupovich or his deputy would give him a ticket for driving too slow or too fast for conditions. Kenny wouldn't be detained for long, and he would continue on to Chicago. He'd survived a night in Orville, left on his own terms, and he was more or less safe now that morning had come to this valley in Illinois.

~

The church bells began to ring. Sister Damien, in keeping with her custom, bowed her head and recited an Ave Maria in silence. She'd inhabited this world of bells and prayers, a perfect roundness that unraveled in a single night. *Hail Mary, full of grace* . . . She could still recite her praise, but all around, in the background and foreground, in the delicate air over the steeple and under the river and the town, a queer little voice said, *I like Indians, I like Blacks, I like Kenny Jefferson.* So she nodded to Ruth Dempsey, long buried, who prophesied on Krapalna Street and on the shore of the Illinois River: *Negroes will return to this place, Indians too, thousands of braves and women and children.* Poor Ruth, like Sister Damien, was whiter than the belly of a fish. She would've loved Kenny, though, the same as any honest woman. How could a human being, holy or not, withhold love from someone beautiful and true?

Acknowledgments

For a detailed account of "sundown towns" in northern states from the 1890s to the 1980s, see James W. Loewen's excellent *Sundown Towns: A Hidden Dimension of American Racism*.

The following quotations are from the indicated sources:

"Save me, O God, for the waters have come in unto my soul": Psalm 69, King James Bible

"I want to be with those who know secret things or else alone": "I Am Too Alone," in *The Selected Poems of Rainer Maria Rilke*, translated by Robert Bly

"Every shut eye ain't asleep": Michael S. Harper and Anthony Walton, eds., *Every Shut Eye Ain't Asleep: An Anthology of Poetry by African Americans since 1945*

"Give him a blood trail to follow . . . / That's all he wants for Christmas": Robinson Jeffers, *Thurso's Landing*

∿

I am grateful to Dennis Lloyd, Sheila McMahon, Ann Klefstad, Jacqueline Krass, and everyone at the University of Wisconsin Press. A deep bow to my parents, especially my mother, for teaching me kindness. My thanks to Uong Chanpidor and numerous friends and readers, including the Zuni Mountain Poets, Scoby Beer, Nancy Brink, Kate Brown, Jim Coleman, Christy Crowley, Tom and Ethel Davis, Vicki Dern, Ellen Garms, Ellen Greenblatt, Michael Job, Ellen Levine, Pat Mayo, Gianna Mosser, Robin

Rose, and Marydale Stewart. In part, the courage of Keith Mather and Mike Wong inspired the chapters of *What We Don't Talk About* that take place in Canada. A special thanks to Lee Swenson and other war resisters who appeared in the documentary film *The Boys Who Said No*. The Veteran Writers' Group led by Maxine Hong Kingston has informed and inspired my writings for almost thirty years.